D0842336

DO NOT FIX OR REPAIR
Contact the library

DISCARD

Liberty Lake Municipal Library

LITTLE THIEVES

ALSO BY
MARGARET OWEN

The Merciful Crow

The Faithless Hawk

LITTLE THIEVES

MARGARET OWEN

HENRY HOLT AND COMPANY
NEW YORK

Henry Holt and Company, *Publishers since 1866*
Henry Holt® is a registered trademark of Macmillan Publishing Group, LLC
120 Broadway, New York, NY 10271 • fiercereads.com

Text copyright © 2021 by Margaret Owen. Border art and tale-opener illustrations
copyright © 2021 by Margaret Owen. Animal skull art © 2021 by bazzier/Shutterstock.
Moon art © 2021 by Sundora14/Shutterstock.
All rights reserved.

Our books may be purchased in bulk for promotional, educational, or business use. Please
contact your local bookseller or the Macmillan Corporate and Premium Sales Department
at (800) 221-7945 ext. 5442 or by email at MacmillanSpecialMarkets@macmillan.com.

Library of Congress Control Number: 2021906595

First edition, 2021
Designed by Angela Jun
Printed in the United States of America

ISBN 978-1-250-19190-8 (hardcover)

1 3 5 7 9 10 8 6 4 2

To the gremlin girls,
I would like to tell you something inspiring,
but the truth is,
when life closes a door for us,
it doesn't always open a window.
The good news is:
That's what bricks are for.

AUTHOR'S NOTE

This is a story about many things, beautiful and ugly, painful and true. There are discussions of child abuse and neglect, navigating abusive environments, and trauma from a past attempted assault. For many of us, these are wounds, and I have tried to give them air here without tearing at the hard-won stitches. Still, I trust you to know your scars.

*The little thief steals gold, but the
great one steals kingdoms;
and only one goes to the gallows.*
—*Almanic proverb*

PART ONE:

THE CURSE OF GOLD

THE FIRST TALE

GOD-
MOTHERS

ONCE UPON A TIME, ON THE COLDEST NIGHT OF MIDWINTER, IN the darkest heart of the forest, Death and Fortune came to a crossroads.

They stood tall and unfathomable in the glass-smooth snow, Death in her shroud of pyre smoke and shadows, and Fortune in her gown of gold and bones. More than that cannot be said, for no two souls see Death and Fortune the same way; yet we all know when we meet them.

On this night, a woman had come to do just that: meet them. Her dull carrot-colored curls twisted from under a woolen cap, her wind-burnt red face as worn as the threadbare cloak over her shoulders. One hand clutched a dimming iron lantern, which smoldered just bright enough to catch the snowflakes flitting by like fireflies before they melted back into the dark.

Her other hand was locked around the ragged mitt of a little girl beside her.

"Please," the woman said, shivering in snow up to her shins. "We're stretched thin to feed the twelve other mouths already, and this one—she's ill luck. Wherever she goes, the milk spoils, the wool tangles, the grain spills. Whatever she touches falls to ruin."

The little girl said nothing.

"She's only . . ." Fortune tilted her head, and the wreath of coins about her brow shimmered and flipped, changing from copper to coal to silver to gold. "Three? Ten? Forgive me, I never know with you humans."

"Four," Death said in her soft, dark voice, for Death always knew.

Fortune wrinkled her nose. "Young. The proper age to be spilling grain and breaking things."

"She's the thirteenth," the woman insisted, shoving the lantern higher as if to drive her point home like a stubborn cow. Weak firelight caught on Fortune's coin wreath, on the wispy hem of Death's hood. "Like me. That makes her the thirteenth daughter of a thirteenth daughter. Her luck's rotten to the core."

"You told your other children you'd take her into the woods to seek her fortune." The Low God plucked a coin from her wreath and let it dance about her fingers, flashing copper and silver, gold and black.

"In truth, you were seeking me," Death finished in her dark-velvet voice, and the woman's features crumpled with shame. "Yet here you have found us both. You have come far, through the dark and through the frost, to ask our favor."

"Asking a blessing of the Lady of Luck. Risky. No way to know what that would be." Fortune's face slipped between cruelty and sympathy as her coin slipped through quick fingers, flashing day and night, red and white.

Death, on the other hand, did not stir. "You know my gifts, and so you know though there is plenty I can take, little can I give. But I will tell you: Only one of you will go home."

The woman drew a sharp breath.

Fortune smiled, and her coin flashed like the sun and the snow, like shadow and like blood. "You sought Death in the woods. Did you think the way back would be easy?"

The woman said nothing. The flame in the lantern burned lower.

"Ask," Death commanded. "What will you have of us?"

The lantern shook in the woman's hand, her knuckles cracked with callus and cold. "I want what's best for—for everyone."

"Choose," Death commanded again. "Which of you will return?"

The woman let go of her daughter.

Fortune lifted the girl's chin She found two eyes of sharpest black in a pale, freckled face, two braids the color of the lantern's flame tied off in bits of rag.

"What is your name?" Death asked as the woman turned and fled the crossroads, stealing away the last scrap of firelight.

"Vanja" was the first thing I said to my godmothers, "my name is Vanja."

ꞔARD ꞠAMES

I̶T HAS BEEN NEARLY THIRTEEN YEARS SINCE DEATH AND FORTUNE claimed me for their own, and I have come far enough through winter and cold that almost no one calls me Vanja now.

Thump-thump. Two raps of gloved knuckles against the carriage roof. The driver's muffled voice carries down to me inside. "Almost there, *Prinzessin.*"

I don't reply. I don't have to; I learned long ago that princesses don't owe their servants answers.

And for most of the last year, that's the face I've worn: the princess.

Or to be precise: Gisele-Berthilde Ludwila von Falbirg of the Sovabin Principality, *Prinzessin-Wahl* of the Blessed Empire of Almandy. Soon to be *Markgräfin* Gisele you-get-the-idea von Reigenbach of the empire's largest territory, the border march of Bóern, once its margrave gets around to a wedding.

Though not if I can help it.

(We'll come back to that.)

I squint out the gilt-trimmed carriage window, studying the timber-and-plaster blocks of Eisendorf Manor as the horses draw us closer. Shadows pass behind the first-floor windows, turning them to rosy eyes winking into the frosty twilight gloom. It looks crowded already, even for a Sunday-night party. Good—a princess ought to be the last of the von Eisendorfs' guests to arrive. There was a reason I dawdled in my bedroom at Castle Reigenbach: to make sure we hit peak Minkja traffic when we left an hour ago.

But I have more motive to survey the manor's scenery than just making sure the *Prinzessin* arrives fashionably late. Lit windows are fewer on the third floor, but I still spot two bracketing the double doors where the master bedroom lets out onto its telltale grand balcony.

The real question tonight is whether it's the *only* balcony.

It is not. Balconettes frame it on either side. Lamplight gilds only one of the balconettes, spilling from an adjacent room that looks to share the fat main chimney with the master bedroom.

That chimney is currently chugging smoke into the dimming sky. One might wonder *why* the von Eisendorfs would keep a fire going up in their bedroom when they'll be busy entertaining guests downstairs all evening.

I'd bet three solid *gilden* that they're heating the guest chambers next door instead, in case I—well, in case the *prinzessin* needs a respite. An opportunity to suck up to the margrave's bride-to-be can't be missed.

One also might wonder why I care about chimneys, balconettes, and suck-ups. It's because tonight, the von Eisendorfs are handing me an entirely different sort of opportunity.

And I would *loathe* for either of those opportunities to go to waste.

The faint reflection of my grin cuts across the glass. A moment later it vanishes as my breath clouds the pane in the late-November chill.

I should play it safe, settle back into my seat, resume the serene, graceful façade of the *prinzessin*.

Instead I size up the remaining distance between us and the first guard we'll pass, and quickly draw a simple, distinct set of curves in the fogged glass. *Then* I sit back and smooth my grin down to a placid smile.

When we pass the first guard, I see him do a double take. He elbows the guard beside him, pointing to the carriage window, and I'm pretty sure I hear: ". . . *an arse!*"

"And no one will ever believe you," I hum under my breath as the fog melts from the glass.

The jingle-stamp of the horses stops when we draw even with the manor's stout oaken front door. I sneak a look under the opposite seat and confirm my satchel, an unassuming toilette bag, is still stowed away. For now, it will stay there.

Then I close my eyes, swaying with the carriage as the footman jumps off, and think of three playing cards dancing facedown across a table. It's time to begin my oldest game, Find the Lady.

There are many tricks to running the game, but the absolutely ironclad one is this: Only one person should know where the Lady is at all times. That person is me.

I run my fingertips over the string of heavy, perfect pearls around my neck. It's habit more than anything; I would know if they were unclasped. I would *know*.

The carriage door opens. In my mind, I flip the first card faceup.

The *Prinzessin*. Silver eyes, pale-golden curls, pristine pearls under glacier-blue velvet and burgundy brocade, a gentle smile with a hint of mystery. Even the name *Gisele* is an intrigue, shunning sturdy Almanic for the Bourgienne pronunciation, with its honeyed vowels and a butter-soft *G*. It's just the sort of pretentious affectation Dame von Falbirg loved to dish out, knowing people like the von Eisendorfs would eat it up.

This is how the game begins, you see. Step one: Show them the card they're looking for.

The *prinzessin* descends from the carriage like a vision. Ezbeta and Gustav von Eisendorf are hovering in the entrance hall, faces lighting up when they see me finally gliding toward their open door. It's not just about arriving on my own schedule, of course. It's about making sure the *other* guests see Ezbeta and Gustav waiting for me.

I alone see the surest sign that this night is going to go off without a hitch, for when Fortune is your godmother, you can always see her hand at work. Faint, dull clouds like coal dust are coalescing around the von Eisendorfs as they flutter in the hall. It's an omen of the ill luck I'm about to bring upon their house.

The Count and Countess von Eisendorf are celebrating their twentieth anniversary tonight—well, commemorating, at least. "Celebrating" may be too strong a term. All I'm saying is that there's a reason *Komtessin* Ezbeta is already ruddy-cheeked and stashing a goblet behind an urn on the entrance hall's credenza.

Something about her always puts me in mind of a stork, though I've never put my finger on why. She's pale-skinned like much of the Blessed Empire, with middling brown hair and angular features—*aha*. That's it. Ezbeta has a habit of pointing with her chin, and with her long neck and a tendency to cock her head, it gives the impression that she's scouring the area for a frog to snap up.

She's dressed to impress, at least, her wrists and throat gleaming with a small fortune in gold and emeralds. It's almost certainly the most expensive jewelry she owns. My fingers fairly itch: It's another opportunity, perhaps.

"Oh, *Markgräfin* Gisele, how good it is of you to come!" Her voice carries like a trumpet, and I hear a fleeting hush of anticipation dart through the crowd inside as the countess sweeps her forest-green samite gown into a curtsy.

"It was ever so kind of you to invite me," I reply, extending a hand to Gustav.

He mashes his lips to my doeskin-gloved knuckles. "We're absolutely delighted."

Komte Gustav is a withered ghoul of a man in a tunic pricey enough to feed Eisendorf Village through Winterfast, and yet *incredibly* it does nothing to help the piss-puddle where his personality should be. Nor does the wet smudge he leaves on my glove.

I pull free and bounce a teasing finger against the tip of Ezbeta's nose. "I'm not the *markgräfin* yet, you know. Not until my darling Adalbrecht returns and makes me the happiest woman in the Blessed Empire."

My *darling* betrothed, Adalbrecht von Reigenbach, margrave of the sprawling march of Bóern, has spent the entirety of our year-long betrothal at his share of the southern and eastern borders of the Blessed Empire of Almandy. He's been instigating skirmishes like your garden-variety *invade-a-kingdom-because-Papi-didn't-love-me-best* nobleman, all while I wait in his castle. And for all I care, he can stay there.

"Well, you're already the most generous," *Komtessin* Ezbeta simpers as a servant takes my cloak and gloves. "The cushions you sent are positively divine!"

"I could hardly let such an occasion go by without gifts. I'm just glad they arrived safely." It isn't even a lie, I *am* glad. Just not for the reason they expect. "Was the spiced mead also to your liking?"

Gustav clears his throat. "Indeed," he says with a faintly strained air. "I thought to serve it tonight, but my wife took a . . . significant liking to it, in fact."

"I can't help it if Princess Gisele has impeccable taste." Ezbeta winks. Saints and martyrs, if she's already soused enough to be winking at me, she might just hand me that absurd necklace herself before the party's over. "Come, come! Everyone's waiting for you!"

I let her lead me into the manor's main parlor, which is overflowing with minor nobility. Much of the crowd are knights and landed gentry who serve the counts, but the von Eisendorfs have also managed to attract a handful of Adalbrecht's vassals equal to their own rank. I see *Komte* Erhard von Kirchstadtler and his husband, and Lady Anna von Morz in a plum satin atrocity that could charitably be called a gown. Even Minister Philippa Holbein has traveled into Boérn from the nearby Free Imperial State of Okzberg.

I scan for one particular face and find it thankfully missing. Godmother Fortune may have tilted the odds in my favor, or maybe Irmgard von Hirsching thinks she's too good to get drunk with the von Eisendorfs. Either way, that's one less problem to deal with tonight.

"I hope the guards didn't give you too much trouble, *Prinzessin*," Lady von Morz cackles, sauntering up to me with a goblet of *glohwein* in each hand. She tries to pass one off to me and fumbles a bit until I steady her grip. "Really, Gustav, even the margrave doesn't post this many soldiers at his front door."

Gustav gives a disgruntled wheeze. "No such thing as too cautious these days. They say the von Holtzburgs lost nearly fifty *gilden* to the Penny Phantom."

We all gasp. That's no trifling sum; a skilled tradesman would be lucky to amass fifty *gilden* over one season. "I'd no idea the *Pfennigeist* struck them too," I say, wide-eyed.

Ezbeta nods, leaning in closer. "Oh, *yes*. Holtzburg Manor was robbed back in January, but they didn't know what the red penny meant until Dowager von Folkenstein said they'd found one after *their* burglary. We think the von Holtzburgs may have been the first victims."

"How dreadful," I murmur. "And their bailiff never found anything?"

"No. He swears only a ghost or a *grimling* could have broken in without a trace." The delight-tinged pity on the countess's face congeals into syrupy comfort. "But never fear, Princess Gisele. We've taken every precaution, just as we promised you. The *Pfennigeist* won't get so much as a button off your gown."

Lady von Morz snorts into her *glohwein*. No one has ever caught the Penny Phantom. No one has even *seen* the Penny Phantom. Not even my betrothed could keep the devil from Castle Reigenbach, where Marthe the maid found my jewelry box cleaned out, with a single red penny left behind as a calling card.

And if even the margrave's walls can be breached, what chance do the von Eisendorfs have against such a creature?

I make my rounds through the crowd, clasping hands and admiring outfits, discreetly emptying my goblet into a vase when the coast is clear, only to make sure everyone sees me flagging down servants for many, many refills. *Komte* von Kirchstadtler wants to know when the wedding will be (not until Adalbrecht returns), newlywed Sieglinde von Folkenstein natters my ear off about how poorly she's felt in the mornings (I make a note to commission a baby rattle), and Minister Philippa Holbein offers apologies for her husband's absence.

"Kalsang fell behind on paperwork over the sabbath," she sighs, absently thumbing the tassels of a pair of white silk cords twisted together and draped over her shoulders. Congregants of the House of the High typically just wear the cords for their sabbath prayers, but those among the public officials tend to keep theirs on day and night.

I suspect it's for the same reason her husband, a soft-spoken Gharese tea merchant who's much happier at home with their two little *apso* hounds, is avoiding this party. Dealing with a bunch of red-faced, competitively self-important Almanic aristocrats would make anyone pray for divine intervention.

His absence is fine by me. I like Kalsang and Philippa. I know exactly what's about to befall Eisendorf Manor, and I'd rather their part in it be minimal.

I spend the rest of the hour making small talk and seemingly chugging *glohwein* like it'll cure boils. (Not that Princess Gisele ever gets blemishes. The pearls see to that.) All the while, I keep an eye on *Komtessin* Ezbeta.

At last, I see my opportunity and start moving toward the parlor door.

"*Nooo*, Gisele!" A hand latches on to my brocade sleeve: Ezbeta has taken the bait. By now, she has had at least one glass of *glohwein* for every glittering emerald in her heavy necklace. That would be roughly seven more than I've had and, judging by her flaming face, about five too many.

And that is why I waited until now to head for the exit, when I knew she would make a tipsy scene.

Ezbeta, of course, obliges me. "You cannot leave us so soon! We've a five-course supper, just for you!"

One might wonder why I'm about to visit such misfortune upon my gracious hosts. Why tonight, on their anniversary? Why them, when they've been nothing but eager to please?

And the truth of the matter is this: If they saw me without the pearls and the face of the *prinzessin*, if they had *any* idea who I really was, they wouldn't give a damn if I was staying for supper or scraping it out of the swine trough.

That's why.

I hiccup in her face, then burst into giggles. My billowing skirts rustle as I wobble in place like a ship in an uneasy harbor. "Of *course* I'm not leaving, silly goose! I simply need . . . I need . . ." I trail off, twirling a pale-blond curl around a finger. The goblet of *glohwein* lurches in my other hand and spills a few drops onto my bodice. Not enough to ruin it, of course, only to sell the idea that I am at least as drunk as the good *Komtessin* Ezbeta.

Sure enough, Lady von Morz shoots me an amused look and mutters something to *Komte* von Kirchstadtler.

"What was I saying?" I ask, my gaze sliding dreamily around the room.

"You should lie down a moment, perhaps," *Komtessin* Ezbeta says, "to recover your faculties before we dine. We have a lovely settee in the guest parlor. *HANS!*"

Half the room gives a start, staring at both of us. Ezbeta is too drunk to notice. I take the opportunity to pat my cheeks as if marveling how warm they are. In reality, there's a layer of rouge beneath my talc face powder, and as I dab the talc away, my cheeks redden like Ezbeta's. While everyone's eyes are still on us, I let off another round of sloppy giggles for good measure.

I need every guest here to witness this mess and think it prudent to exile Gisele von Falbirg from the party. To take the *prinzessin* off the table. I need twenty minutes to myself, and since Gisele cannot leave a party without notice, she will leave with good cause.

"*HANS!*" Ezbeta bellows again. A beleaguered man in a servant's uniform is already at her elbow, wincing at his name being sounded like a bugle.

"What does m'lady desire?" Hans asks with a bow.

"Escort the *mar* . . ." A befuddled look muddies the countess's face as she tries to remember the proper form of address. You can almost see her doing the math, in fact. Too soon for *markgräfin*, not officially a princess-elector; you could say I'm in between titles. For now Ezbeta plays it safe. "Escort the princess to the guest parlor."

I take Hans's arm and stumble toward the door, hiding a smile. Ezbeta von Eisendorf has gotten many things wrong tonight: I am not drunk. I do not need to lie down.

I am not Gisele-Berthilde Ludwila von Falbirg.

But the countess has gotten one thing correct: As far as everyone knows, I'm still Gisele, not a baseborn peasant imposter. And that means for now, they call me *Prinzessin*.

As a final touch, I discard the goblet of *glohwein* on a table by the door, perched haphazardly on the edge. A moment later a clang tells me it's crashed to the floor.

Now everyone behind me will swear to the High Gods and the Low that tonight, Gisele von Falbirg was a senseless drunk, and utterly incapable of the villainy to come.

Poor Hans endures a lurching stroll with me through the dim upper corridors of Eisendorf Manor as I sing praises of his master and mistress. The sour look on his face tells me that praise is wholly unfounded. I can't say I'm shocked.

"*Marthe,*" I slur as Hans opens the door to the guest parlor. A maid is stoking the roaring fire inside, but she scurries away as he walks me over to the settee Ezbeta had boasted of. It truly is a lovely thing, stuffed spring-green velvet warmed by the fire.

Even better, it's been adorned in the gold-tasseled cushions I sent them for an anniversary gift. Just as I'd expected.

I flop gracelessly onto the settee, flapping my arm at Hans. "My maid, Marthe, fetch her for me. She'll be in the scullery. Or the chapel, pious as she is. She wears a . . ." I make a vague gesture toward the crown of my head, staring glassily at the ceiling. "A cap. Reigenbach blue. I need her *at once.*"

"Right away, *Prinzessin*." Hans bows and excuses himself, shutting the parlor door behind him. I wait in place, holding my breath, until the clipped beat of his footsteps fades down the hall.

Then I roll off the settee and onto the floor. I yank up my skirt to free a tiny knife tucked in one of my elegant leather boots.

For this first part, I have five minutes at least, ten minutes at most. Last time I hosted the von Eisendorfs, Gustav would *not* shut up about their new chapel, so I know it's on the opposite side of the manor from the scullery. Hans, tragically, will not find Marthe in either. And that means I have at least five minutes until he returns to apologize.

I snatch up one of the cushions I sent and carefully slice it open. Cotton batting blooms from the gash. When I reach inside, I find a small linen drawstring bag, a dark cloth sash, and two slipcovers identical to the one I just slit open, down to the silken tassels.

I gut the other cushion just as quickly. This one holds a linen shift and a simple steel-blue woolen servant dress, which I stashed inside before gifting the cushions to the von Eisendorfs. Tucked in one sleeve is a dark gray kerchief. Hidden in the other is a modest little cap of distinct Reigenbach blue.

Five minutes later, the new cushion covers are stuffed with my petticoats, chemise, and expertly folded gown; most of my jewelry; and a respectable handful of *other* people's jewelry. Anna von Morz's slim gold bracelet, nabbed while she passed me the *glohwein*. Minister Holbein's earring, to help her avoid suspicion. Rings and baubles picked from the crowd, just enough to let them know the thief passed through their midst.

There's a chance they'll blame the servants of Eisendorf Manor. It's happened before. The bailiff comes in, lines them up, shakes down sleeping pallets, and turns out pockets. But not so much as a trinket will fall to the flagstones, so they'll walk away more or less unscathed.

And I know terribly well that is far, far from the worst thing that can be done to a servant.

I chuck the ruined slipcovers into the fire, where they catch almost instantly, giving off a faint singed-hair smell from the silk. I try not to breathe it in as I braid my hair and tuck it under the Reigenbach-blue cap. One of the burning cushion covers also has the smears of my face powders on it, for no handmaid would own such things . . . and my time as the *prinzessin* is waning.

The final touch, though, demands a mirror—not because I need to see what I'm doing, but because I need to be sure it works. Luckily, Gustav von Eisendorf loves nothing so much as showing off, and expensive full-length mirrors are well in supply in his guest parlor.

I stand before the nearest one and look my reflection over: From the neck down, I am a maidservant in an unobtrusive Reigenbach uniform, filling it out nicely with curves that would be called *ambitious* in a maiden of nearly seventeen like myself. From the chin up, a few wisps of platinum hair twist from under the blue cap, and silvery eyes blink back at me from a heart-shaped face. Even without powders or rouge, twin roses bloom in my smooth ivory cheeks, and my pert lips flush with a natural shell-pink glow.

The hair like sunshine, the eyes like moonlight, they are both key to the image of the girl the march of Bóern knows as Gisele von Falbirg.

So is her signature string of perfect matched pearls.

I reach back and unclasp it from my neck. The effect is immediate.

My face lengthens, thins, mottles with a dusting of freckles; my eyes darken to black; the few loose tendrils of hair burnish rusty orange. The uniform dress hangs a little looser, though I've put on weight from a year's worth of finally eating my fill, and it hangs a little longer, for eating well still cannot replace the inches I lost to years of meager fare in Castle Falbirg.

I am plain. I am forgettable. I am what I was for ten years: Gisele's perfect servant.

I slip the pearls into a pocket and button it tight. I will not risk leaving them hidden in a cushion. Not when I'm so close to being free of them, and of Gisele, for the rest of my life.

Right on cue, Hans's footsteps echo down the hall. I hunch my shoulders forward, lower my head, and slip through the door, donning a look of worried vexation.

In my mind, the second card turns over: Marthe the Maid.

"*There* you are," Hans says. "Marthe, *ja?*"

I jump as if he's startled me, then shut the parlor door and bob into a curtsy. My voice takes on a high, whispery rasp. "My apologies, it seems my mistress sent a few people to look for me in her need. I'm afraid she's had"—I watch as the smell of burnt silk reaches Hans—"an *accident*," I finish with just enough peevishness to suggest this is not an unusual occurrence. Hans's face softens with camaraderie. "I can't leave her, but I need my toilette satchel from the carriage."

Hans sighs, and his voice lowers. "Fine, I'll fetch it. And if the von Falbirg brat has any further accidents, try to make sure they're cheap ones."

I curtsy again. "My thanks." Once he's started down the hall, I duck back into the parlor and call in my drunken-Gisele voice, "*Marthe!* What in the Blessed Empire of Almandy is taking so long?"

It is *certainly* loud enough for Hans to hear. If he is a dutiful man, he will hurry to the carriage house, which is even farther away than the new chapel.

But if Hans is as spiteful a servant as I was in Castle Falbirg, he will take his time.

Ten minutes at the least. Fifteen minutes at the most.

Marthe the Maid and Gisele the Princess fall back into their dance on the table in my mind's eye, circling the third and final card I've yet to reveal.

This is how you win the game, you know. Show them what they want to see, let them think they can win, let them follow the cards. Keep their eyes where you want them.

And never, ever lose sight of the real mark.

I trade the cap for the dull gray kerchief to cover my inconveniently bright ginger braid. Then I take up the linen drawstring bag and fold it into another pocket, checking one corner for a familiar weight: a single red penny.

It's there. And it's time.

I turn my final card. It is a shifting shadow, a blur in the night, a faceless specter. It could be a ghost. It could be anything.

After all . . . no one's ever seen the *Pfennigeist*.

Once upon a time, there was a girl as cunning as the fox in winter, as hungry as the wolf at first frost, and cold as the icy wind that kept them at each other's throats.

Her name was not Gisele, nor was it Marthe, nor even *Pfennigeist*. My name was—is—Vanja. And this is the story of how I got caught.

CHAPTER TWO

THE GUEST

GODMOTHER FORTUNE IS TRYING TO GET MY ATTENTION.

She'll roundly deny it, insisting that I would have found the candle on my own with or without the glimmers of golden good luck in my sight. But one of the few benefits of being the goddaughter of Death and Fortune is that I can see their hands at work.

Fortune's fingerprints have been all over this party. I've seen smudges of good-luck gold when I debated snatching a ring, clouds of coal-dust misfortune warning me not to empty my *glohwein* into an urn right before a knight turned to look my way. She and Death are supposed to leave me to my own business these days, but when Fortune's in a mood, she can't help but meddle.

I have yet to see Death's hand at work here, and that's probably for the best. It's Fortune's nature to poke at my boundaries, but when Death has business with you, she never needs an invitation.

And *I* don't need my godmothers' help. Even if I did, I can't ask. They saw to that themselves.

Nine minutes left now.

I scowl at the luck-shine around the candle, but there's no time to find another out of spite. I carry it over to the parlor's balconette door and tip the lit end over each hinge. Drops of tallow run down the brass. I need to remember to check the hinges when I return so I can clean up the hardened fat. When I lift the door's latch, it swings open glass-smooth and dead quiet.

I slip out into the night. This is my second-least favorite time of year, all damp and drizzle, with bright autumn leaves now sodden clumps of muck, and soil that can't decide if it wants to freeze or not.

It's still only second-worst. For me, the worst time of the year, despite all its Winterfast festivals and cheer, is midwinter.

But that's something for Vanja to deal with; it's not the *Pfennigeist*'s concern.

A blanket of fog has spread over the muddy fields, and the new moon sheds no light. My breath clouds in the chill, but I can only tell when it catches the glow of torchlight two stories below. A murmur of low voices wafts up from the ground level.

The handful of guards outside will keep their backs to the walls and their eyes on the mist, perhaps looking to the fingerbone boughs of Eiswald Forest beyond.

They will not be looking up at the manor itself.

I size up the distance between the parlor's balconette and the full balcony of the count and countess's bedchamber. They told me themselves of their precautions against the Penny Phantom, posting not one but *two* guards outside their solar and swearing it was the only way in.

They'd even had a priest of Eiswald's patron goddess bless their chambers to ward off ghosts.

I could have told them there were no ghosts, just me and a few creative rumors. I could have told them there were several ways into their bedchamber, they'd only ever just walked in through the solar. I could have told them not to squeal about their security measures to *anyone*, even if they believed Princess Gisele was too well known, too well off, to bother stealing so much as a copper bit from them.

But I *didn't*. Because here's the thing about stealing from people like the Count and Countess von Eisendorf: Odds are they deserve it. And instead of sitting around gathering dust, their riches can go to someone who deserves to be rich.

(Me. That's usually me.)

There's a saying in the Blessed Empire: Little thieves steal gold, and great ones steal kingdoms, but only one goes to the gallows. I'm not sure I agree. I've little interest in kingdoms, but even less in dancing with the hangman. And I've gotten very good—*great*, you might even say—at stealing gold.

There's still more distance between my balconette and their master balcony than I'd like, but it's manageable. Besides, I did not send the von Eisendorfs so many anniversary gifts just to leave empty-handed.

I climb onto the balconette's railing, then inch over to the timber ledge along the wall at my right. It's not wide enough to shimmy across, but it does offer a small foothold. I steel myself, then half leap into the open air, planting my right foot on the timber and pushing off the final few feet to the master balcony. I collide with the balcony's sturdier balustrade with a soft *oof* and wrap my arms around the cold stone, then roll over it as quick as I can and hold my breath, listening through the pounding of my heart.

There's not so much as a fracture in the guards' quiet conversation below.

I push myself back up to my feet and carefully try the handles on the balcony doors. They're locked. I figured they would be, this close to Winterfast.

Hence the gift I knew Ezbeta would keep for herself: the spiced mead.

It's no secret that Ezbeta overindulges, and that she loves nothing so much as a good spiced mead on a midwinter night. She's also in her forties, and likely prone to night sweats. If she's anything like Dame von Falbirg, they're worse when she drinks.

I check the window closest to Ezbeta and Gustav's bed. Sure enough, it's been left unlocked.

No dust on the sill, so she must use it as often as I suspect, and as I gently push the panes open, the silent hinges confirm it. They've been well greased so as not to wake Gustav when his wife needs a breath of fresh air.

It's child's play to climb in. There's an entire solar between the bedchamber and the guards, so I don't have to shed my leather boots, just step quietly. I did that for years in Castle Falbirg anyway.

Typically, the bedchamber would be left dark to conserve candles and oil. If I were a servant in this manor, though, I would leave the lamps burning on a night when my mistress was sure to stagger into her bedchamber half pickled in *glohwein*.

The Eisendorfs' servants have done just that, giving me plenty of light to see by. I cross the room to the vanity, barely making a sound.

I find a story spilling from Ezbeta's jewelry cases on the vanity, as I often do. An open box of rings to the side, with seven sitting outside it in a heap, all of them extravagant gold to match her gown's trim this evening. All seven rings removed at once, likely at Gustav's insistence that she not cover up her wedding band on their twentieth anniversary. Her earrings, bracelets, and necklaces lie in a similar state of disorder, but only a few have been removed from the case, like she'd chosen in a hurry in order to make up for the lack of wealth on her hands. A few precious stones, but the most valuable piece is around her neck.

She may or may not keep that one. We'll see if Fortune decides to keep meddling.

I admire the splendor a moment, noting the angles of the cabinet doors, the tilt of case lids. Then I pull out the linen drawstring bag, slip its lone penny into my dress pocket, and begin the harvest.

The *Pfennigeist* has been hard at work all year, picking jewelry off Bóernische gentry like apples from an untended orchard. (They've certainly left enough lying around to rot.) I'd never get away with this in the Free Imperial States, where Almandy's most cunning and ruthless train for years to join the Order of Prefects of the Godly Courts, who serve as instruments of the Low Gods' laws.

But in the nobility-governed principalities and border marches, the local bailiff is usually someone's slack-jawed brother-in-law who won't fuss when a *komte*'s tax ledgers don't add up. So if I get caught in the march of Bóern, it'll be my own damn fault.

I still won't. I can't afford to. The von Eisendorfs are among Adalbrecht's wealthiest vassals, and I'd secretly hoped tonight's haul would be my last, but the sum of my efforts is still short of where it needs to be. I've mustered just over seven hundred *gilden* so far. The magic number is one thousand.

That will be the price of my safety. Of my freedom.

You see, there are two things they don't tell you about having gods for godmothers:

First, nothing is freely given, even a mother's love.

And second, it is very, very costly to run out on a debt to a god.

I eyeball the gold, silver, and jewels as they slither into my bag. I can't say for certain—I take what my fence pays—but I'd guess after tonight, I should have between eight hundred *gilden* and nine.

Not enough, but almost there.

There's a trick to it, packing away the little things first so they settle at the bottom, rather than clinking around the bag. Rings, earrings, brooches; then the bracelets, then the necklaces, sometimes a girdle or a tiara if I'm feeling lucky.

One silver blur tumbles out and rolls off the vanity. I barely catch it before it hits the flagstones. It feels heavy in my hand, heavier than it ought to be. When I unfurl my fingers, I find a ring at odds with the rest of Ezbeta's collection. It's not silver but cool pewter wrought like talons, a perfect moonstone nestled in their grip.

Now *this* looks like a different story entirely.

A rumble reaches my ears from the drive outside. At first I ignore it; the ring is much more interesting than the arrival of a late guest.

Then the rumble grows louder than it has any right to be. Dozens of horses, maybe half a hundred. The Eisendorfs are wealthy, but not nearly important enough to merit a visitor that commands such an escort.

A horn sounds, and I hear a commotion on the ground level, which means the party has noticed their surprise caller. And that means my window of time to finish this job is shrinking, for that courtyard below is about to fill with gawking guests.

I don't have time to ponder the ring or anything else; instead I shove all the jewelry into the linen bag and cinch it shut. I *do* bother to arrange all the boxes, cases, and lids just as I found them, like a gold-eating ghost simply swept through the vanity.

No, not a ghost. A phantom.

I leave the finishing touch in the crushed-velvet lining of an empty case, as I've done a dozen times now: a single red penny, crown-side up.

Then I double-check the knot on the bag and tie it up in my sash. When I climb out the bedroom window, I see banners of fore riders stabbing through the fog.

A white wolf rears on the banners, collared in gold, stark against an unmistakable field of Reigenbach blue.

It's the personal insignia of Adalbrecht von Reigenbach, margrave of Bóern.

Gisele's betrothed.

"*Scheit*," I breathe.

I jerk the window mostly shut behind me, scramble up onto the balustrade, and hurl myself back onto the guest parlor's balconette before I can dwell too long. My memories of Adalbrecht will strip the *Pfennigeist* card from my hand if I let them. It's impossible to think of lockpicks and pennies and clever plans when every bone in my body wants simply to run.

But there's one key to getting out of a tight corner, one that never changes. That trick is to *not panic*.

I've been in worse pinches before. I think. Maybe not. If I blink, I see the dust of ill fortune at the corner of my sight, for my luck has decidedly turned.

It can't be too bad, though, for I don't see the hand of Godmother Death. Yet.

Don't panic.

The hoofbeats are loud enough now that I don't need to worry about the guards below hearing me barge back into the parlor. I draw the drapes over the balconette door's glass panes, then untie the linen bag and shove it under the cushions on the settee along with the kerchief.

The *Pfennigeist* card slides away; Marthe the Maid comes out. I'm still yanking the blue cap back over my hair as I rush to the parlor door and peer into the hall.

Hans is just rounding the corner, my trim leather toilette satchel in one hand, the very one I sent him to fetch. He sees me looking and picks up his pace. "You must make haste, *Frohlein* Marthe, the margrave is coming—"

I seize the satchel from him, careful to block his view of the parlor. "I heard. Thank you for your help. My mistress will be ready in five minutes."

I shut the door before he can protest. I know what he will say: No one in their right mind would ask Adalbrecht von Reigenbach to wait for a heartbeat, much less five minutes. I just need an excuse for the noises about to come from the parlor.

"*Maaaarthe,*" I groan in the drunk-Gisele voice, knowing Hans will pass what he hears on to the countess, "make me *pretty*."

Then I tear open the satchel and get to work.

Inside are clay jars with labels of powders, ointments, tonics—the picture of toiletries a noble lady might call for at any moment. In reality, they're all just half-full pots of lard, lantern oil, or powdered chalk, scented with whatever oils and vile-smelling herbs I scrounged up. It's the perfect way to transport stolen jewelry: buried in goo that is heavy enough to muffle clinking, too opaque to see through, and so viciously perfumed that no one will care to inspect it very long.

Once my haul is stoppered safely in the pots, I pull the rest of my stash out from the cushions and change as swiftly as I can despite the faint sheen of sweat gluing my dress to my skin. The satchel has a false bottom panel, and I pry out a knotted-up bundle of batting and replace it with the rolled-up servant uniform.

Voices rise in the courtyard as the hoofbeats quiet. Adalbrecht must be at the door. Nausea sours my belly. I suppose that will only help me look sick from wine.

I can't quite make out Count Gustav's wheezing as I cut the batting knot open and stuff the new cushions. I *do* catch a round of laughter from the guests.

Stall, I beg silently, *stall as long as you can.*

I cram the last bit of batting back into the cushions and button them up, then rush to the mirror, pearls in hand. The manor door lets out a tortured creak as it swings open downstairs.

Do not panic, I order myself, and slip the string of pearls around my throat. Panic would make my fingers tremble, and no one has time for that. Instead I find the necklace clasp and lock it tight.

My cheeks turn smooth and rosy, my hips and bosom swell, and the color bleeds from my hair as I comb out the braid with my fingers. The platinum locks roll themselves into perfect, sleek sausage curls that I only loosely pin back, since Gisele will certainly have mussed her hair in her drunken stupor. I do one final glance-over: the leather satchel sitting neatly by the settee, the new cushions plump on the velvet, the old cushion slipcovers burned to ash—

The tallow. I forgot the tallow on the hinges. I swipe the small knife from where I'd left it on the hearth and dash to the balconette door, scraping the telltale fat from the brass.

Conversation bubbles up from the nearby stairwell, and thunderous boots crack on the floorboards.

I flick the tallow crumbs into the fire, throw myself onto the settee, and jam the knife back into its sheath in my bootheel. My foot crashes down just as the parlor door shudders with a knock.

To my surprise, Ezbeta's voice carries through the wood. "Gisele, come quickly! There's a messenger from the margrave!"

I let out a breath like a bellows deflating. Just a messenger? But I *have* to be sure. "Darling Adalbrecht! Is he here?" Hopefully Ezbeta reads the tremor in my voice as lingering wine-stupor.

"No, *Prinzessin*." Ezbeta opens the door and hurries over as I stifle my relief. "He's sent a messenger for you. Quick, quick!"

Ugh. Trust a blowhard like Adalbrecht to send a princely escort with a mere courier, just because he can. Though . . . I saw the warning from Fortune, the coal-dust clouds. There must be *some* cause for concern.

I let Ezbeta help me wobble down the flights of stairs. Hans is waiting on a landing, head bowed as we pass. I catch his sleeve and slur, "Marthe went to get me wwwwwater. Take her satchel . . . to the carriage . . . there's a good man." I pat him on the cheek. With any luck, he'll be too annoyed to think about much else.

When Ezbeta half drags me into the main parlor, Adalbrecht's messenger has commandeered the room by virtue of his livery alone, the rest of the guests buzzing and murmuring. They've already formed something of an audience for the man, who straightens and bows to me, then unfurls two pages of a letter and begins to read aloud:

"'From Adalbrecht Auguste-Gebhard von Reigenbach, Lord of Minkja, Margrave of Bóern, High and Noble Commander of the Legions of the South, Loyal Servant of the Blessed Empire of Almandy: *Greetings*.'"

Saints and martyrs, that has to be *half* the letter alone, right?

"'It is my deepest sorrow to have kept my dearest treasure, the lovely and gracious *Prinzessin* Gisele, waiting while I secure our empire's borders.'" (More like expand them for entertainment.) "'But our long winter of the heart is at an end. At last, we two shall become one.'"

Delighted gasps sweep the room, and every eye turns to me. Even the messenger pauses.

I'm going to vomit. *Long winter of the heart?* Whatever minstrel he consulted with for this garbage, I need to track them down and strangle them with their own lute strings.

"Nothing would bring me greater joy," I say sweetly. No one has to know I mean murdering the minstrel.

The messenger continues, stone-faced. "'I myself will be returning to Castle Reigenbach on the morrow, and we hope you all will join us in Minkja for the wedding in two weeks' time. Guests will be received . . .'"

I don't hear what he says after that, too busy trying not to look like I've been sucker punched. Two weeks? Two *weeks*?

No wonder I saw the warning of misfortune. I only have a fortnight to scrape together the last two hundred *gilden* and make my getaway.

Don't panic.

It's harder than it looks.

No, no, I—I can manage this. I'll just need to pull one more job, maybe two. I can still get out.

The manor door belches a hideous squall as it swings open again, admitting a hulking, rather drab fellow. There are two insignias embroidered in silver thread over the breast of his plain black cloak. One I recognize: the three stars of an official of the Free Imperial States. The other I can't quite place: a set of scales with a scroll on one side, a skull on the other. I've heard of such a symbol, but *where*?

The courier spots him and shuffles to the other piece of paper. "The margrave also wishes to pass on the following: 'This is the time for celebration, not sorrow. His Lordship understands Bóern has been plagued by a persistent phantom of late. Now that, too, is at an end.'"

Oh no. Now I know *exactly* what that symbol means. Who that man is.

I may have two weeks to leave Almandy, but I need to get out of Eisendorf Manor as fast as I can.

"'By special request, Bóern has received dispensation for the investigation, arrest, and trial of the *Pfennigeist*, by the Order of Prefects of the Godly Courts.'"

CHAPTER THREE

Rubies and Pearls

THERE IS ONE KEY THING THAT HAS KEPT ME FROM BEING CAUGHT until now, and that is the fact that rich nobles don't know how to handle being robbed in their own homes.

I'm not going to lie, it bothered me when I robbed the von Holtzburgs and they just carried on like nothing happened. Only later did I realize they weren't going to admit to being victims. At least, not until it was in vogue. For nobles who have lived their entire lives assured of their own safety, it's embarrassing that someone—the *same* someone—keeps breaking through their money and their status and taking what they hold dear.

(I know why I left my first red penny, but if I'm being honest, that's why I *keep* leaving them. I want them to know it's me, always me, hitting them where it hurts.)

But the nobility has no way to stop it. That slack-jawed bailiff will just wring his cap at the sight of empty jewelry boxes and mutter about ghosts and *grimlingen*. They can clap obvious criminals in the stocks, but they've no notion how to sniff out wilier culprits like bloodhounds.

The brute in the entrance hall now has been trained to do precisely that. The prefects of the Godly Courts come from the Free Imperial States, where the people elect their leaders, like Minister Holbein—or at least, whoever the Low Gods *advise* them to elect. The Godly Courts are their judges, juries, and executioners, and the duty of a prefect is to find all the facts of a case so the Low Gods themselves may render judgment.

It's said the prefects know where to look, what to ask, who to listen to; it's said they wield tools and powers of the Low Gods themselves to uncover the truth.

I've heard of prefects being summoned into the imperial principalities and marches, but it's for nothing less than the worst of villains, like child-snatchers or doxy-butchers. For one to be brought all the way to Minkja for a mere thief means three things:

First, Adalbrecht has rattled sabers and tightened fists to make this happen.

Second, I need to get out of Eisendorf Manor before Ezbeta's empty vanity is discovered.

And third, I *might* be able to pull off exactly one more theft before I have to clear out of Bóern—and hopefully Almandy itself—for good.

The small crowd draws back to make a path for the prefect as the messenger calls out, "'My friends, I give you Prefect Hubert Klemens—'"

"*Junior* Prefect." The voice from the entryway is muffled by layers upon layers of wool and fur, but it still reaches us clearly enough to stop the courier mid-sentence. Probably because it sounds a good deal younger than any of us expected.

A moment later, a doorman helps the prefect—*junior* prefect—out of his cloak and scarf. It's like popping an olive pit from the flesh; what looked like a bear of a man is abruptly whittled down to a scarecrow of a boy of no more than eighteen. His dark wool jacket sits loose on his shoulders, a uniform that belongs on someone . . . bulkier. What I can see of a gray waistcoat and dark breeches seem to fit marginally better, though *that's* a low bar to clear; his black hair is cut short like a commoner's, but parted on the side and combed as neatly as any noble's. All in all, he gives the impression of a collection of billiard cues that unionized to solve crimes.

From what little I remember of my brothers, this boy looks precisely like someone they would have thrown into the pigpen for fun. The effect is only magnified when he fishes in a breast pocket, removes a set of round spectacles, and places them on his pale, narrow face.

"Junior Prefect Emeric Conrad at your service," the boy says, blinking his dark eyes owlishly. Then he seems to recall he's not in the Free Imperial States anymore, and adds a nervous, "Sir."

My panic begins to subside. At least, it does where the prefect is concerned.

"The margrave requested Prefect Klemens." Adalbrecht's messenger says it like an accusation.

The boy bobs his head in apology, shoulders hunching. With the pearls on, I can nearly look him in the eye. I *think* he'd have a couple of inches on me if he stood straight, but his primary goal seems to be taking up as little space as possible. 'Y-yes, sir, he was held up in Lüdz. I was sent ahead to begin the preliminary investigation." He produces a small journal and a stick of paper-wrapped writing charcoal from another pocket. "I'd like to begin by taking statements—"

Komte von Eisendorf holds up a hand. "I doubt anyone here is sober enough to give you a useful account of what happened, Prefect. Won't you celebrate with us tonight, and save the questions until morning?"

I see the boy mumble an aggrieved "*junior prefect*" under his breath before he offers a shrug. "If it suits you. Sir."

It certainly suits *me*, considering that somewhere on this estate, Hans the manservant is unwittingly returning a satchel full of stolen Eisendorf jewelry to my coach.

The next hour and a half are a blur. I'm only half there as we sit down for supper, but it's not hard to keep up the Gisele act, bubbly and glowing and still half drunk as she fields felicitations. All the while my mind whirs like a clock. A few brave souls attempt to strike up a conversation with *Junior* Prefect Emeric Conrad from where he's glumly rooted himself at the other end of the table, only to give up in short order, looking almost as miserable as he does.

For once, it's easy for me to slip away with relatively little fanfare after supper. The rest of the guests are either too busy buzzing about the upcoming wedding, or too gorged and wine-fuddled to notice me quietly asking for my cloak and gloves. (Even Ezbeta is nodding off in an overstuffed damask armchair.) My coachman has been summoned, and a detachment of the messenger's escort will accompany me back to Minkja, capital of Bóern. All that's left is to wait in the foyer for the coach to pull around.

Or so I thought. I'm standing at a window in my cloak of positively angelic mink-lined frost-blue velvet, staring out into the moonless night, when a reflection in the glass shifts behind me. I whirl around.

Junior Prefect Emeric Conrad hovers a few yards away. This close, it's easy to see how he's practically swimming in his oversized uniform. He lets out an awkward little cough. "Apologies if I startled you, er . . . *Prinzessin?*"

I nod, gracious. "Can I help you?"

"I wished to offer my congratulations on your upcoming marriage," he says very quickly, pushing his spectacles up a thin nose, "and to ask if it would not be too much trouble to take your statement tomorrow morning. The Penny Phantom has stolen from you in the past as well, have they not?"

"Indeed," I say, and by that I mean I made sure everyone saw me wearing a couple of Gisele's most valuable baubles, hosted the kind of party the *Pfennigeist* kept infiltrating, and then immediately sold the jewelry to my fence. "I will be happy to tell you everything I know," I lie. Then I let a beatific smile unfurl over my face. *Gisele's* face.

I know what that smile does to people. I was there the first time the enchanted pearls were strung around the real Gisele's throat; I saw what they made her into. I saw the way her smile seemed to light up the room and break your heart all at once, in just the way you liked best.

Years ago, while I was mending Gisele's winter cloak and she was off on a hunt in the woods, I refined a theory about desire. In the world I knew, there were three reasons a person would be wanted: for profit, pleasure, or power. If you could satisfy only one, they used you. Two, they saw you.

Three, they served you.

From what I can tell, the pearls complete the trinity. They find what you might want, what you didn't know you wanted, and make you believe only the wearer can give it to you. You desire their friendship, their company, their approval, and for many, their bed.

And judging by Emeric's faintly stunned look now, I surmise even a prefect of the Godly Courts is not immune.

The wheels of the coach clatter outside on the drive, and the manor door creaks open. That's my cue. I toss a shallow curtsy Emeric's way. "Prefect Conrad."

As the door closes behind me, I catch an uneven "*junior prefect*."

No, I don't think he'll be a problem.

The footman helps me into the Reigenbach-blue coach, and I glance to the corner. The satchel is there, ceramic jars clinking quietly as the coach rocks from my weight. I seat myself nearby, sweeping my skirts over it, and accept a steaming waterskin from the footman. It's been filled with boiling water for heat, and I settle it on my lap as the door shuts, then draw a soft, heavy fur wrap over myself to make a cozy cocoon against the chill. It's going to be a long ride back to Minkja, but at least it will give me time to think.

The coach lurches forward, and I burrow deeper into the fur.

The way I see it, I have three problems.

First: I don't have enough money to leave right now. A thousand *gilden* is enough to last a spendthrift countess five months, a shrewd laborer five years. It's enough to get me out of the Blessed Empire of Almandy, through one of the borders that *isn't* a bloodbath, and it will buy . . . I don't know what. A ship? A storefront? A farm? All that matters is that it will buy me a life far from here.

And it must be far, if I am to escape my godmothers. Far enough for them to lose their claim to me.

Death told me once that she and Fortune are different beyond our borders of the Blessed Empire. That the Low Gods and their believers are like rivers and valleys, each shaping the other over time. In other lands, she is a messenger, a black dog, a warrior queen; Fortune is a horn of plenty, an eightfold-goddess, a serpent-headed titan. They wear different forms, abide by different laws.

So maybe, outside the Blessed Empire, they will no longer be my godmothers. It's the only way I can think to be free of them. Right now, I have just enough to get past the border as is, but I will be a commoner again, alone and friendless and without a penny to my name, and I know what happens to girls like that. I'd planned to solve this problem, with another theft, but . . .

Now that Adalbrecht's on his way back, I have two weeks to handle the money issue *and* figure out how to flee from my second problem: Gisele's husband-to-be.

Ordinarily, the only trouble with solving a problem like Adalbrecht would be deciding between arsenic and hemlock. But that route is cut off by my third problem: the prefects. Well, not Junior Prefect Milksop really, just the impending Prefect Klemens. A full-fledged prefect will be able to trace Adalbrecht's murder back to me, and convene the Low Gods themselves to decide my punishment. I don't think even Death or Fortune could save me then.

It's a puzzle, like picking a lock, trying to nudge each of the tumblers just right until the way is clear. *If* I arrange a visit to another noble family . . . no, Gisele is too high-profile, especially with the upcoming wedding, and will surely be connected to the crime. If we host celebrations at Castle Reigenbach? That could be something . . .

It takes a moment for me to realize the coach isn't moving anymore.

I peek out from the furs. The muted drumrolls of hoofbeats have fallen silent, and beyond the coach windows I only see pitch-black night, and torchlight sweeping down spruce boughs. My brow furrows with confusion. We're deep into the forest of Eiswald, with no need to stop.

Then I see it.

The torchlight is steady, unmoving, like the flame itself has frozen. And if I look carefully, I can see the crumbling ash of my fortune taking a turn for the worse.

There's no sound but my heartbeat rattling in my ears as the coach door slowly, quietly swings open.

Nothing is there.

Prickles run up the back of my neck. This could be the work of a *grimling*, a wicked, hungry spirit looking for a meal.

Then again, a *grimling* wouldn't bother with these theatrics. I've dealt with two Low Gods since I was four; I know when one's at work.

And if I've learned anything, it's that there's only one way to do business with a Low God: Get it over with as soon as possible. I roll my eyes, peel myself from my nest of fur, and draw my hood up against the cold as I climb out of the coach.

Sure enough, an inhuman figure towers in the road outside, wreathed in the forest's mists, perhaps twice as tall as a man. The only reason my escort isn't fleeing is that they don't see her, or anything at all. Every rider, every soldier, every attendant has gone still, their torch flames stuck in place like lanterns of molten glass. That means whichever Low God this is, they're at least powerful enough to halt time a moment.

That does not bode well.

This Low God has a bear skull for a head, twin red-tinged lights glowing in each eye socket. Two antlers branch from the crest of the skull, their tips blooming into blood-red leaves. A strange shadowy sphere floats between them. Long hair falls around the skull, parted perfectly down the middle, fading from jet-black roots to snow-white ends and laced with bands of scarlet hemp. Two gaunt human arms thrust from a heap of shifting pelts like ribs from a long-dead corpse's jerkin, bone-pale everywhere but the joints, which blush an unnaturally deep crimson. A raven is perched on one of the branch-antlers, its eyes also glowing red.

Life and death, beast and vine, blood and bone, the teeth of a predator and the horns of prey. The goddess of this forest, then. Of course Eiswald is strong enough to hold time. Her woods reach nearly all the way to the border itself.

I curtsy with a bit more sincerity than I had for the junior prefect. "Eiswald. What—"

"Silence, thief." It's a howl, a hiss, a snarl all in one.

Oh, that can't be good.

"It's *Lady* Eiswald to the likes of you. Did you think you could come into my lands and take whatever you pleased? Did you think you would never pay?" Eiswald's voice rises to a shriek. I blink and she's suddenly closed the distance, looming taller than even the coach, eyes burning scarlet. *"Did you think you could steal from mine?"*

"I don't know what you're talking about," I gasp, stumbling back.

There's a bang. A glittering cloud pours from the open coach door: everything I took from the Eisendorfs, hanging in midair like hornets.

The pewter ring rises above them all, its moonstone shimmering in cold talons. "This," Eiswald snaps. "This is a token of my protection. It is not yours to take."

"Ezbeta and Gustav don't need your protection," I fire back.

Eiswald only gnashes her teeth. *"Everyone* in my woods needs my protection. They make their sacrifices every solstice. They respect the old ways. They respect *me."*

"Easy to respect a god," I mutter, thinking of the look on Hans's face when Ezbeta screeched his name. "Anyway, your *token* was just gathering dust in the bottom of a jewelry box. They weren't using it."

"But they are far from your only trespass, aren't they, little Vanja?"

The sound of my name knocks any answer from my tongue.

For the last year, I've been Marthe, Gisele, the *Pfennigeist*. I have not answered to Vanja.

I can't remember the last time someone called me by name. I've forgotten what it feels like.

Eiswald pushes closer, and I smell night and yarrow and rot. "Do not think your godmothers can help you now. Take, take, *take*, that's all you've done for the last year, taken whatever you desired. But you have come into my woods tonight, and stolen from those under my ward. So now . . ."

One pale hand reaches out, knuckles flushed red. My hood falls back on its own, the mink trim coiling around my throat like a noose. I try to move, try to scream, but—nothing. I can't even breathe, lungs afire, my sight filling with the coal dust of terrible luck.

A burning-cold fingertip presses to my cheek, just below my right eye. There's a sharp pain.

". . . I will give you a gift," Eiswald whispers, and glides back. "You will *have* what you want."

I suck in a breath like a dagger in the gut. I can move again. My hand flies to my face—and catches on something hard, no bigger than the tip of my little finger.

Eiswald does not have lips to smile with, but the jaws of the bear skull crack a little wider. Torchlight slices along her teeth. "Rubies and pearls you shall *become*, little Vanja, and you will know the price of being wanted. For true greed will do anything to take what—"

"Wait." I strip off my glove and run my bare fingers over whatever she's put on my cheek. It's too rough to be a pearl. "Is this real?"

Eiswald tries again. "To take what it—"

"Is this a real ruby?" I whip out my boot knife and check my dim reflection in the blade.

Sure enough, a fat, impeccable, teardrop-shaped ruby sits below my right eye.

"*Scheit,*" I breathe, and immediately prod at the stone with the tip of my knife. "I could buy five horses with this."

"*True greed,*" Eiswald thunders, "will do *anything* to take what it wants."

I shoot her a pointed look as the blade scrapes against the ruby, perhaps a little too close to my right eye. Admittedly, cutting gemstones out of my own face is not ideal, but . . . *five horses.* "Do you mind? I'm trying to concentrate."

But no matter how I chisel at the jewel, it won't move, as if it's grown right out of my cheekbone.

Eiswald knocks the knife aside anyway, seizing my chin in a grip that makes me squirm. "Out of respect for your godmothers, I give you one more gift."

"*Pass*," I grind out.

"You have until the full moon to make up for what you have stolen," Eiswald growls. "The longer you take, the more your greed will overtake you, until it is all you are."

The thing about Low Gods is they're inordinately fond of talking like a book of doomsday prophecies. You could ask Fortune about the weather and she'd say something like *The wind's loyalty skews, the veil lifts* and that would mean "The rain will clear out by Tuesday." The only way to get a straight answer from them is to spell it out first. "So I'm going to keep breaking out in gemstones?"

"By the full moon, you will *be* gemstones and nothing more. The only way to save yourself is to shed your greed and make amends for—"

"What I took, right, I heard you the first time." I purse my lips. If I'm sprouting jewels like warts, maybe I've solved at least my money problem. "Are they all going to grow on my face, or somewhere less . . . necessary?"

"*Enough.* You grow tiresome." Eiswald flicks a hand, and the raven flutters down from her antlers to alight upon one ruddy fingertip. "My daughter, Ragne, will watch over you until my gift ends, one way or another."

"Your curse, you mean." I eye the raven as the gravity of this situation begins to sink in.

Eiswald tilts her head, and the leaves on her antlers shiver. "It will be what you make of it, little Vanja."

All the floating jewelry falls to the ground, save for the pewter ring, which vanishes. I swear and crouch to begin picking everything up, doing my best to keep the dirt off my pale-blue cloak. The raven—Ragne, I suppose—lands on the road, then hops away as I gather up the Eisendorfs' jewelry. A moment later she returns, dragging my knife. I tuck it back into my boot.

"At least your daughter's helpful," I grumble to Eiswald.

She doesn't answer. When I look up, she's gone.

In her place stands Godmother Death, her shroud bleeding into the mists of the road.

I rise, my hands dripping stolen gems. "Don't give me that look."

Death does not deny it. Fortune can be slippery, but you can count on Death to deal plain. Disapproval is collecting on her like dew on a grave.

I sigh and jerk my head toward the open coach door. "If you're going to yell at me, do it in here. We've still got a long way to go until Minkja."

CHAPTER FOUR

Midnight Oil

"I'm not angry," death says in the seat across from me, "just disappointed."

I stare out the coach window at the passing trees, mouth pinched shut. The coach jolted back into motion once I'd settled inside, my escort carrying on as if we hadn't taken a short break for me to be struck with a deadly curse.

Death waits a moment, then says exactly what I know she'll say. "It doesn't have to be like this. You know I can help."

And that is when Fortune arrives in a jingle of coins and bones, manifesting into the seat beside Death with a flourish of dust and gold. To me, she looks a little like Joniza, the bard from Castle Falbirg, with skin of deep bronze and glossy, tight black curls.

"*We agreed*," she says indignantly. "If we're going to discuss her servitude, we do so together. It's only fair." Then she reaches over and pats my knee. "Hello, Vanja dear."

"I didn't come to speak to her of servitude," Death protests, as annoyed as she ever gets. At least, she sounds like it. I get seasick if I look at her face too long. It's already hard to see beneath her hood, and her features constantly shift, taking on the visage of people about to perish at that precise moment. "I came because she's going to die."

Fortune scowls. "Every human dies. That's no excuse to break our agreement."

"She's going to die in two weeks," Death clarifies. "On the full moon. It was a matter of business, not family."

Fortune relaxes a bit more than I like, given that we're discussing my imminent demise. "Oh, I see. Well then. How did it happen? Your luck's shifted around quite a bit tonight, but I didn't realize it was *this* dire."

"I don't want to talk about it," I grumble into my fur wrap. "I have it under control."

Considering I now have two weeks to amass a fortune, escape one of the most powerful men in the Blessed Empire of Almandy, and evade the highly trained criminal hunter headed my way, *all the while slowly turning into precious stones*, I absolutely do not have it under control. But I'm not going to tell my godmothers that.

Besides, I have a bad feeling about what breaking the curse might entail. And if I have to make up for *everything* I've taken . . . well, timing is going to be key.

"She stole a token of Eiswald's protection from a countess," Death says flatly.

"*Vanja*," Fortune chides, shaking her head. Her wreath of coins lets out a shimmery ring. "You should know better. It's much safer to steal from the helpless."

(If you have been wondering why I am the way I am, perhaps you are learning now. But I will give Fortune and Death their due: They treat the poor and the powerful with equal disregard.)

Death continues. "Eiswald has cursed Vanja in retaliation. If she doesn't lift it by the full moon, Vanja dies."

"A killing curse over a little token? Isn't that a bit extreme?" Fortune folds her arms. "The *nerve* of some gods."

There's a muted croak from the empty corner of the coach, and then I remember it's not empty after all. Ragne is huddled on the seat, feathers blending into the dark.

"Of course not, dear, I'm sure your mother has her reasons," Fortune says quickly. Then she catches my bewildered look and adds, "I'm afraid Vanja can't understand you like that."

Ragne blinks a sleepy red eye at me and caws, then rolls over. Suddenly a black cat is hunching in the raven's place. She shakes her head, then says in a strangled, guttural voice, "Better?"

"I hate it," I say vehemently. "No. No talking animals."

"The Vanja understands now. Better." She curls up tight, tucking her nose into the end of her tail. "Good night."

I bury my face in my hands. I am *not* going to spend what may be my last two weeks alive monitored by a talking feral shape-shifter.

Fortune's voice carries through my fingers. "Will you be able to break the curse?"

"I *said* I have it handled."

There's an awkward silence. Then Fortune ventures, "Well, since we're both here . . . there *is* a way to get out of it—"

"No." I drop my hands to glare at her and Death. "I don't need your help."

"Eiswald would have no claim to you," Fortune insists. "You'll have to choose someday. It's been what, two years? Seven?"

"Four," says Death, for she always knows, "in two weeks."

"*I don't need your help*," I practically spit, seething.

The fact is that I do. I desperately need both Death and Fortune on my side.

But I can't ask for it, not from them.

It turns out all their help has a price.

After my mother gave me up, I lived with them in a cottage in their realm, and what little I recall, I recall fondly. I remember Death telling me bedtime stories of the kings she'd collected that day; I remember Fortune fussing over racks of houseplants that seemed to wilt out of sheer malice. I remember being warm and safe. I think I remember something like love.

When I was almost six, they could not keep a human child in their realm much longer, so they brought me instead to Castle Falbirg. Fortune meddled as she does, and suddenly I was the von Falbirgs' new scullery maid. They left me there with their blessings: Unlike other humans, I could see Death and Fortune themselves at work in this mortal realm, and use that knowledge for my own ends.

When I was thirteen, they came to me again. I was of age, they said; I had been given to them, they said. And now it was time for me to serve.

Their gift to me was a choice. I was to decide whose trade I would take up: Death's, or Fortune's. I would follow and serve one of them to the end of my days.

My answer was what you would expect of a thirteen-year-old who was asked to choose between her parents: *no*.

My godmothers were flummoxed. They were angry. Fortune was the most vocal about it, but I could see the grass withering around Death's feet, feel the hurt seeping from her shroud. I didn't know how to tell them I didn't want to choose which godmother I loved best.

I didn't know how to say I wanted to be more than a servant.

I had no words at all to say I'd thought I was their daughter, not a debt to be collected.

They settled it between themselves, as they tend to do. One day, they agreed, I would call on one of them for aid. I would ask a favor, I would beg for intervention either by Death or by Fortune, and in that moment—I would make my choice.

And so it has been a long, hard four years since I last called on my godmothers.

Death could save me from Eiswald's curse and simply refuse to take my life. Fortune could tilt the world in my favor, let all the answers spill into my lap so that the curse practically breaks itself. But I would rather leave Almandy, and all that I know, than spend the rest of my life serving anyone ever again.

"I won't ask," I say grimly. "I can figure this out on my own. If you've nothing else to say, leave me be."

Death and Fortune trade looks. Then they vanish in a chorus of coins, bones, and whispering shrouds.

"Rude of you," Ragne says from her corner of the seat, and flicks her tail.

I resist the urge to toss her out of the coach. If Eiswald cursed me for taking one lousy ring, she probably wouldn't take kindly to me flinging her daughter into the road like the contents of a chamber pot. "I didn't ask you either," I snap instead, and yank the hood of my cloak over my face until all I see is fur.

Make up for what you have stolen. Low Gods love their riddles, but if Eiswald had meant only the jewels, she'd have said as much.

I stole this life from Gisele. And now, somehow, I have to give it back.

I doze off, but stir awake at the clang of the rising portcullis when we pass through the main gate of Castle Reigenbach. On a gloomy night like tonight, the castle is just columns of dreary stone, but by day it's a vision, all lacy limestone towers and bright blue shingles clustered in the Yssar River's terminal bend. The river makes a near-perfect natural moat around the castle walls before tumbling down a lovely waterfall and winding through the heart of Minkja below.

Ragne stretches and yawns on the seat next to me. I missed her curling up on a corner of my fur wrap while I was asleep.

"I can't just bring a cat in," I tell her. The hoofbeats on cobblestones cover my voice for the most part, but I still keep it low so the coachmen don't think the future *markgräfin* is nattering away to herself.

"Why not?"

Saints and martyrs, her wretched yowling voice unnerves me. "Nobility doesn't pick up strays for pets."

She blinks her bright red eyes at me. There's a faint glow to them even now. "You are not noble."

"And you're not a cat. We're both pretending to be what we aren't." I push her off the wrap. "Hide in the carriage house tonight. You can come find me tomorrow."

"I have a different idea." Ragne crouches and seems to vanish. Then I feel tiny paws grasp my gloved hand and crawl up my sleeve. I yelp.

"Everything all right, *Prinzessin?*" the driver calls out.

"Fine," I call back through gritted teeth, glowering down my sleeve, where a tiny black mouse with vivid scarlet eyes is now wiggling its nose at me.

I hate this perhaps more than I hate the ruby on my face.

That reminds me, I need either an excuse or a way to hide it. Eiswald had the decency to tear the jewelry from my satchel without ruining the jars inside, so I pick the least-foul-smelling opaque ointment and dab it over the stone as we roll up to the castle's magnificent gilded double doors. I'll make some excuse about an insect bite tonight if I need to, and tomorrow I can call the ruby teardrop a new trend.

Besides, castle staff have *much* more important things to worry about.

"Welcome back, *Prinzessin*," the understeward, Barthl, says dourly as he reaches spidery fingers for my cloak.

I register the muffled uproar of servants rushing through the halls. "You've heard about the margrave."

"Yes, *Prinzessin*." Resignation is etched into his long face. He's near Adalbrecht's thirty years, and never approved of me, but I do feel a pang of sympathy. It's his job to make sure the whole of Castle Reigenbach is pristine before tomorrow's surprise inspection. "Will you need anything further tonight?"

"No." No need to make more work for them, and better to keep eyes off me. I force my voice into a semblance of airy disinterest. "I'm retiring for the evening, and not to be disturbed."

"Understood." He bows quickly and hurries away.

I too hurry up the stairs to my wing of Castle Reigenbach. Technically, there's a faster way to get to my chambers, but Gisele isn't supposed to know about that. The servant passages are the domain of Marthe the Maid.

When I arrived a year ago, the first thing I did was filch a servant uniform, stow away my pearls, and run around the castle, begging for directions. *I'm on an errand for my lady, can you tell me how to get to the stables? The ballroom? The library?*

They showed me every shortcut and servant passageway in the castle, too busy to do anything but warn me not to hassle the resident *kobold*, Poldi. Once I drafted an order to the guards to let my maid Marthe come and go as she pleased, no door in Castle Reigenbach could hold me.

I suppose I could have kept the name Vanja, but there is a scant handful of people in Minkja who still know me by that name. "Marthe Schmidt" has no history, no baggage, no agenda. No scars. And I can stop being Marthe whenever I want.

There's a fire in the hearth when I walk into my chambers, and a lit candelabra on the credenza by the door. That's Poldi's doing, for I know the worth of a friendly *kobold*, and the peril of a slighted one. Castle Falbirg's *kobold* nearly lit Gisele on fire when he thought she had laughed at him. My first night in Castle Reigenbach, I scrounged up a bowl carved of boxwood, filled it with grits and honey, and placed it on my hearth with a small goblet of mead.

I awoke in the middle of the night to find Poldi on the hearthstones in the form of a fiery, squat little man no taller than my knee. I sat up and raised my own goblet from where I'd left it on the nightstand. "To your health, and to your honor."

He toasted me back and vanished, leaving an empty bowl and a roaring fire in the hearth. I've been sure to put out grits and honey every night since, and it has always, always paid off.

I light a few more candles, then crash onto the bed facedown. Ragne scurries out of my sleeve and begins investigating the bolster and coverlet, whiskers twitching.

Part of me desperately wants to stay like this, maybe even fall asleep in my fine gown and let the laundresses steam the wrinkles out in the morning. I've burgled a small fortune, temporarily evaded a prefect, been cursed by a god, and been lectured by my godmothers.

It has, you could say, been a *very* long night.

But there's a satchel full of stolen jewels in the carriage house, and I have to get rid of them before Adalbrecht returns. With a groan, I slide off the bed and onto the plush midnight-blue carpet. It's almost as comfy as the coverlet. I make myself stand anyway, then shed my gown and pearls.

There's a wine stain on my shift, so I draw a new one from my bureau. A small sachet falls out, and I tuck it back in with the soft linen.

When Gisele's trunks were delivered to my rooms from Sovabin, I promptly dug out all the sachets of dried lavender that I'd sewn myself months ago, that I'd slipped between layers of cotton and silk, just as she'd asked. Then I threw them all into the Yssar River. I requested the steward bring me every scent I like, dried orange peels, vanilla pods, rose petals, even cinnamon sticks, all riches to me when I'd spent most of my life reeking of cheap tallow-and-ash soap. It was an unthinkable luxury to be as clean as I wanted to be, when I wanted. To decide what I would smell of.

By the end of the month, the last traces of lavender were gone, and every last stocking smelled of *me*.

I wonder if Gisele will return to lavender when I give it all back.

I can't think about that now. I've just pulled the soiled shift over my head when Ragne's voice pipes up. "Were you in a fight?"

I jump and whirl around, clutching the shift to myself. I'd forgotten she was there. Otherwise I never would have bared my back. "None of your business," I snap.

Ragne's taken the cat shape again, loafing at the foot of my bed. She blinks. "Are you angry? Those are good scars. *I* would be proud to survive such—"

"Shut up already." I yank on the clean shift, face burning. "I said it wasn't your business."

Ragne just yawns at me. "You are very odd."

I don't dignify that with a response. Instead I finish changing into a servant uniform, hiding my hair under a plain knit cap this time. I also clasp my dowdy woolen cloak with a badge that marks me for a servant of House Reigenbach. Depending on what part of Minkja I'm walking, that badge can make me a mark or it can make me untouchable. My fence, Yannec Kraus, works in a tavern right on the border between them.

When I check my reflection in the vanity mirror, I see the ruby peeking through the ointment. That's no good. Yannec has one rule: Everything I steal, I sell to him and him alone. He's also a superstitious man, or at least gods-fearing enough that if I admit the ruby's a curse, he won't risk vexing a Low God by doing business with me.

There's a small medical kit hidden in the vanity for any scrapes I collect on my heists. I plaster a bit of gauze over the ruby and hope it'll stick better than the ointment did. As I do, something in my reflection catches my eye.

A ghost is in the mirror, a girl haunted by familiar unease and doubt now that the enchantment of the pearls can't cover it up. I thought I left that girl back at Castle Falbirg.

"Where are you going?"

"*Scheit!*" I jump again, rattling the vanity. When I look back to the bed, Ragne doesn't seem the least bit contrite. "Out," I say shortly. "On business. Stay here and don't talk to anyone."

"Why not?"

"Because animals don't talk." I start lacing up my boots.

"Or you do not listen." There's a rustle and a suspicious quiet. "Can I talk to people like this?"

When I look up, there's a human girl sprawled over the coverlet, her skin pale as bone, her slit-pupiled red eyes glowing at me from beneath an uneven mess of black hair. Somehow Ragne looks my age and ancient at the same time. She's also as naked as the day she was born.

(I'm assuming she was born. For all I know, she was conjured out of cobwebs and a goat heart.)

"*No.*" I avert my eyes, patience wearing threadbare. "You absolutely *cannot* talk to anyone like that. We wear clothes."

"Not all the time." Ragne sits up. "You are uncomfortable?"

It's not that she's nude—I used to bathe with the other servant women in Castle Falbirg. But I knew them most of my life. I have no idea what to do with someone who bares themselves without hesitation. Without fear.

I point to a dresser. "Either change back or put some clothes on. There are nightgowns in the bottom drawer."

By the time my boots are laced, she's wearing a nightgown . . . as pants. Her feet stick out of the sleeves, the bottom hem hiked up to her neck. Ragne wiggles her toes at me. "Better?"

At this rate, if I leave her here, she's just as likely to wander into the hall wearing only a girdle for a hat. "No. Fine. You can come with, *if* you change into an animal—a small one—and *if* you keep your mouth shut."

Ragne clamps her teeth together with a click.

"I meant no talking," I tell her. "Not unless we're alone, understand?"

She nods and vanishes, the nightgown crumpling to the floor. A moment later, a black squirrel emerges from the fabric, scrabbles up my cloak, and rolls into a ball in the hood. I try not to shudder as I let myself out of the bedroom and slip into one of the servant stairways.

First, I head down to the kitchens and get grits and honey for Poldi. Once those are left on the hearth in the bedroom, it doesn't take long for me to fetch the satchel from the coach (*my lady forgot her toiletries*) and pass through the main gate (*my lady needs an urgent order placed with a seamstress for the wedding*). The guards even light my lantern and offer a splash of schnapps to keep me warm. I politely decline.

They also offer a small dagger with the seal of the margrave's guard in the hilt. That I accept.

Minkja is many things: a city, a dream, a promise kept, a promise broken. But it is never safe, and least of all by night.

The guards of Castle Reigenbach have earned their easy posts through valor and commendation. Adalbrecht is much, much less discerning with the Minkja guard; he lets his army's washouts work off debts or sentences by handing them a cudgel, a uniform, and the nickname of "Wolfhünden." Then he lets them off the leash.

In letter, they keep the peace. In spirit, they're just a gang with a stupid name. ("Wolfhounds"? Groundbreaking.) They've fingers in every flavor of Minkjan crime, from poppy-dust to protection rackets. You want your rival's bakery to go up in flames? Wolfhünden. You want a city council member to slip on a bridge and vanish into the Yssar? A Wolfhunder will provide.

And if the Wolfhünden find out I've stolen and fenced nearly a thousand gilden worth of jewelry in the last year without paying them a "protection fee" . . . well, at least I wouldn't have to worry about the curse anymore.

I see the looks the gatehouse guards trade as I tuck the dagger into my boot. (Ironically the boot that already has a hidden knife, but they don't need to know that.)

"Stay clear of Lähl, Marthe," one finally urges. "Or we'll never see you again."

I want to scowl at them—what kind of business would a lady like Gisele have in Lähl?—but instead I bob a curtsy. "I'm staying within the High Wall, thank you."

That appeases them only a little, but it doesn't matter. I have to offload the Eisendorf jewelry before Adalbrecht arrives tomorrow. And the illusion of Gisele . . . well, she is a demanding mistress.

With my knife and my lantern and my satchel of stolen jewels, I leave the castle behind.

CHAPTER FIVE

Dealing Clean

Minkja isn't so much a city as a hostile architectural take-over. It once was little more than a sleepy monastery and a handful of farmers who traded wool and wheat for mead and cheese among themselves, and everyone was satisfied with the arrangement.

At some point in the forging of the Blessed Empire, the Reigenbach family looked at the long arm of the shoal-thorny Yssar River and saw an opportunity in its few safe crossings. That was how the city within the High Wall came to be, with its crowded rows of milky stucco walls, scrolls of trim, and frost-silvered timbers. The buildings fan out from busy plazas the way fungus shelves sprout on stumps, stripes within stripes of brown and white climbing as high as they can. The skyline is capped off with dark ruffles of shingled roofs so crowded they almost threaten to spill over the High Wall.

And as a matter of fact, Minkja did just that a century or two ago. Houses and inns and muddy lanes began congealing beyond the wall until the Reigenbachs were forced to fence off the city yet again. On a clear day, from Castle Reigenbach you can see old Minkja within the High Wall, young Minkja within the Low Wall, then the farmlands beyond that, and finally the blue snow-capped wall of the Alderbirgs to the south.

Tonight, though, there is only fog and shadow beyond the High Wall.

I hurry through the dark, down the crest of the hill Castle Reigenbach perches on, and over the High Bridge that straddles the Yssar, pulling my cloak tighter against the frigid spray of the churning waterfall below. The High Bridge continues on as the eastern Hoenstratz viaduct, a kind of stone land bridge built to let traders march right over Minkja's winding alleys and straight to the markets they need.

I, however, need to get on Minkja's level. I cut down a brick stair-case and skirt the Göttermarkt, where candles burn in the windows of mismatched temples ringing the broad plaza. A few *sakretwaren* stalls are still open to peddle votives, offerings, and assorted charms to anyone seeking divine assistance at this decidedly ungodly hour. Many also sell witch-ash to those seeking to take matters into their own hands.

Magic is a deadly thing, though, and even deadlier for the desperate. Witches take their power by the dose. They collect bones, fur, and anything else shed by Low Gods, spirits, or *grimlingen*, burn it to ash, and add a pinch to their tea when poultices and rituals won't suffice. (It also doesn't have to be tea. There's a streetwitch in the Obarmarkt infamous for her witch-ash pastries.)

But it's not the domain of humans, and too much witch-ash poisons the mind and body both. Powerful enchantments, like the one on the pearls, require the workings of a warlock. Instead of witch-ash, warlocks draw on the power of a spirit bound to them, usually with some nasty caveats. Back in Castle Falbirg, the resident bard, Joniza, always spoke of them with equal parts pity and mistrust.

"My mother has a saying," she would tell me. "Terrible power, terrible price."

At least the *sakretwaren* stalls don't deal in warlock bonds. I'm not sure Minkja could afford to pay the cost.

A handful of evergreen garlands are strung over doorways and windows in the Göttermarkt, but the real Winterfast decorations won't start going up until next week. The temples, offerings, and souvenirs of the market are primarily for Almanic gods, whether it be shrines to different Low Gods, or the House of the High, which worships them all as manifestations of an unnameable High God. Still, more than a few venues cater to deities from outside the empire. Traders frequently get stuck in Minkja while Ungra or Öst- heckle the empire over the more profitable border crossings; sometimes the merchants decide, for whatever reason, that they like it here, and settle down.

The vendors of the Göttermarkt don't so much as blink at me hurrying past. Heavy mist is rolling off the Yssar, and between the cold and the damp, we've all made a tacit agreement to mind our own business.

Unfortunately, I have to go even deeper into the fog. Yannec's tavern is right on the docks of the Untrmarkt, which deals in more mundane goods like livestock and produce. The taverns along the docks tend to fill with boatmen swilling one more *sjoppen* of beer before they pole back down the Yssar to their villages; this late, I suspect only the meanest and drunkest of the lot will be left.

Yannec's tavern squats in the mist ahead, a brute plaster-and-timber affair making no attempts to convince anyone otherwise. Matching *loreleyn* have been painted on either side of the door, their coiling, scaled tails faded to mildew green. The wall's gray plaster shows through their chests, where drunkards have run sweaty hands over their exaggerated bosoms so many times the paint has worn off. Any port in a storm, I suppose.

I pull off the Reigenbach servant badge and stow it in my satchel.

The sour smell of cheap beer and cheaper men slaps me in the face when I walk into the tavern, but at least it's warm. Sure enough, the handful of people in the tavern are about as drunk as I imagine *Komtessin* Ezbeta to be right now, huddled over wooden *sjoppens* because they're no longer trusted with ceramic.

Two in the corner are in a bleary, heated debate, and from the sound of it, they're agreeing, just too angry and beer soaked to know it. Ragne chitters with displeasure, likely at the pungent air, but she falls silent when I jab at the hood.

Yannec isn't working the kegs, but I hear his off-key singing back in the kitchen. The barkeep is mopping up spilled beer and waves me on. I don't know what lie Yannec told her, that I'm a daughter or a lover or a friend. I am none of those, but she doesn't ask questions, and in the interest of keeping it that way, neither do I.

Behind us, wooden stools clatter to the floor, and grunts and swearing tell me the not-a-debate has erupted into violent agreement. The barkeep tosses her sodden rag at the men, then shakes her head and ducks around the bar to deal with the fight hands-on.

I slip past and head toward Yannec, a great salt ham of a man with the thick arms of someone who spends their days wrestling stew. He's greasing a heavy iron pan in the dank, too-small kitchen. A thin kerchief covers his crown, where I know his bald spot has to be spreading beyond containment. His eyebrows quirk up when I slip through the doorway and clear my throat.

"*Rohtpfenni*," he grunts.

"Marthe," I snap back. I'm too tired for this. I have plenty of names he could use, but he insists on using the one I hate. Probably because he knows why.

Yannec jerks his head at the door. "Just finishing up here. Come on, let's talk in the back." He sets the pan down and picks up a colander and a tin pail full of dishwater, then slouches through the door. I follow.

"He stinks," Ragne whispers. I just poke the hood again. She smacks the back of my neck with her squirrel tail, and I choke on my own startled curse.

We hole up in the back office, where Yannec keeps books for the tavern owner. It's a cramped room, no windows and only one other door to the alley, with a heavy bar keeping unwelcome visitors out.

Yannec sets the pail down and gestures to it. I didn't bother packing away the jewelry into individual jars again after Eiswald's mess, just bundled it all in the servant uniform hidden in the satchel. I pull it out and shake the jewelry into the colander, then submerge it in the dishwater. The oils and pastes float and coagulate into a skin of scum that's easily scraped off.

I pass the dripping colander to Yannec, who runs his fingers over each ring and bracelet, mouthing sums to himself.

You might be wondering why I would trust a man like Yannec, and the truth is, I don't. I've known him since Fortune sent me to his scullery in Castle Falbirg; I trust his resentment and I trust his greed.

I know when Yannec rode with me and Gisele to Minkja, it was to serve dinner to fine ladies, not to sling grease in this dingy tavern.

I trust that Yannec thinks he *deserves* better than this, even though it's his own damn fault for thinking the best cook in backwater Sovabin could hold a candle to traders from all over the world. (If anything, his success was Joniza's doing, for sneaking spices into his pans when he wasn't looking.)

And I trust the trinity of want: I bring him profit and, since he's my only fence, power. He sees me, even if it's just as a resource, and he won't jeopardize his cut of the profit.

"Hundred and sixty," he finally concludes. "After my cut. This's a good haul."

That still leaves me short, like I'd feared. "Would you consider . . . loaning me money?" I venture. "Against a future job?"

(Am I planning a future job? No. Does he need to know that? Also no. I'll be long gone before he figures it out.)

He opens the strongbox and shakes his head, counting out stacks of coins. "*Ja*, but not tonight. We just paid out wages, so we've only eighty *gilden* in cash. You get the eighty now, and I'll take the goods to the buyer before dawn and have the other eighty for you tomorrow."

I press my lips together, trying to smother a frown. I don't like it. Eighty *gilden* is a lot of money to leave on credit. And it's also too much for a tavern to have lying around *after* paying wages.

Joniza was the one to teach me the trick to sleight of hand. There was one person I trusted in Castle Falbirg, and that was Joniza, because the bard taught me how to lie properly. Or, more romantically, she saw a little girl exhausted and covered in soot and grease, and decided to share a bit of her magic.

"Your hands must always be moving," she explained, slipping cards through her elegant brown fingers. "Both of them. People know it's a trick, right? So they try to watch your hands to see it for themselves. But they can only watch *one* hand at a time."

Joniza taught me the tricks behind card games like Find the Lady. How to palm a tin coin and slip it into someone's pocket. How to pluck a silk daisy from behind someone's ear.

But what she was *really* teaching me was how to read a person.

How to keep their attention where you want it. How to make them see only what you want them to.

Yannec never bothered learning any of that. So he doesn't give me anything to look at other than the strongbox he's rummaging in, the one he claims doesn't have more than eighty *gilden* to it. According to his mumbles, he's counted out twenty *gilden* already.

I can see at least another hundred *gilden* in there in hard yellow coin. Another fifty in rolls of white pennies.

I don't know why he's lying and I don't care. There are all manner of things a man could spend coin on in Minkja, for good and for evil. What matters is that he thinks he can lie to *me*.

"If you only have half the money, then you get half the jewelry," I tell him coldly.

He slams the strongbox shut. A glitter in his eye says his temper's stirring. "You got another fence, *Rohtpfenni*?"

There are plenty of other fences down in the Lähl district, but we both know I can't go there alone by night, and a Reigenbach servant has no good reason to go there by day. Besides, they all owe a cut to the Wolfhünden, and that cut will come out of my share, not theirs.

Still, I won't be yanked around. "You sure don't have another supplier," I return. "No one else is bringing you hauls like this. Deal clean with me, or you won't deal with me at all."

Nothing stokes his ire like jealousy, but in the past, he's caved easy enough at a threat. Tonight that glint in his eye sharpens. He's staring narrowly at me—no, my cheek. One meaty finger jabs my way. "What's that?"

I feel a draft where the gauze hid the ruby teardrop. A moment later, a white square flutters onto the desk.

For the second time tonight, a hand clamps around my chin like a vise.

"Who else are you selling to?" Yannec demands, dragging me up to the tips of my toes. Ragne lets out a startled chirp and squirms in my hood. "A stone like that's worth *twice* what you brought me! *Who is he?*"

"Bold of you to assume it's a he," I squeak, trying to wriggle free to no avail, "but it's no one, you dolt. The margrave's coming back tomorrow, and this is a gift for the wedding. I can't sell it."

"Pig shit." He digs at the ruby with his free hand, but it doesn't budge, only grating a little, like a molar rooted to my cheekbone. "What devilry is this? Why won't it come off?"

"I *told* you, it's a gift, it's a special kind of glue—"

He whips me by the jaw like a wet rag. My teeth ache from slamming together.

"*Stop lying*," Yannec growls, breathing hard. He leaves off picking at my face to grasp about the papers on the desk. My breath catches when he finds what he's looking for: a dull knife.

You will know the price, Eiswald whispers in my memory, *of being wanted*.

Considering the first thing *I* tried to do was pry the ruby off my own face, I suppose I could have seen this coming.

There is precious little point in struggling against a Low God who has you by the jaw, but Yannec is just a man, and a greedy, desperate one at that. I thrash until his grip loosens, then sink my teeth into the web of skin between his thumb and forefinger. He howls and lets go completely.

I stumble back, wiping blood from my teeth. Ragne is chirping her alarm in my hood, but I ignore it. "Are you *mad*?" I sputter. "I don't want to do this, Yannec!"

He points the knife at me, grip shaking. There's a sheen of fine powder along the edge.

Suddenly I know why he's so eager to try pulling a shell game with my money. For a horrible second, I fear the powder is witch-ash—but if it was, I'd already be turned to stone or the like.

"Give it to me," Yannec half sobs, half snarls. "Why won't you just *give it to me?*"

No, he's not looking for power, just the escape of poppy-dust. Eighty *gilden* will buy enough to keep him in dreams for the rest of winter. The ruby teardrop will buy even more.

Sweat's breaking out on his upper lip, a symptom of withdrawal, along with paranoia and violence. I should have noticed the signs, and now I'm about to pay the price.

He stumbles around the desk, and I dart to try to keep it between us. "Stop! We can talk this through."

"I'll cut it out if I have to," he whispers. Belatedly I realize I've made a terrible miscalculation: He's standing between me and the door back to the kitchen. I can still reach the door to the alley, but by the time I can work the heavy bar free, he'll be on me.

There's a sudden weight around my neck, and claws dig briefly into my shoulder. A black cat springs off me and lands on the desk, tail bushed out and lashing to and fro.

"She told you to stop," Ragne yowls in that horrid, screeching cat voice.

Yannec gapes at her, then sweeps his knife in an unsteady arc. "Get back, devil!"

"Stop helping, Ragne." I try to catch her by the scruff, but she twists free, shooting me a bewildered and indignant look. "Your mother—"

"You're in league with a *grimling?*" Yannec's face is slick with sweat now.

"You are insulting me, stink man," Ragne hisses. "I am no *grimling*. Give the Vanja what you owe her."

"I'll not pay a red penny to a wicked creature"—Yannec slashes the knife Ragne's way, but misses by a country mile—"nor its *thrall*!"

He lunges for me. Ragne leaps off the desk in a swell of black fur, landing between us as a bristling wolf. Her teeth snap a warning in the air. Yannec flounders back, stumbles, topples to the floor—

—then goes horribly still with a choking gasp. The hilt of his own knife protrudes from his chest.

Ragne sits on her haunches. Then she cocks her head, one wolf ear flat against her skull, the other perked up. "Oh! I think he is dead now."

Her dog voice is even worse than her cat voice.

I slide down the wall, and for a moment all I hear is the pounding of my own heartbeat. Then I see the hilt of the extra knife the guards gave me peeking over the top of my boot, and let out a laugh of disbelief. I'd completely forgotten it was there.

Not that it would have helped any more than the other knife hidden in my bootheel. Poppy-starved men will walk over broken glass for another taste. Men starved of anything, really. Especially gold.

Death appears over Yannec's hunched body, paying no heed to the spreading pool of blood. Ragne's teeth bare in a canine grin. "Hello! It is good to see you again so soon."

"Likewise," Death answers. I feel her eyes on me.

I slide my hands down my face. "I *don't* need your help."

By the time I look again, she's gone. I brace myself against the desk, staring at the lump on the ground far, far too close to me.

Yannec is dead. Yannec, who I did not love and who did not love me, but he was my last link to Castle Falbirg. At least, the last one I still speak to.

Spoke to.

Yannec, who tried to kill me for a ruby, so he could buy enough poppy-dust to forget his own disappointment. I knew being my fence gave him profit and power, but that was not enough. In the end, I was still something to be used.

Yannec, whose body is now one more problem I need to solve. Along with the Eisendorf jewelry. And making it to a thousand *gilden* in the next two weeks. And breaking the curse before it kills me—or before I am killed for it.

The body problem, at least, I can solve.

"Ragne." I push myself back to my feet, inch by weary inch. "Have you had dinner?"

CHAPTER SIX

The Great Breakfast Awakening Of Junior Prefect Emeric Conrad

I FORGOT TO LOCK THE BEDROOM DOOR. I FIND THIS OUT THE HARD way the next morning.

"I'm so sorry, Princess Gisele, but you have a visitor."

I throw an arm over my face as one maid ties the curtains back to let in a cascade of light and another bustles in with a breakfast tray.

"What time is it?" I mumble, then roll onto my stomach. Gisele's pearls click around my neck, for I sleep in them just in case of situations like this: unexpected intruders.

"Nearly nine in the morning, *Prinzessin*."

"They can wait," I groan into the pillow, then stuff down a startled curse as I abruptly find fur in my mouth. There's a squeak. Ragne has burrowed between my pillow and the next one, a black mouse once again. I glare down at her.

Last night I set out a perfectly good chair for her to sleep on, in whatever form she thought best. By no means, I told her, was she allowed on the bed.

Half of my pillow is covered in black cat hair. My *pillow*. You know, where I put my *human person face*.

"Begging your pardon, but he, er, says he made an appointment with you last evening."

I squint at the maid as she finishes opening the curtains. Her name is Trudl, and she was the first to offer me her services as a lady's maid. (Politely declined.) I'm positive she thinks Marthe is doing a terrible job.

"A young man?" Trudl shrugs apologetically as the other maid ducks out with a curtsy. "Emeric Conrad."

"Who?" I croak.

She shrugs again. "He says he's here to take a statement for the Godly Courts, but he looks awfully young for a prefect."

I cannot smother a sigh of immense disgust. "*Junior* prefect. Right. He must have left after I did."

"No, *Prinzessin*. He says he left Eisendorf Manor this morning. He must have skipped breakfast to make it here so early." Trudl helps me sit up. "Shall I fetch—oh."

"What's wrong?" I ask, afraid she's spotted Ragne in the pillows.

She shakes her head. Her gaze has sharpened slightly. "Nothing at all. I was just surprised by . . . well, it's a lovely ruby, *Prinzessin*."

Scheit. Maybe she'll buy the excuse Yannec did not. I stumble to my feet. "I thought it would be nice for the wedding. Stays on with a special glue. It's all the rage in Thirol right now."

Trudl nods. I can guess what she thinks of my having a small fortune pasted to my face. "Very well. Shall I fetch Marthe to help you dress?"

"No," I say quickly, bracing myself on the bedpost. "I told her to wake me at nine, so she'll be along shortly."

Last night . . . well, it didn't end like I'd hoped, in about five hundred different ways, and I am in no shape to run around pretending to be two people at once. My reflection in the vanity says that's a wise choice: Even with the magic of the pearls, Gisele looks a mess, platinum curls as bed-rumpled as the nightgown. Granted, the pearls make it all look deliberate, but . . .

That gives me an idea.

"Send the prefect up to my personal parlor," I say, "and get him breakfast, same as what I'm having. Take my tray there too." Then I scan my breakfast. It's missing the final touch. "And one more thing . . ."

Two minutes later, I stroll into my guest parlor only marginally more put together than when I woke up. I've donned slippers and pulled my hair back into a positively devilish tail dripping down one shoulder, but all I'm wearing is a rich scarlet brocade dressing gown bundled over the nightgown. It's heavy enough that I'm not worried about letting anything slip.

It's still *wildly* inappropriate. A young *prinzessin* has no business receiving guests in her nightclothes. Especially a young *prinzessin* about to marry the ruler of the largest march in southern Almandy. Granted, the pearls don't work the same on everyone, and I didn't want to take for granted that the good prefect would have that sort of interest in women, let alone anyone. But judging by the vaguely terrified transfixion of Emeric Conrad as he stares from the table set for two, he is still far, far from immune.

He nearly knocks over his chair bolting to his feet, then jerks into a stiff bow. "P-Princess Gisele. I—"

"Is it to your liking?" I glide into my own seat and let the question dangle a moment before flicking my hand at the spread of soft brown pretzels and pumpernickel, fans of sliced cheese, pools of spiced applesauce and sweet mustard. "Your breakfast, that is."

Emeric gapes a little too long, taking in the ruby, the dressing gown, the nightgown *under* the dressing gown, and finally catches himself. He half sits, half wilts into his chair, then fusses about his oversized uniform jacket and extracts his little notebook and charcoal stick with excruciating effort, the charcoal's paper wrap crinkling beneath unsteady fingers. "I, erm. It's very kind of you, *Prinzessin*. If you would not mind, I would like to—"

He's interrupted by a knock at the door.

"Come in," I call.

Emeric clears his throat. "I would like to—"

The parlor door swings open to admit a man bearing a sizzling platter of long, fat, *extremely* suggestive red sausages. They wobble scandalously as he sets the platter down between me and Emeric. "Your *rohtwurst*, m'lady."

"*Divine.*" I reach over and gleefully spear one on my fork.

Emeric drops his charcoal stick.

I wave the *rohtwurst* in his direction, its crispy skin crackling with pork grease. "A favorite in Sovabin. Reminds me of home."

"I see." Emeric's voice cracks. Conspicuously.

This is the part where I must admit that I have no idea what to do with someone's . . . *personal rohtwurst.* I mean, I've heard plenty of gossipy details and dirty jokes, and Joniza explained the mechanics when I was the proper age. I would even say there's some appeal in the idea, at least with the right person. But I've had different priorities even longer than I've had an interest in, well, *rohtwurst*, and those priorities come first.

Which means I'm not quite sure what messages Gisele is about to send poor Junior Prefect Emeric Conrad this morning, only that his ears are turning very red, and he looks both fascinated and deeply, deeply concerned when I deposit the sausage between the applesauce and the pretzel on my plate.

"What were you saying, *Meister* Emeric?" I ask innocently. I break a bit off the pretzel and pop it into my mouth.

He's staring at the ruby again. Eiswald did say something about the price of being wanted; maybe there's something in the curse that draws out people's greed, the way the pearls draw out desire.

Emeric fixes his gaze on the table with an admirable amount of determination. "I would like to take notes while we speak. And Junior Prefect Conrad, if you please. I haven't been fully ordained yet."

I chew slowly, swallow, and smile. "I see."

He ducks his head, then cracks open his notebook and flips through the pages. "Er. Let's start with . . ."

"You're not eating." I pout.

Emeric blinks at me over his spectacles, then butters a slice of pumpernickel, seemingly just to appease me. "C-could we begin with confirming some basic facts, please? My superior, Prefect Klemens, is not well versed in Bóernische . . ." The knife slips a bit. ". . . relations."

"Go on."

Tidy black hair falls over his brow as he frowns at his notebook, and I'm amused to realize he may have skipped breakfast at the von Eisendorfs', but he did not shirk personal grooming before he departed. "A little over a year ago, *Markgraf* von Reigenbach traveled to Sovabin to request your hand in marriage, correct?"

No. He all but mugged Castle Falbirg. He did it in the way Almanic nobles rob things from each other, mentioning how every salt road in the southern half of the empire passed—by design—through Minkja. He regaled Gisele's parents, Prince and Dame von Falbirg, with stories of his great armies at the borders, and how sometimes they just *had* to close off every trade route leading into Sovabin, *for safety*. He smiled his wolf's smile and said a jewel like Gisele belonged in a crown.

And then he *requested* her hand.

"Correct," I answer.

Another glance darts up to me, then away. "Shortly after, you came to Minkja with . . ." He checks his notes. "Three servants from Sovabin: your cook, Yannec Kraus; your bard, Joniza Ardîm; and your personal maid, Vanja Schmidt. Correct?"

My fork clinks clumsily on the plate.

That's the second time I've heard my name from the mouth of a stranger in the last twelve hours. I don't like it. It's the difference between waltzing in here in Gisele's pearls and a dressing gown, and having someone walk in on me—the real me—in the bath.

I recover quickly enough. "Not quite. Yannec left my service when we arrived. Joniza came to Minkja after me, and decided to search out other opportunities. I wish them both nothing but the best of luck."

I smile benevolently, like I *didn't* roll Yannec's body into the Yssar River about nine hours ago.

That was how the night ended, by the way. I tossed the office to make it look like a burglary gone wrong, and took the *gilden* in the strongbox, along with the Eisendorf jewels and the tavern's ledger. It would have been easier for Ragne to handle the body herself, but it turned out her assistance had two limitations.

One was that she's apparently a vegetarian.

"It will make me sick," she explained, lumbering out of the alleyway as a black bear with Yannec's body slumped over her shoulders. "What if I ate him and then made myself human? Would I have human meat in my human belly? *No*, I would not like that. Besides, he is a stink man."

The other limit was more literal. We made it halfway to the end of the nearest dock before she wobbled in place and abruptly shrank back down to a squirrel, squalling until I shoved Yannec off her.

"It is hard, big shapes on the new moon," Ragne mumbled, then curled into a ball with her fluffy tail over her nose, eyes sliding shut. "Good night."

It was a strange moment, being stranded on the dock with the body of one of my oldest acquaintances. There's something bitter about parting with someone who had a hand in who you are now; it's even bitterer when that hand left scars.

I said a few words about how he wasn't a good man, but he'd only raised a hand to me once before tonight, and maybe Death would commend him for it. I wedged a red penny between his teeth so he'd have fare for the Ferryman to take his soul onward.

Then I pushed him, the last man in Minkja who knew my real name, into the river, and watched the dark Yssar waters swallow him whole.

"And Vanja Schmidt?"

Emeric's voice brings me back.

"Vanja is gone," I half lie, a little too fast. "She took her leave before we arrived here. I don't think Minkja suited her tastes."

Then I slice the tip off the *rohtwurst*.

Emeric goes very pale, then very red. "R-right, then. Do you know where any of them are now?"

"No." That's an outright lie. I delicately lift the bite of sausage to my mouth. "But my darling Adalbrecht has seen to my *every* need."

I've decided to try to make Emeric's voice crack again before he's finished his questions.

He clears his throat and thumbs through his notebook with a rewarding air of desperation. He's definitely shaking; I *think* he might be sweating. "Thank you, I'm sure Prefect Klemens will find this quite . . . illuminating. Could you tell me about the theft that occurred here?"

I can, but I would like him to be distracted for it. I nudge the platter of *rohtwurst* his way. "You're still not eating! Aren't you hungry?"

The sausages jiggle menacingly on the plate. He tugs on the plain starched linen *krebatte* knotted at his throat. "Forgive me, *Prinzessin*, of course. The burglary, if you could . . . ?"

"Ah, yes." I let the dressing gown slip to the edge of a shoulder and tear off another piece of pretzel, staring vapidly into the distance. "It happened in April, I think? Perhaps the end of March? I was hosting a party for the spring equinox. Do they do those where you're from? Equinox parties?"

Emeric has just taken a large bite of buttered pumpernickel. He half nods, awkward, one hand over his mouth.

"Well, mine was superb. You should really stick around for the wedding, it's going to be an absolute spectacle." I wriggle in my seat, a smug little smile curling my lips as I twirl a pale curl around a finger. "Poor Sieglinde von Folkenstein. She just got married on All-Gods' Eve, and now I'm afraid her wedding's going to look like a peasant revel next to mine."

This is the trick, you see. Everyone assumes thieves are desperate and destitute. The margravine-to-be has everything she needs and more; why in the name of the Blessed Empress wouldn't that be enough?

"Please." Emeric swallows. "The—the burglary."

"Right. Dreadful business." I prod at the *rohtwurst* with my fork, scooting it around the plate. Emeric's interpretation of that is either very lewd or very misguided, but he looks sufficiently flustered either way. "Well, it was just like the rest. I"—*scoot*—"came back here after the party"—*scoot-poke-scoot*—"and my jewelry box was right where I left it, but completely empty." I leave off so he'll at least remember this detail: "Except for the red penny, of course."

"And the castle guard saw nothing?"

I shake my head. "No one's seen the Penny Phantom, you should know that."

(They've seen Marthe, Gisele, and Nameless Servant Number Thirty-Seven countless times, but Emeric won't hear it from me. Or them, probably.)

He leans back and futzes with his *krebatte*, frowning. "Did you notice anything unusual that night? Any uninvited guests, any sullen servants?"

"*Sullen?*" I ask incredulously, surprised by my own flare of annoyance. High Gods forbid a servant look unhappy with her lot as she empties the fifth chamber pot of the day.

Then I catch myself. Gisele, of course, would see it differently.

I force a laugh. "What a funny joke, Pref—*Junior* Prefect Conrad, excuse me. My servants have never said so much as a cross word to me!" I tear the last bit of pretzel in two and wink at him. "No, I don't recall anything out of the ordinary that evening. Ezbeta von Eisendorf was quite in her cups, but that's hardly what I'd call unusual."

Emeric scrapes a spoon into the applesauce. "And the von Hirsching party, do you recall anything from that?"

I resist the urge to roll my eyes. You would think even a junior prefect would do at least a minimal amount of research. "The von Hirsching . . . Oh, their little garden party in midsummer? I'm afraid I was feeling poorly, and unable to attend."

It would have been terribly suspicious if Gisele was at the scene of *every* burglary, of course. Hirsching Manor is close enough to Minkja that I was able to borrow a horse to "run an errand for my poor ailing mistress" and be back before sundown with the contents of Irmgard von Hirsching's vanity.

"Unfortunate," Emeric mumbles under his breath, sounding resigned. "Can you think of anyone at all who might hold a grudge against you, or any of the other families?"

If he had asked Vanja the maid, I could have told him these families practically foster grudges in their servants, and in their subjects, and in anyone they consider beneath them, which is most of Bóern. I could have told him it's their own damn fault for treating us like we're invisible, except when they treat us like toys.

I could have told him where the scars on my back came from. How Irmgard von Hirsching put them there simply because she was *bored*.

But sweet, vain Gisele lives in a world where only wicked creatures would resent someone like her. And Vanja . . . For him, Vanja is gone.

So I say, "No."

And then I jam my fork into the *rohtwurst*, lift the whole thing, and take a hearty, vicious bite off the end, staring Junior Prefect Emeric Conrad dead in the eye as grease rolls down my chin.

"Oh," he says, very faintly.

Then he reaches for his mug of coffee with a little too much zeal. It topples over.

I'm surprised to hear him swear as we both leap to our feet. I call for Trudl, then rest a hand on my cheek, wide-eyed and shocked. "Such *language* from a representative of the Godly Courts."

"Forgive me," he says again, flicking coffee off his notebook as Trudl bustles in to clear up the mess. "That was unseemly. I have only one more question, *Prinzessin*, and then I will trouble you no more."

"It's no trouble at all." I let my dressing gown slip a little more to see if I can get him to drop the notebook.

He only fumbles it a little, tragically. "Do you still have the penny, by any chance?"

I tilt my head. "The penny?"

It could be my imagination, but I'd swear there's a flicker of bad-luck coal dust in the air.

"The red penny the thief left." Emeric tucks the charcoal stick behind an ear and dabs at the notebook pages with a napkin. "Prefect Klemens has a special-issue spyglass that's enchanted to utilize the principles of secular possession to reconstruct the sequence of—er. That is, it will be able to lead us directly to the Penny Phantom."

"What?" I can't have heard that right.

"In simple terms, it's spelled to reveal an object's chain of owners. We can use it to find the previous owner of the penny, which would be the *Pfennigeist*."

"Oh," it's my turn to say, very faintly. Then I do what I do best: lie. "I'm sorry, I gave it to the castle *kobold* on the solstice. Good luck, you know."

Misfortune is *definitely* clouding between us now.

"Unfortunate," Emeric sighs again. "All we have is the Eisendorf penny."

"Do you need more than one?" I ask, trying to disguise my hope as curiosity. "I could inquire with the other victims."

He glances at me, then closes the notebook with a definitive *snap*. "No. I was hoping to cross-reference it with another to be certain, but just the one is enough. I must take my leave. Thank you very much for the breakfast."

"Godspeed." I wave vaguely at the door, and he follows Trudl out.

They're gone not a moment too soon; there's a sharp, quick stab of pain in my belly. I can't hold back a gasp. When I touch where it hurt, I feel something small, smooth, and hard.

I stumble back into my bedroom, close the door, and lift my nightgown. A pearl the size of my thumbnail has bloomed in my belly button.

"*Eugh.*" Somehow it's worse that it grew there of all places. I let the nightgown fall again and sit down on the raised hearth, resting my head on my knees.

I thought I had a loose plan: Break the curse before Prefect Klemens arrives, swing one last heist before the wedding, and get out of town before anyone can climb from the rubble in my wake.

But Fortune's been clear enough: The spyglass changes things. If Klemens can catch me mere *minutes* after arrival, if he can follow me . . .

If not for the damned curse, I'd already be gone. And if I can't break it fast enough to get away from not just my godmothers, but the Godly Courts, I may never make it out.

CHAPTER SEVEN

HILDE

"RAGNE." I STAND AT THE HEAD OF THE BED, HANDS PLANTED ON MY hips.

She's a fluffy black cat again, lying on my pillow with her paws tucked under her chin. One crimson eye opens as she yawns, "Mmmyes?"

"How do I break your mother's curse?"

Ragne stretches, rolling onto her back. One leg twitches in a kick. "She already said it. Make up for what you took."

"But what does that *mean*?"

"It means make up for what you took."

I let out an irate half snarl and yank the pillow out from under her. "Could you *try* not to be completely useless?"

"I was already useful last night, and now I am tired," Ragne says irritably, curling into a ball. "And you are mean, so I don't want to help you. Good night."

She buries her face in her tail, eyes squeezed shut.

I bury my own face in the pillow to muffle a frustrated scream. Then I sputter and pick cat hair out of my mouth once again. Apparently no pillow is safe.

Make up for what you took.

The obvious answer is Gisele. The *worst* answer is Gisele.

I know she made it into Minkja eventually. She's even come to the castle at least twice, forcing her way through beggars scabbing at the kitchen door for scraps. The first time, I overheard two scullions snickering about the madwoman who'd tried to claim she was the true princess.

The second time she came to my castle, I trailed her out. It wasn't hard; no one really sees me without the pearls.

I told myself it was to make sure she'd at least managed a roof over her head. After all, we'd been friends once, or as close as you could be to friends with someone who can have you whipped like a dog on a whim.

But there was part of me that reveled in the shake of her shoulders as she trudged over the viaduct and into the run-down Hoenring district. Part of me was glad for every slick glimmer of snot on her tearstained face, every fray in her tattered, too-small dress, every stumble as *she* had to move out of someone's way for once.

And almost all of me rejoiced to see her slink into a shabby, squat boardinghouse. I wanted her to know what it was like, sleeping in moldering straw, having only one tatty, smelly frock to her name, living at the mercy of a world that doesn't give a damn. I wanted her to know my world the way I knew hers.

It was selfish. It was ugly. And it was true.

I left her in the Hoenring, and I haven't seen her since.

There's no guarantee I need Gisele to break the curse. Eiswald didn't say I had to *give back* what I took, only that I had to make up for it. But I don't have time to dance around the possibility. Better to rule it out and move on.

I get dressed quickly, picking a plain gown of heavy dove-gray velvet and fixing my hair into an elegant tumble of curls. I have to leave the ruby teardrop exposed, because a bandage on the *prinzessin*'s face would generate more gossip than the rumor of a tacky accessory. Between that and the pearls, the whole outfit is the sort the wealthy favor when mingling with commoners: simple enough to let them pretend humility, expensive enough to remind everyone who's going home to a castle.

I also make sure Yannec's ledger is hidden in my vanity. Once I've put a dent in this curse, I'll see if I can figure out who was buying the stolen jewelry, then take the Eisendorf haul there myself.

I leave Ragne asleep on the bed as I step from my chambers in the riverfront wing. If she gets caught, that's her problem.

The halls are hushed, a sterile kind of still. My pulse picks up when I realize why: The margrave must be close.

You see, Adalbrecht von Reigenbach doesn't walk into a castle. He makes landfall. People send warning ahead when they see him bearing down on the horizon, and you can't figure out why the world suddenly seems so quiet, until you realize every creature with sense has gone into hiding.

I can't hide from him in his own castle. Luckily, I need to get out anyway.

"Ready my coach," I order the guards on duty once I reach the entrance hall. "I'm going into the city."

"Right away, *Prinzessin*."

"Where to?" Barthl's voice echoes off the vaulted ceiling. I turn and find him scurrying down the ladder from where he was dusting the stiff, overlarge marble busts of the last margrave and margravine in their high alcove. He looks as ill-tempered and haggard as . . . well, an understeward who's been up all night orchestrating legions of servants.

But that doesn't mean he can pry into my business. I cock my head at him, frost creeping into my voice "Pardon?"

Barthl bows hastily, but there's an equal warning in his tone. "My sincerest apologies, *Prinzessin*." (Somehow I doubt that.) "The margrave will be here anytime now, and it would be . . . That is, I'm *certain* you wouldn't wish to miss his arrival."

The only reason I would want to be here for that is so I could dump a kettle of boiling pitch over his head. "Certainly not," I lie. "I've urgent matters to attend to, but I won't be long."

"Very well." Barthl is utterly unconvinced. "Should the margrave return before you, though, where shall I tell him you've gone?"

This is getting absurd. No one's spoken to Gisele like this since I took up the pearls; I've practically forgotten what it's like to be challenged as the *prinzessin*. "I'm afraid it's confidential."

Barthl's chin lifts, his mouth set tight. "Ah. Shall I tell him it's further . . . *business* with the junior prefect, then?"

That's not a warning, that's an open threat.

Adalbrecht will be the first person to outrank me in Castle Reigenbach. And Barthl will apparently snitch to him without so much as a flinch.

"No," I splutter, "the prefects and I are quite finished. If you *must* know, I'm . . ." *Scheit*. I can't exactly say I'm haring off in search of the real Gisele. This lie has to be morally and practically impeccable. "I need to . . ." I need innocent, I need humble, I need—

Aha.

"Orphans," I declare.

"You need to . . . orphans," Barthl repeats slowly.

"Charity." I pronounce it like laying down a trump card. Now I can give him an order, and he'll have to leave off with his questions. "I promised to personally deliver a donation to an orphanage in need. Now be a dear and fetch me three *gilden* from the treasury."

"As the *prinzessin* wishes," he grits through his teeth, and stalks off.

I futz with my cloak's ribbon tie, silently congratulating myself on my own stroke of genius. This is the perfect excuse to scout around for Gisele in the Hoenring district.

The coach pulls up just as Barthl returns from the treasury with a scowl and a clinking purse. Judging by the purse's size, he withdrew it in white pennies, which are ten to a *gelt*. And judging by the weight when it drops in my hand, it's a good five pennies short. But there's no time to make him do it over.

"Much obliged," I say tightly, and sweep outside before he can interrogate me further.

The footman opens my carriage's door. "Where to, *Prinzessin*?"

"The Hoenring. Find me orphans," I order, practically leaping into the coach. "Take me to the first orphanage you see."

I settle into my seat as the carriage jolts into motion, leaving the fur wraps piled on the opposite bench for now. Then I nearly jump out of my skin as a tinny wisp of a voice rasps in my ear, "You sound like a *grimling*."

Ragne climbs out of my cloak's hood as a black squirrel again, then launches herself into the pile of furs. A moment later, her pale human face emerges through a tangle of chin-length raven hair. And I mean *literally* raven hair, as it appears to be half feathers. Slit pupils slash through the red of her irises.

"You *look* like a *grimling*," I retort, heart still racing. I yank the screens over the windows before someone sees her in here with me.

"But you are the one hunting for orphans." She cackles as she arranges the wraps over herself, bare legs sticking out, then waves her hands around, fingers crooked like claws. "Grr! Argh! Bring me children to eat!"

"I'm—it's complicated," I huff. "I see you decided to be helpful."

Ragne shrugs. "I know what you know, no more. And I know I am to keep watch over you. What did you take from orphans, that you must make up for it?"

"Nothing. I'm looking for the real Gisele."

"Is she an orphan?"

"No." I see Ragne frown and cut her off. "She might be living near the orphanage. It's an excuse to look for her without people knowing I'm . . . not the real princess."

"What did you take from a real Gisele?"

I press my lips together. "Everything."

"And will you give it back now?"

"It's complicated," I grumble again, pinching my nose. "I don't know if it will break the curse, and if it doesn't, or if it goes bad, being locked in a dungeon will make it a lot harder to make up for what I took."

"They will put you in jail for giving it back?" Ragne's brow furrows.

"Gisele is probably angry with me. And if I give her"—I wave my hand at the carriage—"all this back, she'll have the power to hurt me. Understand?"

Ragne grins sunnily at me with all of her teeth. They are much, much too sharp to be human. "No! I don't."

I roll my eyes. "Don't hurt yourself thinking about it. Anyway, when I get out, you can stay in the carriage or you can come with me, but you have to be small enough to not be seen. *Please* tell me you understand that at least."

She flops over sideways on the seat, still grinning. "Yes. I will be a squirrel again."

I don't dignify that with a response, instead counting through the white pennies. I was right, Barthl shorted me by five. On the other hand, splitting the *gilden* into pennies means I can stretch them if I need to. The more "charity" I dish out, the more it might help with the curse. And I'll pay as many visits as it takes to find Gisele.

There's a terrible familiarity to the silver coins as they slip through my fingers.

My jaw aches. After a moment, I look up at Ragne, who's busy pushing her bare feet against the roof of the carriage. "So . . . are you Eiswald's servant?"

She looks over at me, as baffled by that as by everything else. "No. I am her daughter. Mother saw a human man she wanted in her forests, and he wanted her, and they made me, and I have lived with her since. I can tell you all about her forests, they're full of lots of nice beasts and bones—"

"She didn't tell you to serve her?" I interrupt. "When you turned thirteen? Or make you choose between her or your father?"

Ragne swings her legs to the floor and sits bolt upright. "Why would she be so cruel?"

I have no answer for that. I'd been hoping she would.

The carriage slows. Ragne shrinks to a squirrel and darts back inside my hood as I push the window screen aside. We're past the High Wall, well into the Hoenring, where the houses are mostly smaller, the roads mostly narrower, and the faces unilaterally harder. It's not as bad as the southern Sumpfling district, which spends most of spring at least an inch underwater, but it's still a lean life between the High Wall and the Low.

We pull up in front of a lowly clapboard building with a wooden sign that reads *Gänslinghaus*, bordered in what I think were intended to be daisies, if the painter responsible were drunk and blindfolded. A neglected donation box sits by the stoop, the lid still covered in telltale undisturbed road grime and frost from this morning. Something about the house strikes a faint echo in my memory, but I can't quite place it as I get out of the carriage.

A round face appears in the window, pressing their nose to the windowpane.

"Aunt Umayya!" Even if I couldn't see the child's mouth moving, I'd hear them clear through the glass. "There's a princess outside!"

Immediately five more faces pop into the windows, jostling for a better look. There's a murmur of a lower voice, chiding, before the door swings open. A woman stands there in a faded woolen dress that looks like it's retained more stains than dye, unlike the beautiful indigo Magrabi shawl around her shoulders. She looks to be in her early forties, her gray-streaked dark hair pulled back in a serviceable braid, and the laughter in her lined sand-gold face explains the ease in the children.

"Oh, they weren't joking!" The woman inclines her head quickly, all business. "I am Umayya. Can I help you, *Prinzessin*?"

This is about where I realize that I haven't really thought this through beyond "find Gisele."

"Uh," I say, *very* cleverly.

Just then, a little boy of about nine shoves his way past Umayya. He takes off down the road, yelling, "I'm gonna buy raisin buns!"

"*JOSEF!*" Umayya's face drops. She starts after him, then turns to me. "I am so sorry, their other caretaker isn't here right now, just— don't let them burn anything down!"

She's gone before I can protest. The doorway rapidly fills with at least a dozen other children, all peering at me like they haven't decided if I'm a wicked witch or a fairy godmother. The oldest is a boy who looks no more than twelve, and he's bouncing the youngest on a hip, a baby perhaps a year old. Many of the children look like they're from Almandy, Bourgienne, and the other middle lands, but some have the snowy-blond hair of the Deep North, the soft dark Sahalian features like Joniza, even the jet-black hair and amber cheeks of the Gharese.

"Are you a real princess?" a little girl asks.

"Uh. It's complicated." I look in the direction Umayya ran, but she's nowhere in sight, and the door is still wide open and letting out all the heat.

"I'm going inside," I tell the guards.

"Princess Gisele, is that safe?"

I shoot the man a look of pure disdain. "Are we expecting an ambush from a two-year-old?" I don't wait for his answer, striding inside and closing the door behind me.

The interior is as ramshackle as the exterior. I see a curtained-off privy, a plain little kitchen, and a narrow stairway leading to the second floor. A few lonely toys and books lie scattered in the front room among a loose deck of playing cards, and I can smell the aftermath of breakfast at the long table in the corner, but there are about twice as many children in this space as there should be.

And all of them are looking at me expectantly.

"So . . ." I run a hand down my face. "You . . . live here?"

"Yeah," one says.

Another long silence follows. I am *not* good with children.

"Do you—" I rack my brain for anything to fill the empty air. "Do you like it in Minkja?"

A Sahalian boy nods, his dark eyes solemn. "I like the snow."

Silence.

"Great . . . great." I look around and find a chair to sit in. They're all still staring at me. I get an idea and fish Ragne out of my hood, where she's begun to snore. "Do you want to meet my . . . pet squirrel?"

Ragne only rolls over in my hands, snoring louder. The children are not impressed.

I set her on the table and run my hands over my face again.

"You're not a very good princess," someone mumbles. There's a ruffle of giggles.

"You know what?" I snap. The laughter goes quiet, and instantly I feel a little chagrined. This isn't winning me any favors with *anyone*, not Eiswald, Adalbrecht, nor the ragtag bunch of orphans judging my every move.

I just have to keep them occupied until Umayya returns. Then I can make my donation and see if she knows of anyone in the Hoenring who matches Gisele's description.

Well, if I can't be nice to them, at least I can be interesting. "You want to see a knife?"

"*YEAH!*"

It's like a dam breaking. They gather around the chair as I pull out my boot knife and show them how it fits in the heel.

It turns out the keys to a child's heart are weapons and card scams. By the time Umayya returns, half the orphans are taking turns throwing knives at a log of firewood in the corner (I reclaimed my own blade and made them use the table knives) and the other half are watching as I teach Fabine, an older Bourgienne girl, how to run a game of Find the Lady.

"The key is to keep your hands moving," I'm telling Fabine as Umayya walks in, her hand locked around the runaway Josef's collar. "People are always looking for the trick—"

"You let them throw knives?" Umayya gasps as she shuts the door. "Is that a *rat* on my table?"

Ragne jerks awake as I grab her, but mercifully she stays limp. "Just a, a, a puppet," I lie, stuffing her in a pocket. "I thought they might like it, but they got bored."

"And so they are throwing knives instead." Umayya shakes her head, then surveys the damage. "Ah, it could be worse. At least they're not throwing knives at each other. *No one throw knives at each other!*"

At least three orphans sag with disappointment.

"It's my fault for dropping you into this," Umayya sighs. "All right, everyone, hand over the utensils. What brought you to the Gänslinghaus, *Prinzessin?*"

I hand the playing cards to Fabine and stand, embarrassed. "Well, I'm looking for an old friend—"

The back door in the kitchen swings open. A familiar voice hits me right in the gut.

"Good news, Auntie," Joniza half sings as she sails in from the back alley, jingling a coin purse, "it's payday in Südbígn, and our last three performances sold out!"

I can barely breathe at the sight of her.

Not long after I arrived in Minkja, I nearly ran headlong into Joniza in the Obarmarkt, ducking behind a barrel of herring just in the nick of time to escape notice.

Then every day that week I came back, waited for her to pass, trailed her to a Sahalian restaurant in Trader's Cross. I'd watch her get balls of sticky plantain dough and groundnut stew, and wash them down with a carafe that was more milk than coffee. She looked happier than she'd been in Castle Falbirg. Happy enough without me.

Eventually it hurt more to see her than to not, so I stopped. But now—it's like we're right back by the great hearth in Castle Falbirg, and she's teaching me how she snuck spices into Yannec's stews when he wasn't looking, or humming a lively ballad as I practice unfurling silk flowers from thin air. Her black hair is in long, thin, gold-threaded braids now instead of loose curls, and she dresses finer than before, but it's still her, the one person I trusted in Sovabin.

She sees me standing near the table and stops in her tracks, mouth dropping open.

"We have a guest," Umayya says tightly.

Another figure bustles in behind Joniza, oblivious, in a cloak as stained and faded as Umayya's dress. "Really? Who—"

Her hood falls back as she jerks to a halt. She's sixteen, broad-shouldered and taller than me; her dark blond locks have been braided too tight to do her rough-hewn face any favors, and her gray eyes are granite-hard when they land on me.

"*You.*" Her voice is a blast of frost. The room goes silent.

She looks almost exactly like she did the last time I saw her, over a year ago, when I left her stranded and furious on the muddy riverbank.

"Hilde, do you know Princess Gisele?" Umayya asks, perplexed.

Is that what you're calling yourself now?

"We need to talk," I begin.

That's a mistake. Cloudy misfortune begins to tumble through my sight.

Gisele-Berthilde Ludwila von Falbirg stares at me, bright red splotches blooming in her cheeks.

Then she lunges for me, screaming, "*YOU LITTLE BITCH!*"

I grab my chair and swing it between us, shouting over the shrieking children. "*Stop*—I'm trying—"

"*GIVE THEM BACK, YOU FILTHY LITTLE—*"

I jab the chair legs at her like a busker with a performing bear. "I can't—Stop, I'm here to help—"

"*LIAR!*" Gisele rips the chair from my hands and tosses it aside. "You're just a horrible little thief!"

"You're *NOT LISTENING!*" I bolt around the table, Gisele on my heels. Fury rattles in my skull, spilling unbidden from my lips. "You *never* listened," I snarl, "you only ever cared"—I duck under her arm— "about *using* me"—she swipes for me to no avail—"to get out of *your* messes!"

"You stole *everything* from me!" she half screams, lunging again.

I kick the chair back into her path. "Why do you think I'm here, you damned clod?"

"You tell me! I have nothing left for you to take!" One look tells me everything I need to know: There's a fire in her eyes, in her bared teeth, and it will not die easy.

I need to get out. I stumble toward the front door, only to trip on my hem and crash to the floorboards. Gisele is on me in an instant, hands scrabbling at my throat—she's going to choke me—

No. Worse. She's going for the pearls.

There's an ungodly howl. A black cat—*Ragne*—squirms under Gisele's arms, hissing and screeching until she jerks back. It's enough for me to scuttle away and scramble to my feet.

I dive for the door and manage to shove it open before something seizes my cape and drags me back. I hear my footman shouting for guards.

Then two men in Wolfhünden uniforms barrel through the doorway. One shoves Gisele to the ground. The other helps me up.

"All right there, Princess Gisele?" he grunts.

I brace myself on the doorjamb to catch my breath. "Y-yes, thank you."

The real Gisele is still glowering at me, nothing but rancid hate burning in her eyes.

Until the other Wolfhunder speaks.

"Laying a hand on the Golden Wolf's bride . . . men have hanged for less." He raps his cudgel against his palm. "If the lady says mercy, we'll settle for the whipping post."

The room goes quiet again, save for the quiet sniffles of the children old enough to know how bad this can go.

Gisele looks to me, startled, seasick dread sparking in her face.

No one lives in the Hoenring for a year without seeing the recreational cruelty of the Wolfhünden. I can tell she still has only a bystander's understanding of the lash. Doubtless she's told herself if she keeps her head down, though, if she minds her business, if she follows the rules, she won't wind up bound to a post.

She won't wind up screaming in barebacked, bloody agony before the crowd. She won't wind up torn between terror for the next fall of the whip, and hunger for it to bring her closer to the whipping's end.

She won't wind up like me.

Only someone raised as a princess could believe that following the rules would protect her.

And now, only I can stop this. Only I can call off the hounds.

I can do what she *never* did, not all the times her mother had too much mead and struck out because I was just there, not when Irmgard had me whipped for nothing, not even once.

I can save her. Like she never saved me.

And she and I both know I have absolutely no reason to do it.

It's, embarrassingly enough, the sniffling orphans who tip the scales. I grew up tiptoeing around the trip wires of nobility accountable to no one; these children don't need to learn those cold lessons yet. And something about having Gisele *know* she's at my mercy like this— that satisfies the ugly part of me.

"Not necessary," I say, frigid and smooth as a glacier lake, even as I avoid Joniza's stare. "Leave her be. You can't beat sense into a creature gone mad." I drop the coin purse on the floor. "I just came to leave a donation. Happy Winterfast."

Then I sweep out the door. No wonder I thought the Gänslinghaus looked familiar. When I tailed Gisele here months ago, I'd just assumed it was a boardinghouse.

"Back to my castle," I call to the driver, loud enough to carry inside. Extra emphasis on *my*.

Ragne is waiting for me in the carriage as a black cat, nearly blending into the pile of fur wraps. As we pull away, I press a hand to my stomach. The knot of pearl is still there.

Of course Gisele isn't the answer. She never has been before.

"Well, I tried," I mutter.

"You did?" Ragne cocks her head.

I shoot her a dirty look. "Yes. I gave Gisele money and tried to make amends and it didn't do anything." I slump against the back of the carriage seat, turning the curse in my mind like a dead bolt, poking at the tumblers. "I guess it's not about just giving back what I took from people. Since most of them deserved it, that makes sense . . . So the next move is giving to other people. We'll go get money from the trea- sury and try again."

"That was the Gisele?" Ragne asks after a moment.

"Yes."

"I don't think she likes you very much," Ragne yawns, curling up for another nap.

"No," I agree, "she doesn't."

"She smells nice, though."

"So does cyanide." I think of white pennies, and I think of red ones, and I tell myself it was Gisele's own choices that landed us both where we are.

THE WHITE PENNY AND THE RED

O NCE UPON A TIME, BETWEEN THE SNOWY MOUNTAINS AND THE deep, dark forest, two little girls lived in a castle.

One slept in a soft, warm bed and wore soft, warm dresses, and the words spoken to her were soft and warm as well. They called her the *prinzessin*.

The other girl slept on the hard, cold ground in the pantry, to keep away the rats. It didn't always work.

Her only dress was too small, for no one wanted to buy her a new one when it would just be stained and torn too, and quickly outgrown. The words she heard were cold and hard: scrub this, empty that, clumsy oaf, don't let the guests see you so dirty. The hands she caught were harder.

They called girls like her *russmagdt*, soot-wench, for that was all they were good for: cleaning soot off pans, and wearing it.

In the castle lived a clever and beautiful magician who knew the ways of enchantment and charm, and one night she took pity on the little *russmagdt*. She taught the girl tricks to help her impress the masters of the castle through flattery and cunning, and helped her practice night after night, even when both of them were weary to the bone.

And then one day, a great lady came to visit, and a serving maid fell ill. The *russmagdt* was given a rough bath and a clean, too-large uniform and sent to take the maid's place. When the great lady had gone and the castle was beginning to settle once more, the soot-wench was asked to help the *prinzessin* get ready for bed.

The soot-wench saw the golden hand of Fortune reaching for her, and knew this was a chance she would not see again.

"Of course," said the *russmagdt*, "but—there's something in your hair, m'lady."

She pulled a silk daisy from behind the *prinzessin*'s ear.

The princess's mother burst into astonished laughter. "How clever! Did Joniza teach you?"

Both mother and daughter were delighted. By week's end, the *prinzessin* had a new lady's maid, and the (former) *russmagdt* had a clean new dress and a straw pallet beside the hearth.

And for a while, that was good enough.

The *prinzessin* and her maid were together every day. The little maid learned more of the magician's tricks to dazzle the masters of the castle, handstands and somersaults and making salt bowls disappear. At the *prinzessin*'s insistence, the maid also learned to read and write and do her sums.

Then, of her own volition, the maid began to eavesdrop on the tutors sent to school the princess-elector-to-be in history and politics and all things a ruler ought to know. The maid learned of who lived in a castle. Who cheated their way into one. Who took coin from whom, and why.

The two girls became friends in a strange kind of way, for when it was just the two of them, they could have been cut from the same cloth. They shared secrets and dreams and jokes. They climbed the same trees, read the same books, and sometimes the princess snuck sweets off her plate for the maid. To find one was to know the other was not far away. The dame even began to call them *Rohtpfenni* and *Weysserpfenni*, the red penny and the white.

But the seam split whenever anyone else was there, for they were two little girls of almost the same age, but one had been born to own the castle, and the other called her *mistress*.

When I was nine, and new to the higher stories of Castle Falbirg, I thought the dame called me her red penny for my bright copper hair.

I remember the day I was dusting the bookshelves as Gisele's tutor droned on about the importance of standards in minting coins. I remember furtively rolling my eyes at Gisele, and trying not to giggle as she pulled a face behind the oblivious tutor's back.

"It used to be there were only white pennies," the man was wheezing. "Silver through and through. But then the *komte* of Kaarzstadt started sneaking copper into the coins to stretch his silver further, and the practice spread, and no one could agree on what a silver penny was worth when it wasn't pure. The Blessed Emperor Bertholde, your ancestor, declared any copper in a coin made it a red penny, worth one-fiftieth of a white penny. The mints sorted themselves out in short order after that."

I remember the startled, awful look on Gisele's face then. It matched the feeling in my chest.

It was the first time we understood why she was called the white penny, and I the red.

And it would not be the last.

CHAPTER EIGHT

The Golden Wolf

BEFORE WE GO MUCH FURTHER, THERE ARE A FEW THINGS YOU should probably know about my betrothed, *Markgraf* Adalbrecht von Reigenbach of Bóern.

First: He is all things a nobleman of the Blessed Empire should be, handsome and charming and bold. He's won favor by expanding his march's borders—and thus the empire's—biting off mouthfuls of the kingdoms of Thírol and Östr in the south, even nibbling at Ungra to the east. He has *kept* that favor with an easy smile, a hearty laugh, and an iron grip when he clasps hands with other noblemen.

Second: Adalbrecht is still alive because he's not a direct threat to the Blessed Empress. Long ago, the noble houses of Almandy were given a choice: the crown or the sword. Houses that chose the crown, who kept their eligibility for the Blessed Throne, had to give up most of their armies.

Houses that chose the sword ceded their claims to the Blessed Throne, but in exchange, they were given control of both the empire's armies and its borders.

House Reigenbach chose the sword, and thus, the *Kronwähler* cannot elect Adalbrecht to the imperial throne. The *Kronwähler* assembly itself is a revolting knot of internal politics and recreational backstabbing, comprised of one princeps-elector for each of the seven remaining royal bloodlines, and anywhere between thirteen and twenty-seven other delegates and cardinals, depending on how good that week's assassin is. But only the seven *princepz-wahlen,* including Gisele's father, can be elected emperor.

When Adalbrecht was eighteen, the Blessed Empress sent him to the southern battlefront to die anyway, like his two brothers before him, because that empress took no chances.

Instead, for five years, Adalbrecht made a name for himself: the Golden Wolf of Bóern. (He's a blond, and House Reigenbach's symbol is the wolf. What can I say? Soldiers aren't usually prized for their command of poetic imagery.)

He survived. His father did not; nor did the ailing empress. The *Kronwähler* elected someone a little less cutthroat in her stead, and the new Blessed Empress Frieda had no interest in a feud with someone who could never have her crown. The eight years since have been remarkably quiet.

The third thing to know about Adalbrecht: If you've kept up with the math, you now know he is nearly twice as old as me. Plenty of nobility shrug off a winter-spring romance for political gain, but I was raised to be a maidservant, not a princess. A maidservant learns quickly that when a full-grown man desires a girl half his age, it is not out of love, but hunger.

Fourth and finally, this is the thing you must know if you wish to survive: Adalbrecht von Reigenbach hungers most of all for that which he should not have.

That is why, when I see Castle Reigenbach through my carriage window, its great entrance hall doors thrown wide open and the margrave's wagons clustered on the drive, I want nothing so badly as to run.

"Stay here," I tell Ragne quietly, trying not to think too hard about the coal-dust misfortune clouding my view. The carriage door opens before she can protest. I steel myself, think of the *Prinzessin*, hold that card like a shield between me and the margrave—and step out.

"*There you are.*" The bass rumble of Adalbrecht's voice ricochets off the hard floor and out through the gaping doorway, made even stiffer by the unnatural hush. He strides toward me, cobalt cloak billowing under a hefty wolf-pelt mantle. "My bride, my *jewel*."

When the Golden Wolf came to Sovabin, I knew it was not simply for want of a young, tender bride. It's the trinity, you see: Gisele offers not just pleasure, but the power of prestige, of marrying the daughter of a *prinz-wahl*.

Last night, I erred in thinking two out of the trinity would protect me from Yannec. I never would have made that mistake with Adalbrecht von Reigenbach.

Servants and soldiers still weave through the hall, unloading Adalbrecht's train, but each one seems to be holding their breath and affording the margrave plenty of room to pass. He seems to take up most of it regardless, a walking monument to conquest who looms head and shoulders over me even with the pearls, a little too big to be lifelike. His pale face is chiseled hard, broad, and flawless; one golden lock strays from his short braid to frame his face like a scroll of gilt filigree, picturesque.

He snatches my hands up before I can hide them. His fingers feel heavier than they should, like shackles locking into place. Each breath fights me harder than the last.

You see, Adalbrecht von Reigenbach is not just dangerous in the common way of Almandy's nobles, the casual threat of working for those who value your obedience more than your life.

No, the danger of the Golden Wolf is that he takes what he wants.

But the *Prinzessin* has no reason for fear yet. I cover my revulsion with a sweet, warbling, "*Darling!* Welcome home."

"You were out." Each word drops like a charge at a sentencing.

I bounce on my toes, the very picture of a giddy, insipid bride-to-be. Internally, I am spewing a string of curses that would make even the most grizzled brothel-keeper in Lähl blush (and, perhaps, take notes for their *mietlingen*).

"I thought you might want to rest after your long journey," I lie, "and with our wedding so close, it seemed the right time to share some of our joy with the less fortunate."

Adalbrecht squeezes his hands around mine.

Here, with so many witnesses, and with the weight of Gisele's name, he keeps a semblance of grace; his face is patient and mild, and the gentle waves of his blond hair grant him a halo in the morning light.

But I know what he is when there is no one around. I know what he is to girls who don't have the protection of royal blood.

I can only imagine he is worse inside his own castle.

Even now his smile is hardening like cooling glass. "I understand you already shared some *joy* with the junior prefect this morning."

Out of the corner of my eye, I see Barthl abruptly busy himself with straightening out a tapestry. A sizzle of annoyance dances in the back of my skull. Of *course* he already squealed on me.

But there's an easy way out. I tilt my head, blinking Gisele's big, silvery eyes. "Why yes, he came to take my statement about the robbery, and it would have been rude to send him away with no breakfast! The poor boy's practically skin and bones."

Adalbrecht runs his calloused thumbs over my knuckles, pressing a little too hard as the wheels of one of his delivery wagons clatter outside. "Perhaps things are done differently in Sovabin, but in Bóern, it's not seemly for a young lady to take guests when she is . . . *underdressed*. You don't want to embarrass me, do you?"

His thumbs push into the backs of my hands, between the bones.

I yank free to cover my mouth with well-bred dismay. "Oh, how—how mortifying! I understand. Never again, darling—"

"Good." His gaze alights over my shoulder. "Ah, here we are. I brought you a present."

Two pairs of soldiers march up behind me, each pair carrying a large, canvas-wrapped bundle nearly as large as a man. "Where do you want them, m'lord?" gasps one man.

"There." Adalbrecht points up to the marble busts of his father and mother in their alcove. "Take those down."

Barthl's long face falls. He looks like he's only refrained from falling asleep on his feet through some unholy bargain. Still, he rallies as best he can. "We have room in the east gallery—"

"I don't care where they go." Adalbrecht doesn't even look at him, overseeing the deposit of his canvas bundles. Once they're lowered to the flagstones, he strides over, flicking a dagger from his belt. It slices through rope and fabric. The first coverings fall away to reveal a golden life-sized statue of a bristling wolf on its hind legs, mid-lunge.

He can't be *serious*.

The second statue is . . . also a golden wolf. This one has its teeth buried in the throat of a shaggy granite goat bleating in terror, garnets spilling from the wounds.

Adalbrecht looks at me expectantly.

"How, er," I stammer, "thoughtful."

He finally acknowledges Barthl. "I want these up within the hour."

"Within—but m'lord, we wouldn't want to damage anything in our haste," Barthl begins.

Adalbrecht's bright blue eyes bore into him. He grips Barthl's shoulder with a ferocious smile. "And I'm *certain* you don't want to disappoint my bride. These are, after all, her gifts."

Barthl looks like his teeth hurt. "Of course not, m'lord."

I would laugh at the absurdity if it was anyone but Adalbrecht. Instead I clasp my hands together. "They're truly exquisite, darling, I can't thank you enough. Now please, you haven't been home for a year, so don't let me keep you another moment. I'll go bring some more charity to Minkja while you settle in."

"Hmm." Adalbrecht's glass smile turns brittle. "Charity from my treasury?"

Oh, *scheit*, I should have seen this coming. Well, I don't need to pull all one thousand gilden from the treasury, just enough to test if charity will cure the curse. "I wasn't thinking more than fifty *gilden*. Nothing too dear, of course, just a few coins for the needy and poor."

"The poor are rarely needy," Adalbrecht drawls. "They need fewer handouts, and more of a boot to the a—forgive me, I must remember I am not in a war camp. A man will forget your money once he wastes it on drink, dice, or *mietlingen*. A kind act will go further than any amount of coin."

Spoken like a man who gives neither.

"Barthl. My lady may have five *gilden* from my treasury." He pats my cheek like I'm a too-eager hound as Barthl bows and hustles away. "Make them stretch. The ills of the poor will not be cured with money, my little dove, but with deeds."

The gold of his signet ring is unsettlingly cold against my cheek. I cover his hand with mine and make myself smile before tactfully peeling his fingers away. He finally seems to notice the ruby below my right eye, staring a long moment as if wondering whether his treasury paid for that too.

Slowly that gaze begins to simmer with something much, much too close to hunger.

I swaddle his hand with my own to distract him. It works. Adalbrecht steps back as a clatter of wheels announces the arrival of another of his wagons, and every new inch between us loosens the vise around my ribs.

When he pulls his hand away, his signet ring stays hidden in my palm. He doesn't seem to notice its absence at all. Nor does he notice as I slip it up a lace-cuffed sleeve.

I think I'll drop it down a privy, just to give him a headache.

Barthl lopes back into the hall with another purse just as Adalbrecht flicks his hand at the two soldiers stationed by the door. "You. Accompany my lady on her errands today, and make sure our charity is . . ." He lets the pause hang as he turns, headed for a corridor. ". . . practical."

The little purse lands in my empty hand with a *clink*, and then Barthl follows Adalbrecht without another word.

For a moment I stand in the entrance hall, fist tightening on the leather. The *Prinzessin's* façade slips from my grasp.

I hate him. I hate him *so much*. I hate how he talks, how he touches me, how the whole castle freezes around him.

I hate how we can be standing in broad daylight, with dozens of people careening around us, and still he knows how to make it clear that with him . . . I am utterly on my own.

The trinity of want will not protect me from him; nothing will, save myself.

But Adalbrecht went to the trouble of annexing Gisele from the von Falbirgs for a reason, of that I am certain. As long as I wear the pearls, he thinks he needs me alive.

All the same, I won't forget to lock my bedroom door tonight.

I make myself focus. Better to break the curse and get out as soon as I can. The weight of the purse in my hand is promising . . . until I open it up and find it full of dull bronze *sjilling*, each worth a fifth of a white penny, and maybe three *gilden* all told. Barthl's shorted me again.

If Eiswald is measuring my penance in coin, this will barely put a dent in what is owed. You could melt it all down and still have barely enough to buy a single stick of *one* of the seven gleaming silver candelabra in this hall.

I blink.

The candelabra are faintly sparkling with good-luck gold. Fortune's in a mood again. But why—

Then I get it.

There may be a better use of the margrave's signet ring than dropping it in a privy. I will get away with this *exactly once*, but it will be worth it if it lifts the curse.

Besides, Adalbrecht said he doesn't care where the old décor goes.

I plaster the biggest, most empty-headed smile over my face and whirl to face the two soldiers assigned to keep an eye on me. I even snap my hips just right so my skirt and cloak flare in an explosion of petticoats, and clap like a delighted toddler. "Oh, my *markgraf* is the wisest of all men, isn't he! *Deeds*, not coin. Of course. Will you assist me?"

They do. They're not paid enough to say no.

When the coach leaves for town, it's with four tapestries, six bronze statuettes, two fine lace curtains, three porcelain urns, five marble busts (not including the elder von Reigenbachs, who aren't exactly travel-sized), and all seven silver candelabra bundled in the thick, soft imported Bourgienne carpet and stuffed inside. There's just enough room for me to wedge myself into a corner while Ragne clambers over it all as a squirrel.

Essentially, I took almost everything in the entrance hall that wasn't nailed down. Adalbrecht has no reason to return there for a while, so by the time he hears about it, the goods will already be scattered across Minkja. And if he's angry—no, not if—*when* he's angry, I will flutter Gisele's long lashes, cry prettily, and say I just thought this was what he meant by *good deeds*.

We head for the Salzplatt, where the city hall, courthouse, and other municipal buildings wreathe a wide brick plaza. A great bronze statue of Kunigunde von Reigenbach, the first *markgräfin* of Bóern, towers atop a marble column in the middle of the square, closely watching the weighing of salt and stamping of crates.

A few hundred years ago, Kunigunde herself had the idea to ban the sale of any salt in Bóern unless it bore the seal of Minkja, forcing every salt merchant to pass through Bóern's capital city or take a costly detour around the entire march. That brilliantly brutal bit of maneuvering made Bóern the most powerful territory in the south, and kept Kunigunde's memory alive . . . in more ways than one.

No one's quite sure if her statue is haunted, or if a Low God has simply taken up residence there, but periodically the statue brings her spear down on the marble with a *crack*. Then she points it at whoever is trying to cheat the salt clerks at the moment. Right now she stands motionless under the flat gray sky, but I doubt anything in the plaza escapes her notice.

And we certainly don't escape the notice of the rest of the Salzplatt, rolling up in the ludicrously lavish Reigenbach coach. We come to a halt by the city hall, a great limestone building that bristles with spires and gargoyles (though the gargoyles are mostly napping). A line of shabby, pinched people wraps around the entrance, waiting to plead for forbearance from the Debtor's Magistrate.

Adalbrecht's warmongering makes him popular with the gentry of the empire, but he's squeezing most of Bóern to keep his battalions fed, clothed, and well armed. Resentment wars with curiosity in many of the faces that turn toward the coach.

"Wait here," I order Ragne again, then throw the door open and watch the pearls around my neck melt that resentment away. Flickers of gold tumble over their heads, seen only by me: Their luck is about to drastically change.

"You," I say, reaching for a hollow-eyed woman with the hunched shoulders and impeccably mended clothes of a seamstress. "My dear woman. Who do you owe?"

She drops into a curtsy, head bowed. "My apologies, mistress, I'm—I'm late on my taxes, it's fifteen white pennies, but I can't—"

"Lovely. Come with me." I turn to the rest of the line. "In fact, if you're late on your taxes or otherwise owe money to the margrave, please step aside and wait a moment. Everyone else . . ." I pull a candelabra out of the coach as people break away from the line, then toss it to one of the debtors still queuing. From the look on his face, it's worth at least a season's income. "Happy Winterfast. Next?"

The guards trade uneasy looks. "Princess Gisele," one starts, "the margrave—"

"Yes, just as Adalbrecht said," I say merrily, passing a priceless urn to a wide-eyed farmer. "*Deeds*, not money. This is all very practical. Who wants a tapestry?"

Once the carriage has been emptied, I lead the rest of the debtors into the city hall, straight up to the bewildered clerk's window. "Hello," I say brightly. "I am Gisele-Berthilde Ludwila von Falbirg, betrothed to Margrave Adalbrecht von Reigenbach, and I need you to draw up some papers for me."

"O-of course," the clerk stammers, scrambling for a clean parchment. "What does m'lady require?"

"I think you'll need a few pages." I gesture to the small crowd of people behind me, then hold up Adalbrecht's signet ring. "In the margrave's name, I am forgiving the entirety of the taxes, fees, and any other civic debts owed by these people here."

There are gasps and cheers, and an outburst of general chaos as debtors cluster at the window, desperate to make sure their names are on the list. Even the magistrate leaves his chambers to survey the commotion.

I only stay long enough to dictate the order and press Adalbrecht's ring into the wax. Then I start extracting myself from the throng, smiling graciously and clasping hands and retreating to the door. The mood is a distinct kind of joy, the static crackle of a miraculous reprieve, and I see tears in a few eyes.

I try *not* to see them, fussing with my cloak's ribbon ties. Barely over a year ago, that would have been me, weeping for so trivial a windfall.

Just then, a familiar heap of sad black wool stumbles into my path.

I stop short. "Junior Prefect. Whatever are you doing here?"

Emeric Conrad opens his mouth, closes it, then remembers to bow and immediately drops a charcoal stick as he does so. "L-Lady—er—*Prinzessin*. Hello. I was just speaking with the administrator of the city watch. That is, about the *Pfennigeist*, of course."

"Were they helpful?" I ask. They absolutely were not, of that I am *quite* confident. The only people who want to bury word of my robberies more than the victims are the Wolfhünden. Wouldn't want any other thieves getting ideas about evading their protection fees.

Not to mention that, as representatives of the Low Gods, the prefects are one of the few entities who can investigate local law enforcement, regardless of the territory. The Wolfhünden aren't about to help Emeric turn over any rocks when they know exactly what will come crawling out.

Sure enough, Emeric adjusts his *krebatte*, flustered. "They were . . . eager to have the Order's assistance."

What a terrible liar he is. I decide to show him how it's done. "I'm delighted to hear it."

"If I may, what brings you to city hall, *Prinzessin*?" He tucks his charcoal stick away somewhere in the depths of his enormous uniform coat. Then, incredibly, he places a hand on one of the stanchions sectioning off the debtors' line, and executes the most premeditated and ungainly attempt at a casual lean I have ever seen in my entire life.

I give a coy, tilting smile, just to see if I can make him tip over the stanchion. "Why, nothing nearly so *thrilling*." The stanchion wobbles. "Just sharing a bit of comfort with my people." Emeric is nodding a little too hard. "I do love being able to touch them so, it's such a *pleasure*——" And there it goes. The stanchion hits the floor with a clang. Emeric almost falls with it, only catching his balance by a hair. "Oh, goodness. Well, I'd best be off. Best of luck with your hunt for the *Pfennigeist*!"

I sail out of city hall, fighting down a grin. Tormenting the poor boy aside, between the forgiven debts and the valuables I've doled out, I feel like I've done quite a lot of good today. That was a few hundred *gilden* worth of charity right there.

But when I press a discreet hand over my belly button, the pressure of the pearl is still there. My heart sinks.

This is just——just——*rude*.

"Where to now, Princess Gisele?" the coachman asks as I hurry down the stone steps.

"Ah . . . give me a moment," I answer, and climb back into the coach to panic.

No, not panic. *Think*.

"Did it work?" Ragne pokes her cat head out of the fur wrap.

"No." I chew on the tip of my thumb. I just gave away a not-too-small fortune for absolutely no reason. Maybe it didn't work because the total value wasn't enough. Or maybe because the money wasn't mine. Or because I haven't technically spent any money yet at all. Or . . .

There are too many possibilities. I need to start whittling them down.

I bury my face in my hands and groan.

And then I try again. And again. And again.

We drive to the nearby Obarmarkt along the Yssar's northwest bank, where I try to commission my wedding dress from a struggling seamstress, only for her to burst into tears and decline because she can't make it in time. I try to arrange for wedding pastries from a baker. Since the wedding's on a Sunday, he miserably declines as well, as he wouldn't be able to start baking until after sundown Saturday. Worse, he all but throws a basket of ginger cookies into my arms and refuses payment, claiming my visit is advertisement enough. (Ragne, at least, is more than happy to claim the cookies for herself. Unfortunately, that means I have to watch her eat them, which is a little like watching a gingerbread-family massacre.)

We drive east over the Yssar and into the Göttermarkt to leave offerings for Eiswald. I consider scouting for beggars in the Untrmarkt below, but it's closer to Lähl and the Stichensteg islets, where Yannec's body may have washed up. I don't want to be any closer than I have to.

Instead we head up into the Südbígn district nestled in the upper bend of the Yssar, across from Castle Reigenbach, where wealthy merchants dump their spare change into the arts. I sign up House Reigenbach to sponsor a troupe of amateur actors. I commission a play for the wedding feast from a company about to go under. I even book a quartet of musicians from a concert hall run by a local monastery.

In desperation, I cave and have us drive to the border between the Göttermarkt and the Untrmarkt, as close to Lähl as I dare. I take the purse of *sjilling* and fling the coins out the window at the feet of paupers who shout with surprise and glee.

None of it works. None of it seems to matter.

I dispense the last of the money myself, pushing *sjilling* into the hands of the proprietor of an indigent sanctuary. The ruby and pearl do not budge.

As I trudge back to the coach, the driver asks timidly, "Back to the castle, m'lady?"

I want to lean my head against the door and try not to think about the next ruby or pearl that could be growing in me at this very moment. Even more, I want to avoid thinking about what—or who—is waiting for me now at Castle Reigenbach.

But I don't have time for any of that. I need to crack this curse.

"Back to the castle," I confirm grimly, and climb into the carriage.

CHAPTER NINE

Ten Of Bells

WHEN I RETURN TO CASTLE REIGENBACH A LITTLE AFTER NOON, the entrance hall has been hastily reoutfitted in older furnishings that don't quite match the rest of the décor. I can't say I'm sorry to have made more work for Barthl, though the golden wolf statues are certainly the centerpieces of the hall now. It makes me feel better to be a thorn in Adalbrecht's thumb, even if it hasn't done a damned thing about the ruby in my face.

There's a note waiting for me in my chambers. It's in Adalbrecht's writing.

I leave it on the credenza and instead drop into the chair by my vanity, burying my head in my hands.

I don't know what Eiswald wants from me. I don't know how to break this curse. I've stolen the signet ring of one of the most powerful people in the Blessed Empire, stripped a room full of his treasures, and gone on a spending spree, but none of it matters. And the moment I unfold that letter, I will begin to pay the price.

For a long moment, I sit there and just breathe. *Don't panic* has gotten me through so many crises, and while this is above and beyond any I've navigated thus far, it helps.

Think. I have around eight hundred and fifty *gilden* now. If it gets dire, I can take it and run. It won't be enough for the life I want to lead, but it's better than nothing.

Especially if that life only lasts until the full moon.

I have an emergency plan, something to fall back on if all is lost. And I have a little over thirteen days left to figure out how to break the curse, so I can't waste much more time. I make myself get up and fetch Adalbrecht's message.

It's brief and domineering. He says Gisele is not to leave the castle again without his permission. That she is not to give anything to anyone without clearing it with him first. That she will join him for breakfast tomorrow morning and spend the rest of the day with preparations for the wedding.

He does not mention the signet ring, which means either he didn't notice it was gone or he doesn't know I took it. I decide to hold on to it until he brings it up.

I blow out a breath and look at the silver sky. It's half past noon, still light out; this close to winter solstice, I only have another four hours or so before sundown. Gisele may be restricted to the castle, but Marthe is not. I can try to puzzle out some answers with what little daylight I have left.

So long as I stay clear of the Gänslinghaus, I should be fine. And it's not like being nice to those orphans did anything for me anyway.

Ragne flops onto the hearth. "None of it worked?"

I shake my head, too frustrated for words.

"Why not?"

"Ask your mother," I snap. "I helped orphans, I tried making amends with Gisele, I gave away money, but I guess none of that was *good enough*."

Ragne frowns. "Why would giving money help?"

"Because then they can use it to buy things and I . . . can't . . . hmm." My anger deflates a bit. Really, I've given away *Adalbrecht's* money, not mine. Gisele can't claim so much as a penny, never mind even earn one.

I've failed breaking the curse as the *Prinzessin*. Maybe I have to do it as the *Pfennigeist*.

I stow the pearls, change quickly into the servant uniform, and go make excuses to the castle's chief stewardess: Gisele is feeling sickly and will remain in her chambers for the evening, not to be disturbed. Gisele's "sensitive stomach" is well known among the servants. I have gone to some truly revolting lengths to convince them that barging in while she's ill can only end in tragedy and a change of clothes.

Then I snag a stale pretzel and dried *wurst* from the kitchens, change into a plain dress and knit cap in the bedchamber, and slip mouse-Ragne, gently snoring again, and a deck of cards into my satchel. This time I've covered the ruby teardrop with not just gauze, but a medicinal paste that won't budge easily. If anyone asks, I'll say Gisele made me try a glue for the ruby first, one that left a burn.

I take the servant corridor out of the riverfront wing and hurry down what seems like too many flights of stairs. In reality, Castle Reigenbach is as expansive belowground as it is above, with vaults and ballrooms carved behind the cliffs it's perched upon. Gisele's rooms are only two floors above the Yssar River, but by the time I break into the open air, I've descended nearly six stories.

Mist blows into my face, a reminder of why I only take this route while the sun's up. This particular exit lets out at the base of the water-fall. The river itself tumbles off an anvil-shaped shelf, leaving room for a narrow footpath to cut behind the frigid cascade, but it's slippery and impossible to see by night. At this time of year it's even deadlier, with thin coats of ice.

I pick my way across the footpath and up the opposite bank, then sally over to the Göttermarkt. It's chaos by day, the bells and chants of dozens of temples sounding off in no particular order and in frequent conflict; a bonfire roars in the middle, where visitors can write their misfortunes on scraps of paper and cast them into the flames; and supplicants stumble around in various rituals, some with runes painted on hands and faces, others in horned masks or blindfolds. Between lines for the *sakretwaren* stalls, pilgrims flocking to popular shrines, and a small crowd gathered around a wedding canopy at the House of the High, there's barely enough room to swing a broom. In one corner, children are being led through a Winterfast pageant by a woman who looks positively exhausted.

It's unbridled anarchy, and thus, perfect for my needs.

I find a beggar and give him a white penny. I promise him five more if he shills for me.

A few minutes later, I've dragged an empty crate over to one of the Göttermarkt's stone benches. It'll serve as my dealing table. The playing cards make a pleasantly familiar *flipt* noise as they shuffle through my hands, and I begin to lay them onto the crate. Ragne, too, climbs out, perching on the bench beside me as a curious little starling, pitch-black but speckled in white spots.

My beggar shill approaches with his white penny. He wagers a fifth of it on a round of Find the Lady, just as we discussed.

The game begins: He loses the first round, of course, and lets out a shout of dismay. Just as we discussed. I offer him another round and double his wager. He takes it up—and wins. Once again, he's loud about it. Just as we discussed.

We go back and forth long enough to attract an audience, and then honest gamblers get in on the game. They win when I decide they can, which is only enough to keep them coming back. They lose when I want them to, which is most of the time. I'm careful to palm my winnings into the satchel so no one can see how much coin I'm amassing.

By the time I've earned almost a *gilden*, the sun's touching the horizon. I pack up my cards and wait for the crowd to disperse, then hand off all the winnings to the beggar shill. He takes the money and leaves.

Nothing happens. The ruby and pearl don't so much as twinge.

"*Ugggghh*." I slump over and let my head hang a moment as Ragne chirps from the bench. "What does your mother *want* from me?"

I don't have to speak bird to understand that Ragne doesn't know either.

A knot swells in my throat. I try not to think of where the next outbreak will be—Pearls in my lungs? A ruby tongue?—but what wells up in that hollow is the sudden, terrible thought that in two weeks, I will be dead.

I will be dead, and no one will mourn but Death and Fortune, for the loss of a servant.

"Who taught you to play cards, *frohlein*?"

I've heard that voice before, but I can't place it. I look up.

Junior Prefect Emeric Conrad is standing before me once more, bundled up to the point of absurdity in his enormous dingy cloak and scarf. His arms are full of wrapped parcels with the stamp of the Order of Prefects.

The *well-funded* Order of Prefects.

The lock pins slide, just a bit, with hope. I've stolen nearly a thousand *gilden*; perhaps I didn't notice a change because I only earned and gave away one.

"A friend," I say, straightening up, and fan the cards out on the crate once more. This isn't a job for the *Prinzessin* or Marthe, but the *Pfennigeist*: faceless, nameless, whatever I want to be. Right now, I need a shifty grifter. "Fancy a game of Find the Lady, Prefect?"

I'm pretty sure he mouths "*junior prefect*" before shifting the packages in his arms. "Maybe. I have some questions you might be able to help with."

Junior Prefect Conrad, always on the case. This might be an opportunity to steer him off my trail. I gesture to one of the barrels the gamblers used for chairs.

He manages to drop every single one of his parcels as he takes a seat, then shakes his head in resignation, straightens them into a pile, and tucks his hands into the oceans of fabric under each arm. "You seem like someone who may take a few liberties with the law, *frohlein*," he says stiffly. "And you might hear about . . . other liberties being taken."

It's different, the way he talks to me without the pearls. I'm used to it. It still stings every time. But the *Pfennigeist* is nothing, no one; it's one of the perks of being little but shadow and whisper. Nothing can leave a mark.

"That's a devil of an assumption," I drawl, shuffling the three cards over the crate at a snail's pace. Fleecing him will *dramatically* improve my mood. "But sure, maybe I hear things."

"You ever hear of the Penny Phantom?"

I jerk my chin at the cards and lower my voice to a conspiratorial whisper. "I heard of ten of them. Ten to play a round."

He leans forward, enthusiasm igniting him like a candle. "Ten . . . ? Right." He drops a stack of copper bits on the crate.

I wait.

"Oh. You meant . . ." Emeric wavers a moment, then produces a *sjilling*. "Here."

I keep waiting. We both know the Order has cash to spare.

The junior prefect caves and slices another nine over.

"Good man," I cackle with a wicked grin, the picture of a shady dealer.

Ragne chirps, then hops to my shoulder. I turn over the cards on the crate to show him: Ten of Bells, Knight of Shields, Queen of Roses. Then I flip them over and begin the shuffle in earnest.

"Ten," I repeat in my peak grizzled-street-urchin voice. "You're not looking for a Penny Phantom, but the Red Penny Gang. Didn't hear it from me, *ja?*" Emeric nods, wide-eyed. "Look in Lähl, near the Stichenstegs, for a tavern called the Ten Bells. There's a secret entrance in the alley. Heard it's marked with a red stone."

Not a single word of that is true, but it'll keep him out of my hair for a few days. And honestly, you have to appreciate the sheer poetry of it, him paying the *Pfennigeist* for a wild-goose chase.

Then I line up the three cards, facedown. I've switched the Queen of Roses more than enough times for him to have lost her. "Figured out where the Lady lies?"

Emeric reaches out, then stops, hovering between the queen and the Knight of Shields. His hand drops on the knight. I turn it over and sweep his *sjilling* into my satchel.

"Unfortunate," he grumbles. "You've been very helpful. Thank you for your assistance."

The sun ducks behind the rooftops as he gathers his parcels and leaves, and my glee turns bittersweet. I've bought time away from an overeager prefect, but now I have to take the harder way back into Castle Reigenbach. The icy waterfall path is too treacherous in the dark, and I can't exactly stroll in through the entrance hall looking like a street urchin.

I use some of Emeric's money to buy a mug of steaming *glohwein* while I wait for proper night to settle in, trying to puzzle out what I've learned about the curse, prodding at that riddle of a lock with pick after pick and trying to nudge the tumblers into place. Ragne chases other starlings around the Göttermarkt until the temple bells start bellowing for evening services.

By then it's dark enough for me to be on my way. Ragne perches on my shoulder as I climb the stairs onto the Hoenstratz viaduct, cross the High Bridge to the foot of Castle Reigenbach, then hop the wall and slip into the roadside bushes when the guards aren't looking.

There's another footpath here leading up to the castle proper, behind the barracks and storehouses. Trudl told me about it with a bawdy wink (well, she told Marthe, before she decided Marthe was lazy), calling it the Lovers' Road. I found out exactly what she meant when the spring turned warm enough for couples to sneak off at night, and suddenly every private hedge with a view of the Yssar waterfall was . . . occupied. Loudly.

This night is too cold for lovers, though, so I'm the only one making my way up the winding dirt track. Finally it levels out upriver from the waterfall. The path curves around the corner of the icehouse, but I split off there, pressing close to the limestone wall of the castle itself.

Castle Reigenbach is built so close to the river, there's but a thin strip of land to scoot along between the wall and the cold waters of the Yssar, so meager the guards don't bother patrolling it. When I first arrived, they had stationed Gisele in the guest wing, too close to Adalbrecht's chambers for my comfort, and too far from any escape routes. Within the week, I had them move me to the riverfront wing, into a room with a veranda framed by sturdy rose trellises, and gave myself another way out.

Or in. After a few minutes of creeping along the narrow bank, I reach the trellises and shake out my hands. I've kept them in tight fists to try to stay warm, and they're still limber despite the chill. I find my handholds in the wooden brackets and begin to climb.

Sometimes I wonder, in moments like this.

I don't remember my siblings all that well; twelve is too many for a four-year-old to keep track of. I know they were rowdy and quiet and sweet and bold, and some of them looked like my father, a smith, and some of them looked like my mother, a weaver.

I wonder . . . I wonder what they would think of me. Would my sisters like that I climb trellises, sneak in and out of castles, wear gowns of the finest silks? Would my brothers like that I can steal the signet ring off the Golden Wolf himself, and lie as easy as breathing?

Would my mother still believe I'm bad luck?

I wonder if I would have been the same person sleeping in a crowded, smelly hut as I was sleeping with the rats in the pantry.

Ragne pokes me in the ear. "I'm going to go get dinner," she announces, and a moment later a bat flaps away, up into the air.

"I thought you were vegetarian," I grumble. Maybe insects don't count. I don't know that I want to ask.

I reach the veranda and hoist myself over the balustrade. Firelight glows through the curtained panes of the door, a reminder that a little kindness to a *kobold* goes a long way. I'm more than ready to scrounge up some dinner of my own and doze off in a toasty room.

I let myself in and reach for the lamp next to the vanity—

—and something cold clamps around my other wrist.

My free hand closes over the first thing in reach on the vanity, but then it too is yanked behind my back. There's a metallic *clank*. When I try to jerk free, I meet unforgiving iron shackles.

My captor's still at my back. "I'll scream for the guards," I hiss. "I—"

The veranda door clicks shut behind me. "No, I don't think you will."

This time I recognize the voice.

Junior Prefect Emeric Conrad steps in front of me, little more than a silhouette against the hearth, firelight catching along the round lenses of his spectacles.

Coal dust whirls around us. My luck has once again turned for the worse.

"If you called for the guards," he says mildly, "you'd have to explain to them why *you're* here, carrying Gisele von Falbirg's pearls, and why Gisele von Falbirg is not."

Then he picks a book up off the vanity chair and motions for me to sit. "Now then, if you please, *Prinzessin*. I have a few more questions for you."

CHAPTER TEN

DEAD TO RIGHTS

I TRY NOT TO GAPE AS EMERIC WALKS TO THE FIREPLACE, WHERE HIS too-big uniform coat has been neatly folded over a chair, and sets down the book in his hands.

No, it's not just any book; he has Yannec's ledger. The one that I need to find his buyer.

That means Emeric's found the secret cupboard in my vanity. Which is also where I've hidden my store of *gilden* and the Eisendorf jewels. Sure enough, they're in an orderly stack beside the vanity chair.

Which means he's a *lot* better at this than I thought.

This is not the fumbling boy who I could bully with a plate of specific and evocative sausage.

He *looks* much the same: black hair neatly combed, not so much as a wrinkle on his linen shirt, tidy *krebatte*, and charcoal wool waistcoat.

But he's rolled up his sleeves, businesslike, and now that he's no longer drowning in that enormous coat, he looks less like a gawky academic and more like a . . . well, still a gawky academic, but with better posture and at least five knives on him that I can see.

"I can speculate where all these *gilden* came from," he says crisply, "but we both know that's the Eisendorf jewelry. Let's see . . . '*Removal of property with intent to steal, of the sum value of one* gilden *or greater, shall be considered grand larceny and punishable in accordance with local laws.*' I'm fairly certain that jewelry's worth more than one *gilden*. You'll have to tell me, though, what they do to thieves in Bóern."

There's a reason the coins are all stamped with a crown on one side, a skull on the other. One side's for the great thieves. You can guess which side is for the little ones.

Don't panic. Don't panic. Don't panic.

There's one role I can always fall back on, and that's the helpless, gobsmacked yokel. I crumple my face and collapse into the vanity chair, keeping my breath shallow to force blood to my cheeks. "*P-please*, sir, it's not my place to ask where she goes, I'm just her maid—"

"Vanja." He's consulting his little notebook, which still has coffee stains on the edges. "Vanja Schmidt, I believe? That was the family name they had for you at Castle Falbirg."

"That's my cousin, she got me this job so I could feed my mother, she's sick, *please*, sir—"

Emeric sighs. Then he reaches over and yanks the bit of gauze off my cheek.

The ruby teardrop twinkles in the firelight.

Emeric flicks the gauze aside, pointedly. And he waits.

"*Scheit*," I mutter after a moment.

Emeric folds his arms. "Mm-hm."

I slouch back in the chair with a defeated scowl. "All right, Junior. When did you know?"

I ask for two reasons. One is that he looks very pleased with himself. That means he's absolutely certain he has me dead to rights, and I want to know *how*.

The other is that I managed to grab a hairpin from the vanity, and I think I'm ready to start picking the shackles.

"I confirmed it last night, at Eisendorf Manor." Emeric walks back to the hearth and takes a spill-stick from the copper urn on the mantel.

He glances back at me, and I look sufficiently sulky and humbled. It's not entirely artificial; I'm a little embarrassed he caught on that fast.

"Though truth be told, I've had that theory a week now," he continues, and he even *talks* different, words clipped and precise, holding the end of the spill-stick to the fire. The long, thin scrap of wood kindles, and he walks it over to another candelabra, his leather-bound notebook tucked under an arm. "I took the liberty of visiting Sovabin first."

"Cheater," I grumble.

"Dame von Falbirg gave me a very clear account of her daughter, Gisele," he continues as if he didn't hear me, though an eye roll says otherwise. "Soft-spoken." He lights a candle. "Preferred the outdoors to socializing." Another candle. "Fond of books." The third candle lights, and he gives me a significant look from across the room. "Not fond of drinking."

What an insufferably melodramatic little bastard he is.

"Have you *met* Adalbrecht?" I ask dryly. "You tell me you wouldn't dive headfirst into a wine cellar if you were marrying that."

He raises his eyebrows. "Fair point. However, the thefts started in Bóern only after Gisele arrived, implicating either her or someone from her entourage. The dame told me about the pearl necklace she gave her daughter, but that enchantment alters only the wearer's appearance, not their personality. Besides . . . there was the matter of the pennies. You couldn't stop leaving them, could you?"

That hits me in the throat. The flush on my face is real now. "Anyone can leave a penny."

"But you left twelve of them, crown-side up, in the homes of twelve noble families, after you robbed them blind. That's *personal*, Miss Schmidt. You wanted them to feel helpless. You wanted them to know it was you." He sounds like he's reading a prescription, like I'm a strange insect under a glass, and I despise how clinically he's saying aloud something I've never spoken of to anyone. "Gisele had no reason to hold a grudge like that against other nobility. But her chambermaid, the one who conveniently vanished?"

He's trying to make me angry. And it's working: It feels like he's casually rifling through my wardrobe, getting too close to the ugly things shoved in the back. How much did the von Falbirgs tell him? Did they explain their humiliating nicknames? How they made a lonely little girl sleep with the rats?

How I came by the scars on my back?

If I let him get to me, I'll get careless. Last month, I managed to listen to Irmgard von Hirsching talk for five solid minutes without slapping her into a fountain. I can keep my head now.

"I don't buy it," I lie, knowing that sheer bullheaded denial has to annoy him. Sure enough, his shoulders tense. "Typical, trying to blame the servant, since you could barely walk in a straight line around Gisele."

He scoffs. "Hardly. From the moment we met, you were expecting a nervous, enamored schoolboy. I just showed you what you wanted to see."

"Big assumption that I *wanted* to see you," I mutter. Then I raise my voice to cover the scrape of the hairpin in the manacle lock. "And don't be so smug. You asked me about a party Gisele wasn't even *at*."

"To see if I could make you slip again." He's lit enough candles now for me to see something unsettlingly familiar in his dark eyes: the haughty, muffled thrill of knowing you're two steps ahead.

I know it because—because—

Because it's how I feel every time I leave a red penny.

"You nearly threw your coffee on me when I slandered your fellow servants." Emeric returns to the hearth and tosses the charred spill-stick into the fire. "You *did* slip again when I mentioned the Eisendorf penny. The break-in wasn't discovered until after 'Gisele' had gone, but you weren't surprised in the least."

One manacle lets out a rasp as it slides loose. I quickly slump in the vanity chair, wiggling my arms to rattle the chains and explain the noise. "Fine, *maybe* you got me there."

Emeric picks up Yannec's ledger and tucks it into the satchel at his side as he walks back over to me. "I did. All it took was making you think you'd be caught once Klemens arrived, and you panicked just like I expected. I'll admit I didn't anticipate the charitable extravaganza, though—"

"Wait. The—the spyglass thing. That wasn't true?" I stare up at him, feeling a good deal more foolish than I like. "Klemens won't— you *can't* follow the penny?"

Emeric shrugs as he comes to a stop a few feet in front of me. "All a lie. I'm sure you're familiar. People get sloppy when they panic."

"*Sloppy*—" I begin, indignant.

He cuts me off. "Yes, sloppy. Need I remind you which of us is wearing the manacles right now?"

"I think I get it now," I announce with an air of discovery. "You're what happens when an encyclopedia wishes on a star to be a real boy, if that encyclopedia was also an absolute prick."

"Uncalled for." He pats his waistcoat and pulls out the writing charcoal, thumbing open his notebook. "Now then, *frohlein*, I wasn't lying about having more questions—"

"You really don't have *any* way to trace the thefts back to me?" I demand.

Emeric frowns down at me, and I can tell I've cut to the bone this time. "It's never that simple. If it were, the local bailiff could handle everything. There'd be no need to call in a prefect like me."

The remaining shackle slips open.

I huff a laugh of disgust. "*Junior* prefect."

Then I kick him in the shin as hard as I can.

He curses and staggers back as I spring for his hands. Emeric is clearly more used to clapping people in irons than avoiding the clap-pening, because it's easier than it should be to slam his own manacles around his wrists. I only come up to his chin without the pearls, but it's just as laughably easy to trip him with a strategically placed boot, send-ing him crashing to the carpet between the hearth and the veranda door.

Then I put a foot on his chest to keep him there.

"Here's the deal, Junior," I say, icy. I pull the string of pearls from my pocket and hold them up. "You make a single unsolicited peep and I will scream like every *grimling* in Bóern is coming in through the win-dow. And then I'll put these on, and *you* can explain to the guards what you're doing menacing Gisele von Falbirg in her own bedroom."

He regards my boot with a sneer. "This is highly unnecessary, Miss Schmidt."

"I bet you say that to all the girls." I lean on his chest until he winces. "How did you find me in the Göttermarkt?"

"I wasn't looking for you at all," he grits out. "I was checking in with the outpost of the Order of Prefects. I would have told you that if you just asked, you *really* don't have to keep stepping—"

I don't ease off. "You never saw me without the pearls before this afternoon. How did you know it was me?"

"The ruby."

I shake my head. "The ruby was covered up."

"I can still see the curse on it," Emeric wheezes. "And the god-marks of Death and Fortune on you. With or without the pearls."

I go still. "You can see the curse?"

"From Eiswald." He nods.

For a moment, I waver.

This *immediately* proves to be a mistake. Emeric whips the manacle chain around my other ankle and yanks. I tumble to the floor. The pearls fly out of my hand and roll out of reach. I wrench over onto my back just as Emeric lunges for me—

And cold iron grinds against my throat. He's pinning me down with the manacle chain, one hand planted on each side of my neck, and he looks both exasperated and oddly uncomfortable.

"I would really . . . rather not . . . keep doing this." His voice scrapes a little as he catches his breath, glaring down at me. "I have spent the last ten years training to apprehend far better criminals than you. We can come to an arrangement if you surrender."

Better criminals. *Greater thieves,* I think. The kind he doesn't have to send to the gallows.

Here's the thing about people like Emeric Conrad: They don't know what to do when they're not the smartest person in the room. He thinks he won because he fooled me for a day, never mind that I've been fooling half of Bóern for a year.

He thinks he can apprehend better criminals than me, because he's never met a criminal quite like me.

So I blink my big black eyes up at him, and say: "*Poldi*."

A ball of flame bursts from the fireplace and slams into Emeric like a charging bull.

I am going to owe him *so much* mead.

Emeric hits the ground, winded. Poldi grabs him by the collar.

"*Where do you want him, Lady?*" the *kobold* grunts in a voice that pops and crackles like dry firewood going up in smoke.

"Outside."

The veranda door flies open as I get back onto my feet and dust myself off, rather savoring Emeric's sputtered protests. Poldi hauls him out with less than an abundance of careful handling. I close the veranda door behind us and point to the balustrade.

Poldi's form has settled into a stout, fiery little man again, but he moves like no man can, climbing the air like it's a staircase and taking Emeric up with him. Emeric's boot tips just touch the railing.

"Here's my arrangement," I tell him. "You've got less than a minute before Poldi burns through that collar of yours. It would be wise to tell me *everything* you know about Eiswald's curse first."

"Again," Emeric says irritably, "you *could have just asked*."

I fold my arms with a cold-blooded smile. "But then I wouldn't be holding your life in my hands. Where's the fun in that?"

His manacle chain clinks as he tries to gesticulate angrily. "There is something *very* wrong with you."

"And there's a"—I lean forward and squint—"thirty-foot drop, give or take, before you hit the Yssar. Tell me about the curse, Junior."

"I already told you everything I know."

I nod to Poldi. Emeric slips a little.

"It's the truth!" he insists. "I can see it's a curse, and it's from Eiswald—"

My voice rises despite myself. "What about how to break it? Or what Eiswald wants from me? *Anything* else?"

"Only . . ." Emeric flinches. ". . . that it will kill you by the full moon."

A razor-thin crescent is inching over the horizon.

"I'm aware," I say grimly. "So I don't have time to waste with you. Poldi, do the honors."

"Wait—the margrave—" Whatever Emeric has to add, it's lost as the *kobold* lets go.

There's a shout, then a splash, and Junior Prefect Emeric Conrad is officially the Yssar's problem now.

I peer over the edge of the balustrade, hands on my hips. "Think he knows how to swim in those irons?" I ask Poldi.

Poldi and I wait a moment, watching the river. The surface doesn't break.

"*Doesn't look like it,*" he hisses.

I give it another beat or two, then turn and head back inside. "Eh. He'll figure it out. Hopefully before the waterfall. Let's go get you some mead."

PART TWO:

THE LIE OF PEARL

THE THIRD TALE

A RUBY RING

ONCE UPON A TIME, A PRINCESS LIVED IN A CASTLE WITH HER BEST friend, the loyal maid. She took the maid when she ran to explore ruins in the hills. She took the maid when she rode to hunt in the forest. She took the maid everywhere, even when it made her mother frown.

One day, when the princess and her maid were nearly thirteen, another young girl arrived. She was the daughter of a count in the land to the east, who was visiting for the fortnight to discuss dry, boring matters of state with the princess's parents. The little countess was the prettiest girl the princess and the maid had ever seen, with hair of glowing chestnut, twin roses in her porcelain cheeks, and eyes as blue as the heart of a glacier.

The little countess wanted to be friends with the princess. She wanted to be the princess's *best* friend. Her *only* friend.

And the little countess was bored.

At first, she bothered the princess's maid in small ways, pinching her when no one saw, tripping her as she passed, pulling her braids. If the maid protested, the little countess said it was an accident, and she was terribly sorry, and she was *so embarrassed*, and then tears would well up in her eyes, and the maid would run away before someone scolded her for making the little countess weep.

Then the little countess got the princess to help.

The little countess did not want to read or climb or hunt. Instead the little countess came up with a game. She said it had to be boring for the maid, doing the same thing every day, and they could make it more interesting for her. And at first, the princess thought that was a fine idea, for her friend *did* have so many dull chores, and perhaps they could make her work more fun.

It started by inches: springing out from behind a corner to startle the maid. Switching the lye and the wood polish when she wasn't looking. Then the cruelty crept in, stretched the *game* to new heights. A spider down the dress. A nail in the broom that scratched the wood floor. A nail in the shoe.

And if the maid was upset, the little countess would fill her eyes with tears, and say it was all just a jest, and there was no need to be so *mean*.

One day, the maid woke to find the little countess standing over her pallet, giggling and pointing at the blankets. "Is that why they call you the *red* penny?"

The maid didn't understand until she felt an ache below her belly and saw blood on the straw, and realized her first monthly blood had come at the worst imaginable time. She fled to the washroom as quick as she could. For the rest of the day, the little countess made a point of calling her *Rohtpfenni*, until the maid thought she might push her into the fire.

This was when the princess realized it was more than a game.

The princess asked her parents to send the count away, but they could not, for the same reason they asked her to be friends with the little countess: Count von Hirsching controlled a key trade route in and out of Sovabin. It was a lifeline they dared not sever.

So the princess tried to help her maid, and asked the little countess to apologize.

The little countess hung her head and said she was very sorry if the maid's feelings were hurt. She even pulled a ruby ring from her finger and said it was a gift, to make amends.

And the poor little maid believed her.

Night fell. At supper, the little countess gasped aloud and declared her ruby ring was missing. She pointed at the maid and called her a thief. When they turned out the maid's pockets, the ring, of course, was there.

I will never forget that night, how I kept insisting through my tears that Irmgard gave me the ring, that I would never steal from them, until Dame von Falbirg backhanded me into silence. Gisele's father promised Count von Hirsching that I would be punished.

And Gisele—Gisele said nothing.

She said nothing as the von Hirschings demanded I be whipped for a thief. Twenty lashes for a girl not even thirteen.

She said nothing as the guards brusquely bound my hands to a wooden post and ripped my shirt down the back.

She said nothing as they made Yannec deal me thirteen bloody lashes. She said nothing as Joniza pled for mercy, voice rising above my screams. She said nothing when that mercy was granted, sparing me the final seven, even as Count von Hirsching grumbled about spoiling their supper.

And when Gisele appeared in the kitchen after, where I'd been laid facedown on a rough wooden table like the final course, she said nothing.

Yannec was busy plating custards, shamefaced, and Joniza had gone to fetch the local hedgewitch to see to my wounds. Joniza knew a thing or two about herbs, but this was beyond her. Where she came from, they did not whip children.

The hedgewitch would cost her a month's wages, but she hadn't hesitated. All I could think in my haze of pain was that I would need to pay her back, and I didn't know how.

Gisele's eyes were wet and glittering as she slipped through the doorway. I wanted to ask her why she hadn't said anything. Why she hadn't said Irmgard was lying. Why she hadn't stopped Irmgard sooner.

Why Irmgard's tears mattered more than the blood on my back.

But I knew Gisele. She didn't have answers for any of that.

So all she did was stumble in, set something on the table beside me, and then rush out, red-faced and choking back tears. When I turned my head, I saw a dab of bright silver gleaming on the wood: a single white penny.

I closed my eyes.

It would help pay for the hedgewitch, at least.

"Suppose you'll have to do better the next time you try to make a bit of coin," Yannec finally mumbled.

I let the grain of the wood push into my face. Anything to distract from the searing fire of the welts on my back. "I didn't steal the ring," I whispered, voice ragged from weeping. "She was lying. She told me it was a gift."

Yannec hissed as a custard threatened to slide off its plate. "Then you won't fall for that again. But here's a word to the wise, girl. The world's full of nobles like that. You can play by their rules all you like, but they'll still find a way to beat you down and call you a thief. Even the little Miss Gisele. It's just a matter of time."

I didn't say anything. It had all been enough, once.

I'd thought I could be Gisele's maid, her friend, maybe for the rest of our lives. She'd marry another noble, and I'd run her household and maybe find a handsome groomsman or the like, and we would be like—like family, and that would be enough.

Yannec sighed and set the plate down. Then he walked over and patted my sweat-stiff hair, brief and rough, more to comfort himself than me.

"What I'm saying is, you're going to be whipped again, *Rohtpfenni*. If not whipped, then robbed, blinded, whatever they feel like doing, whether you steal from them or not. That's the way of the world. All you can do is make it worth it. Next time they knock you down, make sure it's not for one lousy ring, but a pocket full of gold."

At midnight, Death and Fortune came to me.

They told me I had turned thirteen, and so it was time for me to choose one of them over the other.

They told me one would claim me as a servant.

They said nothing of claiming me as a daughter.

They had nothing to say about the fresh welts on my back, or how I'd *flowered* into my monthly bleeding, or even the black eye from Dame von Falbirg. Gods don't care about such things, you see. Not even godmothers.

I did not want to stay at Castle Falbirg. I was terrified Yannec was right, that Gisele would let me be hurt again, that one day she might even bring down the whip herself.

But far more dreadful was the idea of serving Death or Fortune, and waiting for the day one of them reached for the lash.

They couldn't even offer a white penny after.

So I told Death and Fortune *no*.

And I started thinking of pockets full of gold.

CHAPTER ELEVEN

A Weight Off The Chest

RAGNE RETURNS JUST AS I REALIZE I HAVE MADE A TRULY UNFORTU-nate mistake.

Is it that I just dropped another human being into an icy river in manacles and thus (probably) to his death? Hardly. I think we can all agree that the encyclopedic prick had it coming.

It's that right now, his satchel is (probably) sinking to the bottom of the Yssar with him. And inside that satchel is Yannec's ledger. The one I need so I can find Yannec's buyer and get rid of the Eisendorf jewels.

I've only just walked in through the veranda door when I make the realization. Ragne flaps inside from behind me. She's a black barn owl now, blinking in the candlelight as she perches on a bedpost.

I hurriedly point back out the door. "Ragne. There's a boy in the Yssar, and I need his bag. Can you take care of it?"

She hoots and launches herself out into the night. I run my hands over the tangled mess of my braids, trying to think.

Poldi crackles politely as he swings his legs, sitting on the hearth.

"Right. The mead." I slap paste and gauze over the ruby, duck into the servant corridors, race down to the kitchens, and return with a bottle.

By the time I make it back up, Ragne has returned, human again. She's also stark naked and dripping on the carpet.

"Just . . . why?" I ask, exhausted.

"Humans dry faster. No fur."

"Humans use towels. And clothes." I hand Poldi the bottle. "Thank you for your help."

He snatches it up and vanishes into the chimney. "*I'll keep the fires warm for the half god.*"

I turn back to Ragne and set about finding her a towel. "Well?"

"I took care of it," she says brightly, and shakes her head. Water flies everywhere.

"Where's the satchel?"

"With the boy."

I frown as I pull a clean towel from a basket. "And where is the boy?"

"On the other side of the river."

"Is he . . . ?" I draw a finger across my throat.

Ragne tilts her head, confused.

"Did he drown?" I clarify.

She pokes at her own throat. "Why would you drown like that? Does he have gills?"

"Dead! It means dead. Like having a throat cut. Is he dead?"

"Oh. I don't understand." Ragne plants herself by the fire. "He's still alive."

I throw the towel at her. "What part of that is *taken care of*?"

"The boy," Ragne answers, bewildered. "I pushed him to the shore and—"

"I needed you to get his bag, Ragne!" I throw up my hands. "I didn't care what happened to him, I needed the *bag*!"

My fingers twitch with pinpricks. I swear and shake them out, and find a dusting of tiny rubies erupting over my knuckles.

"I can see that," Ragne says.

I shoot her a dirty look. "I liked you better before you figured out how to do smartass." Then I drop into the chair by the fireplace and untie my disheveled braids, combing them out with my fingers as I think.

So Emeric is still alive. Yannec's ledger . . . hopefully he wrote in charcoal and the pages aren't ruined.

Unless Emeric uses it to dig up anything else he can connect to me.

I'm safe for now—he won't get the drop on me again, and without hard evidence, all he has is his word against that of the margrave's fiancée. I know exactly how that will play out. But I still need the ledger.

The unfortunate junior prefect has left me a few souvenirs as well: In the tussle, he dropped his notebook and one of his knives, and his uniform jacket is still folded over the chair I'm in. I pull it into my lap to check the pockets. There's a few red pennies and *sjilling*, a meticulously folded handkerchief, and nothing more.

I can't help myself from reading the coat like I read the jewelry cases I empty. This one tells an unexpected story: It's much too large for Emeric, riddled in the scars of old and neatly mended tears, even a worn patch or two on the elbow. A small constellation of holes over the breast pocket mark where badges and medals have been removed, and in fine red thread, there's a name stitched inside the collar: *H KLEMENS*.

Either it's stolen, a gift, or a hand-me-down. I can rule out the last one, as the Order of Prefects is too well funded to reuse uniforms. And I can rule out the first, because the impression I've gotten of Emeric Conrad thus far is that it would be physically and emotionally impossible for him to break a single law without screaming. So it's a gift. Sentimental.

There's a sharp, spicy smell to it, oddly familiar, and then I place it: juniper oil. The hedgewitch had worked some into the salve for my lash wounds years ago.

Old anger knots up along the lines of my scars. I stand, toss the coat into my wardrobe, then snap up Emeric's notebook and knife from the ground. At least I can get a sense of what dirt he's got on me, so I can prepare for the worst.

When I flip the pages, though, they're all blank, except for a brief inscription on the first:

PROPERTY OF E CONRAD
If found, please return to nearest outpost of Order of Prefects
of the Godly Courts

Well, at least he's an optimist.

I chew on a thumb tip. This isn't a decoy; I saw him write in it at breakfast—it even still smells like coffee, though the stains are nowhere to be seen. There must be some kind of enchantment hiding his notes. I carry it back over to the fireplace, plopping down on the hearth this time to make use of the bright firelight.

It's a surprisingly well-made little journal considering there's no bookbinder's seal stamped into the buckskin cover. That was my first guess, some charm hidden in an embellishment, for magic usually leaves a mark. It has to be anchored somehow, the way the pearls anchor the illusion of the *prinzessin*. I run my fingers over the cover, the endpapers, even the ink lines of *E CONRAD*, but nothing sticks out.

It makes me angrier than it should. This isn't *fair*. He broke into my room, all but flaunted his excruciating knowledge of my secrets; his stupid little book has no right to keep his. And I am so, so tired of being thwarted today.

I just want something, one *single* blessed thing, to work.

In the distance, the bells of the Göttermarkt begin to chime for the hour. I close my eyes, let myself be angry, tired, temporarily defeated, for each toll. When the seventh and final bell falls quiet, I take a deep breath.

Then I start thinking about how I'm going to pick this lock.

The thing about most locks is that they're more of a stalling mechanism than anything. It's not that they're particularly complex; out of five or six pins, there's just one or two set to give you trouble, and the point is to make you spend ten minutes figuring out which they are. But when you're slipping between gaps in guard shifts, you *have* to be a miser with your time.

I don't have trouble with these locks, because I've gotten very fast at figuring out the tricky pins. The key is to test them one at a time. That's what I need to do now, test this problem pin by pin.

The first one is: What am I dealing with? An illusion, to make the pages simply *look* blank, or an enchantment that truly wiped them clean?

I flip a couple of pages in, then smudge my fingertips down the paper. They come away clean. I do the same to three more pages, with no result.

The first pin slides into place.

Emeric writes in charcoal. If it were only an illusion that makes the pages appear blank, they'd still leave charcoal all over my hands. It has to be an enchantment, one that steals the writing itself. So the next pin is: *Where?*

I poke around the book more, but nothing jumps at me. That is, until I lift my hand to turn a page and find a thin, perfect stripe of gray on the heel of my palm. When I rub at it, it smears away. *Charcoal.*

That second tricky pin is looking very promising.

A line of black bookbinding thread cuts down the crease of the journal in a long, stark stitch. I prod it carefully. My fingertip comes back with another streak of gray.

"Huh," I mutter. Then I pull Emeric's knife from its sheath and cut through the thread.

It's like slashing open a sack of dried peas. Letters spill out from everywhere the stitch pierces paper, skittering into tidy lines, the thread fibers fading to plain white as they empty of charcoal. The pages themselves even crackle and shudder, coffee stains blooming once again, nicks and scrapes carving into the margins. I bark a hoarse laugh.

I may not have cracked Eiswald's curse yet, but this, at least, I can manage.

Once the letters settle, I flip to the beginning of the journal, reading by firelight. The first few pages are useless, dating back to the beginning of the year, before I'd stolen so much as an earring. They're all filled with notes like:

> *Look behind Saint Frieda statue*
> *Widow DEFINITELY lying about the hat order*
> *Writing this just to make suspect nervous, he definitely doesn't like it, still going, I'm going to UNDERLINE this and see if*

And immediately below that:

> *Full confession.*

Smug bastard.

I flip ahead, but my thumb catches on a break in the pages. A folded-up paper falls out, one that definitely wasn't there before I cut the binding thread. It's a letter, short and in a strange hand, dated just over a week ago.

Boy—

Think you've got some solid leads on the Minkja case, but this is a major one. Still, best to do it the usual way. I'll meet you on the sixth and we'll nail this thing down. Remember, cases are built, not just solved. It's not enough to be right, you have to prove it—you've got a good eye, but that's nothing if you can't make others see what you do. Don't neglect the evidence.

H

I frown at the paper. *H*, as in *H* Klemens, as in Prefect Hubert Klemens. Adalbrecht requested Klemens, which means he has a strong record. A standout among prefects would have dealt with the most monstrous criminals in the Blessed Empire.

So why would a man like that call a short string of jewel thefts a major case?

The letter fell from between two pages, and only one is blank. The other page was used to draft a response, with a couple of fitful starts:

Hubert—
~~Don't tell me how~~
~~I know what I'm~~
Noted. I'll handle

It stops there, likely interrupted. So I *did* strike a nerve with Emeric earlier, when I told him he had no proof.

The pages after it are empty. I thumb back earlier and find myself in the entries from last month.

PFENNIGEIST
Started early in the year, shortly after Falbirg-Reigenbach betrothal
Striking only nobility in Bóern
No signs of grimling or godly influence at present
Red penny for calling card—wants attention

Why, that little—I do *not* want attention.

The next page is a packing list. I jump ahead a chunk, irritation simmering in the back of my throat, and find what I'm looking for: the notes from last evening onward.

Imposter carrying marks from Death and Fortune, along with enchanted pearls. D v Falbirg lied, enchantment isn't just for charm but illusion. Will verify identity, whereabouts of former staff in the morning + confirm for Pfennigeist.

He wasn't bluffing about knowing since last night, then. This morning's notes continue:

Imposter attempting to distract from ~~something~~
Distract from everything actually
Imposter has acquired curse overnight from Eiswald, will terminate on full moon; related to Eisendorf theft?

Confirmed: Only missing Falbirg servant is Vanja, the "Red Penny"

Confirmed: Imposter aware of Eisendorf theft, despite leaving prior to discovery

At present, no indication of involvement with AvR + Nmn, Wfhdn

Confirmed: Girl spotted in Göttermarkt, tried to sell false lead; carries same curse + marks as imposter, matches description of V.

Confirmed: Vanja (Schmid⁺?) is imposter

Blood rushes to my face with every line. I never once had him fooled, not until I threw him in his own irons.

He has no right to know this much about me, let alone put it in writing. I hate this. I hate that someone out there knows even a fraction of who I am. I hate that he's not at the bottom of the Yssar right now.

The fire lets out a vindictive *pop*. I stare at the flames, then look back to the journal, contemplating, furious. I suppose it's one way to make sure these notes can't hurt me anymore.

And if I'm being honest, I want that. I don't remember the last time I felt really, truly safe, but I spent most of the last year feeling safe *enough* behind the façade of the *prinzessin*. I forgot how bone-deep the exhaustion goes when you're living in fear.

I want to get back at Emeric for putting one more fracture in my safety. For calling me the Red Penny. I want to burn everything that hurt me until it's nothing but ash.

I shut the notebook, lift it over the fire.

"What are you burning?" Ragne asks, blinking up at me curiously. She's curled up under the towel, hair fanned out to dry on the hearthstones.

It rattles me from the angry fog. Stupid, stupid, *stupid*. I yank the notebook back. "Nothing."

Emeric said he went to Sovabin. I need to know what he knows about me if I'm going to keep one step ahead. If I'm going to keep my distance.

And if he knew about my nickname—what else does he know?

I rub a hand over my face. "I'm getting some sleep. Stay off the bed."

"No," Ragne says. I would argue, but I doubt it'll change a thing.

I lock the bedroom door. Then, as an afterthought, I lock the veranda door too. I hide the Eisendorf jewels and my small chest of *gilden* back in the vanity's secret cupboard, put on a nightgown, and snuff out most of the candles.

I take the notebook and the knife with me to bed, both for the same reason: Emeric Conrad is still alive, and he will likely want them back.

I set the knife on the bedside table, prop myself up on the pillows, and crack open the notebook once more. It takes a few tries to find the notes from Sovabin.

> *Castle Falbirg: lots of recent repair. New funding? AvR paid bribe for G?*
> *Definitely extortion, main town saw dramatic increase in business since betrothal, AvR possibly throttling trade routes*
> *What does AvR get out of it besides G?*

The next line catches me in the gut.

> *Prince + dame openly abusive to staff, insult and threaten wages, potentially violent*

I don't know why I feel so thunderstruck. I suppose—I thought no one else saw it. Or they looked the other way. Or that it just wasn't, well, that bad.

Even now I can feel a tiny voice insisting, *It was only when they were angry, they were scared, they gave you a place in their home, and you could have worked harder, and—and it could have been worse—*

But that voice comes from a part of me that would forgive anything just for a motherly pat on the head. And if I listen, it will eat me alive.

I make myself move on.

The next few lines are tidier, more complete, like Emeric was composing his thoughts at the end of the day.

Almost certain the Pfennigeist is from Castle Falbirg. Will write H proper summary of theories after I interview the servants, but in short:

- *Presence of red pennies → the culprit(s?) wants victims to connect the crimes; they want victims to feel powerless against them*

- *Only targeting nobles → specific class-based grudge*

- *V Falbirgs mistreat their staff and were desperate for money until recently → likely underpaid staff, forcing complete dependency on income to keep them from leaving despite poor conditions*

Overall, suspect is probably someone looking for revenge, humiliated by nobility and wants to return the favor. They know how to navigate aristocratic circles from personal observation, also likely denied basic needs when young and feels compelled to overcompensate now. High-level servant, close to the family, subject to prolonged neglect as a child, possibly abuse.

My ribs have turned to his iron manacles, locked and unforgiving around my chest.

How did he—how *dare* he—

There's a list of names under the word *INTERVIEWS* on the next page. Some I recognize as castle staff, and some are new. A few notes are jotted beside each, like *Bettinger—guard, hired in spring* and *Nägele— new cook, says last one had ill temper*. Emeric crossed out each name as he went along.

Then, halfway down the list, the notes stop at the housekeeper's name. She's worked at Castle von Falbirg since long before I did; she was in the dining hall, watching with a pitcher of wine in her shaking hands, the night I was whipped for the von Hirschings.

The rest of the roster has been crossed out in one broad, savage stroke; she was his final interview.

At the bottom of the page, in large, deadly certain letters, Emeric has written one word:

ROHTPFENNI

I slam the book shut.

Then I wrap the leather string around it as many times as it will go and shove it under a far pillow, out of my sight. My heart is pounding with fury, with shame, and to my shock, my eyes sting.

I haven't cried since I left Castle Falbirg.

I thought I left this girl behind. I made Marthe, the *Prinzessin*, the *Pfennigeist*, all so I could outrun the ghost in the mirror.

Ragne jumps up on the bed as a cat, looks at me, and curls beside my knees without a word.

I belligerently stare at the bed's velvet canopy until the tears burn themselves out.

I will beat this curse. I will keep out of Adalbrecht's reach. I will outmaneuver Emeric Conrad and leave him, and Gisele, and *all of this* behind.

And I will do it . . . in the next thirteen days.

I don't remember falling asleep.

It doesn't take long for dreams to find me. Or for them to warp sinister: Eiswald turning me to limestone that crumbles with every labored step. Gisele pointing at me as rubies pour from her mouth. A golden wolf with Adalbrecht's crystal-blue eyes and a crow in its jaws.

The wolf, however, lingers.

It snaps down on the crow in an explosion of feathers. Then it seizes on a winter-fat marmot. Blood like blue flame gushes from its teeth. Next a fox, a goat, a deer, an elk—

A flick of sharp pain darts over my arm, but I can't move.

The wolf's burning eyes turn to me. It lunges.

There's a flurry of copper, silver, gold, and bone, a note like a resounding bell. I think I hear my name. But as my eyes fly open, it feels like I'm still trapped in dreams.

The low candlelight slices a ghoulish figure from the dark.

A withered, pale-skinned manlike creature is squatting on my chest, tying knots into my hair, sharp teeth bared in bliss. Its eyes smolder a cold sapphire blue.

I try to inhale and it comes out as a choking gag, my lungs screaming as they fight the creature's weight. Ragne is hissing, claws swiping at the thing, but it barely seems to notice, rocking forward.

Gold fortune-glimmer flickers at my side, over Emeric's knife still on the bedside table.

I seize it, shake off the sheath, and jam the steel blade into the creature's side. It feels like stabbing a sack of grain. The withered little man coos and gurgles, rolling drunkenly away into the blankets, but whatever spell it held over me has broken. I throw myself off the bed and gasp out, "*Poldi!*"

The dim hearth swells with fire, like the *kobold*'s poking his head up from a nap. Then it surges angrily as Poldi leaps toward the bed. The creature lets out a quiet, reedy shriek and flings itself onto the wall, scrambling around like a giant, fleshy, four-legged spider as Poldi chases it up to the ceiling.

Then the wretched little man dives for the door, collapses down to almost nothing, and slips bonelessly through the keyhole.

I stare at the door and try not to fall into panic, still catching my breath. "What," I wheeze, "what—*was* that?"

"A *nachtmahr*," Ragne snarls, tail bushed out. "I am sorry, I tried to scratch you awake. Another ten heartbeats, and it would have stolen you."

Sure enough, there's a short row of red lines on my arm. I lean on the bedframe, heart pounding, trying to collect my sleep-dizzy thoughts. It's like trying to gather oil with a sieve.

I've heard of the *nachtmären* but never seen one. They're minor *grimlingen*, lesser goblins that poison dreams and drink them up. If they're not stopped, they take the dreamer from their bed and ride them through the night like a horse. They're not terribly strong, but there can be as many as there are dreamers.

If one ever visited my old family's home, I don't remember, and the *kobold* of Castle Falbirg kept every *grimling* out. Poldi is supposed to do the same.

He floats over, scratching his head.

"*Sorry, Lady,*" he mumbles. "*Dunno how it got in.*"

Fortune's golden silhouette forms near the foot of the bed, just solid enough to see as she picks up the knife's sheath and holds it out to me. Then I remember the rush of her gold in the dream.

Ice runs down my spine. "I didn't ask you to help," I say swiftly. "That doesn't count. I don't owe you anything."

There's a distant, jingling whisper like words spun from tossed coins: "No. Not this time."

I swipe the sheath from her, and she vanishes. I slip it over the knife, then drag the heaviest blanket off the bed and over to the fireplace. I'm too worn out to stay awake until dawn, but—but—

At least for a little while, I need to feel safe.

"Can you keep watch?" I croak to Poldi.

The *kobold* nods, climbing back onto the firewood and pulling a few fresh logs in after him.

I wrap myself in the blanket, wrap my hands around the knife, and, for the first time in almost a year, lay my head down beside a hearth.

CHAPTER TWELVE

ℌchematics

"**Y**OU LOOK TIRED, MY JEWEL."

I contemplate breaking my plate over Adalbrecht's head, but decide it would be too much effort. Especially after last night. He ordained we'd take breakfast in *his* parlor, and while the table isn't as cumbersome as the ones in the dining hall, I would still have to get up and walk around to where he's seated, and that's an awful lot of work.

Besides, Gisele never turned down a plate of *damfnudeln*, not even for such a worthy cause.

Instead I spoon strawberry preserves onto the steamed sweet buns and smile thinly. "I was just so terribly excited about the wedding, I hardly slept a wink."

Scheit, I wish he hadn't insisted on breakfast together. I need to placate him after yesterday's misadventures, I know, *I know*, but it was hard to remember that this morning when I had to drag myself up from the hearth and get ready.

Thankfully, the margrave's parlor is fine enough that a pair of delicate lace gloves is appropriate. I'm not sure how I would have explained my ruby-spotted knuckles otherwise.

Adalbrecht's chambers are on the opposite side of the castle from mine, overlooking Minkja to the west. I can even spot the statue of Kunigunde peering over the rooftops from the Salzplatt. I dearly hope she can't see all the way into his bedroom, and if she can, that it wasn't intentional. Even though the view lies to the west, the parlor is almost painfully bright from light bouncing off painted stucco and limestone and glass.

It doesn't seem to bother Adalbrecht at all as he digs into his *weysserwurst*. I'll admit, it may be my turn to be bullied by sausage, as I'm not too fond of the gray-white *wurst* or how they're served bobbing in the water they boiled in. They *taste* fine, but the usual way to eat them can be a bit . . . distressing.

Adalbrecht, never averse to the distressing, slices the sausage casing open at one end, sucks the meat out through the hole, and adds one more wet sock of skin to the pile on his plate as I try not to gag.

"Good morning, Master von Reigenbach." The castle's chief steward, Franziska, knocks on the door and marches in, understeward Barthl on her heels. She drops a quick curtsy and shuffles the papers in her arms. "I've the documents you requested, and Barthl is here to take notes." Sure enough, there's a slate and chalk in the man's hands. "But before we begin, young Prefect Conrad is here to request an audience."

I almost choke on my *damfnudeln*. Is he seriously going to try to expose me in my own castle?

"Hmm." Adalbrecht glances briefly at me, then discards another empty sausage casing. "He can wait. We've far more pressing matters."

"He was quite insistent on speaking with the *prinzessin*, m'lord. Claimed it's a matter of some . . . urgency."

Saints and martyrs, I'm going to throw him back into the Yssar. But then I find I have a new problem: Adalbrecht is setting down his fork to give me a long, affronted look.

"Wh-what is it?" I gulp and add, for good measure, "My darling?"

Adalbrecht's lip curls. "Is there anything you'd like to tell me about your visit with the prefect yesterday? Anything at all, *my jewel?*"

I shake my head, doing my best wide-eyed airhead stare. "No, nothing."

(The answer to a question like this is always, *always* no, by the way. It's a trick. You might tell them something they already knew; you might confess to a greater trespass than they imagined. If they're going to catch you, make them work for it.)

Adalbrecht gives me another long stare, then turns on Barthl. "Fine. Bring him up here. He can have nothing to say to Gisele that can't be said in front of me."

Oh no. It's happening. "Must we, darling?" I venture. "I would hate to delay planning our special day."

"We won't." He snaps his fingers at me and points to an empty chair at his end of the table, like I'm an errant spaniel. "Move here." He drums his fingers on the table as I grudgingly relocate with my *damf-nudeln*. Once I'm settled in arm's reach, he jerks his chin at his steward. "Franziska. Begin."

The steward, a lean woman in her forties, straightens up and consults her papers. "We've removed the family wedding regalia from storage. The Reigenbach bridal crown is being cleaned and polished, and your father's wedding suit is being tailored to your most recent measurements—"

"I want a new one," Adalbrecht barks.

Franziska pauses. "A new suit, m'lord?" He nods. "What would you like changed from the . . . traditional one?"

Adalbrecht rattles off a list: ermine lining for the cloak, fresh woad dye for the blue fabric, polished gold buttons, on and on. I do my best to maintain a placid expression; as Marthe the Maid, I've been in those chests, seen the wedding regalia. It's already got gold buttons, ermine, bright blue dye. He's asking for the exact same suit made all over again, just because he can.

What a waste.

Barthl slips through the door. Emeric is hovering in the hall behind him, just out of the frame. He seems to have dug up a uniform that actually fits this time, but he's still fidgeting like a premium fusspot.

Though . . . why is he keeping up the act? Emeric caught me last night; he should be marching in here to haul me off to await trial. Yet neither he nor Barthl seems inclined to pay me any mind.

Adalbrecht ignores them both either way, continuing to dictate to Franziska. "Tell me of the schedule."

"Sunday will be the ball, where the assembly will witness the signing of the marriage decree," Franziska says. "Then the full week must pass before—"

"I told you to get around that."

Franziska hesitates, mincing her words and flicking her gaze pointedly to the hallway. "The officials were quite firm, m'lord. All seven days, according to the law."

I barely hold in a sigh of relief. Dame von Falbirg used to claim that the law was to give couples time to reflect on the beauty and sanctity of marriage; Joniza used to say it was to keep nobles from kidnapping a politically advantageous spouse and catapulting them to the altar. (Joniza, of course, had the right of it.)

Adalbrecht glares daggers at the glimpse of Emeric's sleeve peeking through the doorway. I don't know what vexes the margrave more, that he wasn't able to bribe city hall into letting him have his way, or that he can't exactly order Franziska to increase the bribe within earshot of a prefect of the Godly Courts. He grumbles, "Continue."

"There will be an event every evening until the following Sunday, when the marriage will be consecrated in the eyes of the High Gods and the Low." Franziska places an elaborate schematic of the decorations on the table before us. "We will use the traditional chapel here in Castle Reigenbach for—"

"*Pfah*." Adalbrecht throws his napkin onto the drawing. "Any common drudge can use a chapel. I want the Göttermarkt."

Barthl and Franziska trade looks. "Which temple, Master Reigenbach?" Barthl asks. "Also, *Meister* Conrad—"

"I *said* I want the Göttermarkt. Was that not clear?" Adalbrecht's ire has found a new target, it seems. "I want every temple, every chapel, every cathedral. I want *every* Low God's blessing. We'll stage the ceremony in the plaza. You have two weeks to clear out the rabble and make it presentable. Get it done."

The knot in Barthl's throat bobs. "Very well, m'lord. And the prefect is here."

Adalbrecht scowls. "Come in, boy, let's have a look at you." Emeric steps into the parlor, shuffling nervously as Adalbrecht looks him up and down. Unsurprisingly, the margrave is not impressed, because his next question is a terse "When will Klemens get here?"

"M-Monday, sir." Emeric wrings his hands. Now that I know it's a ruse, I can see how calculated it is, how each darting glance to me is as sharp as a needle prick.

Wait. Klemens's letter said he'd arrive on the sixth—Sunday. Why is Emeric lying? To make me think I have more time before I have to face a *real* prefect?

"Hmm." Adalbrecht fishes another *weysserwurst* from the tureen and slices a hole at the end. "Well? What do you want with my bride?"

Emeric looks to me as Adalbrecht begins to suck the meat from its wilting casing. I'm starting to wonder how many consecutive mornings the junior prefect is going to spend being bullied by sausage.

"I do apologize," he says with a bare glint of an edge, "but I'm afraid my notes have been . . . misplaced. I need to retake the *prinzessin's* statement, and I did not think we would wish to disrupt the margrave's day."

Oh, *absolutely* not. The moment we're alone, he'll try to clap me in irons again, that's what he's here for. But I'm not the only one whose cover can be blown. "What grave news. It would be dreadful if *all* your hard work was discovered by the wrong person. Have you tried retracing your steps?"

The faintest hint of irritation flickers over Emeric's face. "Indeed I did, Princess Gisele. All the way back to the Gänslinghaus."

To the—

The smile freezes on my face. That's Gisele's orphanage.

Scheit, scheit, scheit.

He's found her. And unlike all the times Gisele came to plead among the beggars, the Order of Prefects can help her demand an audience now.

How *dare* he stick his nose in this. This should have stayed between me and Gisele, he had no business interfering.

Cold fury washes through me. I decide to give as good as I'm getting. "My parlor was cleared out after we spoke," I say sweetly, "but I'll have my maid Marthe check with the *russmagdt*, see if she found anything in the cinders."

I can tell when Emeric connects the dots, because first he goes white as his starched *krebatte*, then livid red. It doesn't matter that his notes are currently stashed under my pillow; as far as he knows, they're ashes in my hearth, and the glitter of barely smothered outrage in his eyes *almost* makes me feel good as new.

Then a broad hand lands on mine. This time, all of me freezes, even with the layer of lace between us. A distant part of me notes Adalbrecht's managed to replace his signet ring already, its golden edges pushing into my flesh.

My throat tightens. It's been over a year since I learned what sort of man *Markgraf* von Reigenbach is, but a lesson like that lives in your bones.

"Prefect." Adalbrecht drops the empty sausage casing on the pile with his other hand. "My bride is going to be occupied for most of the week. I will let you know if she finds time." Something in his tone shifts even stonier. "Join us at the ball on Sunday. We'll be signing the marriage contract and can always use an extra witness."

A ghost of a furrow appears in Emeric's brow before smoothing out. "I thank you for the honor, sir, but a commoner like myself—"

"Nonsense. You'll be our guest." Adalbrecht grips my hand even tighter. I can't think of an excuse to pull away, there's a panicked, empty fog in my skull like I'm free-falling, I just want him to stop touching me—

"Then I must accept, sir," Emeric says, sounding oddly hasty. "Thank you again."

Adalbrecht lets me go so he can bob for another *weysserwurst*. "Oh, and you're welcome to bring a guest."

Emeric looks dead at me, mouth in a thin line. "You're very generous, sir. I believe I know exactly who to bring."

The absolute theatrical *bastard*. He's going to bring Gisele.

"Good," Adalbrecht says smoothly. "You're dismissed."

A stiff beat passes. Emeric is neither servant, subject, nor soldier of the margrave and he doesn't have to take Adalbrecht's orders. But he evidently knows better than to dispute them either, for all he does is bow. "Good day to you both."

He shoots me another look from the hallway on his way out.

Adalbrecht watches him go, expression darkening. "I suspect that boy's taken an interest in you," he says, sour. "An *improper* one. I won't indulge it."

I stare at Adalbrecht. Somehow, I'd forgotten all about that angle, but I suppose Emeric did just give a very convincing argument in favor. The absurdity shakes a borderline-hysterical giggle from my panic. "That suits me very well."

Adalbrecht's frown deepens. "It should." He wads up the paper of Franziska's plans for the chapel decorations, then tosses it lazily into the fireplace. "I want the schematics completely done over for the Göttermarkt by lunch. Now, the guests . . ."

The edges of Barthl's mouth wilt as he watches the paper burn, but he only jots a note on his slate.

I would feel bad, but by the time this wedding rolls around, I fully intend to be long gone from Minkja, and that's going to be a considerably larger problem for them.

(I should probably feel bad about that too. But given that the alternative is becoming an incredibly valuable, if eccentric, statue, I don't.)

The rest of the morning is spent just as Adalbrecht threatened: in wedding preparations. And by that I mean him dictating everything. We will serve venison at the gala. We will have a breakfast banquet the morning of the wedding. My wedding dress will be Reigenbach blue.

At one point, desperate to escape, I gently offer to go confer with my maids on how to dress my hair for the occasions. Adalbrecht just pats my hand. "Impossible," he says firmly. "I *so* value your input." And then he calls for another round of coffee.

By lunch, I've realized that he intends to keep me trapped here because he can. Not just today, but every day until our wedding.

I don't have time for this. Not with the curse, not with Prefect Klemens due in less than a week, not with Emeric and Gisele at my throat.

While Adalbrecht is droning over some nonsense with seating arrangements, I come up with a plan. The curse is the only thing keeping me in Bóern right now; I can scrape by on the money that I have. Once I'm out, Gisele is welcome to a triumphant return, I just need her to lie low for a few more days. I'm sure she'll agree if it means living in a castle again, especially one like Castle Reigenbach.

Considering she tried to strangle me the last time we spoke, though, I'm going to need someone else to deliver that message.

And that means going back into Minkja. Which means the *prinzessin* must be . . . indisposed.

So when no one's looking, I sneak the tiny jar of milk off the coffee service. Then I stuff a napkin in there to absorb the milk and keep it from splashing, and hold the jar between my hot palms.

When there's a break between discussing the Wednesday hunt and the Saturday gala, I excuse myself to visit the privy.

"Don't be long about it," Adalbrecht barks.

I smile sweetly, the jar safely hidden in my conveniently enormous and lace-shrouded sleeves. "Of course," I lie.

When I reach my bedchamber, I close the door, then set the jar on the hearth and wring the milk back into it from the napkin. The cinders from the fireplace are still warm. They'll keep it just tepid enough to go bad, fast.

My birth mother once said that wherever I go, the milk spoils. I certainly didn't manage that when I was four, but I've figured out the trick of it by now. And I've also figured out the secret to faking a stomach ailment: the smell of rotten dairy.

Before I leave my bedroom, I also work a light dusting of pale-green powder into my cheeks. The pearls make it look like an elegant kind of nausea, at least.

"Saints and martyrs," Franziska says when I return. "Mistress Gisele, are you taking ill again?"

I smile bravely, like I'm auditioning for the role of First Martyr in one of the more gruesome holy pageants, and sink into a chair. "I'll be fine, it's just my poor constitution. Please, don't stop for my sake."

I barely pick at my supper a few hours later. I can see the castle staff pursing their lips; they know a storm is squatting on the horizon, and it's blowing in from the riverfront wing.

The *prinzessin* retires early. My bedroom is already beginning to sour with the rotten-milk smell that's the key to pulling this off. (I warned you my methods are revolting.) I cover the ruby, change quickly into the servant uniform and a pair of worn gloves, and then run down to the kitchens to forage for a real dinner. The kitchen staff don't even bother me, they're so accustomed to Gisele's needs sending me into the pantry at all hours.

Trudl, on the other hand, catches me by the elbow as I pick up a bucket of scraps. Her voice is hesitant but clear. "Marthe. You haven't been here when the margrave is home. You should know . . ." The words hitch, then come out in a rush. "The maids work in pairs, no matter the job, while he's here. Or they walk with another servant. They never go alone. Do you understand?"

My grip tightens on the bucket handle. "I understand."

"It may change once he's married," Trudl adds. "Fortune willing, he'll stay only a few months to make sure he's put a baby in that poor girl, then run back to the battlefield. But whatever you do, don't let him catch you alone."

I stare at a bit of cabbage in the scrap bucket and nod, unsure of how to tell her that he already did a year ago. If Joniza hadn't come around the corner before he—

Well. I learned.

"Thank you" is all I say. Then I take the scrap bucket, and grits and honey for Poldi, and return the way I came.

CHAPTER THIRTEEN

To the Letter

WHEN I TOLD RAGNE I WOULD BE STUCK IN THE CASTLE ALL DAY, she decided to go visit her mother. She's back now in human shape, making a face as she crouches by the fireplace. She's at least managed to don one of my larger shirts this time. "Why does it stink in here?"

"Because—" I stop myself from blurting out something snide. I've been treating Ragne like a buffoon, but the more time I spend with her, the more I suspect she's far cannier than she lets on. She just lives by different rules.

"I'm making vomit," I say, telling the truth for once.

"Can't you just . . . *bleh*?" Ragne sticks her tongue out.

"I can, but this doesn't feel bad." I take the pitcher of water from the washbasin and pour some into the scrap bucket, then add the sour milk, slosh it around a few times, and leave it to marinate overnight in the privy closet. "In the morning, I'll pretend to be Gisele's maid and tell the other servants she's sick. Then we can sneak out of the castle."

Ragne wrinkles her nose. "Confusing. Why don't you just leave?"

"Adalbrecht—the margrave who owns this castle—won't let me. He . . ." I try to think of a way to help her understand. "You know how you don't like to eat meat? Adalbrecht's the opposite. He *likes* to eat other people up, he likes knowing they're in his belly."

"If he tried to eat me, I would leave forever."

"Well, I can't change into a bear, so it's dangerous to leave alone." I rub my eyes. "Did your mother say anything?"

Ragne tilts her head. "I told her it was not fair to give you a curse but not tell you how to break it. She said . . . if you can't figure it out, then that's the problem."

"Helpful as ever," I grumble.

"I don't think it's fair. If the curse wasn't going to kill you, then you could solve it in your own way. But you do not have time, and it is wrong to make you waste your days looking for the answer. So I bothered her until she gave me a hint." Ragne smiles with all of her sharp teeth. "Mother said to remember you are cursed to have what you want."

I pull off the gloves and examine the rash of rubies. They've spread up to both wrists now, little glittering scarlet pockmarks. If this is what Eiswald means by what I want . . .

She's not wrong. But . . . am *I*?

"Am I just supposed to *not* want gemstones?" I scowl. "That's like asking me to not want to eat."

Ragne shrugs. "That's all she said. But we will try again tomorrow. Where are we going?"

I go to my wardrobe and rummage in the very back, under boots and scarves and stockings, until I find what I'm looking for: a tattered dress in faded rusty red. Falbirg red.

I haven't worn it since we left Sovabin. But tomorrow, I will need to throw myself on the mercy of someone who has no reason to give any; she will know this red on sight.

I rock back on my heels. "We're going to find an old friend."

⤮

I almost make it out of the castle without incident Wednesday morning.

The classic spew gambit executes without a hitch, as it always does. When Trudl knocks on the door a little after sunrise to summon Gisele to breakfast, I answer the door as Marthe, with a plaster over the ruby, heavy soot-shadows swiped under my eyes, and an apron and skirt splashed in, well, the contents of the scrap bucket. It is *very* ripe. In fact, Ragne's helping, retching in the privy closet from the smell.

Trudl stumbles back, gasping, "I'll tell the margrave. How bad is it?"

"She's been at it for three hours," I say with a dead-eyed kind of exhaustion. "At least another day. Maybe two. She won't keep anything down but water."

Another of Ragne's gags punctuates the sentence.

Trudl's eyes water. "High Gods and Low lend you strength, Marthe."

And thus I buy myself at least a day to work with. (Maybe two.) I can still smell the fake vomit as I hurry down the servant corridors.

"You there, *frohlein*." Barthl's voice stops me as I'm about to slip out the kitchen door. "Hold a moment."

I turn around, keeping my eyes downcast. I know it's not about the ruby teardrop; I made sure the plaster and gauze was set before I left, and so far everyone's bought the story about the glue burn. Still, I almost never run into Barthl as Marthe, and if he places the old Falbirg uniform under this servant-issue cloak, I'll have to come up with some lie. "Please, sir, my mistress is very ill. I need to fetch her—"

"Yes, yes, you're going into Minkja, correct?" Barthl's voice is all business. I venture a glance up and a tiny nod. His hound-dog face is even more haggard than usual, a slight dusting of stubble on his normally clean-shaven cheeks. Even his short mouse-brown hair looks out of sorts. He shoves a sealed, unaddressed envelope my way. "Take this with you. There is a tavern in the Madschplatt called the Broken Lance. Leave this with the man at the counter."

Well. This sounds shifty.

Barthl seems to recognize that, because he blusters, "They're . . . catering . . . the wedding. One of the events, that is. Don't ask questions."

I never expected Barthl to be particularly adept at lying, but I *did* expect a degree of basic competence there. Clearly I've misjudged.

"No, sir, right away, sir," I say meekly, and leave with the letter. The Madschplatt is in Lähl. This gives me an excuse to stay away from the castle even longer. Not that I particularly need it; I've left the sour milk pail out in the room to keep the entire riverfront wing reeking, and the rest of Castle Reigenbach is already in mayhem with preparations for next week.

I pass through the main gate as usual, but wait until I'm out of the guards' eyeshot to pull a warm forest-green knit cap over my hair. I've wound the two braids into knots that the cap can cover completely, since the last thing I want is for my ginger hair to stick out. A spare yellow hat also waits in my satchel, because on the off chance that someone describes me to the authorities, I'd like it to be with an outdated hat color.

I've also brought Emeric's notebook, knife, and writing charcoal, along with the money I fleeced off him earlier. Hypothetically I'm just going to talk to Joniza, but Joniza taught me herself: Better prepared than lucky.

I head to the Obarmarkt on the northwest bank of the Yssar, which caters to wealthier patrons than the southeast markets. Once I reach the Mittlstratz viaduct, I follow it until it intersects with the western curve of the Hoenstratz, then take the first staircase to the street. I've walked this route often enough that the only thing that gives me pause is the icy stone steps. Ragne takes no chances either, flitting above me as a black sparrow.

Once I'm at ground level, I find myself in the heart of Trader's Cross. If Minkja were a clock face with Castle Reigenbach at the center, Trader's Cross would be squarely where the hour hand points at nine. The neighborhood started with a single spice merchant, some say Magrabi, some say Surajan; all that's certain is her wife sold traditional pastries on the side, until the pastries started outselling the spices. Traders went out of their way to visit before continuing to the Salzplatt just north of here. The traffic laid the foundations for first tea shops and specialty grocers, then textile merchants, pottery dealers, traditional apothecaries. The narrow alleys now bloom with garlands of Gharese prayer flags, bright woven Sahalian baskets, intricate geometric murals on the stucco, little shrines to distant gods tucked into pockets between houses.

I stash myself beside just such a shrine, dropping a *sjilling* into the offering dish before a statue of a winking fox as Ragne perches on the roof over the tiny idol, and wait. Maybe Joniza's changed her breakfast routine, but if not, I'll see her coming down the alley any minute now to toss a coin on her way to the restaurant.

All I need to do is convince her to help me. Well, no. First I need to apologize. *Then* I need to convince her to take my offer to Gisele: I will cheerfully return the pearls *after* the curse is broken, but only if Gisele tells Junior Prefect Emeric Conrad to piss off.

And to add a stick to that carrot: If she turns me down, I'll just as cheerfully chuck the pearls into the Yssar on my way out.

But when I glance up, I discover that Gisele isn't the only one who needs to tell Emeric Conrad to piss off.

Joniza's picking her way through the crowd, bundled up to the point of absurdity in a thick fox-fur coat. (She never did take to the cold.) Right beside her and deep in discussion is the junior prefect himself.

Damn him. I can't believe he already tracked her down. Then again, if he knows about the Gänslinghaus, it couldn't have been too hard.

I yank up the hood of my servant-issue cloak and duck my head, darting into the street. Emeric said he could see the curse on me, so I need to get out of Trader's Cross before he spots it.

But when I reach the corner and dare a look back, he's scanning the passersby, eyes narrowed.

What an unmitigated pain in the ass he is.

I hurry around the corner, through a cramped alley, heading south. After a few more turns I check again; all is clear. I let out a hiss of annoyance.

"Why did you leave?" Ragne chirps, landing on my shoulder.

"I think I was being followed." The bells toll ten o'clock as I lean against a wall out of sight, thinking. "We'll go to Lähl and deliver Barthl's letter, and then I'll come back and try to find Joniza again."

We keep winding south, passing through the gate of the High Wall and into the Sumpfling district; if Trader's Cross sits at nine o'clock on the short hand, I am dragging the long hand back to eight o'clock. Here, the buildings are far from the immaculate timber-and-flower-boxes-and-painted-plaster affairs of the Obarmarkt. At best they match the sturdy brick and plaster of the Hoenring. At the worst . . . well, the Sumpfling floods at least once a year, so many of the lumber buildings are propped up on leaning stilts that I wouldn't trust to hold against a stiff breeze, much less carry the weight of multiple people.

Beyond the High Wall, I trade my servant cloak for the worn shawl in my satchel. In the Obarmarkt, a servant of Castle Reigenbach can go anywhere she pleases, but Lähl is one of the parts of Minkja where that cloak makes me a target.

It's a quick walk along the Yssar to reach the Stichensteg islets, which mark the unofficial border of Lähl. The handful of sandbars aren't sturdy enough for a proper bridge, and the Wolfhünden saw an opportunity, so they control the network of flimsy rope bridges that stitch the islets to each shore. I thankfully only need to cross two, but I still have to pay a red penny to each of the brawny toll collectors stationed at either end of the bridges. There's a minor commotion at the far end of the islets; the rope bridges have a tendency to snag bodies. Odds are a floater has washed up on a sandbar.

Lähl is the kind of district that you smell before you see, a stained and faded seven o'clock glowering spitefully up the long hand of the Minkjan dial. It bristles with docks like the Obarmarkt and the Untrmarkt, but these docks seem to jut into the Yssar a little more salaciously, like a drunk with a coin and an eye for an available *mietling*. A *mietling* used to just mean someone hired for any odd job, but these days it's the politest term for someone whose job sites are mostly in the bedroom. Lähl is also the kind of place where both drunks and *mietlingen* are in plentiful supply.

It's not quite a market and not quite a slum, but busier than both. When I'm not picking my way around puddles of virtually any substance that can be expelled from a human body, I'm weaving around shambling poppy-eaters, pinch-faced streetwitches, and bony old cattle being driven to the tanner.

Ragne has been following along as a raven, presumably to keep clear of the smell of the gutters, but she lands on my shoulder, head cocked. "These people are selling strange wares. One shouted that she is selling the *wurstkuss*. Why would someone pay her to kiss a sausa—"

"It's an expression," I say hastily. "Er, more like a nickname. It means—" I explain in the sparest terms, trying and failing to keep my face from burning.

Ragne blinks a crimson eye, head still cocked. "Someone else said they would roll a penny. What does that mean?"

"Uh, a lot like what I just said. But in other places, for very cheap, and you'll probably get lice."

"What is 'Alms for the Vicar'?"

"No idea."

"What about 'Hide the *Nudel*'?"

"You can probably guess," I say a little desperately, tempted to pull my hat down over my flaming cheeks. "Can we please—"

"Do you know what a 'Five Martyred Johanns' is?"

I hide my face in my hands. "*STOP. ASKING. I DON'T. KNOW.*"

Then I run smack into something. Some*one*, judging by the grunt of annoyance. Ragne squawks and launches herself into the air.

"Watch where you're going, little pig," a low voice snarls as I stagger back. I find a man scowling my way, shaking out his arm. He's about Yannec's age, dusted in stubble a day or two too old to be dashing, and on the back of his hand I spot a stark black tattoo: two lances in an *X*.

That's the mark of a disgraced soldier, either deserter or discharged in dishonor, like most of the Wolfhünden. This one doesn't look to be in uniform, but a standard-issue cudgel swings at his belt nonetheless. He's either off duty or on business they don't want traced back to them.

The Wolfhünden may protect me as the *Prinzessin*, but they're no friend to Marthe the Maid. And if they ever caught the *Pfennigeist*, they'd be pulling my corpse out of the Stichenstegs within days.

So I cast my eyes down like I did with Barthl, tug my cap lower, and mumble, "Sorry, sir, won't happen again."

The Wolfhunder spits at my feet and stomps off.

Only a few minutes later, I see him again as I reach the Madschplatt. He's loudly cursing as his boot lands in one of the many puddles that give the Madschplatt its name. It isn't quite like the other plazas of Minkja, more of a sprawling mud pit left open only because the ground wasn't sound enough to build on. Brothels, slaughterhouses, and charity clinics crouch at the edges, the gaps between buildings grouted in pigpens and rubbish heaps. The smoky air reeks of ovens burning cheap peat bricks and dried dung, and every person hustling through the muck gives the distinct impression that they would sell you to the *grimlingen* for a single *sioppen* of beer. Even the children. Hell, *especially* the children.

Then I catch sight of the tavern sign for the Broken Lance, where I'm supposed to deliver Barthl's envelope. I head in, blinking to let my eyes adjust to the dim, and find an interior as run-down as the exterior. A handful of bleary-eyed customers are scattered at rickety tables, all in the kind of slump that suggests they're close to permanent installations. The barkeep looks up as I walk in, flicking dirty water off his hands. "What do you want?"

I fish Barthl's envelope from my satchel and slide it across the counter. "For the, uh, catering?"

He gives me a wooden nod. "Understood. Now—" The door behind me bangs open. It's the off-duty Wolfhunder, slinging a satchel from his shoulder. The barkeep's face darkens, but with an exaggerated sigh, he turns to the strongbox. "Off with you, girl."

I hurry out of the way, keeping my head down. The Wolfhunder doesn't seem to notice me, shoving his satchel at the barkeep. "Sixty shillings."

"I'll give you white pennies, Rudi. Need the small coins to make change." There's a series of clinks as the barkeep counts out twelve silver *pfenni*. "Where's your boy, Steffe? Thought he was in charge of collecting fees for your route."

"Late," Rudi the Wolfhunder grunts. "And I'm not waiting around for the brat. Got . . . *pressing* matters to see to." A bawdy chuckle.

I sneak a look. There's a crude *X* like the tattoo stamped into the satchel leather. He's collecting protection fees.

"Oh." The barkeep produces Barthl's envelope. "And a message from Papa Wolf."

Papa Wolf? There are a number of names I could call Barthl, but *that* certainly isn't among them. Adalbrecht, on the other hand . . .

But he's the Golden Wolf, shining and upright, and the Wolfhünden already take his orders in public.

So what, precisely, is the margrave of Bóern asking them to do in the shadows?

CHAPTER FOURTEEN

SHORTCHANGE

I WON'T GET THE ANSWER HERE. THE WOLFHUNDER SNATCHES THE letter and shoves it into his jerkin. Then he dumps the white pennies in his satchel and clears out.

I wait to leave until the barkeep shoos me off. Unfortunately, Rudi's still in sight, sidling up to a brothel. I hang back behind a crowd congealing around a doomsday prophet who's shouting at the sky, but I can't help notice the Wolfhunder dip a fist into the collection bag of protection fees.

A *mietling* in a very hardworking dress catches the man's sleeve, running a hand up his arm. "The usual?" she purrs. She lights up when he hands her a white penny. "Ooh, *Rudi*, that'll buy you a whole hour."

"Just gotta wait for Steffe" I barely hear over the prophet, before the Wolfhunder squeezes a handful of the woman's rear end, eliciting a piercing giggle.

I look away, the pins of this lock beginning to slide. I don't need to tell you how much of a colossal fool you'd have to be to skim off the protection fees even *once*. If Rudi's doing it often enough for a *mietling* to know his routine . . . Not to mention that he's lazy enough to rely on this Steffe boy to usually do the collecting. I'm guessing the Wolfhünden don't know about that either.

The clock hasn't even chimed half past. I can't go back to Trader's Cross just yet, and I still haven't figured out how to break the curse. Maybe this is an opportunity to try something new.

When the half-past chimes do clang through the sooty air, Rudi the Wolfhunder apparently decides he's waited long enough. He hangs the satchel on a hook under a red-paned lamp and orders the other *mietlingen* soliciting by the door to keep an eye out for Steffe, then follows his *mietling* inside with an explosion of truly upsetting chortles. I give it another minute before I slip out of the doomsday prophet's audience and hide in an alley, rummaging in my own satchel.

I trade the green knit cap for the yellow, take off my shawl, and, in my head, draw out the *Pfennigeist*. As the Penny Phantom, I am anyone, I am no one. I am whoever I want to be.

Today, I'm Steffe's older sister. And it's time to play a game.

I return to the Madschplatt at a much quicker pace, donning a harried look as I hurry up to the brothel.

"Looking for a good time, girl?" one *mietling* asks.

I decide to take a page from Emeric's book and gulp nervously, tugging on the edges of my knit cap. "Oh, no, miss, I—I'm looking for a *Meister* Rudi? I'm Steffe's sister, he's sick and I'm here to do the collections for him."

The *mietlingen* roll their eyes at each other. The first one points to the satchel. "He's . . . occupied. There's the collection bag. Just go to every door in the plaza, tell them who you're collecting for."

"Thank you." I fumble the bag as it comes off the hook, then clutch it to me and head toward a pawnshop with a fresh, glossy coat of paint on the door and three gleaming brass balls on the sign. I know the type: pawnbrokers like this let desperate people take out a "loan," securing it with something more valuable as collateral. If you need twenty *sjilling* and leave a family heirloom worth thirty, you'll be sure to clear your loan quick. Sounds fair enough, right?

But here's the trick: When the debtor returns to pay, they find their debt doubled in fees and outrageous interest. It will cost them far, far more than their collateral is worth to get it back. So they don't. And then the pawnbroker sells it for what it's worth.

Trinity of want, after all. When all you can offer is profit, they use you.

When I step inside the pawnbroker's shop, my eyes are huge, roaming over statuettes, jewelry, a polished hurdy-gurdy. The clerk at the counter sits up, teeth glinting in a smile. "What can I do for you, *frohlein?*"

I size him up fast: early twenties, no calluses on his hands, oil-slicked yellow curls, a flashy belt buckle. Eager for some break in boredom. Couldn't scream "deadbeat son" louder if he tried. I give a fragile little cough. "I'm Steffe's sister," I say, holding up the satchel, *X*-side out. "He's sick today, so I'm here for the fees? I think it's sixty *sjilling?*"

The clerk's eyes crinkle in amusement at the squeak in my voice. He hunts around for the strongbox—just as I thought, he hasn't been doing this long—and calls from behind the counter, "Shame about Steffe, but with such a cute substitute, I can't complain!"

Ugh. Any hesitation evaporates. I titter, staring at a jewelry case. "The rings are so lovely."

The clerk surfaces with the strongbox, setting it behind him, and leans over the counter. "You could get one yourself," he urges, oozing into salesman mode. I try not to pull a face at his breath. How can it smell like rancid honey and cheese at the same time? "Just a little one. Rudi spends enough on himself down here, he won't know the difference."

I make an anxious little hum but jab my finger at one with a price tag of one *sjilling*. "Could I get that one?" Then I fish around in the collection satchel, emerging with a white penny. "I'm sorry, all I have are white pennies."

"Don't you fret, *frohlein*, we can make change," the clerk says with a smirk. He removes the ring and hands it to me, then takes my coin and turns to his strongbox.

"Oh, and the collection fee's sixty *sjilling*," I add, "or twelve white pennies."

He starts counting out my change, then stops, brow furrowing. "Er. Right."

"Or maybe you could split them, so I have smaller coins? Thirty *sjilling* and six white pennies?"

The clerk brings the strongbox over to the counter, looking a little panicky as he tries to keep count of my change *and* the protection fee simultaneously. "Right away, *frohlein*."

He slides four *sjilling* over just as I pull a *sjilling* from my dress pocket. "Oh! I found a *sjilling* after all. Here, I'll trade you for my white penny."

"What?" He looks about to cry.

"I gave you a white penny, *ja*? And the ring is one *sjilling*, so I'll give you this, and you can give my white penny back." Then I lean over the jewelry case again. "How much for these earrings?"

The clerk looks up. "Ah, three *sjilling*."

"Oooh," I coo, "maybe." Then I return to the counter and pounce on a few coins. "Is this my change? No, wait, you've given me an extra white penny. I can give you nine for a *gelt*? Or we could take it out of the protection fee? This is so complicated!"

A strangled artificial laugh crawls from the man's throat. "Did you want the earrings too, *frohlein*?"

I smile giddily. "You know what? I do."

An experienced pawnbroker would know a shortchange game on sight, but this wastrel has no notion that I'm playing a shell game with his money. I flit around the store, throwing transaction after transaction at him and getting him to overpay my change every time. When I leave, it's with three rings, the earrings, a brooch, a small brass figurine of a ram, a matched set of bronze candlesticks, and a profit of nearly a hundred white pennies in my bag, on *top* of the protection fee.

Then I sell all the goods to the next pawnbroker I find, and short-change her, too, for good measure. It's revenge for making me wait while a weeping widow begged fruitlessly for her wedding ring back.

The wedding ring goes with me when I leave. I accidentally on purpose run into the widow on my way out, then gasp and pretend to pull the ring from the mud. "Oh, I think you dropped this."

The woman bursts into tears once more, clinging to me until I extract myself and hurry off.

Ragne alights on my shoulder again once I'm a reasonable distance away. "That was a nice thing you did for her."

I shrug. "It was easy."

The next part is harder.

I complete my circuit around the Madschplatt, collecting fees and more from miracle cure hawkers, bail bond shops, barber-surgeons, more taverns, even a chapel to a local saint that I'm positive is a front for poppy-dealers. But for businesses like charity shops, pauper's hospitals, and the streetwitch guildhall, I pull the same shell game with change and transactions—but in reverse, leaving them with more money than when I walked in. I even hide white pennies between ledger pages, stuff them into overflowing donation tins, making sure each has enough to cover the next few months' worth of protection fees.

There's still leftover silver when I've left my last shop crammed with secret wealth. I carefully sift it from the red pennies, sneaking it into my own satchel. The satchel will weigh enough to be convincing, at least until Rudi the Wolfhunder checks inside.

The real beauty of it is that Rudi can't strong-arm the shopkeepers to pay again. He'd need the brawn of the Wolfhünden behind him for that, and he can't exactly tell his boss that he got scammed out of the fees. He'd have to admit to letting a hired boy make his collections while he was off martyring a Johann or five, and that would only make them look a little harder at his lines in the ledger. Someone who's been skimming regularly can't survive that kind of scrutiny.

I'm close to the end of Rudi's hour with the *mietling*, so I return the satchel to the brothel's hook and scurry away. When I'm out of sight, I switch hats again and wrap my shawl back around my shoulders. That ought to throw off anyone looking for "Steffe's sister" with her yellow hat. I'll just scatter the white pennies throughout donation boxes on my way out of Lähl.

I pop out of the narrow alley and—

See Gisele.

She doesn't see me. She and a few of the older orphans are waiting in line outside a spindly little chapel down the lane, holding empty bags. The House of the High operates food banks from its smaller neighborhood temples around Minkja, providing decent fare between produce tithes from their farmers and donated leftovers from trusted inns and taverns. As I watch, a kind-faced older woman directs the family at the head of the line to the half of the vestibule where the food is separated by their customs.

I suppose the donation box at the Gänslinghaus was rather sparse. Still, I left them nearly three *gilden*. That should have stretched longer than a day.

A bellow of rage echoes down the alley behind me. Rudi, it seems, has looked inside the satchel.

Gisele glances over to find the source of the shouting. I swiftly turn away, walking toward the Madschplatt. I have to look unbothered, like I do this every day. I have to pray that she's too distracted to recognize my dress is faded Falbirg red.

I duck around the first corner I can and nearly trip on a goat tied up in front of the streetwitch guildhall.

There's a sign listing their services, and I pretend to peruse, keeping an ear out for the Wolfhunder.

Sure enough, Rudi rounds the corner, swearing up a storm. His eyes skip right past me. Good. If he's smart, he'll start running now, and hope his superiors in the Wolfhünden don't care to follow.

He makes a circuit around the Madschplatt, vainly looking for any sign of the culprit, but there's nothing to be found. Realization is just starting to set in when a child's voice tears me away: "'Scuse me, sir, you wanna play Find the Lady?"

Ice strikes lightning-fast through my bones.

Fabine, the Bourgienne girl I taught to cheat at cards in the Gänslinghaus, has wandered into the plaza.

The poppy-eater she's approached only blinks and mumbles a little, slumped against the cracked foundation of a pawnshop. I slowly turn to keep them both in my line of sight. I don't know if Gisele's noticed Fabine's absence, but it's not safe for her here, especially not on her own.

I'll just—keep an eye on her.

Fabine wanders away from the poppy-eater and over to a few *mietlingen* clustered around an open brazier. She holds up the cards, but the women laugh. "You'll find no ladies here," one of them cracks. "Run along, little bit."

Yes, I want to say, *run back to the chapel, go back*.

But instead Fabine wanders right into the path of the fuming Wolfhunder. And just like me, she smacks right into him.

I don't even know I'm moving until I'm halfway across the Madschplatt. I hear Rudi screaming at Fabine, I see his hand raise, I'm almost there—

I yank Fabine out of the way before he can strike. It's not gentle, but it's better than the alternative. "*There* you are. We need to get going. Terribly sorry for the inconvenience, sir—"

Fabine twists free, panic on her face. "Who are *you*?"

And belatedly I remember: She doesn't know me from a stranger. The only time she saw me, I was wearing the pearls.

"Now, don't carry on like this," I say a little frantically, sneaking her a wink. "We don't have time for games. We need to get back to— to—" *Scheit-scheiter-scheiten*. What in the Blessed Empire is Gisele calling herself again? "To our friends," I try.

Fabine gapes at me. Then she opens her mouth and lets out a positively operatic shriek. "*STRANGER! KIDNAPPING! HELP!*"

Good instinct, but *so* unhelpful right now. "No—Fabine—please—"

"Hey." The Wolfhunder steps closer. "Didn't I see you earlier?"

This can't get any worse.

"Is there a problem here?" The voice cuts across the Madschplatt, cold and hard and horribly familiar.

Emeric Conrad is marching toward us. And from the look on his face, he knows *exactly* whom he's addressing.

I decide it may just be easiest to walk myself over to the slaughterhouse and have them deal with me. Maybe they'll make a nice bag out of my hide.

Rudi puts up his hands and shakes his head. "The wench might be a child-snatcher, but you'll find no problems with me, Prefect."

"Then be about your business." Emeric wraps a hand around my upper arm before I can make a run for it. "And Miss Schmidt. I'd like a word."

CHAPTER FIFTEEN

ℝINGER

"**P**ASS," I SAY, TRYING TO YANK FREE OF EMERIC'S GRIP.

He's not giving an inch. "That wasn't a request. Fabine, I'm sure Hilde needs your help more than these people need a card game."

Hilde. That's right, that's what Gisele is calling herself. "How did you even find her?" I grouse as Fabine runs back up the lane.

"Amazing who you run into when you're being dragged out of the Yssar," he answers under his breath. "She was apparently on her way to speak to you. Is there anyone in Minkja you *haven't* robbed, swindled, or backstabbed?"

My mouth twists. "I mean, in the grand scheme of things, isn't funding the extravagance of the nobility through the blood of the commoners the *real* swindle—"

Emeric makes a noise of utter disgust and pushes me into the cramped alley behind the streetwitch guildhall.

His frumpy-bumbling-boy shtick is retired for the moment. I suppose it's a harder sell without Klemens's hand-me-downs anyway, though I have to admit I'm marginally impressed his new black uniform's immaculate as ever, considering we're leaving a plaza literally named for its mud.

"You can run," Emeric grits between his teeth, "and when you do, I will cheerfully escort the real Gisele von Falbirg up to the margrave, and you will hope you can make it out of Bóern with what you have in that bag."

Interesting. It's just like breakfast yesterday: If he wanted to arrest me then and there, he could have. Instead he's threatening me.

In my experience, that means I have something he wants.

The strange thing is, I don't know what. The prefects don't need to worry about profit, there is *certainly* no power I can give him, and no one looks to a girl as plain as me for pleasure.

For the moment, I play along. "You're just mad I tossed you in the river."

"I think it's reasonable to take issue with you nearly drowning me."

"Sure, but you're not mad because you nearly drowned. You're mad because you went to all that trouble to set a trap and stage your big triumphant reveal, and I *still* tossed you in the river."

Emeric doesn't dignify that with an answer, but a muscle jumps in his jaw. *Ha.* I'm right.

We come to a stop between a puddle of—well, I don't care to speculate—and a scattering of rusted round witch-bells, not surprising this close to the guildhall. I guess it's far enough down the alley for Emeric's tastes.

The moment he lets go of my arm, Ragne swoops between us as a raven, then abruptly shifts to human. "Hello again!"

Emeric's chin snaps up as he diverts his gaze skyward, ears burning pink. "Er—hello?"

"Clothing, Ragne. We've had this conversation." I throw my shawl over her. It's long enough to cover the essentials. "There."

Emeric is still avoiding too close a look, but a flicker of curiosity darts through his face. "Wait. Aren't you the girl who pushed me to shore?"

"The Vanja sent me," Ragne says brightly. Emeric blinks at me, startled, only to sour when Ragne adds, "I was only supposed to save your bag."

"*There* it is," he mutters.

"I wanted to say hello again," Ragne continues, smiling very toothily, "and to tell you it's my job to look after the Vanja, even though she is mean. If you hurt her, I will turn myself into a bear and kill you. That's all. Goodbye!"

She leaps into the air in a rush of feathers and alights on a nearby rooftop as a raven.

"Eiswald's daughter," I explain, wrapping the shawl around myself once more. "So, you know. Death is only a rooftop away. Might want to *bear* that in mind."

I didn't think it was possible for Emeric to dislike me more than when I tried to drown him, but by all the saints and martyrs, I think I've pulled it off.

He gives me a look of pure loathing and carries on as if imminent death by bear is nothing new. "What is your business with the Wolfhünden? What are they asking you to do?"

I shake my head. "Nothing. I stay out of their way."

"This would go much quicker for both of us if you would stop taking me for a fool," he says frostily.

"Then don't talk like one, Junior," I snap back. "If the Wolfhünden knew the Penny Phantom isn't paying their protection fee, they'd make an example of me. Several examples, if we're counting all the pieces I'd be in. I keep my head down."

That's not the answer Emeric wants. His brow furrows. "You expect me to believe you were collecting fees for them out of the goodness of your heart?"

"Ask the Wolfhunder about the fees I collected," I return. "Why that bag's full of copper. And when you're done, you can go check with all the charity shops who've suddenly come down with a rash of silver, and then maybe you can start minding your own damn business instead of harassing my friends and stalking me."

Emeric already looked skeptical, but at "stalking," he scowls. "Charter of the Prefect, Article One: '*A prefect is bound to investigate and resolve any case they are assigned by their superiors, to the full extent of their ability.*' It is *literally* my job to investigate you."

"Is it your job to memorize the whole clubhouse oath too, or is that extra credit?" I mutter.

He ignores it. "And the impression I got from Miss Ardîm was that you aren't exactly friends. But for the record, I was actually in Lähl to tail the Wolfhunder you angered. In fact, I had to blow my cover to . . . Why are you—what's so funny?"

I'm clutching my stomach, trying not to die laughing. "You thought you had a cover? Looking like that?" I wave my hand at the grimy walls around us, streaked with soot and scum and a respectable variety of dung. "Do you see where we are? You stick out."

"I do *not*," Emeric says, subconsciously tugging at his spotless black uniform jacket.

"You look like a schoolboy trying to buy his first *wurstkuss*."

He turns an incandescent red. "And *you* look like a murderous little wretch, but the difference is *that's* actually true."

"See? Still mad," I scoff. "And still breathing, so wouldn't you say 'murderous' is a little melodramatic?"

"I'm not talking about me." Emeric pulls Yannec's ledger from beneath his cloak. "Your former colleague, a *Meister* Kraus, just washed up in the Stichenstegs this morning with a knife in his heart and one of your *signature* red pennies in his mouth. So peculiar that his ledger was in your vanity. You really have a nasty habit of dumping things into the Yssar."

I give him a poisonous smile. "Only the trash." Then I lunge for the ledger.

I run right into the palm of his hand. It stays flat on my forehead, keeping me at arm's length. Emeric hoists the ledger out of my reach with the other.

"I don't think so," he says testily. "I have younger siblings, I can do this all day."

"Yannec fell on his own knife," I growl, flailing for the ledger anyway.

"How innovative of you. He fell on his *own* knife. I suppose the penny was just decorative."

"It was fare for the Ferryman, you louse-brained—*pedant*—" I make another fruitless hop.

"And it just happens to be *your* calling card. Sure."

"Think what you like, but it's the truth. He was in poppy withdrawal and lost his balance trying to cut the ruby off my face." I drop an inch and Emeric's hand slips onto my knit cap, pushing it off and leaving him with only a fistful of wool. I duck under his arm as he lurches forward.

Then I freeze.

Godmother Death is standing behind Emeric.

One hand stretches for him.

"*I don't need your help!*" I yell, and hurl myself at his side to knock him out of her reach. I get a brief glimpse of his flabbergasted face before we topple to the ground.

A thunderous crash echoes from where Emeric was just standing.

When I roll off him and look up—

I don't know what I see.

It's something like a warhorse, but with the hairless moldy-pale hide of the *nachtmahr*, its mane and tail like tin smoke. I can see holes in its heaving sides like rotten canvas, and the mud sizzles, bakes, and cracks where its hooves fall.

I've never heard of a *mahr* this large. Never heard of one so solid in the daylight. One that drops from thin air.

But if Emeric's looking for murder, he'll find it in those burning blue eyes.

The *mahr*'s nostrils flare once, twice, as I slowly push myself to my feet. There's a scrape as Emeric rises behind me.

A fat gray-black tongue worms out from between the *mahr*'s decaying lips, baring teeth sharp as a wolf's as it tastes the air.

"Run," I say, "*now*—"

We run.

Hoofbeats and howls rip down the alley at our backs. I look over a shoulder and find Ragne as a black kestrel, swooping and clawing around the *mahr*'s thrashing head.

Then I'm yanked into a gap between houses. It's so narrow I have to turn sideways to thread between the walls of plaster and lumber. Emeric is already squeezing through, headed for the open lane on the other side. I follow. With luck the *nachtmahr* won't fit and we can give it the slip.

Incredibly, I catch a mutter from Emeric: "It *had* to be horses."

"*That's the issue?*"

We're halfway to the street when the *mahr* finds us. It thrusts its head and neck into the gap, teeth gnashing, but its shoulders are too broad, and Ragne is still diving at its eyes, and I think for a moment maybe I'll make it—

Then something horrible happens.

The creature stretches, lengthens like warm, wet clay. Its horselike skull thins, cords of muscle fluttering in ripples under the rotting skin, fangs bared.

I snatch Emeric's knife from my satchel, slashing wildly at the *mahr*. Like before, the steel blade doesn't faze it in the slightest. Every cut that opens along its snout looks weeks old.

Teeth close on my hand.

I scream and pull away, and just in time. The *mahr*'s fangs snag on my raggedy glove and rip it off instead. The knife falls with a clatter.

A much more human grip drags me farther down the gap. "See? Horses are the worst. Do you know if it's a *grimling*?" Emeric sounds both too close and too smug for my comfort, but since we're both wedged between the moldering walls, I have bigger complaints.

Besides, I'm too busy watching those teeth shred the glove to do more than gasp, "*Nachtmahr.*"

"Copper, then," he mutters. A black sleeve thrusts past me as the *mahr*'s neck stretches even longer. There's another knife in his hand, a similar make to the one I just dropped, but the blade is penny red.

This time, when it catches the *nachtmahr* on the snout, the beast screams.

There's a squeal and a pop as windows shatter above us. I hide my face from the shower of glass. Emeric keeps pulling me through the gap, mumbling a rhyming string of words in one of the northern Almanic dialects. I've heard of spoken charms to ward off *nachtmären*, but this creature is either immune or highly motivated, and I don't have time to find out which.

We burst free into the beautifully open lane. There's no time to breathe, though. The *mahr* spills out behind us, wobbling and shuddering until it's broad as a bull again. Screams split the air. Other pedestrians flee into houses, storefronts, emptying the lane until it's just us, the *mahr*, and the handful of poppy-eaters too far gone to know they should run.

The creature pays them no mind, blue eyes still fixed on Emeric and me.

"What does it want?" I wheeze.

Before Emeric can answer, it charges.

I bolt for another alley, Emeric on my heels. Lähl's a labyrinth of sharp corners and tight passages, and if we can't lose the *mahr* through the latter, we'll try the former.

Hollow, smoking hoofbeats chase us down the alleyway. We careen around one turn, then another. Crashes follow in our wake as the beast slams into walls and scuffles to keep its feet.

A sharp jab of juniper spikes my breath. I don't know the source until I run past Emeric, who has slowed to a stop. He's uncorked a small vial, and as I hang back, he dabs a drop of silvery oil to his lips.

Then he rattles off another string of words and flicks a hand at the alleyway. Lines of silver light blaze up the walls like matched streaks of lightning. A moment later, the *mahr* veers into sight—

—And stumbles to a halt once it runs between the lines. The magic splinters into a net, forcing the beast to its knees. It lets out another glass-breaking scream as it thrashes.

"Huh," I rasp, walking closer. "Well. Now what?"

Emeric catches my shoulder, and his face says something's wrong. "That," he says between ragged breaths, "should have banished . . ."

With a furious sobbing wail, the *mahr* forces itself back to its feet, the light-threads straining.

"Banished?" I back away. "I'd call that a stern warning at best."

"Then *you* get rid of it!" Emeric retorts. "At least I'm trying—"

One of the light-strings breaks with a twang.

We reach an immediate unspoken agreement to table this debate, and break into a sprint once more.

The *nachtmahr*'s roar follows us through alley after alley, growing louder the deeper into Lähl we flee. I can see the edge of the High Wall looming closer. It's herding us that way, where there are no tight corners to outmaneuver.

Then, as we tumble into another muddy open lane, I trip into something that lets out a cascade of jingles. We hit the muck with a unanimous grunt.

Emeric hauls me back up, but not fast enough. The *mahr* erupts into the street.

Like before, the bystanders scream and scatter. All save for the heap of a woman I crashed into, who's staring around glassy-eyed as she sits up.

A chorus of bells punctuates the movement.

And the *nachtmahr* whinny-howls, then retreats a few steps.

I look from the woman to the *mahr* and back. She's a ringer, a burnt-out streetwitch, decked out in bells at her wrists, her ears, a wreath around her neck. Each one is the mark of another pinch of witch-ash she should have left alone. Too much at once and you start to see *every* Low God, every *grimling*, the way I see Death and Fortune, until your mind heals. If it can.

They wear bells because the sound drives most spirits away. And from the way the *nachtmahr* is tossing its head, the bells are no friend to it either.

"I need to borrow this," I tell the woman, then lift the jingling wreath from around her neck. The *mahr* shies away with every ring.

I give the bells a hard shake. It rears back on its hooves, screaming. Windows up and down the lane spiderweb with cracks.

"That's . . . something," Emeric says grudgingly. "Will it go away on its own?"

Before I can answer, a loud, cold peal of bronze hammers down over the street. The hour-bells are sounding from the Göttermarkt.

The *mahr*—splits.

No, *splits* isn't quite it. It's like double vision, only the *mahr* breaks into not two identical shapes but untold ones, like a herd of ghosts. Then they all spin back into the solid horse-form again. It's bleeding silver-blue smoke from its teeth.

The bell towers peal again. The beast fractures, thrashing. Before it can reunite, a third toll sounds down the muddy lane.

The *mahr* screeches a final ruinous note, and explodes into dust.

The street is silent but for the rest of the tolls, until the ringer reaches up and tugs at the bells in my hand. "Need those back," she whispers.

I let them go. "Thanks."

Then I look over at Emeric, and burst into laughter.

"*What?*" He stares at me, as if somehow this is the strangest thing he's seen today.

I gesture to the mud on his now-askew cloak, the smears of grime on his face, the spots on his spectacles. Even his hair is so thick with dirt and sweat, it's nearly lightened to brown. For a final touch, I wipe my filthy hand on a sleeve he jerks away. "Finally. You fit right in."

Emeric doesn't seem to find that nearly as funny as I do. "We need to get out of the open. And then we need to *really* have a word."

I fold my arms as Ragne lands on my shoulder. "Counteroffer: You give me back the ledger, I stop making fun of you for looking like a human civics primer, and we part ways as mutually thwarted adversaries."

"Before or after I take the real Gisele to Castle Reigenbach? Now, *a word*." He points to an open doorway nearby. The windows have been boarded over, and the door itself is dangling from its hinges, long in disuse.

It couldn't scream *trap* louder if there was a visible bucket of water balanced over the doorjamb.

Ragne must sense my unease, for she leaps from my shoulder and lands in the mud as a black wolf. Emeric nearly jumps out of his skin. "Remember, if you try to hurt the Vanja," Ragne tells him, "I will bite you, many times. And *I* do not fear the bells."

Then she pads through the doorway.

"You heard the lady," I add, and follow her inside.

I can see why the building's abandoned once my eyes adjust to the dim. The ceiling beams are rotted through, sagging perilously, and the far end of the front room has sunk at least a foot into the mud. But evidently it's good enough for Emeric, for he stalks in behind us. He tries to close the door without success, gives up, and asks me bluntly, "How did you know the *nachtmahr* was coming? You pushed me out of the way."

I debate my answer, but he already knows half of it, and I can't think of a danger in him knowing the rest. "I was given to Death and Fortune as a child; that's why their marks are on me. They're my godmothers. I can see their hands at work."

"So you saw Fortune working against me?"

I shake my head. "I saw Death."

It's another answer he didn't expect; he turns from keeping an eye on the lane outside to give me a startled, almost-indignant look. "Then you saved my life."

"I . . . suppose." The idea is wretchedly uncomfortable, especially since I'm almost positive Death was trying to help me. I retreat to more familiar ground: exploitation. "That has to at *least* be worth a measly ledger."

Emeric stares at the floor, and I don't think he caught that, or he'd be making a face at me. Then he looks up. There's a hungry edge in his dark eyes, like he's about to take a gamble. "Margrave von Reigenbach is responsible."

"What?"

"Klemens and I aren't after you," he continues in a rush. "Not really. The *Pfennigeist* case is a cover so we can actually investigate von Reigenbach and the Wolfhünden. And I'm almost certain he sent that *nachtmahr* to kill me before I find out what he's up to."

"Wait. Stop. Wait." I put my hands up between us. "You *aren't* try-ing to arrest me? What about that whole Winterfast pageant you put on when you broke into my room?"

"I thought I could blackmail you into spying on the margrave."

For a moment I contemplate asking Ragne to tear out his throat. All that time I spent stressing over the looming threat of this day-old breadstick with a thirst for justice, and it was all a bluff.

But I'm loath to admit it worked.

"You really know how to make a girl feel special," I just grumble instead. Then the back of my bare hand catches my eye. Frowning, I take a closer look.

Emeric shrugs. "You've been living a double life for what, a year? I need someone to get close to von Reigenbach, and someone who can steal the signet ring off his hand is much more likely to get the evidence I'm looking for. Besides, it's not all blackmail. We'd ask the bailiff to reduce your sentence, and the Order might have information that could help you with your curse."

I'm only listening with half an ear as I pull off my other glove.

"I *was* going to tell you all this before you dropped me into—"

"Don't need it," I breathe, staring at my knuckles.

The dusting of rubies has vanished.

Something—*something* I did today—worked.

That's the third time I've given Emeric an answer he neither wants nor expects. "What?"

"Don't need it," I repeat, grinning like a fool. "No thanks. *Pass.*"

I can cure the curse, I can get out of the empire, I can leave this all behind. And I can do it *myself*.

I'd better hop to it, then. "Come on, Ragne."

Emeric's right hand twitches toward something at his side—the ledger, I'm guessing. Then he clenches his fist. "It wasn't a request. I *will* take Gisele to the margrave."

I can't help a little twirl as I waltz toward the doorway. He's been bluffing about bringing in Gisele the whole time. It's absolutely *delicious* to call it.

"The scary one you think's shacking up with *nachtmären* and what-not? *That* margrave? I doubt it." I flick a little mud off his shoulder as I pass by. "Appreciate the offer, though."

He catches my other hand halfway to the ledger in his pocket. *Damn.* That really would have been the crowning triumph of today.

Ragne rumbles a growl until Emeric lets go. He gives me a livid, almost desperate look. "Von Reigenbach's a monster, Miss Schmidt. He could bring down the empire."

"Don't I know it." I all but dance through the doorway, into the harsh winter daylight, and tip him a mock salute in dismissal. "Good thing I'm on my way out."

CHAPTER SIXTEEN

Pearls in Vinegar

A LITTLE OVER A DAY LATER, I AM DECIDEDLY LESS CONFIDENT.
It's not just that when I snuck back into the castle and took a bath, I found new pearls blooming through the mud on my ankles. It's that when I think back to everything I did before losing the rubies from my hands, the options for how I undid that much of the curse aren't great.

I . . . *redistributed* funds away from the Wolfhünden. I tried to help Fabine, disastrous as it was. I guess I saved Emeric's life. (Almost certainly a tremendous mistake.)

And now that it's Thursday, I have four days left to narrow it down and break the curse before Klemens arrives and I have a *real* prefect to worry about.

The *prinzessin*'s sensitive stomach can only get me out of so much. I was really hoping to squeeze two full days out of the most recent performance, but Adalbrecht had a message delivered to my chambers this morning: The first wave of wedding guests will be arriving less than an hour from now, and I am to attend the welcoming reception. Worse, I'm to do it in the gown he chose for me.

Here's the thing about playing the role of both maid and lady for a year: I pick what I wear specifically so I can manage dressing myself. There are some things, like bodice laces, that are tricky but doable. Other things, though, require a second set of hands. Like sleeves that have to be tied over the chemise, in multiple places, along both arms.

Would you like to guess what kind of sleeves are on the gown Adalbrecht has *requested* I wear?

This is why when Ragne paws at the balcony door as a cat, she finds me fighting with an elbow tie as I let her in. Her head tilts. "Would you like help?"

"No, I've got it." I wedge my arm against a bedpost to hold one of the ties in place. "Did you see anything?"

"The Gisele stayed inside all day, with the children. They like her very much." Ragne slinks into a nightshirt I left for her on the hearth. A moment later, her human head emerges, limbs sprouting from the appropriate sleeves. She's still forgotten to change her slit pupils, but at least she's getting better at clothes. "I did not see the Emeric Conrad at all. And it was very cold."

"You volunteered," I remind her. A bitter chill swept over Minkja last night, leaving the rooftops gilded in frost. I'd still planned on spending at least the morning staking out the Gänslinghaus, but Ragne offered to do it for me.

"Yes." Ragne sprawls over the warm hearthstones, then squints at me. "Are you sure you do not need help?"

"You really don't have to do everything on your own, dear."

Fortune's voice cascades into the room like a coin purse bursting at the seams.

I look up and find her standing with Death at the foot of the bed. "*You*," I bite out, pointing at Death. "You almost killed someone for me yesterday. Even if I wanted your help, I wouldn't want it like that."

Death catches at her ever-shifting cowl with an ephemeral hand. "That wasn't me. I mean, yes, I was there for the boy, but only because he was about to die on his own."

"So . . . I did save his life?" I pause dueling the sleeve ties. I *don't* like the idea of being responsible for that. Whatever Emeric does next better be virtuous as a saint, or Eiswald better not hold it against me.

Fortune steps closer. "There are dangerous forces at work here, Vanja, and you are too close to the heart of it all." She tips my chin up. "Death and I have been talking, and we decided . . . You don't have to choose between us."

Any protests die on my tongue.

If I don't have to choose, don't have to serve, I won't need to flee the empire, I won't need to keep running from them, I could *stay*, I could—maybe I could make something like a home—

"You can serve us both," Death adds. "We agreed. We—"

"*NO!*" I jerk away as Fortune reaches for the sleeve ties.

Fortune draws back like I slapped her. "We're trying to be reasonable here, Vanja. Eiswald can't hold a curse on one of our servants. You can trade off between us, serving me one week—"

"I never wanted to be your servant!" I almost scream. "I wanted to be your *daughter!*"

Silence locks the room.

"All we want is to protect you." Death sounds hurt. I don't know why I expected a god to understand. "Please, Vanja. Just let us help."

I shake my head, willing iron into my spine even as I feel my throat tighten. "You don't help. You bargain. All you offer has strings attached. If you have nothing to give freely, go."

There's no answer. The room falls quiet save for the crackle of the fire, and the afternoon feels colder despite it. They're gone again.

I hear Ragne sit up, but she doesn't say a word.

I shove my shoulder back up against the bedpost and go back to the sleeve ties. "Is . . ." My voice breaks, and I clear my throat hastily. "Is your mother like this?"

"No," Ragne answers. Some part of me crumbles a little. "She is nice, sometimes, and she is cold, sometimes, but she does not expect anything for her help." She crosses the room and starts working on my other arm. "I do not either."

I want to yank free and do it myself . . . but the sun is only an hour from the horizon. The guests will be here any minute.

"Thanks," I mutter instead.

"The Gisele didn't barter for her help either."

I frown at her. "When did Gisele help you?"

Ragne deftly cinches an elbow tie. "When I pushed the Emeric Conrad out of the river. The Gisele was crossing the bridge and she ran to help us. She said she was coming to see you, but she helped the boy instead, since it was cold and he was very wet. She didn't ask for anything in return."

"Glad she finally figured out how to do that," I snap. "Don't trust her to keep it up."

"I think she might be nice," Ragne insists. "She was—"

"Then let her help you!" The words explode from me as I shake Ragne off my arm. "Go be her new little pet, and don't come crying to me when she turns her back on you too!"

Ragne stares at me, red eyes wide as saucers. Then she turns into a squirrel and runs under the bed, leaving the nightshirt in a heap on the floor.

I—no.

I *refuse* to feel guilty.

I finish tying up my sleeves myself. It takes longer than I'd like. Longer than Adalbrecht would like too, evidently, because there's a knock at the door just as I knot the final point. I check the mirror one last time to make sure the pearls are securely in place, smooth my white-gold curls, and answer.

Barthl is standing outside, thin lips pinched like he's stepped in something ripe. "I am to escort you to the lesser reception gallery," he sniffs. "As *expediently* as possible."

When I arrive, Adalbrecht is pacing outside the doors. He all but winches my arm around his and throws the doors open, marching us inside.

"I apologize for keeping you waiting," he thunders. "My little *snow-drop* hasn't been feeling well."

There are murmurs of sympathy from the nobles crowded into the claustrophobic little gallery. It was already overstuffed with tempera portraits of the Reigenbachs clustered on the walls, and statues of them jammed into every corner and alcove, as if we might have forgotten who owns Minkja; now there are even more bodies packed in here.

I recognize most of the faces from the von Eisendorf party. There's also a face I know too well: Irmgard von Hirsching, still precious and hollow as a porcelain doll.

"Oh, dearest Gisele, how dreadful," she simpers, bustling over to us in a gown of wildly ostentatious gold satin. "I *so* admire your courage, coming to greet us in such a state."

For absolutely no reason whatsoever, I think about the knife in my boot. And the bottle of arsenic in my vanity. And the golden chain she's wearing around her neck—if you don't have your own garotte, you can always borrow a friend's.

"Anything for you, Irmgard," I say.

Adalbrecht abruptly drags me toward the wall of official portraits. There's a plain sheet draped over a frame on the wall, obscuring a painting I haven't seen before. It is . . . conspicuously larger than the portrait of Adalbrecht's parents. "I have another surprise for you, *pet*. Everyone! Your attention!"

He already *was* the center of attention, so there's an awkward little shuffle as everyone tries to look even more interested somehow.

"My loyal subjects, you have the honor of being the first to see our official portrait."

I have just enough time to think, *I don't remember sitting for a portrait*, before Adalbrecht whips away the sheet. My jaw drops. A collective uncomfortable inhalation whiffs through the room.

Certain artistic liberties have been taken. For one, I sincerely doubt Adalbrecht actually posed on a pile of dead enemy soldiers with three howling wolves against the full moon; for another, the painter has been *extremely* generous with Adalbrecht's breeches, particularly the suggestion of his, er, *weysserwurst*. The most prominent dead soldier at Adalbrecht's feet also bears an uncanny resemblance to the portrait of his father a foot away.

You know, *subtle*.

The crowning glory is that there *is* a platinum blonde clinging to Adalbrecht's arm, but it very clearly isn't me. Or, rather, not the image of the *prinzessin*. The body is detailed enough, outrageous curves in gauzy white silk that borders on indecently translucent. The face, though . . . to call it a rush job would require more charity than I dispensed in Lähl yesterday. It looks closer to the self-portraits Gisele tried to draw as a child, a nose like an anemic carrot pressed against her face, lumpy folded ham slices for lips, the eyes positively crooked.

"*Incredible*," I breathe, with complete and perfect sincerity.

But when I look out to the assembled guests, I find Irmgard's face twisted with pure, seething fury. Then it's sucked under like a spider drowned in icing.

Adalbrecht makes me stand around while he extracts admiration from his audience, arm linked through mine like a bolt in a shackle. All I have to do is smile vacantly while he prattles on to some count or other, so I let my eyes wander.

They land on a painting from Adalbrecht's childhood. He stands between his two older brothers, looking remarkably sullen for a boy of seven. It's downright inspirational, the way the artist has managed to capture his blend of entitlement and constipation at such a tender age.

Something seems off, though. I can't quite put my finger on it.

Once we have a break in fawning vassals, I say under my breath, "Darling, do the von Hirschings *really* have to stay until the wedding? Irmgard is such a tiresome little gossip."

Adalbrecht's mouth pinches. "Yes, they're staying. They're guests in my castle. Don't let me hear you speak ill of them again."

Then he marches me over to a knot of women clustered around Irmgard, all perched on settees and ottomans, and discards me like a soiled napkin.

Ugh. Well, if I have to put up with Irmgard, at least I don't have to be sober for it. I lift a goblet of *glohwein* from a passing tray and sink onto the only open settee, which is unfortunately beside Irmgard.

"So," I say in tones of utmost scandal, "*what* was Anna von Morz even doing in that hat last week?"

"Exactly what I want to know." Irmgard launches into a spirited condemnation. I'm barely listening, only offering an occasional nod.

Why does Adalbrecht care about the von Hirschings? For the von Falbirgs, the answer was simple: They needed the trade route that passes first through Hirsching territory, then through Sovabin. But the von Hirschings and the von Reigenbachs have a mutually parasitic relationship. Very few goods come through Hirsching territory without stopping in Minkja first. There's no need to suck up to them.

And if I'm being honest . . . well, it's not that Emeric's words stuck with me, so much as one very outlandish theory of his: why *nachtmären* are suddenly sprouting in Minkja like daisies.

"Where did you get it, Gisele?" Irmgard's voice barges into my thoughts.

Scheit. No idea what she's asking about. I give a slow, imperious blink. "I shouldn't say."

Sieglinde von Folkenstein delicately brushes some crumbs from her mouth. "Please, *Prinzessin*, my husband might let me get a topaz one while we're in Minkja. Can't you at least tell us the jeweler?"

Oh. The ruby teardrop. My lips thin in a warning smile. "I am sworn to secrecy."

"Seriously. How does it even stay on?" Irmgard leans forward and wraps a hand around my collarbone. There's a thorn-sharp glint in her eye.

Sieglinde also scoots closer. So do the other women, crowding in, cut-glass gleams in every gaze, every gaze locked on the ruby. "Tell us," one urges. "Tell us, Gisele. It's not fair you have the only one."

"It's not fair," Irmgard echoes, that spidery rage punching one tiny, bristling leg through the surface.

There's a faint manic haze, like—like when Yannec tried to cut the ruby from my face. It's Eiswald's curse spilling blood on the roots of their greed, forcing it into full, savage bloom. This is the price of their want: to be devoured.

Irmgard's finger suddenly jabs in my face. "Can I touch it?" She doesn't wait for an answer, pushing at the teardrop until it aches against my cheekbone, and I am almost thirteen again, and she is laughing as I step on the nail she hid in my shoe—

"Oops," I say flatly, and dump my goblet of *glohwein* down the front of her gold satin dress.

She flies back with a little shriek. The haze breaks.

"Oh, Irmgard," I coo, "you've had an *accident*."

Irmgard stares at me, breathing hard, fury scuttling behind her eyes, until—she lifts her voice. "*Markgraf*, our *dear* Gisele isn't feeling well."

The little *snitch*. A large hand wraps around my upper arm.

"My sweet bride," Adalbrecht says sternly, "I fear you are still ill. Let's get you back to your sickbed, hmm?"

He practically drags me from the settee before I can say another word.

"I'll return shortly!" he calls over his shoulder, voice merry and hard. "Just tending to my poor ailing snowdrop."

But when we reach the vestibule, he doesn't head for the stairs to the riverfront wing.

Instead, he keeps an iron grip on my arm and steers us up the opposite set of stairs, toward his chambers.

I find myself thinking about my boot knife again, but for a very different reason now.

"I will give you a tonic to settle your nerves," Adalbrecht says. "Since you find yourself so agitated by my guests."

Oh, *that's* not sinister at all.

But I can get out of this myself. Or at least, I can . . . manage it. He still needs a bride, after all, so whatever he's giving me won't be lethal. The worst part will be being alone with him, and even that—well, the pearls protect me. He's brave enough cornering a servant girl alone in Castle Falbirg; there are consequences if he harms Gisele.

I can handle this myself.

Adalbrecht's guards shout a salute from the top of the stairs. He lifts a fist in what looks like a return salute—but then I hear a tiny, brittle *crunch*.

I blink, convinced I imagined it. Then, as we pass the guards, two thuds echo down the hall. When I sneak a look back, they've both collapsed to the ground, eyes shuttered.

Before I can process that, Adalbrecht pushes open a door I've never bothered with and pulls me into his study.

I don't know what I expected: Skulls on pikes? Bubbling cauldrons? Walls oozing with pitch? But really it's quite . . . boring. Tall, arching windows with thick blue velvet curtains, Kunigunde's distant stony crown in the Salzplatt visible through the lattice of diamond-shaped panes. Walls hung with stuffed animal heads and tapestries. Bookcases, maps, stuffed chairs by a respectable fireplace. Sunset drapes the room in red-hot light, like everything it touches is iron and this room is the forge.

Adalbrecht lets go of me and heads toward a credenza near the window, letting something drop from his fist onto the desk. I squint. I think I see fragments of bone, a tiny rodent jaw—

"This will put your mind at ease." Adalbrecht is standing over a surprisingly robust collection of bottles on the credenza. Some are clearly mead and schnapps, others tinctures stuffed with sprigs of laurel, thyme, borage in liquids of different shades. He pulls out a bottle no taller than the length of my hand, something flickering like flame in the clear liquid.

Adalbrecht, I discover, is a lot like Yannec.

(And not the way I'd prefer, which is dead in the Yssar.)

I've known since I met him that he believes the world owes him a

tithe simply for being born a noble of Almandy; he likes to feel powerful and to remind others that they are not. And like Yannec, he knows
nothing about sleight of hand.

So he gives me nothing else to look at but his chosen bottle while
he pulls a crystal goblet from a nearby cupboard.

I have not spent the last twelve months curating a respectable poison collection to not know Augur's Tears when I see it. The flickers
are the giveaway: flakes of gold leaf dancing in the clear bottle in slow,
perfect spirals, catching blazing sunset light. Those perfect spirals are
a curious property of the tincture, and the gold draws out its potency.

It's not necessarily a poison. It's made from the tears of the Low
God Truth, and when augurs prophesize, they take a thimbleful to strip
away the veils of the world and see things as they are—at least, for an
hour or so. Longer than that will drive one mad, and more than a sip
will kill you.

Adalbrecht is currently pouring much more than a sip into the
crystal goblet.

And that's when I realize: I may not be able to manage this after all.

Whatever the Golden Wolf has sunk his teeth into . . . it does not
require the *prinzessin* to be alive.

The last bit of security, the last bit of leverage I had against him, is
dissolving like a pearl in vinegar.

Adalbrecht walks over to me and holds out the glass. Dying poppy-
red sunlight drenches us both, leaving razor shadows beyond its reach.

It's just me and the margrave. I'm on my own.

"I'll just take that to my rooms, then," I say, half turning to the
open door. "I don't suppose you have a lid—"

He twitches the glass just out of reach. "It's part of a set that stays
here. Drink it now."

I—

I don't know what to do.

I could spill the glass, but he has plenty more left in the bottle.

I could run, but he commands the guards.

I could call for Poldi, but Adalbrecht is the master of this castle.

I could try to get to the boot knife in time, I could kick him, I could . . .

He's a trained warrior, leader of the armies of Bóern, head and shoulders taller and heavier than I am. And he will eat me alive.

I'm alone, and nothing and no one will save me but myself.

Maybe—I can pretend to drink it and spit it out after I go. That's the best I've got.

I take the glass.

And Godmother Death appears at my side, only to me.

Her hand is on the rim of the crystal goblet, and for once, her face isn't shifting as it warps between people about to die.

Her face is mine. My *real* one, not the illusion of Gisele.

"Ask me for help, Vanja," Death pleads. *"Please."*

I don't want—I *won't* live out the rest of my days as her servant.

I will do this myself. Even if it kills me.

I raise the goblet to my lips and drink.

CHAPTER SEVENTEEN

ℌAUNTED

"ᐯANJA!"

I ignore Death. I think—I think I can pull this off.

I let only the one sip go down my throat. It burns like liquor, but with a strange salt-and-copper aftertaste. If I'm right, it's close enough to the dose the augurs use that I'll just have a very eye-opening hour.

I make a show of coughing and wrinkling my nose. "Oh, this is dreadful. I think I'll——"

"Drink your medicine," Adalbrecht orders. "*All* of it."

I blink at him.

And then I blink again. I see it now, what was wrong in the portrait of him as a boy. He and his brothers all had hazel eyes.

Now Adalbrecht's are blue as the heart of a flame. If anything, they look like they're almost glowing . . . no, burning . . .

The room around us wobbles like jellied broth. I catch my breath. Then—then—

It's as if the walls, the floors, Adalbrecht, *everything* is blistering and peeling away. I see coats of paint on the walls, decades of paint, I see blood on a carpet that hasn't been there for forty years. The wall of hunting trophies is all old dead things but for one beastly skull burning with the same blue fire that's in Adalbrecht's eyes.

When I look at him, I don't see the face of a man but a horse's head nailed to his shoulders, a crown of more iron nails floating above, teeth bared, eyes of cerulean fire.

"*Drink*," he thunders, blood and blue flame spilling from his mouth. But I see, I *see*—

I see a spill of golden hair in a bloody battlefield by night, a soldier of no more than twenty lying motionless, blood sluggishly streaming from a whistling wound in his chest, hazel eyes half lidded in pain and delirium. Every agonized breath is a curse on the wretch of a general who lost this battle, a curse on the empress for sending him to die among the chaff, a curse on his father for letting her. Weak. His father was weak. House Reigenbach was once a house of *kings*. And now—

He is the last of his brothers, meant to be the greatest. Now he's just nothing but the greatest corpse in the dirt.

He was good as any prince. He deserved to be a king.

I see a *nachtmahr* crawl onto his sternum, giggling as it paws at his face. I see a crow hop over, pecking curiously at his ear.

Weak. He can't stop it. The breath is crushed from his lungs.

Weak. Just like his father.

His eyes fly open. He seizes the crow, snaps its neck in one hand. The *nachtmahr* lets out a squeal, form writhing, and suddenly it's no longer a little man but a half-rotted crow.

It looks to the soldier for orders.

The soldier sits up, his wounds limned with sapphire-blue flame. And now—now I see that same blue ignite in his eyes.

He was born to wear a crown, even if he must make it himself.

Now I see him slaying beast after beast for the *nachtmären*, trading their lives for wicked deeds and borrowed crumbs of their power. A marmot buys the death of the general, a fox for his father, a goat for the empress, too many more to count. Now I see him swearing to keep them fat on terrible dreams as he whips his soldiers into battle after battle, laying the cornerstones of a kingdom, claiming what was always meant to be his.

Now I *see* the margrave standing before me in the study, reaching for me—

There's a scream that sounds like a cat and a child and a woman all at once, and a blur of black fur and red eyes streaks into the study from behind me. I jump and drop the goblet in earnest.

The blur claws its way up Adalbrecht's legs as he howls, makes a couple of loops around his torso, then launches itself onto his desk, sending papers flying. It's Ragne. *Ragne* saved me.

She hurls herself onto the mantel, still caterwauling, and tears down a tapestry, dragging it into the fireplace. Flames eagerly gnaw through the embroidered wolves. The carpet below starts smoking as well. Her final coup de grâce is to knock over the water pitcher on her way out the door, leaving Adalbrecht very little to douse the fire.

"I'll—I'll go get help," I gasp, and run out of the study on Ragne's heels. I think Adalbrecht shouts after me, but when I dare a look back, he's trying vainly to stamp out the flames.

The hallway is even worse than the study. I see ghosts, I see memories, I see what the von Reigenbachs have done here and the scars and stains they've simply hidden behind portraits, all laid bare by the Augur's Tears. I don't feel drunk, but I *certainly* don't feel stable either, the walls shifting around me through centuries of change.

I stumble to the nearest servant corridor. It's deserted, as I hoped. Everyone is too busy waiting on our guests downstairs, and I understand now why Adalbrecht knocked out the only two guards on duty.

The dark, cramped corridors are only slightly better, but finally I make it back to my room in the riverfront wing. It, too, boils with ghosts, and I can *hear* every speck of floating dust, every stitch of fabric on the bedspread, every spiral of frost creeping over the cold windows.

I drop to my knees, shaking, then curl up on the floor. How am I supposed to do this for an *hour*? I want the world to steady out, I want to feel safe again, I want my mother—any of them—

I catch myself before the unspoken plea can fully manifest. I know that price. I won't pay it. I won't.

Something soft pushes at my hand.

"No, you need to get up," Ragne yowls. "You are sick, you need help."

I open my eyes. She's hard to look at, like when the *nachtmahr* in Lähl split into a thousand versions of itself at the toll of the bells. Only each of Ragne's forms is different, and I see all of them at once, anchored in twin dots of burning red. A moon hangs over her head, waxing from dark to full.

I see blood on snow, a tiny, wriggling ball of shadows cradled in Eiswald's cold hands. I see Ragne rolling and crawling with the beasts of the forest, learning their ways as she learns their forms, but never quite settling in. Her mother is a Low God, and her father is a human, and she is not quite either, and she is not quite kin with anything, and she is not quite of any world.

I hear her excitement to venture with me into the world of her father, singing through every heartbeat.

I hear her disappointment when the first human she meets is bent only on gold, and on saving her own skin.

"You helped me," I whisper. "Why?"

"Because that's what people do," she says, as if it's the most obvious thing in the world. "Humans just make it complicated. Up, now. You drank too much."

I feel so heavy. "I'm sorry I yelled at you. I was angry, but it wasn't your fault. It was . . . mean."

Ragne doesn't answer a moment. I think I see her tail lashing. Eventually she says, "It was mean, but your godmothers are cruel, and I think the Gisele hurt you. But don't do it again. Please, get up."

I roll over. The room spins. Somewhere above me, a couple is arguing in a time when this was a guest room. I can see the volcano that made the lava that turned to stone that tumbled through the mountains until it was dug up, cut into a square, and built into the wall beneath the plaster.

"It's too much," I wheeze.

Ragne bumps my hand with her head again. "I will go get help. You have a few hours before this reaches your heart and kills you."

"Oh. Fantastic."

"I will be fast," she promises. And then she is gone.

"*Lady? Can I do anything?*" Poldi asks from the hearth.

I cover my eyes. "Stay there. I've had Augur's Tears, and if I see the truth of you, I think my brain will break."

"*Right you are. Careful what you say, for as long as the Tears hold you, you'll speak only the truth.*"

What a fun, terrible new complication.

Every moment I lie there with my eyes closed, the truth digs into my other senses all the more viciously. I hear the wind in the forests of the timbers that built the bedframe. I taste Irmgard's lies like rotten milk. I can't . . .

I can't stay like this.

I make myself get up. The floor *does* feel like it's swaying now. I stagger to brace myself on the bedpost, then look up, and find—

The vanity mirror.

I see myself.

I see my own face beneath the pearls, I see the dress sitting wrong because it doesn't *fit* me, it fits Gisele, all of this fits Gisele and I'm just a thief and a liar and too much of a coward to be—myself. I see the hand of Death and the hand of Fortune, one on each shoulder. I see my birth mother behind me, just the same as she was the night she left me in the woods, and the shapeless ghosts of my siblings behind her.

A moon hangs over my head, waning from full into dark. The inverse of Ragne's. The mark of Eiswald.

I see a bloody, malignant teardrop below my right eye, veins branching from it and blazing all over me, to the pearls at my ankles, to my belly button, to dozens of other pinpoints. When I press my finger to the end of one in my arm, I *feel* a bump, a knot that wasn't there, waiting to burst through the skin.

In the mirror, the veins swell with every heartbeat, glowing brighter scarlet. Rubies and pearls erupt from my spine, my eyes, my scars, swallowing me in gemstones, until there is nothing left.

Nothing but my greed.

It's a reflection, the coward in me insists, just the reflection—just the mirror and the poison, nothing more.

I don't know if it is real, but what matters is that it is true.

Tears spill from my eyes, and in the mirror, they look like pearls.

There is no *Prinzessin*. No Marthe. No *Pfennigeist*. No matter how many cards I lay between myself and the rest of the world, no matter how many lies I tell, how many lives I steal, it will never be enough. I will never escape the ghost in the mirror.

I will never escape her, because I am haunted by myself.

I see myself for what I am: a scared girl, alone in a cruel world, abandoned by family and friend, who would rather turn herself to blood-stained stone than let anyone get close enough to leave another scar.

A girl who would rather die than serve anyone ever again. Even myself.

And it is killing me.

The tears burn as they roll down my face. I can't look any longer.

Ragne isn't back yet. How long has it been? She said hours. Maybe something happened to her. Maybe I can't wait. Adalbrecht is trying to kill me. How long until he's at my door?

I can't stay here. I need—I need help.

All my options come with a price. All I can do is choose which one to pay.

I can't do this myself. Not anymore.

I need help.

I need to get out.

It's a long, tortured process changing out of the dress (as I see the hands that spun the thread that . . . you get the idea), and it involves running into a lot of things. I think I lose at least ten minutes to staring at a tapestry. By the time I've changed into a plain dress and a cloak, the sun is gone and a sickle moon is slicing through the seam of the dark, deep sky.

I am almost completely delirious now. I see wheels in the stars, I see eyes in the walls, and maybe that's the truth of them but it makes no sense to me.

I choose to take the servant passage down, because at this rate, I'll get stuck on the trellises, staring at the dead roses until I freeze to death. Ghosts and memories watch me go, and I could swear the stairs are winding me in a spiral, but—I've gone this way a thousand times. I know what I'm doing.

I *have* to know what I'm doing.

But when I fumble out of the exit at the bottom of the stairs, I realize I should have taken my chances with the roses.

The night is bitterly cold, the frost thicker here at the base of the waterfall, where layers of frozen mist have built up. And the narrow path that cuts behind the curtain of water is now carpeted in ice.

I stand there a moment, wondering if my breath's coming in short, harsh gasps from the stairs, or because the Augur's Tears are getting close to my heart.

I need help. And I can't stay here.

I step out onto the icy path.

Yssar, the Low God himself, watches me from below the surface of his river, I see that truth. I've no idea what he makes of it as I choose each step like a drunken surgeon trying to sew a wound, trying to ignore the eons of history, the trysts and murders and everyday people passing along the track before and after me.

I should have known it for a fool's errand. I barely make it halfway across before I slip.

There's no room for error with a waterfall. My foot slides, then I slide, and before I can even scream, I'm gone.

It's not a long drop, but it's horrifically cold, and the sledgehammer of the waterfall drives me right to the stony bottom of the river. My lungs contract on their own from the shock, trying to drag in air but pulling in choking froth. I thrash and push up until I break the surface, spewing, and manage only half a breath before I'm torn between two currents, sucking me back to the waterfall and pushing me away at the same time. My lungs are burning, boiling, and all I want to do is *breathe*, some animal part of me is panicking—

A distant part of me feels the slightest bit guilty for wishing this on Emeric. I don't know what's more annoying: that I might actually die here thanks to my own series of terrible decisions, or that with the Augur's Tears in my blood, I know this guilt isn't a lie.

Something about that annoyance steadies me out. *Don't panic* might as well be carved into my bones, and that, at least, I can count on.

I need to get away from the waterfall first, or I'll never get out. I splash and kick until the waterfall's pull lessens. Something presses against my spine, helping me rise faster. I break the surface.

I hear voices over my own violent coughing, and I'm dimly aware of being pushed toward a nearby dock. Then hands reach down to pull me out. Beneath the water I see the dark blur of an otter's snout, glowing red eyes. Ragne found help after all.

I'm hauled up onto the sturdy planks of a dock, where I collapse in a sodden heap. A comically large cloak is wrapped around my shoulders.

I make the mistake of letting my eyes fall to the wool.

I see a bear of a man passing through a town by the sea as the trees spill gold and red leaves into the wind. I see a boy stopping him on his way out of an inn, clutching a knapsack much too large for a child of eight, hair neatly combed and dark brown eyes sharp as flint behind their oversized spectacles. I hear the boy say he has a petition for the Godly Courts.

I see the boy leave with the man, the youngest recruit in the history of the prefects.

And other recruits won't let him forget it. The boy can follow the threads of a crime, connect what no one else sees, but he can't puzzle out how to get his classmates to eat with him. He doesn't understand why his teacher barely hides a sigh every time his hand shoots up, because shouldn't he have the answers? He doesn't know to watch his steps until the third time he's tripped in the library, and everyone watches him pick up his broken charcoal sticks, snickering into their books.

This is how he learns having the answers is not enough.

I see the man hand off his cloak and uniform jacket years later, when the boy makes history again, the youngest to pass the first rite of initiation.

I see the cloak and jacket stay with Emeric until he reaches Minkja.

Shame rushes through me. I *shouldn't* see this. It's not mine to know.

". . . Schmidt. Can you hear me, Miss Schmidt?"

"She needs to get out of the cold as soon as possible." A firm grip on my shoulders keeps me upright, even as that voice sends one more chill through my gut.

If there are two people in the Blessed Empire who I *don't* want to see the full truth of, they would be Emeric Conrad and Gisele von Falbirg.

My teeth chatter as I clap my hands over my eyes. I try to find the words, but they come out strangled and stunted: "I can't—I can't look at you."

Emeric curses under his breath, and I can hear every emotion in it like it's been dissected on a table: vexation, distrust, urgency, concern, fear. "The poison's gone too far. She won't make it back to the Gänslinghaus." I taste-smell a whiff of juniper oil and witch-ash. "Miss Schmidt, this . . . isn't going to be very pleasant, I'm sorry. But you have my word that it's going to help you. All right?"

"What will I owe you?" I slur.

I can hear his confusion in the silence. Finally he says, "Nothing," the same way Ragne said people help each other, like it ought to be plain as the nose on my face. And the ugliest truth tonight is that I wish I could understand that.

I'm not a good person.

I don't know if I said that aloud. Everything feels like it's slipping away.

"Miss Schmidt—" One hand is peeled from my face. "*Really*. You are far too aggravating to die here. I'm going to make a small cut on one of your fingers, understand?"

I make myself nod, shivering, eyes squeezed shut. There's a sharp dart of pain on the tip of my left forefinger. I hear Emeric pull in a breath, as if bracing himself. Then he says, "I *swear* this will help. And it should be over fast."

Have you ever felt the sting of a sliver, looked at it, and realized it's going to hurt almost as much coming out?

Have you ever pulled a loose thread, only to see the cloth bunch and wrinkle?

Have you ever looked at the veins and arteries in your hand and wondered how many of them branch through you, fragile and immeasurable as roots in soil?

Now imagine that delicate network of blood vessels is full of splinters, and they are *all* being pulled out the way you would pull on a loose thread, and your nerves are the cloth crumpling in their wake.

This is how I learn that Junior Prefect Emeric Conrad has a gift for understatement, because *it's not going to be very pleasant* does not *begin* to cover what this feels like. The only mercy is that it's quick, too quick to fight. If Gisele wasn't holding me upright, I'd be keeling over into the Yssar.

There's a sick little *splat*, and suddenly it's as if I've gone from being trapped in a burning theater while the orchestra still plays over the screams, to falling into a snowbank in the middle of an empty forest. Everything feels muffled, dulled now that I'm not tasting the sound of infinity and whatnot.

Scheit, it's cold.

I peel my eyes open and see a nasty little puddle on the dock, marbled in the blood still dripping from my finger. My heart is thrashing against my ribs, I'm still gasping for breath, and overall every inch of me somehow feels seasick, but they're familiar and mundane kinds of hurt.

A fat snowflake lands on my hand and melts. I blink in time for another to catch on an eyelash. Of *course* the first snow would fall tonight.

"Tell me," Emeric says unsteadily, "that you didn't drink Augur's Tears to try to find a cure for the curse."

I shake my head, pulling the damp cloak tighter around me, and finally let my gaze wobble up to him and Gisele. "Adalbrecht . . . t-tried to kill me . . . or Gisele . . . I thought—Wh-What's wrong with you?"

There's an odd sheen to Emeric's eyes behind the spectacles—no, it's a glow. Not in the same way that Adalbrecht's eyes burned blue, but rather the way a hedgewitch's do when they eat witch-ash, white of the eye and all, as if it makes a lantern of their skull. Astonishingly, a sweat has broken out over his pallid face even in the snowy night, gluing a few strands of hair out of place, and he hasn't even tried to fix them.

Emeric waves it off, though, pushing himself to his feet with unusual effort. "Later. We're taking you to the Gänslinghaus before you freeze to death."

Ragne heaves herself out of the water and onto the bank, shuddering and shedding until she rises as a great black horse. Then she kneels, tossing her head, and the message is clear: *Get on.*

I expect a grumble about horses from Emeric. It doesn't come. He and Gisele each take one of my elbows, but it's Gisele who does the heavy lifting.

Whatever Emeric's done to himself, he's in worse shape than he's letting on.

Everything grays and blurs as I try to stand, only to topple over. I hear voices as if through water, like I'm back in the Yssar, but they don't sound panicked, only tense. Gisele's voice warbles through: ". . . meet you there. Go."

Then I see burning red eyes and a dark mane, and I am seated sideways over broad withers, barely upright. It's snowing harder now, the flakes spinning in drunken whorls like gold leaf in Augur's Tears.

The world lurches and jolts upward, but there is something warm and steady to lean on, there is an arm before me and another at my back, both fists anchored in Ragne's mane. The last thought I have before I fade away is that if I were anyone else at all, this might have been nice.

CHAPTER EIGHTEEN

Keep Your Enemies Closer

THROUGH THE HEAVY GRAY OF SLEEP, I HEAR A VOICE, VELVET SOFT and inevitable.

"We were trying to help."

I think a hand lays against my brow, smooths my hair back. I don't know. I am drifting in the fog.

"We saw you suffering in Castle Falbirg," Death continues. "We can't keep mortals in our realm for long, you know that. But if you were sworn to serve one of us . . . we could protect you. We could have taken you away from there."

A long pause. The weight of her hand almost aches, not because it's heavy, but because I've wanted it for so long.

"We don't understand mortals. We can't, really, if we're to do our jobs. But we thought we knew what we were asking. We just didn't know what we were asking . . . of you."

Death's hand lifts.

"Gods can't be wrong, Low or High. We can't make mistakes, can't go back on our bargains. So long as you are our child, there will be a day when you must decide who to serve." She sighs. "Fortune and I will stop pushing you for now. We can wait."

I open my eyes.

I don't know what I expected to wake up to, but the walls of a bathtub are not it.

I also don't expect to wake up *sweating*. Especially because I seem to be wearing a large nightshirt and not much else. But I've been cocooned in a heap of blankets, and the air beyond them seems unreasonably warm.

Death is nowhere to be seen. I'm alone in a dim, plain room barely bigger than a closet, an iron chimney running from floor to ceiling nearby. My shift, dress, stockings, blouse, and cloak have been pinned to a clothesline next to it.

Panic grips my throat until I see a familiar weight in the pocket of my dress. At least I remembered to button the pearls in there, loopy as I was.

Hushed murmurs seep up from below the floorboards, too muffled to make out the words. I think I remember hearing something about taking me to the Gänslinghaus, but it's too quiet—unless it's later than I know.

I slowly, painfully lever myself from the tub. Part of me very much wants to sneak out, run from the reckoning I'm due. But if I saw anything with the Augur's Tears, it's that I can't make it out of this mess on my own.

Getting dressed is harder than I expect, and going down the stairs is even harder. The muted conversation falls quiet at the first creak of the steps.

Two faces are turned my way when I hobble into the kitchen, lit only by lantern light and coals: Ragne, sitting on the counter in another nightshirt, and Gisele, standing over a steaming kettle at the stove. There's a huddle seated at the long table that I'm fairly sure is Emeric, asleep in a mysterious pile of folded papers.

"Tell me he didn't undress me," I croak.

"That boy passed out about a minute after he dragged you in." Joniza doesn't look up from where she's seated at the other end of the table, frowning at a paper, her mass of gold-trimmed braids piled atop her head. I know that thoughtful scowl; she's working on a new song. "Though since he *did* sleep in the tub Monday night, you could say you were in his bed."

"Ew," I mutter.

"You are better now!" Ragne says brightly, then hunches, sheepish. Her voice lowers. "I'm not supposed to be loud."

"You're fine. The children should be well asleep by now." Gisele smiles, her cheeks rosy from the stove. Then she turns to me, and full winter turns her stone-cold. "Is there anything you'd like to say to Joniza or me before I wake up *Meister* Conrad?"

Joniza glances up. The look on her face says very plainly, *Do not involve me in this.*

My belly tightens with an old, resentful ache. I know I did this to Gisele, but she has no business acting like I didn't do this *for* her too. I remember her exact words on the muddy riverbank a year ago. I remember how she begged.

The pearls bump silently against my thigh.

"I drank poison meant for you," I return, just as frosty. "From *your* fiancé. That's what I have to say."

"Tea, anyone?" Joniza asks innocently, pushing back from the table.

"Yes, please." All of us jump as Emeric sits up, accidentally knocking over a stack of paper. He pushes his spectacles into his hair and rubs his eyes.

"Me too." I hang my cloak on a hook and head for a mug rack on the wall. A soot-mote pops out of the first one I take down, scuttling behind the stove with a hiss. I suppose there's no *kobold* here to keep them out.

Gisele shoulders past and pointedly pulls off a single mug. "I'll make my own."

If I could roll my eyes any harder, you'd hear it all the way in Sovabin.

A minute later, I slide tea over to Emeric as I sit down across from him. (Does he need to know he got the soot-mote mug? Absolutely not.) He lifts his head from his hands, bleary-eyed, and rasps, "Thank you. Any . . . ill effects?"

"Don't ask me to do cartwheels anytime soon," I say dourly. "What happened to you?"

"I'm not technically supposed to do magic until I complete my initiation rites as a prefect," he admits, and settles the spectacles back on his face. "The witch-ash we use has a, a kickback of sorts. You only get the charm to minimize it *after* the second initiation, to keep fools like me from throwing it around two days in a row. It's for emergencies only, and"—he pinches his nose—"between the *nachtmahr* and the Augur's Tears, there have been an unprecedented number of emergencies."

"That was rather brave of you, then, to risk it for Vanja's sake." Gisele drops into the chair beside him.

He shakes his head as Ragne settles on the stool next to me. "Very kind of you, but I don't believe in bravery, just unpleasant alternatives."

"Not *that* unpleasant," Gisele mutters into her tea.

"I don't have to be here," I shoot back. "I don't owe you anything."

Ragne cocks her head at me. "You were dying," she says, as if explaining it to a small child, "very bad, a lot."

"Fine, yes—"

"You were poisoned, and you almost drowned, and if you had not come here you probably would have frozen—"

"I *get* it, Ragne."

"You're here because you have nowhere else to go," Gisele says icily. "So a little gratitude won't kill you."

Joniza clears her throat. She's returned to her song but is maintaining her not-to-be-involved face.

Emeric glances from Gisele to me, sizing us up like two feuding tavern drunks who might take a swing at any moment, then straightens his folded papers. "Right, then. Given that *Markgraf* Adalbrecht von Reigenbach has now attempted to murder both of us and, by proxy, Princess Gisele, I think"—his mouth screws up like he's bit into a rotten lemon—"*cooperation* is in all our interests."

"Aren't *we* just giddy as a bridegroom," I drawl.

He looks down his thin nose at me. "Charter of the Prefect, Article Seven: '*In the event that it becomes necessary to seek aid from a criminal or miscreant in resolving an investigation, the association should be as brief as possible, to avoid tainting the prefect's evidence, character, or judgment.*' Collaborating with a criminal like you should be my absolute last resort. The entire point of our job is to make sure the law applies to everyone, not to disregard it when it's inconvenient."

Something about how he says "criminal" bothers me. It's not disgust; it's almost closer to dismissal. Before I can stop myself, I'm sniping back. "Oh *no*, wouldn't want to disappoint Papi Klemens."

Emeric bristles more than I expected, but he reins it in, taking a sip from his mug. "Hubert will be more interested in results. Besides, this is all standard for us. I arrive first, looking like a fresh-faced pushover, and solve the case because everyone buys the act and lets down their guard."

The *exactly like you did* is implied. I decide I was completely justified in giving him the soot-mote mug.

"So like it or not, I don't believe any of us are in a position to turn down assistance right now, especially not Miss Schmidt. At the very least, we should start by sharing what we know. Is that acceptable?"

"Vanja goes first," Gisele says immediately. "Otherwise, what are the odds she goes last, then extorts us in exchange for what she knows?"

"Eh," I say. "Decent." Emeric makes an exasperated noise, and I shrug. "What? She's learning."

He just digs another charcoal stick from under his papers and pulls one sheet out of the stack. "Start with the margrave."

My hair's falling loose around my shoulders, so I split it into two sections and start braiding to keep my hands busy. "He proposed to Gisele last year, sent soldiers to get us, and by the time I got to Minkja, he was already back on the frontlines. I didn't even know he was return-ing until his messenger showed up on Sunday and declared the wedding was in two weeks."

"That's . . ." Gisele starts, then folds her arms and looks away, as if she won't lend me any more credibility than she absolutely must.

"Princess Gisele?" Emeric prompts.

She still doesn't look at me. "It just seems, I don't know, too fast. He's the most powerful noble in the southern empire, and Sovabin is a royal principality, even if it's tiny. A wedding like that should have months of preparation."

"A rushed wedding and he's still trying to kill the bride before-hand. Interesting." Emeric jots something down and looks back to me. "Perhaps something changed. Tell me about the poisoning. Did you see anything with the Tears that could be of use?"

I sum it up for them, from Adalbrecht's protection of the von Hirschings to him insisting I drink the Tears. Then I remember. I shoot out of my chair, slamming my hands on the table. "His eyes!"

Joniza shushes me. "So help me, I am *not* playing another hour of lullabies if those little monsters wake up."

I lower my voice and lean in. "There's a painting of him and his brothers as boys. They all have hazel eyes. Now his are blue. And with the Tears, they glowed like a *nachtmahr*, and he had a horse head, and there was a skull in his study, and—"

"Hold on." Emeric raises a hand, scribbling frantically. "He had a *what?*"

"A horse head. Like the *mahr* that attacked us, but nailed to his shoulders." I describe the vision of Adalbrecht dying on the battlefield, the *nachtmären*, the dead beasts. Then I snap my fingers. "And the night you tried to surprise me, I was attacked by a *mahr* in the castle."

"But a *kobold* would keep them out," Gisele says suspiciously.

Her suspicion is contagious, because Emeric gives me a skeptical, irate look, like I'm wasting all their time with a fib. "I am *excruciatingly* familiar with the *kobold* of Castle Reigenbach, Miss Schmidt."

I stiffen, rocking back on my heels. Something jumps at the back of my throat. I know they both have reason to doubt me, but there's an old, choking kind of panic when I'm telling the truth for once and no one believes me. It catches me like missing a stair, and for a moment I'm back before the von Hirschings, swearing in vain that I am not a thief.

Ragne perks up beside me. "I saw the *mahr* too. I tried to scratch the Vanja awake." She points to my wrist, where the red lines peeking from my sleeve are still vivid enough to see by lantern light.

The moment passes. The panic loosens its grip.

"Maybe Adalbrecht brought it in. I don't know." I sit back down and awkwardly half shrug to Ragne in thanks. "Oh. And his understeward, Barthl, had me deliver an unmarked letter to the Wolfhünden."

"*That's* why you were in the Madschplatt," Emeric says.

"Er. Part of why. I was working on the curse." I catch myself scratching at the ruby teardrop, and resume braiding instead. "Full moon's coming. Anyway, that's all I have."

Emeric looks like he wants to say something but changes his mind, folding his paper again. Somewhere under the pile he finds a heavy needle and waxed thread, runes carved on the wooden spool. "Thank you, that was genuinely helpful."

"You don't have to sound so shocked."

"Don't I?" He threads the needle and starts pushing it through holes punched into the crease of the papers. "I'll go next. Obviously this would be better if I had my notes, but *someone* burned them." He shoots me a look of palpable grievance. "Six months ago, the Order of Prefects received an anonymous tip about the death of the previous *Markgraf* von Reigenbach. All records say he died in his sleep eight years ago, but we needed the steward of the castle to verify it, and he was nowhere to be found. When Klemens and I finally tracked him down, he'd left all family and friend behind and retired to Rósenbor."

"That's a long way to go for an easy retirement," I say. Rósenbor is about as far north as you can get in the Almanic Empire.

Emeric pulls the thread taut. "Exactly. He wouldn't even open the door for three days. Finally he told us that when he found the former margrave's body, the feet were"—he grimaces—"worn to tatters. There were bloody human footprints leading to the bed from the window, which was locked from the inside."

"So a *nachtmahr* rode him to death." Joniza's abandoned her lyrics for the moment. She scoots closer to Gisele.

"It would seem so. Klemens didn't think we had enough evidence to summon the Godly Court, but *Markgraf* Adalbrecht's had the Order's attention for a while now. He's driving his own march into debt to fund his wars, the Minkjan city guard are little better than his personal gang, he gains almost nothing from an alliance with Sovabin—"

"You *don't* think he's marrying for love?" I fake my shock. "The pearls are very compelling."

Gisele sets her mug down a little too loudly. "*Yes.* They are."

"Anyway," Emeric says quickly, "there have also been rumors in the last few years that none of his soldiers can clearly remember their night raids, despite those being his most successful battles. Collectively, that all was enough to open an investigation, and then we took his *Pfennigeist* case as a cover."

"Why, though?" Joniza taps her quill on her parchment. "Why would he invite prefects into his own home?"

Emeric shakes his head as he slips the thread through another group of folded papers. "That I don't know. My best guess is he's keeping his enemies close, so he can control what gets reported back to the Order. I also don't know how the Wolfhünden factor in. Money *has* moved from his treasury to their coffers in the last day, outside of the normal payroll, so something's afoot."

"How do you know that?" I ask, fascinated.

He gives me a long look, drawing the thread through another set of punctures. "I think we all know why I'm not going to tell you. Princess Gisele, anything to add?"

Gisele stares at her mug, mouth in a tight line. "The streets are talking about the *nachtmären*. We've seen more in the last week than all year, but no one's connected it to the margrave's return, and no one's seen another beast like the one that chased you in Lähl. Besides that . . . I suppose I could see if there's anything unusual about the guests, if you can get me a roster."

Emeric sets down his papers and thread, and now I can see it's starting to take the shape of a new notebook. "All told, I think we can safely say the margrave is behind the *nachtmären* attacks, with something ambitious and unpleasant as the end goal. Now . . ."

"You don't have proof," Joniza points out. Emeric stiffens. She just shrugs. "I mean, you're the prefect, you tell me, but it sounds like your word against his. Can you even use what Vanja saw with the Tears?"

He shifts uncomfortably. "It's . . . complicated. Truth attends every session of the Godly Court, but they're, well, fluid, because the truth is different for everyone. They can only confirm whether the witness believes their testimony is true. So, Miss Schmidt can testify that she *believes* the margrave ordered a *nahr* to kill his father. The former steward can testify that it *looked* like a *mahr* killed him. But that's not enough to prove he was killed by *Merkgraf* Adalbrecht's *nachtmahr* specifically."

And I know too well how my word will stand against Adalbrecht's. "We need more evidence, then. All we have so far is an old painting of him as a miserable, constipated child, everything I *hallucinated* while poisoned, and a bunch of coincidences."

"What if you didn't hallucinate all of it?" Joniza asks. "You saw him knock out the guards with magic before you went into the study, right?"

I chew on a thumb tip. "Right. He crushed something like a rat skull."

Emeric sits up straighter, twirling his charcoal stick. "Anything like that would help. At the very least, there may be more leads in his study."

"There are guards at the main entrances, but I could sneak you in through the servant corridors," I say slowly. "We could break in during the ball on Sunday. You already have an invitation, after all."

Gisele frowns. "A margrave inviting a commoner to his wedding ball? That sounds like a trap."

"Oh, no, it's—well, it's kind of a trap," I say, trying and failing to keep a straight face. "Just Adalbrecht being a bastard. He thinks Junior here has an *improper interest* in you. I mean, me pretending to be you. Us? There was the whole breakfast incident."

"*Breakfast incident?*" Gisele's voice rises to a squeak.

Emeric's ears go red as he stabs the needle back into his notebook-in-progress with an alarming amount of enthusiasm. "*Anyway.* I know what to look for, if Miss Schmidt can get me to the study."

"But the bride-to-be can't just leave her own ball," Gisele protests.

"I could take the Vanja's place," Ragne offers. Then she does an odd little shiver—and suddenly I'm looking at the *Prinzessin* in a nightshirt, down to the ruby teardrop under my—*her*—eye, an alarmingly guileless smile plastered over her face.

"Have you been able to do this the whole time?" I demand.

Ragne shakes her head. Then her hair singes ginger and freckles bloom over her face, until I'm looking at my mirror image. "I grow and fade with the moon. By the full moon, I will be greater still."

Now that I think about it, she isn't napping as much, and she's held larger shapes for longer. "Terrifying," I say. "Can you talk like me, though?"

Ragne turns to the rest of the table and screws up her face into a garish leer. "I am the Vanja. I take things and I am mean for no reason."

Emeric has an abrupt coughing fit; Gisele and Joniza make no such pretense, clapping hands over their mouths as they nearly fall out of their seats laughing.

I just scowl. "False. I'm always mean for a reason."

"*I'm always mean for a reason,*" Ragne mimics.

"Cute, but she still has to make small talk," Joniza says. "Ragne, what would you say if Countess von Folkenstein told you that she was expecting?"

Ragne blinks. "Expecting what?"

"Sieglinde's pregnant?" Gisele blurts out at the same time.

"Maybe there's your answer." Joniza looks from me to Gisele. "Give back the pearls. Gisele can be, well, herself."

I'm surprised to hear Gisele say "*No*" at the same time I do.

"You don't want the pearls?" I ask, incredulous.

She pushes back from the table, shaking her head. "Not while the margrave's trying to kill me. It's not safe."

"Right, better to lose a red penny than a white," I say coldly.

"That's not what I'm saying—"

"That's *exactly* what you're saying."

"I can protect the Gisele," Ragne interrupts, shifting until she's back in her own human shape, raven-haired and red-eyed. "At the ball. I can hide as a maid, or as a mouse, or almost anything at all. I can keep the Gisele safe."

I start to throw out something acerbic and catch myself. Gisele and I have too many miles of thorns between us to cross right now, and we will happily keep tearing each other to pieces until sunrise.

"That could work," I say instead. "I guess you're bringing her to the ball after all, Junior." Then I blanch. "No. Wait. Irmgard will be there. If you come as a guest, she'll recognize you without the pearls."

Gisele flushes. "Then how am I going to get in?"

"It's getting late." Emeric knots off his thread. "And we all could probably use some sleep. We'll come up with a plan tomorrow. Let's reconvene—"

"We're not done," Gisele interrupts, sudden frost in her tone. "What happens to Vanja after this?"

I narrow my eyes. "What do you mean?"

"I mean Prefect Klemens should arrest you," Gisele spits. "You stole my name, my betrothal, my face, and apparently almost a thousand *gilden* worth of jewelry. You don't just get to walk away from that."

And just like that, we are back in the thorns, and I don't care how much I bleed if it means I can wrap some around her throat.

"I stole a face that wasn't yours to begin with," I hiss. "You want your cute little husband back, you can have him. And yes, I stole your name and some jewelry, but I'd call that back pay for what your family owes me."

Gisele stands, planting her hands on the table, voice rising. "You had food, clothing, and a roof over your head. My family gave you *everything*."

I'm on my feet before I know it, a feral, explosive rage roaring down every vein. The world ruthlessly contracts to just her and me in this room, the white penny and the red. "If we're keeping ledgers, then I hope there's a line for the scars on my back. I hope there's a line for my damn childhood, Gisele, because your family stole that and got away with it. You're angry over losing a year, I'm angry over losing a *decade*."

She stares at me, stunned into silence. High Gods and Low, it feels good to say this to her face. It feels even better that no one at the table is coming to her rescue. I want her to feel that lonely, awful terror. I want her to feel it in her bones.

"What, no white pennies to hand out this time?" I snarl, enjoying her flinch a little too much. "You *wanted* me to take those pearls. You should be *begging* me not to throw them into the Yssar once I'm—"

Wrenching pain blazes up my backbone. I can't hold back a cry, bracing myself on the table. Emeric half rises from his chair.

I wave him off and straighten, awkwardly reaching to pat between my shoulder blades. Sure enough, my fingers find one hard knot of stone, then another. I won't know for sure until I get to a mirror, but from the angular edges, I'm guessing a line of rubies now runs up my spine.

"It's nothing," I mumble, "just the curse."

The stairs creak, and Umayya's round face appears, peering down into the kitchen. "Is everything all right?"

"Fine," I lie. "I'm leaving. Tomorrow you can expect a charity visit from the *prinzessin* so we can nail down the plan."

Joniza stands abruptly. "I have a gig tonight in Südbígn. I'll walk you as far as the Göttermarkt."

I falter at that. "You don't have to, Ragne's coming with me—"

"I'm not doing it to be nice," she says, reaching for her fox-fur coat. "I can get Gisele into the ball. But I'm not telling you how until I get one hell of an apology."

CHAPTER NINETEEN

Try, Try Again

We WALK TOWARD THE HIGH WALL IN SILENCE FOR A MINUTE OR two, snowflakes drifting around us, Ragne riding on my shoulder as a black cat so she could leave her borrowed clothes behind. I'm trying to think through what exactly I'm supposed to be apologizing for.

The fact that there are multiple possibilities is, perhaps, part of the problem. Finally I clear my throat and take a guess.

"I'm sorry I didn't try to get you work while I've been pretending to be Gisele."

Joniza blinks at me, slowly. "Try again."

Scheit.

"Uh," I say. "I'm—I'm sorry I used what you taught me to steal."

She lets out a little huff. "You think I give a single damn about those rich crapsacks? Try again."

"I'm sorry I . . ." I'm running out of ideas. "I never finished paying you back for the hedgewitch? Hold on, I might have some change in my pockets—"

Joniza spins on a heel as I surface with a white penny and a few *sjilling*, and I have to duck out of the way of the Sahalian five-string *koli* strapped to her back. "I never *cared* about the money," she snaps. Then she swipes the coins from my hand anyway. "That's a lie. Give me that." They vanish under the fox fur.

There is no *Try again* this time. I brace myself.

"Do you know how scared I was when I arrived at Castle Reigenbach last year and they said Gisele didn't want to see me?" Joniza asks, pacing in the street. "I thought that blond bastard had murdered you both, until I saw Gisele riding around in his carriage. Then I was angry. I thought I would have a *home* here with you and her. I barely had enough coin to keep off the streets. I worried myself sick about what had become of you."

"But you were fine!" I insist. "I—I saw you in Trader's Cross, I saw you every day for a week, and you were fine! You were fine without me!"

Joniza shakes her head. "You never learned, did you? I guess I can't blame you, not with the hell we went through in Sovabin. Just because you can survive without someone doesn't mean they're unwanted. I was so afraid what that monster might do to you. Then, a month after I get here, the *real* Gisele shows up at my door to tell me everything. And you know what? I understood why you did it."

"You did?" I ask, startled.

For a moment Joniza just stares at the line of street lanterns leading to the High Wall. "No matter how bad it was in Castle Falbirg, the margrave would have been worse. You saw a way out and you took it. I don't blame you." Her gaze cuts over to me. "I *do* blame you for thinking so little of me that you'd shut me out and try to do all"—she waves a hand vaguely at me—"*this* on your own. I could have helped you. And now look at the mess you're in, cursed by a god and poisoned by a margrave and—"

"I know," I groan.

"*Don't* interrupt me." It's the tone specifically calculated to remind me she's a decade my senior. "And don't sulk about being at the bottom of a pit you dug yourself. Nothing stolen is ever really yours. And you still have to answer for what you took, who you hurt. Including me."

"That's what people keep telling me," I mumble. "They just never say how."

Joniza lets out a breath that plumes in the cold, shivering despite her fur coat. She never did take to the chill. "Come on, I'm going to be late."

Another stiff quiet falls between us. I think I'm supposed to apologize again, but I still don't know what to say. I know how to beg forgiveness and curtsy and tug my forelock like a good little maid trying to keep her job, but I don't know how to apologize like I mean it.

That reminds me of the other thing I can't muster words for: Yannec. Did they even speak anymore? Does she even know he's dead?

I . . . I don't think I can break it to her. Not tonight, at least.

"I have a question," Ragne says suddenly. I feel her tail lashing against my back.

That's odd. Ragne may be an open book, but this is the first time we've flipped to *nervous*. "Yes?" I prompt.

"What do I do if I like a human person?"

Joniza and I trade wide-eyed looks. I open my mouth and she immediately claps a hand over it. "Absolutely not. I wouldn't let you give relationship advice to my archnemesis."

"You haf an arfhnemefif?" I garble through her fingers.

She lets me go. "I do. Keeps trying to upstage me every time we play the same venue. I hate him. Also: illegally handsome. *Anyway.* Ragne, do you like this person as a friend, or is it different? How do they make you feel?"

Ragne wiggles on my shoulder. "Floaty? And warm. And like I want to laugh a lot. And like I want to put my mouth on—"

"Right, yes, understood. You've got it bad." Joniza laughs softly. "Well, humans are . . ."

"Complicated?" Ragne suggests.

Joniza and I both laugh at that, and it's almost a relief. "Yes," Joniza says. "So sometimes your feelings can make them uncomfortable, if they don't feel the same. But not always. And sometimes they do feel the same." She cracks a grin. "And then you can put your mouth wherever they want you to."

"*Ew,*" I mutter.

"You say that like I didn't catch you kissing your pillow and pretending it was Sebalt the stable boy."

I bury my face in my hands. "How *dare* you."

"How do I know if someone feels the same way I do?" Ragne chirps. I am, for once, grateful for her one-track mind. I think Joniza may be thawing, but I am so, so afraid of spoiling it.

"That's also complicated." Joniza purses her lips. "Here's the secret with humans, Ragne. There's a lot of really, really bad ones. And a lot more who aren't really good *or* bad. But sometimes you find people who prove they're worthy of you, who prove they deserve your trust. And you can always tell people like that how you feel. You should, if you want to keep them around."

"Subtle," I say under my breath. Joniza lightly slugs me in the arm.

And just like that, there's a knot in my throat

"I really missed you." The words spill out, splintering a little, and I can't stop the tide. "I thought you'd move on and I'd be fine with it, but I missed you so much, I'm sorry I made you worry, I'm sorry I pushed you away, I'm—"

Joniza wraps me in a fierce hug, and there is nothing more I can say.

It's the first time I've been held like this in . . . I don't know how long. At least a year. Maybe longer.

"Fine, fine," she says after we've both dried our faces. "Apology accepted. I promised you a way to sneak Gisele in. It isn't a ball without music, right? So the first step is getting me into your rotation . . ."

"*A-r-d-î-m*," I spell out to Franziska the next morning as I march up the stairs to Adalbrecht's wing, "with the accent on the *i*, you know, one of those fun little hats. I'd like her to play after the marriage contract is signed but before it gets *too* late."

"Yes, m'lady," the chief steward says, jotting a note on her slate. Then she blanches as she sees my destination. "Oh, *Prinzessin*, the margrave wanted a private—"

"What's that?" I ask innocently, then throw open the door of Adalbrecht's parlor.

". . . don't see why you had to *pois*—" Count von Hirsching is saying before he cuts himself off. He and Adalbrecht are alone with their breakfast, not even an attendant on hand to clear the plates. "Position . . . the . . . floral arrangements," the count falters, "like . . . that."

Interesting. Can't say it's a shock the von Hirschings are in the mix; I file that away to tell Emeric. (Maybe for a price. Waste not, want not.)

Adalbrecht, for his part, started choking on his coffee the moment I blew through the door.

"Oh, darling, I feel *so* much better," I trill. It's only half a lie. Physically, I still feel like I've been run over by a wagon. Emotionally . . . Well, the horror Adalbrecht's trying to stifle right now is adding years to my life. "I slept so well! What was that medicine? Why, I could drink a whole bottle."

He's still coughing into a napkin, and holds up a hand.

"Why don't you join us for breakfast, *Prinzessin*," Count von Hirsching says with the strained smile of a man thumbscrewed by decorum. Adalbrecht glowers at him, but the count's gaze is locked on the ruby teardrop, sharpening just as his daughter's did the afternoon before.

I give a tinkling laugh and steal a sweet roll off Adalbrecht's plate. "No need, I can't stay long. I came across the most darling little orphanage the other day, and I thought I'd bring over Winterfast sweets and spend some time with the children. They're so bright. *So* full of potential."

"Charming," Adalbrecht wheezes, still flustered. He's not going to fight me on it, though, if it gets me out of the parlor. That gives me another idea.

"Did I hear there's an issue with the flowers? Franziska was just here!" Any excuse to derail his little scheming session with a witness. I bellow over my shoulder, "*Franziska! FRANZISKA!* The margrave needs you!"

"It's fine." Adalbrecht barks.

"But we want everything to be perfect! For the special! *Day!*" I squeeze his shoulder as Franziska hurries in. "Ta-ta! I'll be back in the afternoon to receive the next round of guests."

And just like that, I've bought myself the morning. Even better, it's an excuse to stay out until the halls of Castle Reigenbach are teeming with scandal-famished aristocrats.

I have to keep playing this part, the empty-headed, noble-hearted version of Gisele, because if he thinks I'm a true threat, I'll be dead before dawn.

But as I sweep from the parlor, taking a bite out of the sweet bun, I know I've sent the message I want: Gisele already survived his poison and his *nachtmahr*, and if he wanted her dead, he should have tried harder than that.

For a man who has repeatedly tried to murder his bride, I'm a little surprised Adalbrecht wants this many witnesses to see us sign the marriage decree at the ball a day and a half later.

Strains of violins and flutes rise through the wine-soaked air to tangle in the ballroom's chandelier tapers, wafting into the ceiling's network of murals sectioned by geometric stone arches; boughs of holly and silver fir froth over drapes of Reigenbach blue on each wall, and gilded ivy climbs every marble column.

The decorations have plenty of competition for flash. Everyone's saving their finest for the wedding itself, but their *second* finest is nothing to sneeze at. Vivid silks, rich brocades, and pounds upon pounds of glittering jewelry spin past in a lively Bourgienne tordion.

My fingers itch as I wait beside Adalbrecht for the tordion to wind down. There's just *so much* I could be stealing right now, if I didn't have social obligations with the man who tried to poison me earlier in the week. And if it weren't for the curse. And, I suppose, the law, though really we all know my concern for that is cosmetic at best.

But the image of the *Prinzessin* doesn't waver, putting on a brave, gracious face while Marthe and the *Pfennigeist* wait for their turn.

The marriage decree is laid out on a small table before us. I've snuck glances every chance I can. Between Emeric, Joniza, Gisele, and me, not a single one of us can think of why Adalbrecht would try to kill Gisele before the wedding but still throw an entire ball just so everyone sees us signing the paperwork. A small party is customary for signing the decree, not . . . this.

The best explanation is that something in the decree is off. Every official Almanic wedding needs a signed decree, but they're especially critical for unions between noble houses, laying out limits so people like Adalbrecht don't go around on a marry-and-murder spree to acquire their deceased spouses' property. The language is clear: If Gisele dies, Sovabin's title stays with the von Falbirgs. There's even a grotesque little clause to address the fact that Gisele technically isn't old enough to be considered an adult by imperial law. Until she turns seventeen in April, she'll legally be considered Adalbrecht's ward.

But skin-crawling as that is, it's standard-issue for a marriage decree.

"You look nervous, my little . . ." Adalbrecht pauses, eyeing my gown, then lands on: "strawberry."

I picked my dress for the evening and didn't give him an opening to dictate otherwise. It's a luscious wine-red velvet, trimmed in white lace shot through with gold thread, and the important thing is that if at any point the thorny rubies on my spine poke through the fabric, they will look like a fashion statement.

"Just thinking about a week from now," I say sweetly. It's not entirely a lie. I've wasted a whole week; only one more remains before the curse kills me, if he doesn't beat it to the punch.

Adalbrecht isn't really listening, eyes following something. I trace his gaze to the far side of the ballroom, where Emeric is glued to the wall beside a veritable waterfall of evergreens, awkwardly declining an invitation to dance. He's a bit of a novelty, a plain spike of uniform black in all the flash and glitter. I'm sure there are more than a few nobles who want to titter over the joke of taking him for a spin around the floor.

That's the point, really. Adalbrecht has invited the commoner to remind him of his place. And mine, even if my bridegroom doesn't know any better.

"Something wrong, darling?" I ask, bland.

The lines at the corners of his mouth cut a little deeper. "I'm afraid your little admirer isn't getting the hint. He's been ogling you all evening."

I do *not* need Adalbrecht keeping a close watch on Emeric. "I'm sure someone else will catch his eye soon enough. But if you'd like, I could dance with him and step on his toes. I'm sure that would quite cure him of any interest." It would also give me an opportunity to yell at him for being so obvious.

Adalbrecht's true smiles are as rare as they are cruel. One sharpens his face now. "I think you'd have to break his feet, little berry . . . but you might be onto something."

Thankfully, the music wanes to quiet and the tordion slows to a halt before my betrothed can pursue that thought any further. It's time to sign the decree.

There's a quick speech (all Adalbrecht, because of course it is) and the steward, Franziska, comes forward with a ridiculous ostrich-feather quill (studded in sapphires along the shaft, because of course it is). We sign the parchment. Just like that, it's official: A week from now, once the wedding ceremony has been completed, Gisele will be *Markgräfin* von Reigenbach in the eyes of the gods and the empire.

But once it's done and the music strikes up again, Adalbrecht snaps for Franziska. Before I realize what's happening, she's been dispatched to fetch Emeric. He trots over, looking positively miserable. "You called, sir?"

"You've barely danced a step, boy." Adalbrecht grabs me by the elbow. "Surely you won't refuse a turn about the room with my bride."

"Oh, er, sir, I wouldn't want to——" Emeric's playing up the nerves, but I can spot a flash of annoyance. We all know this plain, schoolyard kind of malice. Adalbrecht wants to rub Emeric's face in what he can't have.

"Wouldn't want to?" Adalbrecht echoes, teeth baring in that true, terrible smile. "Are you saying my bride isn't to your liking?"

"Of course not. I——I would be honored." Emeric bows and holds out a hand as Adalbrecht pushes me forward. I let Emeric lead me onto the floor, ignoring the snickers from the likes of Irmgard and Sieglinde. (Sieglinde has managed to convince her husband to let her glue a topaz on her face after all, just as she'd threatened. It's hideous.)

"What," Emeric grits through his teeth, "did you *say* to him?"

Long, piercing notes soar through the air, striking up a pavane. *Ugh.* The entire point of the pavane is to show off what you're wearing and who you're dancing with. Since Emeric's only in a slightly nicer version of his uniform, I've no doubt Adalbrecht arranged for that as well.

"I said I'd stomp on your toes if we danced," I hiss back. "Because he noticed *you* were staring at me."

We fall into two lines of dancers, each couple facing ahead, hand in hand as they glide forward. Emeric already looks pained, and I haven't even managed to kick him in the shin yet, like I'm aspiring to. His voice stays low enough not to carry beyond us. "I was watching *him.*"

"It's not like he's going to stab me in the middle of the ballroom."

"How sure are you about that?"

We split apart, weaving back through the other dancers before meeting again. This time we have to stand facing opposite directions and walk in a slow wheel.

"Sure enough." That's a complete lie, but I'll be a stone-cold corpse before I concede a point to a sentient fireplace poker with an undeservedly high opinion of itself. I lift my palm to his. "Follow my lead."

"I know how to dance." Emeric sounds faintly insulted.

I give him a dubious look. "Where does *that* fall in the prefect curriculum?"

We switch hands and directions. "It doesn't," he says curtly. A beat passes before he elaborates. "My sister lost most of her sight when we were young. She wanted to learn and needed a partner." I scowl at him, and his eyes narrow. "*What.*"

"I can't make fun of that, you inconsiderate ass," I grumble. "But if you keep looking like your teeth hurt, Adalbrecht won't stop making us dance until he can get you to cry." Emeric frowns deeper, and I roll my eyes. "Just *try* to look like you're enjoying yourself. I know the pearls are helping."

He deftly whirls me out of the way of a careening Ezbeta von Eisendorf, who is making a strong case for the virtues of abstinence. Emeric's face has gone from outright misery to an uneasy discomfort. All he says is "Not the way you think."

Before I can interrogate *that* further, a cheery, brazen run of notes riffs off the unmistakable strings of a Sahalian *koli*. Joniza strolls onto the stage, gold paint flashing on her lips and on her fingertips as they fly. The piper she's interrupting looks both delighted and furious, and I have to agree with her earlier assessment: Her archnemesis *is* unreasonably handsome.

Just like that, it's a musical duel. Joniza's striking up a jovial galliard, but the piper keeps trying to wrest the song back to the stately pavane. And the ballroom floor is *chaos*, as no one knows which dance to stick to.

Just as we planned.

That's our signal. It's time to start the game.

CHAPTER TWENTY

Self-Evident

Emeric drops my hands like hot coals.

I try not to take that personally, craning around him to make sure Adalbrecht's distracted. "If he asks, I——"

"Went to powder your nose, I know. Go."

There's a line at the privy closest to the ballroom, which we expected. I make a show of frowning and hurrying off, headed for a different privy farther away, just off the entrance hall.

No line. And Gisele is waiting for me inside.

You see, some of the musicians have assistants to carry their instruments, stage costumes, songbooks, and so on. Gisele might have been recognized at the ball, but no one, especially no one like Irmgard, will be looking at the servants.

She's carrying the satchel I readied ahead of time and wearing the

Reigenbach servant uniform we hid under her cloak. "Sorry, miss, just looking for my mistress's earring," she calls as I walk in, then double-takes. "Ugh. I'll never get used to that."

"You'd better," I say tersely. I unclasp the pearls and hand them over. "Put those on last."

We trade dresses, and then we both dig in the satchel, me for paste and gauze to cover my ruby teardrop, and her for face powders and the fake ruby. It wasn't as hard as I expected to find a bit of red glass in the right shape, because my *accessory* has become a full-blown trend for anyone who can afford it. There are certainly no shortage of imitators tonight.

It doesn't take Gisele long to replicate my cosmetics, and once she's done, I use my pinkie to rub powder off a patch below her right eye. Then I drop a bead of glue on the red glass, hold her chin in one hand, and press the teardrop on with the other.

"Hold still," I tell her. "It needs to set."

Gisele closes her eyes, fingers knotting in the undone bodice laces; the seams will split if she tries to lace it before the pearls cut her down. I see a nervous flush rising up her neck. "How . . . how big is the crowd?"

"Hundred people, maybe? Half the wedding guests haven't arrived yet. I already did most of the talking, you'll just have to dance and smile and nod. Adalbrecht is being fussy about Emeric, but just laugh it off and he'll settle down."

She lets out a breath. "Then . . . I think I can do this for twenty-five minutes. Thirty at most."

"If it takes longer than that, we've got bigger problems." I let go of the false ruby, and it stays put. "There. Now put on the pearls. They help with the hair."

I realize my mistake as soon as the pearls are on. The image they produce is the same no matter the wearer, but how they get her there is the opposite of me, narrowing Gisele's shoulders, carving out curves instead of adding them, even taking an inch or two off her height. Dame von Falbirg must have asked for this specific form when she bought the enchantment. I never said anything to Gisele about it, but it's eerily close to the older portraits of the dame as a younger woman.

Those portraits don't have a charm that makes me want to forgive them, oblige them, on sight, though. The pearls do.

For nearly four years, there's been a rotten kind of simmer in my blood when it comes to Gisele. It's been there so long, I don't know who I am without it. But the moment those pearls clasp around her neck, I remember how happy I was to serve her.

I turn away, fingernails digging into my palms. "You can do your own hair."

Then I yank one more servant uniform from the satchel, toss it onto a chair, and get out before I indulge anything so dangerous as for-giveness.

A black cat yowls by the door, blinking red eyes at me. I only hold the door open long enough for Ragne to slip in, then continue on my way back to the ballroom.

My scalp stings as I braid my own hair a little too tight.

Emeric's affixed himself to the wall near the closest exit, studying a penny-sized pewter coin in his palm. I'm sure that's doing nothing helpful for Adalbrecht's paranoia.

I duck out of sight before he spots me. The last thing Adalbrecht needs to see is Emeric leaving the ball early and Gisele showing up min-utes later, breathless and rumpled like she's fresh from a rendezvous with a besotted junior prefect.

Something about that thought makes me unsettled. I don't know why. And I don't *want* to.

I don't have to wait long for Gisele to arrive, Ragne one step behind her in her own servant uniform, hair neatly tucked into a bun and red eyes darkened to brown. We've coached her on her role: If anyone asks, she's Gisele's handmaiden and is not to leave her side.

Once they walk in, Emeric ducks out, heading down the hall. I fall into step behind him, only to realize as his head swivels that he doesn't know I'm there. We make it almost to the vestibule before he stops and fishes the pewter coin out of his pocket.

I whisper, "*Boo.*"

I didn't know it was possible to make a vertical leap all the way onto a staircase landing, but Emeric proves me wrong.

After he's done swearing at me, I observe, "You know an awful lot of big-boy no-no words for a man of the gods."

"You are an absolute *terror,*" he snaps. "At this point I'm frankly amazed nothing else cursed you before now."

I shrug. "Who's to say they haven't tried? Come on, we've got half an hour at most."

He grumbles but follows me to a tapestry tastefully obscuring a doorway that blends right into the masonry. It leads us into the servant corridors, where it takes a moment for my eyes to adjust to the dim. The torches are spaced farther than in the normal halls, just sufficient to navigate by and no more.

Emeric catches my shoulder. His voice drops to a whisper. "Wait—do you hear—"

"We're not alone," I tell him, heading down the narrow passage. "Don't worry about it."

"What do you mean, we're not—"

He's cut off by an extremely distinct species of giggle-gasp echoing from one of the pathways splitting off to the right. The shadows cast by distant torchlight lay out an equally distinct explanation.

"You see," I say gravely, "when two people love each other very much, or at least think the other's passable if they squint—"

"*Yes I understand now thank you.*" I can practically hear his blush.

"You realize if we get caught, that's our excuse, right?" I point out. "We're just a couple of squirrelly youths who got turned around looking for somewhere to, er, canoodle."

"Then I'd rather not get caught," he says, grim.

I force a laugh as I lead us toward a flight of stairs. "That makes two of us." Then I flash his own coin at him. For someone who's supposed to be a highly trained supersleuth, he's awfully easy to pickpocket. "What's the deal with this? Special gift from Papi Klemens?"

He snatches it out of my hand. "Will you *please* refrain"—I pass him his writing charcoal—"from robbing me"—and his makeshift notebook—"while I'm *working*?" Then he lets out an exasperated sigh. "I need my spectacles to see, Miss Schmidt."

I'm too busy holding them up to the nearest torch, impressed with how the lenses distort it. "No kidding. Nearsighted? That seems appropriate."

"You're the first to make *that* joke," he says with absolutely no sincerity, plucking them from my hands. "They also let me see things like enchantments, magical traps, and your curse, so it's in both our interests to leave them on my face."

"You didn't say what this is." I toss him his own coin again. It's incredible how he just put it back in the same pocket.

He catches it with a scowl. "Later."

We exit the servant passageways into the hallway of the margrave's wing. Just as I suspected, there are no guards in sight, and if I strain, I can hear faint conversation far beyond the bend of the corner. Adalbrecht doesn't want anyone closer to his rooms than they have to be.

The study door is locked, so Emeric keeps an uneasy lookout while I break out my picks. It's almost laughably simple to crack, just a few taps on the tumblers and a twist of the tension rake, as if the margrave's confident that his reputation alone would deter anyone from crossing him.

It's pitch-dark inside. Even the drapes have been drawn to shut out the rooftops of Minkja below. Still, I hear Emeric draw in a sharp breath. "Ah. *That's* what you meant by a skull in his study."

"Sure? Poldi can light some candles——" I turn to double back and run into Emeric instead.

"Wait." There's a rustle of fabric, then a glimmer of ghostly light spilling between cupped fingers. It's the coin, glowing like a tiny moon in Emeric's hands. He sets it on the credenza, where it brightens enough to shed chilly light throughout the study. I see his jacket has already been laid at the base of the door to keep the telltale light from shining through.

Well. I'm not generous enough to say I'm impressed, but I can respect his foresight.

"Every prefect has a coin like this." His voice stays low as he rolls up his sleeves, heading toward the wall of hunting trophies. "The engraving also changes when there's a message for me at the nearest outpost. *That's* the deal with it."

Ah. Wonder what he's waiting on.

"What are we looking for, exactly?" I ask.

"That's a very bold *we*, Miss Schmidt. Just stay out of the way and don't steal anything. How much time do we have left?"

I shove my hands in my pockets, annoyed, and annoyed that I'm annoyed. "Sorry, I don't speak Sanctimonious Coatrack."

"That doesn't even make sense. The time, Miss Schmidt." When I don't answer, he releases a drawn-out, waspish sigh of pure martyrdom. "We want evidence or leads. *Nachtmären* paraphernalia, correspondence from the von Hirschings, anything that seems out of the ordinary. And for the love of High Gods and Low, try not to disturb anything."

"Twenty minutes at the most, fifteen at the least," I say primly. "I'll start with the desk."

There are no papers left in sight on Adalbrecht's desk, no decorations of any kind; inkpot, drying salt, and quills lined up perfectly at the head. Just as much a curated façade as the *Prinzessin*. I won't find anything here he doesn't want seen.

But knowing Adalbrecht, he'll still keep his secrets within reach. I plant myself behind the desk and slowly look around. There's the credenza with its bottles, tapestries of family trees and past conquests, bookshelves full of military history and volumes of Almanic imperial law . . .

There. Something catches my eye: a clean stripe in the shelf's thin blanket of dust.

"He isn't letting the servants in to clean," I tell Emeric. "And he's only pulled one book off this shelf since he got back."

Emeric's got his hands full with an elk head he's carefully lifting off the wall. "Can you write the title down? My notes are—you know where they are."

I do know: exactly in the pocket where I left them. I fetch the charcoal and notebook-in-progress from his discarded jacket, listening a moment at the door to make sure we're not in for an unpleasant surprise. Nothing.

I jot down the book's title and volume number, then check to see if Adalbrecht's marked any pages. Sure enough, there's a folded slip of paper tucked inside at SECTION 13.2: FILIATION AND GUARDIANSHIP; SUBSECTION 42. "'Adrogation and Intestacy,'" I read aloud. "What's that?"

Emeric tilts his head. "That's inheritance law. But why would he . . . ?" He trails off, then keeps mumbling to himself like I'm not even here. All I catch are fragments like "coparcenary" and "chain of title" and "ultimogeniture," which I'm pretty sure is something you pay a *mietling* for.

I consider throwing his charcoal at him, but settle for sticking my tongue out at his back. Then I return to the law book, writing down the section and subsection, and finally unfold the paper. It's a list of names in Adalbrecht's handwriting.

"Interesting."

This time it's my turn to jump, almost knocking the inkpot off the desk as I discover Emeric looming over my shoulder. "Do you *mind*?" I hiss.

"Sorry," he says, not even trying to hide a smug little smirk before he taps the paper. "I think these are all border towns . . . to the north. Write those down too."

I shove the charcoal his way. "You've got perfectly good hands. Write it yourself."

He tears a clean paper out of the notebook and snaps the charcoal in half, then points at the trophy wall. "We have ten minutes at most, and I need to document those runes."

I look up. The elk head is sitting on the ground, and in the void left behind, a bleached horse skull has been nailed to the wall. Runes are scorched into it in wheels and patterns that make me seasick if I try to focus on them for too long.

It's the one I saw with Augur's Tears. I guess that much was real.

"What if we just smash it?" I suggest. "There's a poker by the fireplace."

Emeric shakes his head as he walks back to the trophy wall, then draws one of his knives. "From your vision, it sounds like his arrangement with the *nachtmären* is to sacrifice an animal every time he wants one to do his bidding. This is similar, but . . ." The blade flashes with a veneer of gold as he uses it to prod the skull.

"Worse?" I suggest.

Emeric nods. "I'm fairly certain at least part of that is a binding spell, like a warlock's. Binding himself to a single *nachtmahr* wouldn't do much, though. If we knew the horse this skull came from, we could get answers from its ghost, but without it we're just guessing. I think we'd better know what the margrave's bound himself to before we cut it loose, don't you?"

"You take the fun out of everything." I start copying the town names down. "Is it enough to summon the Godly Court?"

"Not yet. A warlock can legally bind themselves to whatever manner of creature they like. We have to prove he's using it to do harm. Besides, we should wait for Hubert to get here so he can call the court."

"What, Papi Klemens doesn't let—"

Emeric's voice turns sharp, sharper than I've ever heard it. "*Please stop calling him that.*"

I flinch, a dart of panic zipping through my veins. Hot embarrassment flushes on its heels. A year is not enough to undo the instincts of Castle Falbirg.

"Fine, you don't have to be a beast about it," I mumble.

Emeric doesn't speak for a moment. There's only the scratch of charcoal on paper. Then he says, "My father passed away about ten years ago. It's not particularly funny to me."

I remember what I saw through the Tears: a little boy standing before Klemens, saying gravely that he had a petition for the Godly Courts. A pin in the lock begins to slide.

"Huh," I say, cunningly.

"And we need Hubert because a fully initiated prefect is allowed to lose the occasional case. I'm not."

There's enough weight there that I don't push.

"When's Klemens supposed to arrive?" I know it's in the letter in his old notebook, but I can't remember for the life of me, and even if I did, I can't let on. Those notes are supposed to be cinders in my fireplace.

Emeric glances back at the glowing coin on the credenza. "Eight hours ago."

That's why he's been so on edge.

I decide it's getting a little too tense for both of us. "What are the chances he has a soft spot for charming and unrepentant jewel thieves?"

Emeric's shoulders loosen. We're both more comfortable on this ground. "You never know. Did you see if von Reigenbach altered anything in the marriage decree?"

We spent a decent amount of time on Saturday going over what to look out for in the decree language, since I'd be the only one guaranteed a chance to examine Gisele's. "No, it all looked typical."

"We're missing something," Emeric says through his teeth as he hoists the elk head back into place. "Especially since he's looking into inheritance law. His heir by Gisele could be eligible for the imperial throne, but Gisele would need to survive for significantly"—he ducks a branch of antlers—"longer than the wedding. And I can't think of why he would want Sovabin's immediate alliance."

I shrug. "You saw yourself, he's apparently been throttling trade routes. If he hadn't bribed the von Falbirgs, I don't know that they could even afford to come out for the wedding."

Emeric goes very quiet. When I look up, he's fixed me with the riveted stare of a cat that's spotted a dangling string. Somehow he's managed to acquire a charcoal smudge over a cheekbone.

"I never told you that," he says. Each word is faster than the last. "I only put it in my notes."

Scheit.

But he doesn't seem angry. If anything, there's a genuine bounce in his step as he crosses the room. "You read them, didn't you? Did you see my theories about the Wolfhünden? I *knew* von Reigenbach was—"

"I only read some of them," I snap, biting off each word.

"Which parts? Do you think I missed anything?" Then he cocks his head, frowning. ". . . Miss Schmidt?"

I shove the list of names back into the book and jam it onto the shelf. "I read your notes on Sovabin and the von Falbirgs." I can't look at him as I collect the papers from the desk. "Didn't miss a thing. You got it all completely right."

Every bitter, festering detail.

I've done my best to keep this at arm's length until now, to pretend he doesn't know the old wounds under this uniform . . . but I suppose that was never going to last.

I dare a look up in time to catch comprehension break across Emeric's face. He goes pale, making the scuff of charcoal stand out even more. I'm sure he's enjoyed speculating and theorizing and read-ing the tea leaves, but—it's my *life*. They're my scars.

And I will not, *cannot* stomach his pity. I think of snow, of frost, of a dark forest with a lone lantern at a crossroads, and I let that cold run down my veins. "Except for one thing. I don't want attention."

Then I hand him the notes and broken charcoal, and slip past, headed for the collection of bottles.

"Miss Schmidt—" he begins, and his voice is so startlingly soft it's almost cruel.

But he's cut off as a shouted salute echoes down the hall.

It's the guards stationed at the entrance to the wing.

Adalbrecht is coming.

CHAPTER TWENTY-ONE

An Unlikely Passion

WE SCRAMBLE FOR THE DOOR. I TOSS EMERIC HIS JACKET FROM THE floor as he douses the coin light. The guards are posted at the entrance to the wing, so if they saluted Adalbrecht on sight, we have just under ten seconds to get out of here before he turns the corner in the hall.

I crack the door open, let Emeric out, and flip the latch as I close the door behind me so Adalbrecht doesn't wonder why his study's unlocked.

A distinct voice echoes from down the hall: Irmgard.

We might not have another chance like this again.

I spot an unobtrusive linen closet a few yards away. The door's unlocked when I test the handle.

Emeric wheezes a perplexed *oof* as I yank him in after me and pull the door mostly closed. "What are you—"

I plaster a hand over his mouth and whisper, "Eavesdropping, *obviously*. Irmgard von Hirsching is with him."

Just enough torchlight creeps in through the open door for me to see Emeric's brow furrow. I pointedly hold a finger to my lips as the voices grow louder, and try not to think about how cramped it is in here. It's generous for a linen closet, but not *that* generous.

". . . painted over *my face*."

"It was necessary," Adalbrecht rumbles as a halo of candelabra light waxes across the carpet. I hear the scrape of a key in a lock, then the door hinges, and the light moves out of the hall, into the study.

I take my hand off Emeric's mouth before it gets distracting. Not that it would. It's just that I feel it every time he exhales, and that's . . .

Distracting, a pesky voice says. I shove the idea away and let the closet door ease open a little farther.

"That was supposed to be *our* portrait," Irmgard whines from inside the study. "When you fix it, everyone's going to think it was just redone for me."

"I need to keep up appearances. Now, do you actually have an update from your father, or are you here to complain about a painting?"

I hear Irmgard huff. "We're a little confused, and hoping you can clarify: Are you going to kill Gisele or not?"

"I'll remind you, our original timeline . . . *concludes* sometime the week after the wedding. I won't have the von Falbirgs trying to contest the legitimacy."

Emeric shifts beside me, and I can nearly hear him silently cursing that there isn't enough room to dig out his notes.

"You were willing to kill her Thursday."

Ire pushes more thorns through Adalbrecht's voice. "Don't try your games with me, girl. You told me yourself Gisele's wearing some kind of illusion. A stand-in could play her part through the wedding easily enough."

Now I'm the one silently cursing. At least it hasn't occurred to them that it already happened a year ago.

"I acted because her behavior was growing erratic," Adalbrecht continues. "She's course-corrected since. We'll go back to the original plan."

There's a tense little pause. I can hear the honeyed bite in Irmgard's voice. "I hope you aren't growing soft on her, *Markgraf.*"

She's baiting him, as deranged an idea as that may be. But Adalbrecht knows better, or he doesn't care, because his answer is a cold, flat, "I am not."

"Then I really don't understand the delay. The decree's already signed, and my father—"

"The damned *kobold* is protecting her, or she'd already be dead. Every hearth in the castle may as well be her guard dog."

(I owe Poldi an entire cellar of mead, apparently.)

Irmgard's voice rises. "I'm sorry, I thought we were in Castle *Reigenbach.* The little goblin should answer to you."

An uncomfortable silence. Then Adalbrecht says shortly, "She formally acknowledged the *kobold* before I did."

Too close to me, Emeric breathes, "Oh, *awkward.*"

"Then fix it," Irmgard sniffs. "My father is not in the business of investments that don't pay out."

"It's going to be resolved after I deal with the prefects." Adalbrecht sounds like his patience is running perilously low. "I have no desire to keep her alive past the wedding night, and the Wolfhünden are standing by if opportunity arises in the next week."

There's a flicker of shadow in the narrow strip of visible hallway.

Then, to my surprise, I see a sleeve inch into sight—the sleeve of a servant uniform.

Barthl is creeping close to the study door. I think he came from the servant corridor.

What is *he* doing here?

"Do you absolutely need the wedding night?" Irmgard pries.

"I won't have another for a while," Adalbrecht answers. "You'll have to forgive me my indulgences."

Saints and martyrs, of all the things to listen to a few yards away while I'm jammed in a cramped linen closet with a boy who smells— ugh, *yes*, distractingly—of juniper. It doesn't help that he makes the exact same muffled noise of disgust I do at "indulgences."

Barthl is lingering too close for my comfort. He hasn't noticed us, fixated on the study doorway, spidery fingers gnarling in his *krebatte*.

"Fine. But no more excuses. If there's an opening to eliminate her, you take it. We've put a significant amount of effort into identifying and organizing sympathizers, and committed more of our treasury than you have any right to."

"I'll decide what I have a right to." Adalbrecht's voice leaps to a crescendo; she's struck a nerve. "I am the margrave and your *superior*—"

A loud and unmistakable floorboard creak splits down the hall. The study falls silent.

Barthl blanches, then scuttles back toward the servant corridor.

"Hello?" Irmgard calls out. "Who's out there?"

The coal dust of bad luck begins tumbling through my sight.

Emeric and I look at each other, wide-eyed. The linen-closet door is still conspicuously ajar. I hastily pull it as close to shut as I dare, but if that latch clicks it'll sound like a thunderclap in this quiet.

"Stay here," Adalbrecht orders. Footsteps fall like the stroke of an executioner's axe, passing the closet. From the angle he's at, it's hard to spot that the door's cracked open, but when he comes back, it'll stick out like a sore thumb. And I know he'll spot it, because misfortune rains around us.

We're trapped.

I steel myself and whisper. "Well, this is happening. Canoodling youths it is."

Emeric wrings his jacket in his hands. "There has to be an alternative—"

"We get caught and probably die, that's the alternative," I hiss back. I pull his jacket free and toss it haphazardly on a shelf, like it was discarded in the throes of a very unlikely passion, and undo a few buttons on my blouse to add to the illusion. Then I make myself grab a fistful of his shirt and pull him closer. "If it's any consolation, this isn't how I envisioned my first—"

"No." He braces a hand on the shelf behind my head, leaning away like I'm poison. "I don't—*I don't want to do this.*"

I let go, a little staggered.

He doesn't want to kiss me.

No—not just *doesn't want*. The notion is so repellent, he would rather get caught by Adalbrecht, the monster at both of our throats.

Oh gods, I want to *die*. I want the floor to cave in. I want to shrink until I'm small enough to hide behind the towels. It's not that I want to kiss him—I don't think I do—it's just gutting to be reminded that without the pearls, I'm not . . .

Not Gisele.

It doesn't mean anything, I tell myself.

I don't know what I expected.

I may not be a good person, but I know too well how it feels to have something forced on me, and I won't do that to anyone. "We don't have to, actually, *you know*, it just has to look close enough," I say in a rush. "Just follow my lead. All right?"

Adalbrecht's footsteps have reached the end of the hall; he'll be doubling back any moment now.

Emeric gives a pained nod. I swipe some of the charcoal smudge from his cheek onto mine. Then I move his free hand to my waist, wrap my arms around his neck, and give his hair a quick tousle for good measure. "Head down."

I should have pinched my cheeks before this, but I'm pretty sure I can hear all of my blood rushing to my face anyway. What a fool I was, thinking it distracting when Emeric only exhaled on my hand. It's *much* worse when I can hear his every uneven breath an inch from my ear, feel the heat of it on my throat.

"I'm . . . sorry," he mumbles into my shoulder, "I—"

The closet door swings open.

I let out a squeak and make a show of pushing Emeric away. He stumbles back, and the shame and flush on his face really helps sell this lie, even if it's wretchedly authentic.

"Prefect Conrad," Adalbrecht says slowly. "This is unexpected."

"Junior prefect," he mumbles, "sir."

I drop my head and curtsy, staring at the floor. "I'm so very sorry, m'lord, I must've taken a wrong turn in the servant corridors, I don't know this wing at all . . ."

Rough fingers clamp around my chin and tilt it up. I keep my eyes cast down, even though I'd love nothing more than to bite Adalbrecht's miserable hand off.

"I ran into you at Castle Falbirg, didn't I?" he asks. "You're my lady's personal maid."

Ran into. I almost scream. He found me in a hall alone, pinned my hands to the wall with just one of his, and had half my bodice undone before Joniza came around the corner and he simply went on his way. It was fast and detached, like he'd had plenty of practice. Like I was just another appetizer on the von Falbirgs' table.

And then the next morning, he demanded—*requested*—Gisele's hand in marriage.

"That is correct, m'lord." The tremor in my voice is humiliatingly real.

He releases my chin with a nauseating little chuckle. "If you intend to sample my goods, Conrad, we can provide you with a guest room."

Emeric ducks his head, and I can't tell if his face is burning with mortification or anger. "That won't be necessary, sir."

"Then let's get you back to the festivities, eh?" Adalbrecht claps him on the shoulder and flicks a hand at me. "Run along, girl. Actually—go wait in the entrance hall. Maybe wine will help the prefect find his courage."

"Right away, m'lord." I have never been so happy to leave a linen closet. I'm not mad at Emeric, I just . . . don't want to look at him right now. Or for the rest of the year. Maybe a century.

I still make myself walk down the hall behind them instead of taking the servant corridors, calculating my distance like weighing a ballista. You learn how to judge these things, growing up with a family that might strike at you simply because they've had a bad day and you're there.

Adalbrecht might be acting cordial, but he'll cut Emeric's throat between here and the guards if it makes life easier. I keep close enough to be a concern as a potential witness, but far enough behind that if Adalbrecht makes a move, he won't have time to catch me before I scream for the guards.

Every time he glances back at me, I drop my eyes to the ground and know I was right to follow.

I trail them all the way to the entrance hall, then plant myself there as I've been told. I feel a little sick, if I'm being honest, and I need time to think, and to breathe.

When I took the pearls a year ago, I learned within the first hour the difference between navigating the world as someone desirable, and as . . . myself.

It wasn't just Gisele's status, it's never been. All of a sudden, people were smiling at me, laughing at my jokes the way they did with Irmgard; they were making sure I was comfortable and bringing me little gifts simply because I was there.

For the last year, I've only taken the pearls off when I want to go unnoticed. Unwanted. I know what I am without them.

Until tonight, though, I have never felt so *unlovely*.

"Miss Schmidt."

Oh, *fantastic*, Emeric's managed to get away from Adalbrecht.

I want to bury my face in my hands, and only resist out of sheer willpower. I don't know why I give a damn about the opinion of a boy I threw into the Yssar less than a week ago. "We need a better place to wait," I babble, looking anywhere but at him, "and did you see Barthl—"

"It's not you," Emeric says at the same time. "I mean—I didn't want—or *not* want—" He runs a hand through his hair and doesn't seem to care that it leaves a strand sticking straight up. "You're right, we need to find a better place than this."

I purse my lips, then wordlessly head to an alcove in the vestibule Gisele will eventually pass through. I tuck myself into a corner out of sight, sliding down until I can rest my chin on my knees. Emeric hovers outside the alcove a moment, then folds himself to the ground in the opposite corner, knotting and unknotting his fingers.

"I," he says unsteadily, "I've never understood people like . . . back in the servant corridors. I don't know what it's like to, to want—*any* of that—with someone you don't really know. And I can't fake it. I—I just can't."

I have a very uncomfortable thought, and that is that I understand it *perfectly*. I've read fairy tales, of course, and listened to plaintive love songs, but I never understood why anyone would wake up after a hundred years and marry the prince who broke into their bedroom for a kiss. Or dance with a stranger once and decide to spend the rest of their lives together. I always felt a baffled kind of melancholy when others raptured over love at first sight, like maybe something was wrong with me, maybe I didn't know how to love someone at all.

I didn't know it wasn't just me.

"It was my problem," Emeric says. "I'm sor—"

"No," I interrupt, faster and rawer than I intended. "I . . . know what you mean. You have nothing to apologize for."

He grimaces. "I feel like I do."

This conversation is getting vastly more personal than I was prepared for. "*I* made a miscalculation. You don't owe me a consolation . . ." I wave my hand. ". . . canoodle. That's not how it works. Ever."

Emeric's mouth twists. "A consolation canoodle," he repeats slowly. "You've actually done it. I really, truly don't think I've heard that one before."

I am *not* going to smile at him. I refuse on principle. (The principle is: I've already met my emotional-availability quota for the day.) Instead I bite my lip and lean to look out into the hall. Still no sign of Gisele.

"How . . . how do you do it?" Emeric asks. "You said that would have been your first kiss. You don't care that it wouldn't have been real?"

Fire rushes to my face. Of *all* the things for him to remember . . . That's the worst part, really. Listening to other girls gossip about lovers they'd kissed behind the stables, or at a festival, or by moonlight in secret. Listening to them whisper the word *tongue* like it was an act of delicious treason. Wondering if I was ever going to giggle like that, and telling myself I didn't care.

For a dreadful moment, my mind simply goes blank, because at this rate I'm *over* quota. I don't know how to put this ugly truth into words that won't burn coming up. But for some reason, I feel like I can say this to him.

I *want* to say it to someone who understands.

"It would have mattered," I say quietly. "Like it would have mattered to you. But you heard how they were talking about me. About Gisele. We know what Adalbrecht is. It's like what you were saying about there being no such thing as bravery. I've made it this long because I'm used to all my choices being unpleasant."

He huffs a bitter laugh. "You must think me a terrible coward."

"Not really. Just someone who values his principles more than his own lifespan."

Emeric cracks another smile, and despite everything, I find myself violating my own principles and grudgingly allowing one in return.

"For the record," he says awkwardly, "I think we both would have deserved . . . something better." Then he sits up straighter. "They're coming back."

Gisele and Ragne are climbing the stairs, and I know my cue. I stand and brush myself off. "See you in a bit, then."

I slip from the alcove and catch Ragne's eye. She nods and splits off toward Emeric. I showed Ragne the way to the bedroom through the servant corridors earlier, and once they've collected his cloak and scarf, she'll smuggle Emeric up so we can all compare notes. This way, the servants in the riverfront wing won't wonder why Princess Gisele's being waited on by a stranger instead of Marthe.

Still, something catches in my throat as I fall in behind Gisele. It feels cramped and familiar, this—me a plain little accessory with my head bowed, her in the fine gown and the pearls to protect her, chin high as she glides up the stairs. Adalbrecht's booming laugh echoing at our backs.

Those damned pearls easing the thorns from my heart.

It feels like I'm sliding back to who I was, what I was, when I still thought Gisele would take care of me, her loyal maid. And this time, I may not be able to climb out.

THE WOLF AND HIS WIFE

ONCE UPON A TIME, THERE LIVED A PRINCESS AND HER MAID, AND they once had been friends.

If you asked the princess if they still were, she would say yes. What happened when they were thirteen was unfortunate, but her maid was the strongest, cleverest maid she knew, and within a few weeks, she was good as gold.

If you asked the maid if they were still friends, she would tell you she wasn't sure they ever really were.

Or maybe she wouldn't say that; she would smile and say of course. Or she would say yes and then ask after your family. Or she would laugh and get on with her chores.

The maid was learning to lie, you see, because she had learned the truth would not protect her. She was learning to pick locks and to grease hinges, and as she dusted the castle's meager handful of treasures, she was thinking through all the ways she could sneak them out.

It was only a game, she told herself. It was only if she needed it.

One day in deepest, reddest autumn, the castle got word that a great and terrible wolf was coming to their home. The prince seemed to think he wanted gold, soldiers, power . . . but the dame looked at her daughter and knew the wolf hungered for something else.

The princess was not plain, but she was not pretty in a way that made creatures like the wolf feel good about themselves. If the wolf sought a huntress, he would find one in her.

But he did not want for a huntress. He wanted for a wife.

And the dame knew he would take what he wanted.

Before the wolf arrived, she hid all portraits of the princess, save for those from when she was but a sweet morsel of a babe. She took the last of the gold from the treasury. And she left.

When the dame returned, her hands were empty save for a string of enchanted pearls.

The maid watched as the pearls were clasped around the princess's neck. The maid saw them cut down the princess until she was small, sand down her edges until she was soft, bleed the color from her hair and eyes until they were faint remnants of what had been.

And the maid realized, once the pearls were locked tight, that she and the princess were friends again. They had always been friends, hadn't they? Why wouldn't she want such a lovely friend?

The dame's eyes welled with tears of joy and relief. "This will protect you," she told her daughter. "Men will be cruel, but they will be less cruel when you are beautiful."

"I don't want to marry him," the princess said. The tears in her eyes were neither of joy nor of relief.

"No one ever does." The dame made sure the clasp would not falter. After a long quiet, she said once more, "But beauty will protect you."

The wolf came to the castle. And the dame was right.

He sniffed around their doors and their rooms. He sniffed around their tables, their feasts. He sniffed around the princess's skirts. But he did not close his jaws, because the princess's beauty soothed him so.

Then that night, he found the maid, and sank his teeth into her, because she had no pearls to protect her. He left her bleeding in the hall when her only friend ran him off.

In the morning, the wolf announced he would carry the princess away for his bride, and she wept, and she, too, was learning to lie, because she called them tears of joy.

The maid did not weep, for she was the cleverest, coldest maid in Sovabin. She knew the prince and dame would send her with the princess to keep the wolf busy. She knew her godmothers were waiting for a moment just like this, when she was trapped without any hope but them.

I knew I would have to go to Minkja, or the von Falbirgs would cast me out in barren Sovabin. I knew the pearls would only protect Gisele for so long. There would be nothing, no one to protect me.

I knew from the scars on my back that Gisele would look the other way while Adalbrecht ate me alive. She would throw me to the wolves if it meant she would survive another day.

But she never suspected I, her loyal, obedient maid, would do the same.

CHAPTER TWENTY-TWO

The Thorns

By the time we get to my chambers, I can't decide if I want to forgive Gisele or tear the pearls off her neck.

Luckily, she does it for me, unclasping them the moment she steps inside. Her hair darkens, her silhouette fills out. There's a little rip as the seams of the gown are suddenly put to the test. "I forgot how much I hated this," Gisele says tightly, and tosses the pearls on the bed.

Without their charm blunting the edges of my resentment, I don't have to mull it over anymore; it's boiling quite well enough on its own. I begin untying my apron and say brusquely, "Adalbrecht knows about the pearls."

Gisele looks at me, then away, face hardening. "I don't care. I never asked for them."

But she sure cared when *I* wore them. I keep that to myself. "Did you notice anything useful at the ball?"

"I'd rather wait until the others get here."

Well, then. It seems I'm not the only one still harboring grudges.

I walk around her to go get a nightgown out of the dresser, because all I want to do is crawl into bed and not think about what happened tonight—with Adalbrecht, with Emeric, any of it. Then I think twice. Emeric will be here with Ragne in a moment, and even if I put a dressing gown on over the nightgown, I—I don't know that I want him to see me like that.

(It was different with the pearls. It wasn't *me*.)

I pull a plain kirtle out of the wardrobe instead. It's still one for a margravine-to-be, but it's soft, simple pine-green lambswool, meant for a quiet day in the library or a private stroll in the gardens. It'll be comfortable enough over the linen shift I'm already wearing.

"Ragne's sweet," Gisele starts, pauses, carries on. "And funny. She kept coming up with names for everyone. She called Anna von Morz the Scary Dress One, and Irmgard was the Smells-Like-Feet One."

I bark a laugh as I start unbuttoning the servant uniform. "Too bad she can't do all the wedding events. Give me a second, and you can put this on." This is the last part of the plan: The *prinzessin* retires early from the ball, though Adalbrecht will keep the festivities going until late in the night just to prove that he can. Joniza will wait around for Gisele so they can leave together, just as they arrived. (Joniza may also be having a rendezvous with her archnemesis. I'm not sure and I'm too afraid to ask.)

Gisele isn't listening. She's slowly pacing around the room, taking in the deep-blue plush carpet, the rivers of velvet curtains, the view of eastern Minkja spilling out beyond the Yssar. Her fingertips run over the bedposts, the vanity, the mantel above the hearth, careful as though it's all a spun-glass dream, breakable if she presses too hard.

More careful than she'd ever been with me.

The room—all of it, really—is a hundred times more lavish than anything she had in Sovabin. A thousand times more luxurious than the drafty, crowded Gänslinghaus. All of this would have been hers, if not for me.

But she's not wearing the pearls anymore, so they can't make me feel sorry.

I clear my throat and slip my arms out of the servant-dress sleeves, turning my back to her. "Hurry up Ragne and Emeric will be here soon."

Gisele's breath hitches. "Is that the curse?"

Damn it all. I forgot about the rubies on my spine. The thin shift's neckline is low enough on my back to let at least two or three peep over. "Yes."

"How long do you have?"

I suck in a breath, looking through the window at the half-moon staring back. "One week. Unless I make up for what I stole." I shimmy free of the servant uniform. "Turns out that's not as easy as it sounds."

Another quiet falls, and all I hear are the soft pops as Gisele undoes the buttons on her gown. Then she breaks the silence. "I spoke with Joniza about what you said before. I didn't understand—I didn't *see* how bad it was with my parents."

Liar, I want to scream, hands shaking even as I fold the uniform. She was there when they whipped me for the von Hirschings. But it's been a year since we left Sovabin. She's not the same. Neither of us is.

"I'm sorry," she says. "I should have stopped them."

I set the servant uniform on the bed, beside the pearls. Maybe she's learned. Maybe—maybe we can start to close these wounds. "We were young—"

"But you shouldn't have stolen this from me," Gisele continues over me, and my stomach drops. "You took everything, my name, my future, my *life*. You—"

I whirl around, practically spitting with fury. "None of this was yours. You talk like you were owed this but *none of it belongs to you*. You didn't earn your name, you didn't earn this life, there is nothing here except for what you were born into or loaned, and what *I* earned."

"What you stole!" she shouts back, wincing as she pulls the fake ruby off her face. "Do you think any of this belongs to you either?"

"You didn't even want it!"

"I didn't want to marry Adalbrecht! Don't you dare pretend that's the same!"

I can't believe how gullible I was, thinking she might have changed. "So you wanted all this, the jewelry, the dresses, the castle, the servants, as long as I was the one who paid for it, not you. Because that's what the *Weysserpfenni* is worth—"

"My own mother didn't think I was good enough for him," Gisele interrupts, climbing out of the heavy skirts. "She was ashamed of me, because she wanted a daughter like Irmgard."

"And I needed someone to protect me from Irmgard!" I storm over to collect the gown, *my* gown, and even in my rage I'm still taking care to fold it so it doesn't crease, because one year of living like Gisele cannot override ten years of serving her. "I needed someone to protect me from Ada*AAAAAAA*."

Something is wriggling in the skirts.

I drop them and leap back. A little fist-sized gray-white creature scrabbles from under the heap of red velvet. It's a tiny, horrible man, crawling like a crab, blue eyes blazing.

Gisele lets out a shriek.

Ragne bursts through the door, and it's my turn to let out a startled shriek.

Then Emeric tumbles in after Ragne, and Gisele and I both make panicked squawks and dive for the nearest dressing gown at the same time since we're both in nothing but our thin linen shifts, only to find ourselves both trying to yank it on. (A painfully apt metaphor.)

"Sorry—*sorry*—I'm not looking—" Emeric starts to back out of the room, spots the *nachtmahr*, and proceeds to visibly cycle through both fight and flight instincts at a speed heretofore unobserved in the common man. Meanwhile, there's a sound of tearing fabric, and then Ragne lands on the floor as a black lynx, the shreds of her uniform still clinging to her like a caul. One massive paw knocks the little *nachtmahr* from where it was darting toward the bed, then crashes down to keep it in place.

I give up on the dressing gown and grab a blanket, wrapping it around my shoulders. "I don't suppose any of us have bells. Junior, close the door." He does. I shoot him and Ragne a narrow look. "How long were you in the hall?"

"The Emeric said it sounded like an important conversation," Ragne yowls, batting the *mahr* back and forth as it whines, "and we should give you privacy, and we did, but then you screamed."

Emeric looks everywhere but at us.

No. I am not coming out of this night grudgingly liking the smug bastard. I refuse on yet another principle (which is: There's only room in this town for one smug bastard. That smug bastard is me).

Gisele gasps, and I discover I have a new problem.

The *nachtmahr* is swelling, almost bubbling, from a tiny man into some awful hybrid of human and horse. The skull warps ghoulishly, its limbs stretching like horse legs that still end in gray, gnarled hands. As it grows it screams, showing clusters of fangs long and thin as needles.

Ragne snarls, shuddering into a black-coated lioness, but this room was shockingly not designed for three humans, a lion, and a horse-man-monster. To make matters worse, Poldi flares up in the hearth, shouting a string of indignant insults.

"Stay there, Poldi," I shout as Ragne swipes at the now man-sized *mahr*. It wails and leaps for her jugular, but misses, biting into her shoulder instead. She screams, and my heart jumps into my throat.

"Vanja!" Emeric shouts.

I whip around to stare at him. What happened to *Miss Schmidt*?

"Catch——!" Emeric is trapped behind the bulk of lion-Ragne, but he tosses me one of his knives. I manage to snag it in a glimmer of good-luck gold. When I draw it from the sheath, I see it's the copper-coated blade. The one that wounded the *nachtmahr* in Lähl.

This *mahr* sees the penny-red flash and lets go of Ragne. It shakes its head at the knife, whining, tongue lolling, but Ragne and Emeric have blocked the door to the hall, and Poldi and I have the door to the veranda.

It lunges for Gisele.

I don't know what it is that moves me.

Maybe it's reflex, years of putting her first.

Maybe it's the cold lightning calculation of instinct: I have a knife and she does not.

Maybe it's the girl in the mirror, my ghost still haunting myself, the one who still clutches the dying taper of a hope that we can change, we can make it through the thorns, we can stop hurting each other.

I throw myself at the *mahr*. We crash to the floor. It's horridly clammy and almost sticky to the touch, its long fingers furiously yanking my hair into knots. I artlessly jam the copper knife into any part of it I can see, its belly, its eye, between its cracking ribs, until it gives a terrible, wheezing shudder and goes still.

I shove myself off and let the knife fall to the ground, bracing myself on my hands and knees. "All right, Poldi," I say between breaths, "do the honors."

"*You got it, Lady,*" the *kobold* says cheerily, and drags the carcass toward the hearth. There's a series of cracks, crunches, and sizzles that I truly do not wish to investigate.

A pair of impeccably polished boot toes come into view. I look up as Emeric crouches beside me, dropping the blanket back over my shoulders. There's an odd look on his face.

"Fine, maybe you're onto something with the horses," I croak.

He shakes his head, saying stiffly, "The rubies. On your . . ." He gestures to his own back. "They've disappeared."

I reach between my shoulders. The sharp line of rubies down my spine is gone.

"You saved the Gisele," Ragne adds, wincing as she limps over.

For a moment, I hang my head. It's one more reckoning I can't run from. Not anymore. I have to make up for what I took.

"I know how to break the curse," I admit. Then I straighten up and look to Gisele. "Eiswald said to make up for everything I've stolen, and it's not just the jewelry, it's *you*. I have to make it up to you. I have to return your name and give you your life back."

Gisele sits on the foot of the bed, stunned, as Emeric helps me to my feet.

Then she looks dead at me, eyes hard as steel, and says, "No."

THE
LOYAL
MAID

ONCE UPON A TIME, THERE LIVED A FAMILY HIGH IN THE MOUNTAINS, in a crumbling castle, with a daughter who everyone said was kind and wise, and would rule their principality well.

One day, when the daughter was fifteen, a wolf came to their door and whispered that he would gobble their castle up if he could not have her. And so her parents gave her a charm to protect her, and sold her to the wolf.

But in case the charm failed, they sent something else with her: her maid. You see, the wolf had a taste for young blood, and the maid was loyal. She had saved the family before when they needed to placate a cruel count, and perhaps she would save their daughter now.

Perhaps the wolf would eat the maid first, and be satisfied.

The wolf sent soldiers to collect the princess and her maid. They rode in silence for a long, long while, both wordless with fear.

The princess was afraid that she would not please the wolf, that he might trap her in his lair, that he might hurt her.

The maid knew all of those things would come to pass, and worse. And there would be not even a white penny to cling to after.

The maid had plenty of time to think about this, for it was a long way to the wolf's kingdom.

Then one sunset, when they were but a few days from Minkja, the princess could bear her troubles in silence no more. She told the soldiers she was going to the river to wash before dinner, and took her maid with her.

The maid watched as the princess cast her pearls onto the riverbank. The princess's dress tightened, seams stretching, and with a cry of frustration, the princess threw it to the ground too, caring not a whit for the mud that would need to be scrubbed out of the silk, the stitches redone, the buttons found and replaced.

To her, it was freedom.

To her maid, it was one more mess that would fall to her.

The princess dropped her purse and toilette and stormed to the water, tears burning down her cheeks. "I can't marry him! I'll have to go to balls and socials and all those awful parties with people I hate, and I'll have to pretend to like them for the *politics*, and I'll have to keep wearing the pearls for the rest of my life or he'll know I'm—me! I can *never* be me again!"

"That does sound miserable," the maid said tonelessly.

"He's twice my age, and I'm sure he'll want an heir as soon as possible, and Mama said it would be over soon and not to fight—" The princess wrapped her arms around herself, shivering. "I don't *want* him."

The maid was only half listening as she collected the gown and the pearls. The pearls tangled around her hand, smooth and lovely, and she wondered what it would be like to have a mother who would give everything to try to protect you. Even if it was the kind of protection you didn't want.

"I need my kerchief," the princess sniffled, and the maid brought it to her.

The maid saw the cambric shift the princess wore was much the same as her own. Almost identical.

"I can't marry him, Vanja. I don't love him. I—I don't think I can." The princess stared into the river, at the slices of peach and gold light carving into her own reflection, before splashing her face with the icy water. "You have to help me. You *have* to."

The maid didn't answer for a long moment. Then she said, cold and flat, "Fine."

Gisele did not see Death and Fortune standing between her and me on the riverbank that day. She didn't know how they lingered, reminding me that an easy solution lay before us. Death could strike the margrave down, Fortune could keep the wolf at bay through unlikely coincidences, but they would cost my freedom.

And I——I held the pearls.

There was nothing and no one to offer me protection in this world, so I would seize my own.

"I'll do it," I said. I had already climbed into Gisele's gown, and the moment the pearls clasped around my neck . . . it fit perfectly.

Gisele stared at me from the riverbank, mopping up her face. For a moment, she didn't understand. Or rather, she did, in a way that was all von Falbirg. "Oh, Vanja, you're *brilliant*. You can take my place when I need you to, like at a ball, or with . . . with the margrave, I'm sure you can——"

"No," I told her, running my hands over her dress——my dress. "Not *when you need me*. If you don't want this life, I'll take it. I'll take it all."

"That's not funny."

"I'm not joking." I pointed to the Falbirg servant uniform on the ground. They always made mine too big, in case I grew into it. "But I could use a maid now."

"You can't be serious," she sputtered. "Give the pearls back, Vanja. You'll never pass for me, you weren't trained as a lady."

I swept the perfect curtsy I'd watched her practice for years, a furious, toothy smile on my face. "Of course I was. You just didn't notice."

Gisele caught her breath. A flush rose to her cheeks. "Give them back. I'll call the guards."

A bone-deep stab of fear shot through me. Then an impossibly shiny platinum curl fell over my shoulder, and I remembered who I was now.

"Go ahead," I told her.

She screamed for help, haughty and angry and frightened, still oblivious to what it meant to lose the pearls. When the guards came running, I wrenched my face into a mask of hysteria and half stumbled to them first, claiming this madwoman had attacked me, that she was claiming to be the real princess, I was scared, so scared, *help me, please.*

They were Adalbrecht's soldiers all, and not a one of them knew Gisele's true face.

When Gisele shouted who she was, who her *parents* were, red-faced and weeping and clad in nothing but a muddy shift, she lived my lie to the letter.

"You're safe now, *Prinzessin*," one soldier told me, putting herself between me and the thunderstruck Gisele. "She can't hurt you."

"Go on now, leave Princess Gisele be," another guard shouted. "Go home."

She sank to her knees on the muddy riverbank, stunned.

She had always been believed.

I felt a weak stir of pity. It was no match for the years and years of bitterness, but it moved me to one final twist of the knife.

"Let us be charitable," I said gently, "even in times of crisis. Could someone please fetch me my purse?"

Three guards tried to do it at once. Once I had the purse in hand, I opened it and walked over to Gisele.

"Vanja," she whispered. "Don't do this. Please."

I handed her a single white penny.

It would be enough to take her to town, at least.

And then I returned to camp with Adalbrecht's soldiers, and did not look back.

No one asked where Gisele's maid went. Yannec was busy trying to grease up friends among the officers, and Joniza wouldn't leave Sovabin for another week. No one even remembered my name.

The loyal maid was gone.

And a few days later, Gisele-Berthilde Ludwila von Falbirg, future margravine of Bóern, arrived in Minkja to walk into the wolf's jaws herself.

CHAPTER TWENTY-THREE

The Safest Way

I STARE AT GISELE, UTTERLY WINDED. "*NO?* I'M GIVING YOU EVERY-thing!"

"I don't want it. All tonight did was remind me how miserable I was," Gisele says. "Everyone here hates everyone else, and they all think they're smarter and better because they're playing these stupid games to try to tear everyone else down. It's disgusting. I don't want to go back."

I'm rapidly trading astonishment for fury. "Then why are you even mad at me? You *still* don't want this life!"

"Because you took it from me!" Gisele balls her fists in the sheets. "You didn't ask what I wanted. Maybe I would have agreed to something like this, maybe we could have figured something out, but it wasn't your choice to make!"

"I, er. I'll wait outside." Emeric starts scooting toward the veranda door.

Ragne sits up straight, tail lashing and nostrils flaring. "The margrave is coming."

"*Scheit*, already?" I mutter. The *mahr* hasn't been dead for more than a minute or two. "I'll handle him. You." I point at Gisele and swipe Emeric's cloak and scarf from the ground where he'd dropped them coming in. "Give me the dressing gown. And you." I toss Emeric his belongings. "It's too cold out for the veranda. Take Ragne and hide in the wardrobe. Ragne, be a squirrel or something." She shrinks into a black cat and leaps into Emeric's arms as he heads for the wardrobe, and I internally scream at the fact that I've just ordered him into a tight space with my underthings, but there's no time to walk it back now.

I peel the plaster off my ruby teardrop, grab the pearls, trade Gisele the blanket I've been wearing, yank on the dressing gown, and clasp on the pearls just as there's a thunderous knock at the door. It flies open a moment later.

I'm starting to really enjoy the alarm on Adalbrecht's face when he realizes, once again, his naive, empty-headed teenage fiancée has somehow waltzed around a trap.

"My—my dewdrop," he stammers. "I was told there were screams."

I've made a very deliberate calculation: There's no point in pretending I didn't see the monster he just sicced on us. Instead I bury my face in my hands, shuddering. "Oh, it was *dreadful*! There was a hideous little beast in my skirts, and it tried to—it tried to—" I burst into heaving, dramatic sobs.

"There, there." He awkwardly pats my head. "Are you sure you didn't just imagine it, dearest? Your nerves must be in quite a state after such a busy night. Perhaps you nodded off and had a bad dream."

Is he *serious*? I have rug burns and bloodstains from tackling that thing, and he thinks—no, this is how men like him work. They do something wretched and try to convince you it wasn't that bad, then pretend it never happened at all.

Instead I point a quaking finger at the gore-splattered fireplace he's conveniently ignored. "If Poldi hadn't saved me . . ."

The *kobold* salutes us with a dismembered horse hand.

A vein jumps in Adalbrecht's brow. "That's . . . dreadful," he manages to squeeze out between gritted teeth. "I'll go tell the guards to keep alert. We wouldn't want anything happening to the guests."

"Of course," I snivel.

"You. Clean this up." He snaps his fingers at Gisele, then waves at the mess of ruined fabric and blood on the carpet. "I want this room spotless for my lady."

Gisele stares at him with a look I remember from the riverbank.

Just over a year ago, he upended both of our lives, demanding her for a wife.

Now he doesn't even know who she is.

A faint disgruntled hiss slides from the wardrobe. *Damn* it, Ragne, not now. Adalbrecht starts, looking around for the source.

"One of the castle mousers ran in the wardrobe," I say quickly.

"Then get it out of there before I have to replace all your gowns."

"Of course, darling." Why do I feel like I'm apologizing? "Hilde's just had quite a shock, but everything will be put back in order soon."

Gisele snaps out of it and bobs a quick curtsy. She hasn't yet figured out to keep her head down as she adds, "Yes, right away, sir."

It should have been *m'lord*, but Adalbrecht seems to be too preoccupied to notice. He heads toward the door. "Oh, and, dewdrop," he says, catching the doorframe. "Do keep this to yourself. We wouldn't want to cause the guests unnecessary worry either."

Then he's gone. I resist the urge to kick the door shut after him, and make myself wait until I hear the guards shout a salute to close it.

"You can come out—actually, stay in there a moment, please." I toss Gisele the servant uniform, then discard the pearls again and pull the green kirtle on over my shift. This will be a lot easier if we're not trading blankets and dressing gowns.

"I do not like the margrave," Ragne seethes from inside the wardrobe. "I do *not* like how he speaks to you both."

"And, you know, the murder stuff." I fasten buttons as quickly as I can. "At least we learned something. He may be sending the *nachtmären*, but he's not, er, mentally connected to them once they're dispatched."

"How do you figure?" Emeric's voice is muffled behind the doors. Saints and martyrs, I hope he's not looking at anything too embarrassing.

I glance to Gisele. She's almost done with her buttons, so at least I can address the wardrobe situation. I yank open the doors and give Emeric a hand out as Ragne hops down. "The *mahr* was hiding in Gisele's dress. It could have easily killed us the moment we were alone, so why didn't it? Why wait until I found it, unless it was there to spy on us?"

"A reasonable assumption." Emeric brushes a stocking off his elbow that we both are pretending isn't there. "But if they're his eyes and ears—"

I hold up a finger. "Adalbrecht got here too fast. There's no way one of the guards made it down to the ballroom, got his attention, and brought him up here, all in a few minutes. So yes, I think he can feel when one of his *nachtmären* dies, because he bolted up here to check himself. But I *don't* think he can see and hear through them in the moment, I think they have to make it back to report. Because that nasty piece of work"—I point to the fireplace, where Poldi is merrily cracking open vertebrae like chestnuts—"heard me arguing with Gisele. And if it had passed that along to Adalbrecht, he would have known *exactly* who Gisele was when he saw her."

Emeric gets a peculiar look on his face. "That's . . . a very astute point."

"Yes, I make them sometimes." I look around and find Ragne flopped by the hearth, still as a cat. "Ragne? What do you need for your shoulder?"

"I heal when I change my shape," she yawns, "but it makes me tired. I will make sure the Gisele and the Joniza get home safely, and then I will come back here and sleep, a lot."

"Before you go, Princess Gisele—did you notice anything at the ball?" asks Emeric.

Gisele purses her lips. "The noble families in attendance are from all over the southern empire. Even some three or more territories away. But the only Free Imperial State representatives are—"

"*OHHH* they're Bóern's neighbors!" I finish in a rush, frantically swatting Emeric on the arm. "I noticed that too!"

"*Must* you?" He swivels out of range.

"No, Junior—the list from the study, the border towns—"

The match strikes for him. He digs out his makeshift notebook and thumbs through until he finds my copied list. "We'll need a map to confirm, but I'm pretty sure these all border Free Imperial States. What are the odds he has something unpleasant planned for the attending heads of state?"

"Decent," I say grimly.

Emeric studies the list, thinking; I see one hand stray to the pocket where he keeps his prefect coin. Then he sighs. "Hubert may have some ideas . . . but I don't think there's much more we can do tonight."

"And I need to get back the Gänslinghaus to help Umayya." Gisele shakes her head. "I wish I could help you with the curse, Vanja, I really do, but if you're supposed to make up for what you took, I don't see how giving my name back will fix anything. You'd just be forcing me into a life I don't want." She looks at the hearth. "Miss Ragne, if you're ready."

Part of me wants to scream at her. Part of me knows she's right, and I hate it.

I know in my gem-studded bones I have to give her name back to break the curse. But if she doesn't want it . . . Eiswald said she gave me this curse for my greed. And it would be pure selfishness to drag Gisele back just to save my own skin.

By the time I shovel out enough frustration to make my way to a witty comeback, Gisele is already gone, and Ragne with her. Emeric is tactfully bundling himself into his cloak and scarf without a word.

Right. This is the last part of the plan: I get him out of the castle, then I get to go crawl into bed—no, I need to scrub the blood out of the carpet and get Poldi his grits, and *then* I get to crawl into bed and really, *really* not think about what's happened tonight.

I grab a warm woolen shawl from the wardrobe and head for the veranda door. "Come on, this is the safest way out."

Emeric narrows his eyes. "*Is it*, though?"

That startles a laugh from me. "I'm not dropping you into the Yssar this time, so yes. Besides, Poldi's busy."

The *kobold* pointedly snaps a femur in two from the fireplace. "*Not too busy.*"

Clouds have rolled in, and it's snowing again when I step out, hop over the balustrade, and swing onto the trellis, picking my way around the roses. Emeric is watching me, shaking his head in disbelief. "Again: the *safest* way?"

"Just watch out for thorns." I make it to the bottom and wait as he clambers down after me, grumbling curses when his cloak periodically catches despite his best efforts. Once he sets foot on the ground, I catch his shoulder before he takes too big a step back and plunges off the narrow bank.

Emeric stares at the minuscule strip of dirt between the castle wall and the river. Then he looks back up at the trellis. "This is absurd, Miss Schmidt. This is how you get in and out?"

I'm a bit disappointed that we've gone back to "Miss Schmidt," but it would take a knife to my throat to make me admit it. "I took the other way when I was poisoned," I tell him. "Lots of stairs, lets out onto a pathway behind the waterfall that's solid ice this time of year. You saw how that panned out. Now keep your back to the wall and start scooting."

"How have you survived doing this for a year?" he asks under his breath as we inch along.

I snort into the frosty air. "Sheer belligerence, mostly."

"I believe it."

For a moment there's only the scrape of cloth on limestone. Eventually I ask: "What happens if Pap—if Klemens decides to arrest me?"

"Then I will make a very persuasive argument that your assistance has been . . ." Emeric sighs. "Extremely unorthodox, frequently indecent, but nevertheless irreplaceable. Hubert's a pragmatist. I can probably get him to hold off for now."

"I don't like 'probably.'"

"Well, it's what I have." He lets out a breath as we turn a corner and finally reach the wider part of the bank.

"I don't suppose I could convince Klemens to retire early."

Emeric's eyes flash. "No."

I shush him, lowering my voice to a whisper. "It's a joke, Junior." Then I point to a nearby wall. "That's the barracks, and the other buildings you'll pass might be occupied too, so keep it down. You can hop the wall onto the Hoenstratz viaduct at the bottom of the hill. People mostly use this path in the summer, so try not to draw too much attention to yourself."

Emeric frowns at the rocky track. "What do they use it for?"

"It's nicknamed the Lovers' Road," I say dryly. "Take a guess."

"Ah." It's too dark to tell if he's blushing, but the snowflakes catching in his hair almost seem to melt a bit quicker. He starts down the path, then pauses and turns back to me. "Are you going to be all right? On your own?"

One of these days, he's going to stop catching me in the throat with these questions, but it isn't tonight.

"I usually am," I say, with the quickest tremor in my voice. It's a betrayal, a confession I never intended to give, and it hangs between us like his breath clouding the air. He's looking up at me through the falling snow, silent and unsure.

I—I need to get out of the cold. "Don't fall and die."

Then I vanish around the corner before I can think too hard about the look on his face, the same peculiar one from before.

I make it back to my bedroom fine, because I've done this for a year, because I'm *fine* on my own. Besides, I still have to clean up the mess the *nachtmahr* left, and get Poldi his grits and honey. I run my hands through my hair, let out a long, long breath, and go to dig up a fresh face plaster and a servant uniform.

It takes a trip down to the kitchens to fetch a bucket of water and Poldi's dinner, made even longer because I have to detour around a couple who have turned the nearest servant corridor into their own personal Lovers' Road. I elect to cut past the entrance hall on the way back. Adalbrecht's voice thunders down the hall as I draw near. Doubtless he's stationed himself there to see off the guests who aren't staying in the castle.

Then I almost trip as another voice echoes back to me, clipped and precise and completely unexpected.

". . . mishap at the outpost, and I find myself in need of lodgings, sir. I thought I would see if your gracious offer of hospitality was still open."

He *didn't*.

I don't run, because you don't run with a bucket of water in one hand and a bowl of grits in the other unless you want to spend a long time cleaning up both. Instead I walk *very quickly* toward the entrance hall and peer around a corner.

Sure enough, Emeric is there, futzing with his scarf. He must have doubled back after—but—but—Adalbrecht's tried to kill both of us now and it's not safe for him here—what is he *thinking?*

Adalbrecht laughs like a wave crashing. He claps Emeric on the shoulder so hard his spectacles nearly fly off. "Of course, boy. Want me to dig up the little ginger wench?"

Oh no. I try to edge away.

"Not necessary," Emeric says quickly. "Sir."

"Are you sure?" Adalbrecht looks around and spots me. "Look, there she is now. Girl! Get over here."

Emeric looks about as appalled as I feel, ears turning brilliant scarlet. "Really, sir," he says, "I just—"

"She can show you to a guest room." The margrave's not giving a suggestion.

"Right away, m'lord." I bob a quick curtsy, glaring daggers at Emeric. "Follow me, sir."

Another group of guests comes along to distract Adalbrecht, and I take the opening to stalk as indignantly as I can up the stairs to the riverfront wing, Emeric trailing behind me. It's not that I don't understand why he's doing this, I just don't *want* to understand why he's doing this.

I'm fine on my own here. I'm *fine*.

I leave the bucket by my door and march us to the neighboring room. I know it's empty because I've made sure it's empty as long as I've been here, rather than risk someone witnessing me scale the trellis. Sure enough, the door swings open to chilly, undisturbed dark. Poldi pops up in the hearth and sets about helping himself to the logs stacked nearby.

"You are an absolute fool, Emeric Conrad," I tell him, because I will not admit I'm glad he's here, with or without a knife to my throat.

A tired, crooked, *insufferably* smug smile slips over his face, one that says he knows anyway. He heads inside, shrugging off his cloak. "Then it must be nice not being the only one for a change. Good night, Miss Schmidt."

CHAPTER TWENTY-FOUR

FARE FOR THE FERRYMAN

THE DOOR CLOSES, AND I STOMP BACK TO MY ROOM, DEEPLY ANNOYED
with him and even more deeply perturbed at the odd feeling in the
pit of my stomach. I drop Poldi's grits and honey on the hearth. When
he arrives for them, I'm sponging blood out of the carpet.

"*You want me to toss that boy in the river again?*" Poldi asks, seating
himself on the hearthstones.

I shake my head, putting perhaps a little too much enthusiasm into
scrubbing out the blood. "Not . . . not tonight."

Ragne returns as an owl a few minutes later. I was starting to get
worried, though that's pretty high up on the list of things I won't admit
without a death threat. She wings over to a spare nightshirt I've left on
a chair for her and crawls in, emerging a moment later as a human.

"I have another question," she declares, sitting up. "If I put my mouth on a human's face, is it still a kiss?"

I squint at her. "Aren't you supposed to be sleeping, a lot?"

"I will soon. I am very tired." She rubs her eyes. "But is that still a kiss?"

"Uh. Well. It depends where. If you put your lips on someone else's lips, we usually just call that a kiss."

Ragne shakes her head and taps her cheek. "Here?"

"That's being kissed on the cheek."

"I see." She flops back into the chair. "Then I kissed the Gisele on the cheek! And she kissed me, the plain kind. It was very strange and I liked it."

I pause scrubbing to blink up at her. "You . . . she . . . plain as in on the mouth?"

"Yes!"

"With . . . *Gisele?*"

"Yes!"

Many, many pins on *that* lock click into place.

I mean—I need to speak with Gisele first, to make sure I'm not assuming things, but . . . the Prince and Dame von Falbirg were atrociously clear about one thing growing up: The best Sovabin could offer was royal lineage. Gisele's dowry was little more than the promise of an heir who would be eligible to be elected emperor by the *Kronwähler*. But if Gisele prefers girls, the candidate pool would be severely limited, leaving only the few noblewomen able to conceive with her. No wonder she hadn't told her parents.

But I'm jumping to a *lot* of conclusions. There's one thing I know for sure. "Ragne, you know how humans make things complicated when they don't have to be?"

"Very," she says, curling up in the chair.

"Who you kiss is one of them. We should both talk to Gisele before telling anyone else. She might want to keep it to herself. Does that make sense?"

Ragne looks a little forlorn, resting her head sideways on her knees. "I think it does. I would like to kiss her again, though."

I think about the look on Gisele's face when she'd spoken of Ragne earlier. "I'd bet she'd like that too."

Then I push myself up to empty the bloody water off the veranda. I can't help sneaking a glance at Emeric's windows next door; there's a dim light through the sheer curtains and a silhouette hunched over a desk. I hurry back inside. Ragne is coiled in the chair, nodding off.

"Don't fall asleep like that, you'll hurt your neck." I change into a nightshirt myself, douse every candle but one, and crawl into bed. A moment later Ragne climbs up as a cat, settling against my shins. I'm too used to it by now to even pretend a protest.

Instead I search under the pillows until I find soft, sturdy leather and the crinkle of parchment I've kept hidden there for almost a week now.

I tell myself I'm reading through Emeric's stolen notes to make sure there's nothing we're missing. Not because I can hear them in his voice, see him twirling a stick of charcoal around his fingers before adding another line. Not because it reminds me he's one room away, that he came back to the house of a man trying to kill him just so I wouldn't be left on my own.

Not because all of those things are comforting in an entirely terrifying way.

Perhaps a drop of Augur's Tears lingers in me still, though. Because I must tell you the truth of the matter: I fall asleep by the dwindling candle, thinking of the moment before he threw the copper knife, when he called me by my name.

❧

After breakfast the next morning, I decide to give the notes back.

Is it motivated, at least a little, by the fact that rashes of pearls have broken out over my elbows? Maybe so. I think I'm starting to connect the dots on the curse: At least a few gems disappear every time I do something, well, selfless. Like rescuing Fabine from the Wolfhunder, or throwing myself at the *nachtmahr*. I think they're growing no matter what, but they seem to grow faster when I do something self-interested, let's put it that way.

That would explain why my charitable spree last week was for naught; it was all just to help myself. And maybe giving the notes back won't change a thing either, but it feels like—ugh, I can't believe I'm saying this, *who am I*—it feels like the right thing to do.

Unfortunately, it gets a bit more difficult when Emeric doesn't answer his door. I've prepared a short and scathing speech (*I've decided you need these after all, you're clearly helpless without them* is about the gist of it) and come up with a decent ruse (the journal is tucked into a stack of towels that I, Marthe the Maid, am delivering to his room). But I knock once, twice, and there's no answer.

Trudl pokes her head out of another room down the hall. We're due for another wave of guests this evening, and every bed in the castle must be ready. "You can go in. The prefect's not there."

"Junior prefect," I correct before I can catch myself. I decide we're all going to pretend that didn't happen. "He's not in?"

"Hurried out a little after sunrise. Said he got some urgent message or something."

Klemens. He must have arrived.

Trudl misreads the dismay on my face. "Don't worry, he'll be back. The margrave is having us hold the room for him."

She garnishes that with a wink that says word has gotten around about the linen closet incident. *Fantastic.* Just what I need.

I hurry back to my room and toss the extra towels on a chair. I suppose I'll have to face Prefect Klemens one way or another, and perhaps if I graciously return Emeric's notes in his presence, that whole "reformed thief" concept will be easier to pitch.

"We're going into town," I tell Ragne, who, true to her word, even slept through breakfast. At least Adalbrecht had the mercy to let everyone dine in their own rooms; it had to be hellish for the servants, running all those trays up and down the stairs, but working around dozens of hungover and petulant nobles in one of the dining halls would have been worse.

Ragne stretches, cat tail curling, as I shove Emeric's notes into a satchel. "Will we go see the Gisele?"

"We have to find the outpost for the Order of Prefects first. But probably later." I can't hold down a smile. There's something downright sweet about how happy Ragne seems. "You really like her, don't you?"

"Yes." Ragne rolls in a blanket and sits up as human, looking at me earnestly. "I know you don't like her. Are you mad with me?"

I think for a moment, adding the usual suspects to my satchel: playing cards, dice, a knife. "I used to be her friend," I say. "We might be friends again someday. But we both hurt each other. We both *decided* to. And when someone decides to hurt you, no matter how much you like them, it changes things. So no, I'm not mad at you. I mean, your mother cursed me to die, and we're still fr—" I cut myself off.

It's too late. Ragne's face lights up. "Are we friends?"

A week ago I would have thrown *myself* into the Yssar before saying yes. But it's been a long week, and she's been with me for most of it. "Yes, fine, we're friends," I grumble. "Even if you have terrible taste in sweethearts."

"*I* think she tastes—"

I clap my hands over my ears. "*NOPE*. Don't need to hear it."

I leave a message with Franziska that the *prinzessin* is not to be disturbed and head out the gates, waving to the guards as I pass. I have to mind my step; it kept snowing overnight, and while the roads have been cleared, icy patches make the walk downhill more treacherous. Ragne clings to my wool cap as a black sparrow, ready to fly off if I slip.

Thanks to the ice, I make it to the Göttermarkt a little more slowly than I like. It's been transformed in the last few days: The plaza itself has been emptied of bonfires, penitents, and pilgrims, and all the remaining *sakretwaren* stalls have been squashed up against the temples themselves. The clamor has been replaced by the sounds of work crews making over the plaza itself, ringed in a crowd of onlookers and temple-goers.

Easily the greatest attraction is the three ceremonial houses that have been erected for the wedding. Normally they're little tents or quick sheds slapped together, but Adalbrecht of course would not settle for anything less than tiny hollow palaces, and from the looks of it, that's what he's getting. The two smaller ones on the north and south sides of the plaza are to represent House Falbirg and House Reigenbach, and the large, open-faced one over an altar on the east end is for the houses united. There's another platform being constructed at the western end of the plaza, but it must be for a Bóernische custom, because I don't recognize it at all.

I stop by a *sakretwaren* stall for directions, then wind through the crowd, past the temples of Yssar and Time and the Spindle-dam. I can't help but notice the flash of coin and blur of coal at the cathedral of Fortune around a corner, but I give that a wide berth.

Finally I find a steadfast little building wedged between the temples of Justice and the Knight Unseen, looking as hardy as its granite keystones and weathered as the heavy oak door. Over the lintel is a bronze plaque with the scales, skull, and scroll of the Order of Prefects. A barred window overlooks the street, but I can't see anyone inside.

I climb the handful of steps and try the handle. The door opens to a little waiting area lit by thin bars of glowing metal. I'd bet it's the same enchanted pewter as Emeric's coin. There's a desk nearby with a mug of cold coffee and scattered parchment, set up like a reception clerk's, but no one's in the seat. Empty benches line the opposite wall.

A hallway bends out of sight, but muffled voices seep from it like watered-down ink, too indistinct to make sense of yet. I take a deep breath, trying to memorize the layout—the desk, the benches, most importantly the door—in case Prefect Klemens decides a cooperative thief is still a liability and I need to make a quick exit. Unless I'm mistaken, wisps of misfortune are gathering in the corners. Maybe that's just a bad omen that comes with me being inside a law enforcement office. Maybe it's worse.

Then one of the voices rises, and I hear it clear and stark as day.

". . . *should have BEEN THERE!*"

I've never heard Emeric so—broken.

I'm moving before I know it, following his voice with the same kind of weightless purpose that carried me in the Madschplatt. I rush down the hall and find him in a simple little parlor, pacing furiously as another person tries in vain to hand him a kerchief. He keeps running his hands over his face, pushing his spectacles up into his hair. "It's my fault, *I* told him we could split up like usual, *I* told him I could handle this, there's no one to blame but—"

Ragne chirps from my shoulder, and Emeric finally looks up.

There's a strange kind of horror in seeing someone cry for the first time. From the looks of it, he's been at it a while, eyes bloodshot, breath ragged, a faint film of salt speckles on his spectacles.

I'm not supposed to see him like this, raw in a way that feels irreversible. It's even worse watching him try to pull himself together, like someone walking on a broken ankle. "V—Miss Schmidt," Emeric says unevenly, "I, I'm afraid—now is—"

"What happened?" I ask. Ragne flies over to perch on his wrinkled collar, combing his hair with her beak.

He swallows. "They . . . f-found . . ." He can't keep going, covering his face again.

"Prefect Hubert Klemens was found deceased early this morning," the other person says quietly, and finally manages to shove their handkerchief into Emeric's hand. "In the Stichensteg islets."

I suck in a breath. "It wasn't an accident."

"Our coroner is making an assessment." The stranger brushes off their uniform, which is simpler than Emeric's, though it also bears the insignia of the prefects. A pair of silver-threaded prayer-cords drape over their shoulders, lopsided and too fine for everyday wear. More likely they were interrupted at morning prayer, and they haven't had a moment to put the cords away. They tilt their head at me, almost birdlike. "I apologize, but who are you?"

"She's . . ." Emeric clears his throat. "She's a consultant. Miss Schmidt, this is Ulli Wagner. They're the head clerk at this outpost."

"And this is Ragne." I point to where she's still perched on Emeric. "Eiswald's daughter. Sometimes she's a bear."

Ulli raises their eyebrows as a soft chime hums through the room. "I see. Conrad, that's the coroner. I'll be right back." They slip out the door.

There's a dull, aching silence. Then I can't help myself; I put a hand on Emeric's sleeve. "Hey. Junior. Whoever did this, they don't stand a chance. You had me figured out before you even got to Minkja, now you've got me and Ragne to help. And *she* can turn into a bear."

He lets out a shaky breath, and I don't know if it's a laugh, but it might be in the same genus, and I can work with that.

Ulli returns with a grim-faced woman in a doctor's apron and gloves who I surmise is the coroner. She hesitates at the sight of me. "Conrad, is . . . is this your . . . ?"

Emeric recoils from me like he's been caught red-handed in the candy jar. "Just—just my consultant," he rasps hastily, all but hiding the arm I'd touched behind his back. "For this case. I'll vouch for her."

I manage a wordless nod. In the last ten seconds I've whipped from sympathy to embarrassment to indignation to a mélange of all three, garnished with a flicker of bewildering warmth at being vouched for. Any attempt at articulating that is going to come out as a mortal scream.

"Very well." The coroner removes her gloves and produces her own notebook. "We're still conducting the standard tests, but preliminary findings suggest Prefect Hubert Klemens's death was a homicide. The cause of death seems to be a single knife wound to the heart. A prefect-issue knife was left in the wound, so it's likely to be our murder weapon."

"One of his own?" Ulli asks as Emeric covers his mouth with his hand.

The coroner tilts her head. "At this point, I say yes. It was the iron knife, and that was the only one missing from his set. Furthermore . . ."

This, I realize later, is when I should have listened to Fortune's warning.

Cloudy misfortune begins to press in at the edges of my sight. I can't fathom why, and despite everything, I don't want to leave. Not now, not with Emeric like this. He came back for me last night, I owe him this much.

". . . it's custom to leave coins for the Ferryman on the closed eyes of the deceased . . ."

Ice locks around my heart. I remember Emeric in the alley last week, laying out the facts of Yannec's death: *His own knife.*

". . . however, we found a single red penny . . ."

Your signature *penny in his mouth.*

". . . in his throat."

My breath catches.

When I look to Emeric, he's staring at me, face marble-pale.

"I don't—I couldn't—" I stammer.

Emeric's voice goes thin as a razor and sharper still. "A red penny?"

I take a step back. He catches me by the forearm.

My heartbeat rattles my veins faster and faster. The words come out pitchy, and *scheit*, it sounds too much like my gobsmacked yokel voice but it's real, it's real, it's too real. "It wasn't me, I didn't go any-where last night, I don't, I *didn't*—"

I am back in Castle Falbirg, I am swearing I am not a thief—

There's a terrible, betrayed fury in Emeric's face. "How long have you been lying to me?"

"I'm not, I swear!" *Don't panic don't panic don't panic—*

"What did you do to him?"

Ragne drops between us, a snarling black wolf. Emeric lets go as Ulli and the coroner stumble back into a couch.

I can't breathe. They don't believe me, they won't ever believe me, I'm going to get caught, I'm going to—going to—

Break my own most vital rule.

I panic.

And I run.

PART THREE:

THE
RUBY
PRICE

ᴅesᴘeʀaᴛıon

I BOLT DOWN THE HALL, INTO THE WAITING ROOM, OUT THE DOOR, into the street. There's a thunder of footfalls behind me. I know Emeric's at my heels.

If I don't get out, he'll be at my throat.

My mind is plummeting through a sickening red fog, trapped in a panicked free fall, allowing only one thought:

Get away, get out, fast as you can, run, run, run—

Ragne swoops over my shoulder, a raven now. "Follow," she croaks, soaring toward a side street. I tear after her.

Coal-dust bad luck swirls around me like a dirty blizzard.

"STOP!" Emeric's voice rips down the lane. I don't look back. *"STOP HER!"*

I duck around a woman pushing a cart, then nearly run into a construction worker carrying buckets of nails toward the plaza. I don't think, just kick one hard enough to launch nails into the street in my wake. Emeric will have to slow down unless he wants one through the boot.

There's a flurry of cursing, and I know it worked. Ragne takes me around another hard corner, then another, breaking Emeric's line of sight as many times as we can; timbers and doorsteps and window boxes full of frostbitten dead stalks all bleed into a fleeting blur. My lungs burn. My heartbeat slams around my ears like an angry drunk. I don't dare slow down, even for a breath.

"Up," Ragne caws, and I see she's led me to the Hoenstratz viaduct. The road above might be clear enough for her to take the horse shape, and then I can—I don't know, I can think of something—I just need to get away—

"Look out!"

Ragne drops onto my shoulder as a cat, knocking me off balance. I stumble out of the way of a ball of silvery light that's buzzing like a hornet.

It sinks into Ragne's side instead. She lets out a startled chirp and goes limp.

I catch her before she falls, and I—I don't have time to describe how relieved I am when she blinks up at me. But only her eyes move, and slowly at that.

I see Emeric's dark head weaving through the crowd down the street. Half of me wants to run until I've cleared Minkja. Half of me wants to stay behind solely so I can strangle him for whatever he's done to Ragne.

I don't have time for strangling, and I don't know if Ragne does either. I sprint for the stairs to the viaduct, drawing odd looks from people who just see a frantic girl clutching a motionless black cat.

The stone steps are a mess of ice and frozen slush. I try to pick my way up as fast as I can. I'm halfway there when I hear a scuffle below, and I twist to look back.

"*Stop!*" Emeric shouts up at me, eyes blazing with witch-ash glow, still in just his shirtsleeves. The damned fool didn't even bother putting on a jacket. "You can't run from me!"

A second later, he and I both discover that's regrettably accurate.

My boot lands on a patch of ice and skates out from under me. I just barely manage to dump Ragne on a step before I bang down the rest and crash into Emeric. We hit the ground with a crunch.

The sharp smell of juniper spikes the air—followed by blood. Emeric lets out a startled hiss of pain beneath me. Broken glass slides from his left hand, spilling silvery witch-ash oil and stained in red. His vial must have shattered in the fall.

I don't even know if he feels the gashes as he swipes for me. I grab his bloody wrist, only to miss his right hand when it clamps around my collarbone, dragging me down. He wrenches us around to pin me to the ground this time. The weight of him drives me into the filthy snow, cold rivulets of melted slush jabbing in at every hem. He lets go of my shoulder, only to catch my free wrist in an iron grip.

"Let me *go*, I didn't—" I spit, that choking red cloud closing in again as I thrash and try to push him off, to no avail. "You hurt Ragne! What did you do to her?"

Emeric jerks back an inch, alarm darting through his face, only to ice over into cold rage once more. "She'll be fine, it's a paralysis spell. *I'm* not a killer. What did you do to Klemens?"

"*Nothing!*"

"*STOP LYING TO ME!*"

I stare at him, at the burn of witch-ash in his eyes, at his crystal clear conviction that no matter what I say, I am guilty, I am a murderer, I am a liar.

I am one of the little thieves, and he will send me to the gallows himself.

I don't know how I ever thought I could trust him. I don't know why I thought I might—

He was right about one thing last night: It was nice, for a moment, to not be the only fool.

A drop of blood slides over my fingers, the ones wrapped around his left wrist. I see beads of witch-ash oil still marbling his knuckles.

I have to get out, whatever it takes.

I yank his hand closer and flick my tongue over his bloody palm.

It has two immediate effects: One, Emeric goes completely still, gazing down at me not with anger, but something I don't think either of us know, a sudden, stunned desperation.

Two: A thorn of juniper oil sizzles in my mouth, tempered in gritty witch-ash and the tang of blood.

I feel the ash dissolve to lightning in my teeth. I'm not trained in the methods to properly cast magic, but power is power. The cantrips and rituals just make it stronger, lessen the kickback, grease the wheels.

So I glare up at Emeric and gasp, *"Piss off."*

And the magic does the rest.

There's a *crack*. He's thrown off, but I don't see where he lands, because the kickback hits like a sucker punch. I roll onto my knees just in time to vomit into the snow, a fever and a chill ramming down my veins and turning my muscles to little better than wet clay. Belatedly, I remember Emeric mentioning something about the potency of the prefects' witch-ash, but it's too late for takebacks now.

I make myself stand and stagger up the stairs, wheezing, braids swinging, tides of gray ebbing in my vision. My hat is gone, and if my satchel hadn't been buttoned up, I would have lost everything in it too.

I think I twisted my ankle because it keeps twinging, but I can't stop, can't stop, if I stop he'll catch me, if I stop it'll be the lash all over again.

Ragne is still a soft heap of fur on the icy steps. I scoop her up and force my burning legs to carry us the rest of the way to the viaduct. Carts and carriages rattle past, wheels clattering against the stone. I walk as fast as I can until at least I've caught my breath a little, then I make myself run again, trying to keep clear of icy patches. I keep looking back, but I can't see Emeric on my trail.

Some tiny part of me can't help worrying I might have seriously hurt him. I don't know what I'm doing with magic, I just wanted him to let go, what if—

It's the same part of me that just wanted Dame von Falbirg, Death, Fortune, *anyone* to treat me as a daughter. It's the lantern at the crossroads, stealing away into the dark. Nothing waits for me down that road.

The world narrows to my thudding heartbeat, my lungs on fire, step after step after painful step.

And then I make it. I see the wooden sign, the painted daisies that suddenly make sense. Gisele always loved daisies best.

I don't notice how quiet the Gänslinghaus is when I pound on the door. How the only faces peering out windows are on the second floor.

The door swings open. Gisele is there, pale and tense. "What—"

"Help me, please," I nearly sob. "I need somewhere to hide."

Gisele glances off to the side, then nods. "Come in."

"Thank you, I'm so sorry, it's just, just until Ragne wakes up . . ." I nearly trip over the doorstep. The warmth of the front room is such a relief I want to cry, so warm my fingers burn coming in from the cold.

So warm I miss the clinging dusty misfortune dimming my sight.

"What's wrong with Ragne?" Gisele's voice sharpens as the door closes behind us.

Then I hear a deadbolt slide into place.

"Nothing." Emeric's voice rasps across the room.

I spin around. He's by the front door, pale and bloody and shaking. He's been here the whole time.

He knew I'd come.

Of course he did, because he knows better than anyone that I have nowhere else to go.

I look to the kitchen—the long table has been shoved up against the back door. I'd have to drag it away to get out.

I'm trapped.

"Ragne took a paralysis spell that wasn't meant for her." Emeric looks like the witch-ash hit him about as hard as it hit me, but he still beat me here. Grief and fury have carried him farther than the dust of gods and monsters.

"You left that part out, *Meister* Conrad," Joniza says. She's leaning on the dividing wall by the kitchen, winding a braid around her finger, eyes narrowed.

Gisele looks from Ragne to me, then to Emeric. "Take the spell off her."

"It'll wear off on its own momentarily," he admits. "Which is why I'm ending this now, before *she*"—he flicks a finger at me—"gets an angry bear to help her run off again."

I don't even have a name to him anymore.

"Give it up," he tells me. "I'll take you back to the outpost, and you'll be held until a fully ordained prefect can try your case."

"No." I back toward the wall, shaking my head. I can't rot in a jail cell until the full moon. "I didn't do anything—I don't have *time*—"

"Wait." Joniza holds up a hand, steel in her voice. "I agreed to hear you out, and to hear Vanja out. So get to it, boy. What makes you think she had anything to do with your man's murder?"

Emeric's face fractures for a moment; then it's like a north wind blows, and a detached chill settles over him. "Hubert was a threat to her. She asked repeatedly if he'd be willing to overlook her crimes, and was never satisfied with my answer."

"If 'not being satisfied by a man' was grounds for a murder charge, you'd have a lot more suspects," Joniza shoots back. "What else?"

Ragne twitches in my arms.

"Hubert was stabbed with his own knife and l-left in the Yssar." Emeric's voice cracks but he soldiers on. "He was found with a red penny in his mouth. Last week, Yannec Kraus's body washed up——"

"Yannec's dead?" Joniza pushes off from the wall, looking ill. Gisele covers her mouth.

"Stabbed with his own knife, a red penny in his mouth. He washed up in the Stichenstegs, *exactly* like Hubert." He points to me. "And *you* admitted you were there when he died."

"Why didn't you tell us?" Joniza asks, and the look in her eyes makes me want to crawl under the table.

"There——there wasn't a good time," I stumble, knowing how absurd it sounds, but saints and martyrs, between the margrave and poison and *nachtmären* and curses it's true, it's true——

Joniza just lets out a disbelieving scoff.

I'm losing her. Every inch I've dragged myself out of this pit, I'm losing.

"He'd been eating poppy!" My voice rises. "He was going into withdrawal and tried to cut the ruby off my face. Ragne scared him away from me, and he tripped and landed on his knife! I didn't want him dead!"

Emeric isn't giving an inch. "But you wanted his ledger."

"Yannec was fencing my hauls, I wanted to find his buyer——"

"You just threw him in the river?" Gisele asks unevenly. "Like trash?"

"Gisele, *please*——" My back collides with the wall. I still try to retreat, pushing myself along it just to get away, even though I know there's no way out.

"I'm guessing you didn't want to keep paying his cut," Emeric continues, cold and mechanical. "Maybe he got too greedy, maybe he was blackmailing you. Or were the Wolfhünden closing in?"

"No, I *told* you—"

He doesn't want my answers. "You eliminated him because he was a threat. Just like Hubert."

"I didn't—please just—"

I feel Ragne shiver once more.

Emeric sees it too. He's talking faster now, making his case before she can intervene. With every sentence, he steps closer. "You fooled me into"—his voice hitches—"into staying at the castle, so I wouldn't stop you."

"No—I n-never—"

"You came to the outpost to make sure no one connected you to Hubert's murder."

"Will you listen—"

"You didn't know they'd find the penny."

"Just *listen* to me!"

But as I look at Emeric, at Gisele, at Joniza, I can tell: Four years, and nothing has changed.

I hit the corner, and Emeric's voice fades away.

There is nothing to help me. There is nowhere for me to run. I want to throw up again. I'm trembling so hard I can't tell if Ragne's still moving in my arms.

I feel like a stranger is in my body, like I'm watching this happen.

I'm not in this room.

I'm in Castle Falbirg, almost four years ago to the day, and no matter how I scream, no one is listening.

It's four years ago, and I am bound to the whipping post, and I am burning.

It's four years ago, and I am lying facedown on a table in a dim, suffocating kitchen, and Yannec is telling me it's just a matter of time before the world finds an excuse to whip me raw again.

He was right. And now he's dead.

Only it's not four years ago, it's now, and I have nowhere to go, and I can't breathe, and Emeric is shouting, and Gisele and Joniza aren't saying anything, and all I can do is brace for the fire.

Ragne rolls out of my arms.

Then she stands beside me as a girl, yanking my damp cloak over herself and leaning heavily on my shoulder. "That is *enough!*" she yells, slurring a little.

The room falls silent.

"I will not be a bear," Ragne fumes, "because it scares you, like *you* are scaring the Vanja." She points at Emeric. "I have been with her for almost all of the last week and *you are wrong.* The Yannec was a bad, clumsy man who stank of poppy. He tried to cheat the Vanja, then he tried to hurt her, and she did nothing but get out of his way. He fell onto his knife after I surprised him. I could smell that she was sad when he died."

"When *weren't* you with Vanja?" Joniza asks coolly.

"I have left the Vanja three times. Once was right before *he*"— she jabs her finger at Emeric again—"attacked her, once when she was stuck in the castle with the margrave all day, and last night when I helped you and the Gisele go home. There was no time for her to kill a Hubert Klemens. And never have I smelled human blood on the Vanja until *his* blood, right now." Ragne pushes herself up a little taller, chin shaking as she looks at Gisele. "Yes, she is mean, but she is my friend, and she is *trying*. And you are all hurting her."

There's another brittle, jagged silence.

"But . . ." Emeric looks lost. "Why did you come to the outpost?"

I don't know why that's what does it, why that's what breaks me. Maybe it's that I'm hurt and scared and losing the adrenaline that kept those wolves at bay. Maybe it's that I was trying to do something right for once. Maybe it's that I was trying to do something for *him*.

I rip open my satchel so hard the buttons fly off, find the leather journal by touch, and throw Emeric's notes at him. They land at his feet before everything streaks and blurs with tears.

My legs choose this moment to give out. I slide down the wall and bury my crumpling face in my knees. Ragne crouches next to me, a hand on my back.

Every rush of terror boils up, every old wound splits open again, every strain of a strange kind of mourning, all of it surges to the surface. I am spilling over, I am drowning in the taste of blood and ash and juniper oil. I am bawling in a way I haven't in years. I hate that they're all here to see it, but I don't even have room for shame.

For too long, the only sounds in the room are my broken sobs and the whispery rustles as Ragne picks dirt and grit from my hair.

Then the floorboards creak. Ragne growls, "*No.* You stay back."

"I . . ." Emeric's voice is stricken, gutted. "I have to . . ."

"I think you both need some room, Conrad," Joniza says somewhere far away. "You stay here with Gisele, maybe have some tea. I'll take Vanja upstairs and let Umayya know the children can come down now."

Gisele's voice shifts past me, the floorboards groaning as she walks toward the kitchen. "I still don't understand who would go to the trouble of framing Vanja."

"They didn't," Emeric says with the weary, bitter clarity of a man realizing his purse was cut. "Last night, von Reigenbach said he would deal with the prefects. So he framed the *Pfennigeist*."

I hear a soft crinkle as the journal is picked up—then a fleshy little *thud* and Joniza's sharp gasp.

I look up. A tiny *mahr* is flailing on its back at Emeric's feet, where the journal was. It's barely bigger than a beetle.

Joniza freezes halfway between me and Emeric. She lets out a squeak of disgust and stomps on the *mahr* as fast as she can. There's a foul little crunch.

"Oh," Gisele says. "Was it spying—"

She doesn't finish that thought. Blue flames burst out from beneath Joniza's boot like lantern oil catching a spark. Joniza leaps back with a startled curse.

Gisele grabs a pail of sand beside the stove and throws it over the flames.

They go out. Then they flare up again around the sand, blue fire licking across the floorboards.

That's when we all realize: This fire will not die. Adalbrecht means to burn us all down.

"Umayya!" Gisele runs for the stairs. "We need to get everyone outside, now!"

"Up, up—" Ragne helps me to my feet.

Joniza starts for the kitchen door, but there's no time to drag the table out of the way. She doubles back and undoes the deadbolt on the front door, then yanks.

It lurches—then stops. Joniza tries again. It doesn't budge.

Both doors are blocked.

We're trapped.

CHAPTER TWENTY-SIX

House of Fortune

IT'S THE LITTLE THINGS IN LIFE THAT SURPRISE YOU, ISN'T IT? LIKE
how you can be trapped in a burning building, and it'll still seem easier to deal with than being accused of murder by a boy you thought you
might—no.

Blue flames creep over the floor as Ragne hauls me from the corner. I hear Umayya and Gisele ordering the older orphans to get their
shoes on as fast as they can.

Joniza gives the front door another frantic shake. "Come on, *come on*."

"Jammed from the outside," Emeric says tightly. "The windows—?"

Orange flames crawl up the other side of the glass panes, and when
I gasp, it reeks of lantern oil. *Of course.* Adalbrecht wanted to deal with
the prefects. Dozens of Wolfhünden would have seen Emeric run here,
and Papa Wolf never does things by halves.

Ragne lets me go, then swells into an enormous black bear. She lumbers to the door as Joniza clears the way, then hurls her weight against the wood. There's an awful squalling *crack*. One more heave and the door collapses.

There's a scream from the top of the stairs. One of the younger children is hiding her face in Fabine's skirt and babbling about the bear. Ragne shifts down to a cat, running in agitated circles in the front room. "Hurry!" she yowls. "Out!"

I look behind me. The blue flames have reached the pantry door.

Some distant part of me lurches at that—there are over a dozen children, Gisele, Umayya, and Joniza, what will they *eat* if all the food burns—and then a passionless calculation clicks into place.

Joniza's collecting most of the children in the street outside, Umayya and Gisele bringing down the last stragglers. I rush up the stairs, twisted ankle be damned, and grab Gisele's arm as smoke begins pooling on the ceiling. "The money," I hiss, "the donation I left last week, where is it?"

"*Now?*" she shoots back, bewildered. The sobbing toddler she's carrying yanks a handful of her hair.

I don't have time for this. "I know you didn't spend it! Where is it?"

She frees a hand to point down the hall. "Last bedroom, under the mattress on the left—"

I don't wait to hear the rest. I hear her shouting after me as I stagger toward the end of the hall, covering my face with my apron. More smoke leaks between the floorboards, the heat like a knife in my lungs.

I burst into Gisele's room, where two plain beds are tucked in opposite corners. Left, she said *left*, didn't she? I try that bed first. The mattress is heavy, stuffed with straw and rag with more hay beneath it, and it's a struggle to keep it lifted as I run my free hand through the stalks. It's getting even hotter, the air curdling with smoke.

Finally my fingers catch on soft leather. Gisele hasn't even emptied the pennies from the purse. I seize it and crawl from the bedroom, staying low, where the air is clearer.

I'm still racked with coughs by the time I make it to the landing. The downstairs is almost entirely blue flames, the gap of the ruined front door a dimming target. Faintly, I hear Umayya shouting, "*No, stop!*"

Then a silhouette darkens the doorway. I hear the steps creaking in agony as the figure takes them two at a time, and then Emeric's face swims out of the choking shadows, because *of course*. Of course it's him. Who else would believe the absolute worst of me and still run into a burning house to save my life?

He wraps one arm around my shoulders, the other around my waist, and we half stagger, half tumble down the stairs, out into the shocking savage cold. People are yelling, throwing handfuls of snow and buckets of water, but there's no point. Between the lantern oil and the *mahr*, it'll take the Yssar itself to put it out. At least the snow-banked neighboring rooftops won't catch a spark.

I drag in breath after breath of clean air. Emeric's still holding me steady, and half of me wants to stay this way, pretend everything's fine now, we can go back to how it was before this morning.

But I have not survived this long by listening to that part of me. I shove him off.

Immediately hands wrap around my elbows—Gisele, this time. She's wet-eyed and livid "Vanja, what were you *thinking*? It's just money! You could have gotten yourself and Emeric killed!"

"*Just* money?" I gasp through the cacophony, and sweep a hand at the children watching flames devour the Gänslinghaus. Only some of them even have coats on. "How are you going to feed them? Where are you going to stay?" I shake the purse at her. "How are you going to buy a new *house*, Gisele? How can you live like this for a year, and still say it's *just money*?"

"Who's Gisele?" one of the orphans whispers.

"We're going to have another problem," Joniza says, smoke roughening her voice. "The inns are filling up. Between Winterfast and the wedding, there's hardly an empty bed in Minkja."

"No one has family here to help?" Ragne asks, now a wolfhound, tail wagging as a few younger children cling to her sides.

Gisele shakes her head. "It's an orphanage. None of us do."

I stare at the dirty snow in the street, at the purse in my hand.

That's not exactly true.

At the edge of the crowd, I see Wolfhünden lingering, eyes sharp as hunger. There are too many witnesses for them to trample over a bunch of orphans in plain view, but we can't stay here. There is only one place to go.

Scheit, I'm going to hate this.

"I have an idea," I say shortly. "Follow me. And don't ask questions."

We wind up flagging down a passing farmer for a ride along the Hoenstratz viaduct, because it's a long way to go with over a dozen children, and even longer when many need to be carried or kept warm. She's more than happy to pack them into her haycart. The rest of us walk alongside it, an awful, sick silence weighing every step. Ragne sticks close by me but doesn't say a word, only steadies me as the limp from my ankle gets worse.

I don't even try to look at Emeric. It's not out of spite or chill, but self-preservation. If I think about it, about him, if I even pick at the loose ends of that knot, I'm going to start crying again.

We leave the viaduct and the friendly farmer just north of the Göttermarkt. Mercifully, it's not the same staircase I came up earlier, so we don't have to worry about the children tramping through Emeric's blood or my vomit. A few of the younger ones start to whine as we wind through the lanes, but it's not long before I see the telltale spires.

We've come to my mother's house. At least, one of them.

Fortune's cathedral stands large, gaudy, and lined in actual coal dust. Great urns bracket each side of the brass-wrought door. There are four, one for each type of hasty help a passerby might want: gold coins for one's own good fortune, silver for another's, copper coins to relieve one's bad fortune, and coal bits to wish it on another.

(It might not surprise you to know the two most popular urns are copper and coal. Maybe that says something about human nature, but I also think it says something about personal budgeting. Buying good luck? In this economy?)

"You think the priests will take us?" Joniza asks doubtfully. I don't blame her. Fortune's temples *do* provide shelter to those wounded by her caprices, but that's usually in the event of a grand disaster like a flood or a landslide, not one measly house fire.

"They'll take us," I answer through my teeth. I walk up the steps and push the doors open.

It's dim inside, smelling of old timbers, hot coals, beeswax tapers, and frankincense. Threads of delicate smoke weep heavenward from thuribles strung in vestibule corners, sweet and heavy with gardenia. On the far side of the sanctuary, an acolyte looks up from polishing the gold-and-bone archway over the altar.

"Hello?" She sets her polishing rag down and hurries through the truncated rings of pews. "Can I help you? Our evening service won't— *WELL*, now."

Mid-step, the acolyte freezes and shivers. A wreath of flipping coins manifests over her head, and her simple vestment turns to a gown of gold and bone.

I hear gasps from the others crowding in at my back. I ignore them.

"Hello" is all I say.

Fortune plants her hands on her hips. "I suppose this settles it, then? Do you think Death should be here for this?"

Death never needs an invitation. She appears beside Fortune, tapping a foot. "We *agreed* to give her space."

"She came to me!" Fortune protests as another round of startled gasps takes a lap around my company. "With all her little friends in tow! She came to ask me for help, not you, I win, end of story. Oh, Vanja, we're going to have the *best* time—"

"I'm not asking for help," I interrupt.

Both Fortune and Death look at me.

"This is your house," I continue, "so it's also mine."

"Now, wait." Fortune frowns.

I don't let her finish. "I am here to claim my place in your house, as your daughter. I'm not asking for anything that isn't mine by right." Fortune's frown deepens. I keep pushing. "Of course, if you don't want me here, you can renounce me. Give up your claim to me, and I will lose *my* claim to you and yours."

We all know that isn't happening.

Death coughs into a sleeve.

"Stop laughing," Fortune snaps. "It's not funny."

"It's very funny," Death returns.

Now Fortune's the one who looks peeved. Or rather, the acolyte she's possessing looks peeved. "You can't just expect me to host all your friends indefinitely."

"They're my guests, and I brought money. I'll give you two *sjilling* for every day they're here. That should cover food, lodging, and protection against *grimlingen* under this roof."

"Three white pennies a day."

"One." I jingle the purse. "I'll pay you twenty-five up front. That's the best offer you'll get out of me."

It's a rare sight, seeing Death's shoulders shake with silent laughter as Fortune looks more indignantly betrayed than a cat in a bath.

"Deal," she grouches, and I toss her the purse. "Our offer stands, Vanja. You don't have to choose. But you can't run forever."

She vanishes, leaving the acolyte blinking and clutching a leather purse with an extremely generous donation. Death hesitates, then disappears after her without another word.

"I, er," the acolyte sputters. "I need to tell the High Priestess. Can our . . . guests . . . please follow me?"

She leads Umayya and the children off to a hallway branching from the sanctuary. Gisele and Joniza hang back, eyeing me like I might smite them at any moment. Emeric's brow is furrowed, but he says nothing.

"Vanja," Joniza begins, artificially casual, "at what point were you going to tell us about this?"

I look away. "So we're just going to ignore the whole 'don't ask questions' thing."

"Are . . ." Gisele looks almost afraid. "Are *you* a god?"

"If I were, Adalbrecht would be a stain on a floor somewhere," I retort.

Then I rub my eyes. They're dry and they sting in the way that only gets worse after they close, so I leave my palms over them a moment, thinking. There's really no point in hiding it, not with what they've seen, not now.

"My mother thought I was bad luck, because I was the thirteenth child of a thirteenth child, so she gave me to Death and Fortune when I was four. The night the von Falbirgs had me whipped, my godmothers said I was old enough to serve one of them and tried to make me choose. I wouldn't. So they said I would serve whoever I asked for help first."

Someone draws a breath through their teeth.

I lower my hands, blinking until my eyes clear, and say hoarsely, "That's why I've been stealing. If I slip up *once*, I'll be their servant the rest of my life, so I'm trying to save enough money to leave the empire and get away from them." I huff a bitter laugh. "You know. *Just* money. Anyway, this should take care of you until . . . well, until after I'm gone. One way or another."

"Why didn't you tell us?" Gisele asks. She almost sounds hurt.

I stare at her. And then I laugh again, harsh and disbelieving. After all this time, she still doesn't get it. "This ring a bell? *'Once upon a time, Death and Fortune came to a crossroads.'*"

I see it finally dawn in her face.

"You already knew the first part," I almost spit. "You got to fall asleep to my story for years. But you didn't say *anything* when I needed you. Why would I tell you a single blessed thing after that?"

Gisele draws back as if I struck her.

I hear the hour-bells chiming. Somehow, it's not even noon. "I'm going to the castle," I say, exhausted. "There's a social and a dinner party tonight, so count me out for the rest of the day."

I limp for the door. Emeric starts to reach for me, then catches himself. After a beat, he swallows. "I . . . I can walk you there."

"You have other things to take care of," I say, pushing the door open. This time I *am* being cold. I don't know what else to be with him right now. "You have your notes back."

Ragne helps me make it down the waterfall path and up through the servant corridors. By the time I reach my bedroom, I'm practically on my hands and knees.

Now that no one's hunting me and nothing's on fire, there's no distraction from the lingering effects of that drop of witch-ash. It feels like the time I got sick from spoiled meat, like every inch of me turned to jelly just long enough to bruise, then froze over too fast, and my bones will splinter from any sudden moves.

Even without the backlash, as I stagger past the vanity mirror, I see I'm a sooty, bloody, tearstained wreck. My dress is torn in nigh a dozen places, my hat is gone, and my shawl's been half singed off. Most of the scrapes I can cover, but I'll have to come up with a story for the spreading bruise on my jaw.

Maybe not. *I fell down some stairs* is horribly accurate.

"You need rest," Ragne says gently.

I shake my head. "I need to clean up before the social." It's a few hours off still, but moving this slow, I'm not taking chances.

Poldi helps heat the bathwater, no mead required. I need the help, because the bath has to be drawn again after the first round of water goes murky with blood and grime. I fall asleep in the tub anyway. Ragne wakes me an hour before I have to face the guests, just enough time to finish getting ready with the help of the pearls.

The rest of the day grinds by in a grating fog. It's like I'm moving through a fever dream; people are laughing and smiling and clasping my hands, ladling out gossip and boasts and flattery, sometimes staring at the ruby teardrop with a hungry gleam until I excuse myself. All I can focus on is hiding my limp and not shoving my foot too far into my mouth.

The Wolfhünden will have reported back to Adalbrecht by now, but if he's galled that Emeric survived, he keeps it under wraps in front of the guests. I still keep my distance. I can tell he likes me like this: saying little and asking even less.

Enough guests have moved into the riverfront wing that when I finally excuse myself after dinner, I have to maintain the gliding walk, the ramrod spine, all the way up to my bedroom. The hallway's still abuzz with servants and nobles, witnesses all.

Those witnesses work in my favor, though. I see new faces among the castle guards, and flashes of the *X* tattoo on their hands. Irmgard wanted Adalbrecht to take the first opening to kill Gisele; it seems he's resorted to moving Wolfhünden into the castle so they won't miss any chances. I was already careful not to get caught alone as Marthe, but now I'll have to do it as Gisele too.

As I slip the key into my door's lock, I spot Emeric coming around the corner. My stomach clenches. His head flies up, then he picks up his pace, but we both know he can't make a scene with this audience. I hurry inside and close the door behind me. Then I can't help but lean against it, pulling off the pearls and letting out a breath.

I'm sick, and I hurt everywhere, and I'm so *tired*. And I can finally stop pretending I'm not.

Quiet footsteps pause by the door. There's a soft brushing sound, like fingertips grazing the wood—and then it passes. I hear the neighboring door unlock, open, shut.

Ragne is stretching on the hearth as a human girl, in clothes for once. She sits up, feet sticking out at odd angles. "Hello! You made it."

"I did." I throw the pearls on the bed and start on my bodice laces.

"How are you feeling?"

"Awful," I admit. "Like I had the pox for a week. And fell out of a tree."

I flop onto the chest at the foot of the bed as she stands, walks over, and pats my head. "How are you feeling here?"

My throat catches. I stop fussing with the laces a moment and say again, "Awful."

To my surprise, Ragne says, "Me too." When I look up at her, she fidgets. "I like the Gisele very much. But she hurt you again today. And the Emeric is confusing. I am sad for him, and I am very angry at what he did to you."

"That really sums it up," I say with a humorless laugh. "If it helps, I'm confused too."

I trade my fine gown for the first kirtle I see on the floor. Only once I've pulled it over my head do I realize it's the fir-green one from last night, when I showed Emeric the way out.

I can't wear this. I go to dig another out of the wardrobe as Ragne sits on the hearth ledge, stands, looks at the veranda, and sits again.

She's been jittery since I got back. It takes me a moment to sort out why, and only a heartbeat to think of a solution. "Hey, Ragne. I want to make sure everyone's fine at Fortune's cathedral, but I'm in no shape to leave. Can you go check—"

"*Yes!*" She practically poofs into an owl, only to realize the veranda doorknob needs hands to turn it. I open it for her and let her fly out into the night, unconcerned. I'm not going anywhere feeling this sick, and if Adalbrecht tries anything while she's gone, I have Poldi.

I go back to the wardrobe and rummage around for another kirtle, only to touch strange heavy wool.

It's the coat Emeric inadvertently left behind a week ago exactly, when he first tried to arrest me. The one with *H KLEMENS* stitched into the inside of the collar.

My chest tightens. This doesn't belong to me.

I . . .

I tell myself I don't want anything of him left in my room.

It's an excuse, I know it's an excuse, but it's enough for my pride. I fold it automatically, tucking it under an arm, then stop before I reach the bedroom door. Regardless of the Wolfhünden hiding among the guards, there's no good excuse to send Gisele's maid over to Emeric's room to return his clothing. Even if I come up with a ruse . . . I'd still have to talk to him.

I head for the veranda instead. I'll just drop it off on his railing, knock on the door, and get out before he can answer.

Outside, it's the kind of frigid that shocks the breath from your lungs. The only upside is it numbs my throbbing ankle a little as I climb onto the trellis and shimmy my way to Emeric's veranda.

I'm focusing too hard on keeping the coat clenched at my side, and on not putting too much weight on my bad foot, to notice my mistake until after I've knocked snow off his balustrade and started to lever myself over.

Last night, he left the sheer inner curtains drawn across the veranda door and the windows. Tonight, they've been pushed aside. That means I have a crystal clear view of Emeric bent over the washbasin near the door, spectacles hooked on the back of the mirror, splashing water onto his face.

These are the three things I notice, in the order that I notice them:

First, his shirt is. Well. It's not there. That is, I mean, it's not on *him*, where it *should be*, it's been tossed over the desk chair. This is all very—confusing.

Second, he's not exactly built like a fortress, but with his shirt off he looks drastically less like a gawky academic and more like a boy who's ended a few fights himself. He's got a respectable scattering of scars, enough to veer dangerously close to *un*respectable. He even has a tattoo over his heart, something I wouldn't have believed if I wasn't seeing it with my own eyes.

If I had enough time, I could read stories in his marks, like I do with everything else I'm not meant to see.

But I don't have enough time, because the third thing I notice is this: He's been crying again. I know this because his eyes are red. And I notice *that* because even without his spectacles, he's staring dead at me, dripping water all over the carpet.

An agonizing beat passes as we gape at each other. Then he bursts out of the door and onto the veranda. I fling the coat directly into his face and hurl myself back at the trellis. Through the wool I still hear a muffled "*Wait!*"

"Nope," I say, clinging to the trellis, "too cold, good night."

"Please—"

I keep scuttling back toward my veranda.

"I don't want this," he says raggedly. "Us, like this. I owe you an apology, if—if you'll hear it."

There's something arresting there. It's the same as the moment I realized he felt the same solving cases as I did leaving red pennies. Something about that rings in me like a bell.

Neither of us wants to be alone tonight.

But I've survived alone until now, I tell myself.

Then I accidentally put my weight on my twisted ankle. I can't bite back a sharp cry.

Emeric all but leaps for the trellis. "Hold on—"

"Don't," I say, throwing a hand out. He stops, one leg over the balustrade. I rest my forehead against the cold stone, eyes squeezed shut as I wait for the pain to subside. "It won't hold both of us. I'm fine."

He doesn't have to say a word; the *pig shit* is implied.

Instead, he just says, "I can help your ankle."

I finally let myself look at him. The absolute fool is clutching the coat to his chest, his *bare* chest, in the freezing cold. He hasn't even put it on. He barely managed his spectacles, and even those are crooked.

It still hurts, the memory of who he'd been this morning. The memory of who I'd become to get away. I didn't care if I killed him on those stairs.

No, I *did* care. And it didn't stop me.

Neither of us wants to be alone with who we were.

Neither of us has to be.

"Put a shirt on," I grumble. "I'll leave the veranda door unlocked."

CHAPTER TWENTY-SEVEN

Vanja Is Fine

I CAREFULLY CROSS THE REST OF THE TRELLIS AND HOBBLE INTO MY room. The dead roses rattle a minute later as I toss a fresh log into the fireplace.

The knob turns, and Emeric slips inside, back in his shirt and waist-coat, a small leather bag in one hand. "You've got the witch-ash side effects too, right?" he asks nervously. I nod. "Wagner gave me something to help. It needs to steep in hot water. Or cider, because it tastes wretched."

"Wine?" I shamble over to my vanity and pull out a bottle I've been saving for emergencies. I'd say this counts.

"That works."

I pass it to him, then fish out two mugs. He tips a stream of powder from a parchment envelope into the bottle's mouth, swirls it around, then sets the bottle close enough to the fire to heat. Then he pulls another vial of witch-ash oil from the leather bag. At my alarmed look, he says, "This isn't the same strength as prefect-standard oil. I'll be fine."

It's my turn to give him a look *loaded* in doubtful implication.

He ignores it. "Please, sit."

I lower myself onto the ledge of hearthstones. There's plenty of room between me and the fire, but the masonry beneath my palms is warm from soaking up heat all afternoon.

Emeric kneels on the floor by my feet, and my mind can't quite wrap itself around the way that makes me feel. "Your right?" he asks quietly. I nod and inch that boot forward. A strange look crosses his face. "I'm sorry, the boot . . . that is, this works on direct contact."

"Do what you need to," I sigh, tilting my head back to study the ceiling.

Belatedly, I realize I should have thought that through. If I found it disorienting for him to be on his knees, I am in no way capable of reckoning with him slowly, cautiously beginning to unlace my boot.

"There's a knife in there," I blurt out.

"I know. I had a very clear view when you were stepping on me a week ago."

"Oh."

"I've been thinking . . ." Emeric starts, then clears his throat. "Last Thursday, with the Augur's Tears. You said you weren't a good person."

"*Scheit*," I mutter. I'd hoped I kept that to myself. "But it's the truth, isn't it? Otherwise I couldn't have said it with the Tears."

He's being almost painfully careful as he loosens the final row of laces and starts to ease my boot off. "I think there are lives that make it easy to be good. Or what most people call good. When you have wealth, status, family, it's easy to be a saint, it costs you nothing. I can't say if you're a good person or not. But the more I know of you, the more I understand that the world keeps making you choose between survival and martyrdom. No one should fault you for wanting to live."

My foot slips free with a twinge. It almost hurts more, having it out in the open. I stare at the ceiling again, this time because I don't want him to see my eyes welling up.

"I'm sorry," he says again, "the—the stocking—"

"I said do what you need to."

I really, *really* should have thought that through.

Emeric's trying to be as clinical as he can, but I think I stop breathing as his fingers skim up my calf, under the hem of my skirts. They find the stocking tie below my knee and go to work. His head's bowed, and I can't see his face, but a flush stains the back of his neck.

"All that was to say," he continues, "the fact is that your life has been hard because people keep choosing to make it that way. And today I was one of them, and I am so, so sorry. I chose to believe the worst of you, to hurt you trying to prove I was right. I did it, even knowing what the von Falbirgs put you through. I'm no better than they are."

I feel the stocking tie come undone, and if I don't say something to distract myself, I'm going to scream. "If you were as bad as the von Falbirgs, I'd—" About to say *throw you back in the Yssar*, I realize that might not be the best choice, considering Klemens. Unfortunately, what stumbles out of my mouth, shaking with tears, is worse: "I'd have never let you in."

Emeric slips a little. He pauses, fishes out a neatly pressed kerchief, and passes it to me without a word before turning back to my ankle.

I dry my face, trying not to think about the silk sliding down my leg, or the hands guiding it. "Besides. I made it easier to—to believe. If Adalbrecht had tried to frame Gisele, or Joniza . . . If I wasn't . . ."

"Please don't." Emeric looks up at me. The firelight catches in his eyes, stirring embers in the deep brown. "You don't need to justify what I did. You could have been the worst backstreet cutthroat and it wouldn't excuse how I treated you. Or how the von Falbirgs did."

I don't know what to say to that. Some part of me has always looked for how I brought these things on myself. I missed a spot of tarnish on the silver, I missed the way the dame gripped her mead, I missed *something* and set them off and if I could figure out where I went wrong, they wouldn't call me stupid or throw things or strike me.

There had to be a reason for it. That made it something I could control. Something I could hope to stop.

It's the worst kind of relief for someone to say it was never in my control.

Emeric shifts to prop my foot on his knees, and I'm abruptly, *excruciatingly* aware of the stocking slipping off my toes. It was easier to hide under boot leather and silk, but my ankle's a swollen, bruised mess. He breathes out a curse, shame clouding his face. Then he reaches for the vial of witch-ash.

"You're sure that won't hurt you?" I ask.

He shakes his head and uncorks the vial. Thyme wafts from the oil instead of juniper. "The Order's ash is a much higher concentration. This is just for medicinal use." Emeric takes a small swig, then dabs a few drops onto my ankle. "This might feel odd, but it shouldn't hurt."

I brace myself and nod. He hasn't understated it this time: It feels strange when he starts mumbling under his breath, a little like my ankle's deflating, but the ache washes away. I didn't even realize how sore it was until now.

Emeric's looking at a scratch over my knuckles, eyes glowing from the witch-ash. "There's still a little magic left. Do you want . . . ?"

"Sure."

It's also strange, almost hypnotic, to watch him as he moves around me, brushing away the scrapes and scuffs. It feels like another thing that belongs behind a curtain, the concentration in his brow, lips moving almost silently, fingertips trailing faint smudges of thyme oil on my skin. Finally he reaches for the bruise on my jaw.

I have a very unsettling thought as fingers brush the side of my face, as thyme floods my nose. I—I think—

I want him to stay like this. Close to me, touching my face feather-light, like I am something precious, I am worth taking care. Like I deserve to live without wounds, not despite them. I want this moment trapped in amber, so I can hold it tight when I need it most.

He lets me go, and it passes. The cold consolation is that I can finally catch my breath.

Emeric stands and offers me a hand up. "How is it?" he asks as I test my ankle.

"Better." There's an unspoken question lingering like smoke between us. I tuck my hair behind my ears, awkward. "So . . . that was a really good apology."

(Was I *significantly* distracted for most of it? Yes. Am I mulling over the viability of *you have to take the other stocking off now, for symmetry* as a compelling argument? Also yes.)

There's a jolt in my stomach as Emeric presses his lips into a pained smile. "May it be the last I owe you."

"I'll drink to that." I walk over to the vanity to pick up the mugs I left there. "Which of us do you think Adalbrecht's going to try to kill tonight?"

Emeric flinches.

I instantly know why. "Sorry, I wasn't thinking—"

He waves it off, blinking rapidly. "Not . . . your fault. He'll probably come after me. But you should be safe with Ragne, once she returns." He sees my chagrin. "How long will she be out?"

I shrug awkwardly. "She, uh, wanted to go see a sweetheart. I didn't ask."

"That's not ideal." He looks away, troubled. "Still, the castle *kobold*—"

"Poldi."

"Poldi," he amends, "should be enough. Though if the margrave can murder a trained prefect, I'm not sure what else he's capable of."

Poldi himself pops his head out of the logs, looking between Emeric and me. *"Can't watch both your rooms,"* he crackles apologetically. *"Not at the same time."*

"Then I can wait for Ragne," I say.

"No—" Emeric runs a hand through his hair. "I'm not letting him get anyone else." A strained beat passes. "I . . . suppose I could try to stay on watch until Ragne gets back."

I look at the empty mugs, then at the deck of cards on my vanity, and come to a decision.

I've spent most of my life starving for independence. For freedom from Death and Fortune, from reliance on scraps the von Falbirgs tossed me, from the memory of a dwindling lantern in midwinter.

But I'm learning the bitter difference between independence and self-exile. We both have poison to bleed out.

And neither of us wants to be alone tonight.

"Or," I say, passing Emeric a mug, "you could just . . . stay." He freezes in the middle of taking the mug from me, and I realize how that sounded. "Not like that! I mean until Ragne gets back!"

"Of course," he sputters, "I would never—I mean—"

"Careful, you're going to sprain your dignity." I'm a *little* miffed at how swiftly he slammed that door shut, even if I didn't mean to crack it open. I return to the fireplace and settle cross-legged on the carpet, setting my mug on the hearth ledge.

"Just—if that's what you want." If Emeric grips the mug any tighter, it might shatter.

"I do want. I have an idea." I lean forward and pat the carpet a modest distance away. "We were never going to trust each other, right? You're a walking morality lecture with something to prove, and I'm a scoundrel with an unflinching sense of entitlement to other people's property."

Emeric sits across from me in a meticulous knot of limbs, his mouth twisting. "Reasonably accurate."

"We can't afford that anymore. What Adalbrecht did today worked because we don't know each other, and I'm sure it won't be the last time he tries it. So we're going to play Find the Lady." I pull out the Queen of Roses, the Knight of Shields, and the Page of Grails. "You pick the queen, you get to ask me a question, and I have to give you an honest answer. You pick the knight, and I get to ask you."

"And the page?"

I grab a scarf and use it to pull the wine away from the fire. "We drink. Even if this didn't have junk in it to help with the witch-ash, I'm guessing we both need it."

Emeric blows out a breath. "Yes, I think we do. All right."

I fill the mugs, and as he picks his up, I see his hands are shaking almost as much as mine. Well, I can start things off on a lighter foot. I tap my mug to his. "*Proszit.*"

"*Prozt,*" he returns.

I wrinkle my nose at him. "Northerner." Then I take a sip and make a much worse face. The kindest thing that can be said is that the powder gave it a *very strong* bouquet. "Saints and martyrs, Junior. If this doesn't make me feel a hundred times better, I am going to be very mad that I wasted this bottle."

"I warned you," he laughs. I didn't miss the flash of relief when I called him Junior.

"Ugh." I start shuffling the cards, then lay them out. He waffles a moment, then picks the middle. It's the Knight of Shields.

"Here we go," he says. "Ask."

I stack up the cards and flip through them. I don't want to hurt him, but grief is a house on fire. It needs to burn itself down. "Tell me about Klemens."

His throat moves. "What do you want to know?"

"Everything. How you met, his bad habits, his favorite pastry. Tell me why you gave a damn about him."

Emeric stares into his mug, gathering himself. When he speaks, he's somewhere far from this room. "My parents were bookbinders up in the northwest, near the Bourgienne border. My father also kept books for the locals. When he was murdered, the bailiff just said there was no proof of the culprit. But I went through Father's desk. His last appointment was with the bailiff. When I looked through the bailiff's accounts, they weren't adding up. Father kept clean books, he would have noticed . . . but I was eight. The sheriff just brushed me off."

"And you took it to Klemens." I tip my head awkwardly. "I . . . saw a little of it, in the Tears, from your cloak. I didn't mean to."

"I don't mind." Emeric half shrugs. "Hubert was on his way back to Helligbrücke, but he heard me out. It was enough to investigate, and he was the only reason the bailiff faced justice. Then Hubert told my mother I would do well with the prefects."

"You solved a murder when you were eight," I say wryly. "With math. I think 'well' may be underselling it."

He cracks a smile. "The stipend didn't hurt either. I'm the oldest of four, and my mother wasn't ready to remarry. It was a way to keep a roof over our heads without forcing that on her. Besides, I wanted to be Hubert. You know the saying, little thieves and great ones?"

I nod.

"I've always hated it. It's everything wrong with the empire, that we punish people who are usually just trying to survive, when people like the margrave get away with whatever they want. Prefects can make *anyone* answer to the Low Gods. So we moved to Helligbrücke, and Hubert kept an eye out for me in the training academy." Rue seeps into his voice. "I needed it. Turns out no one likes being shown up by a little know-it-all."

This is when I realize: This is why he keeps tripping me up, finding truths that catch me in the throat. Our lives are very different, but we both speak the brittle language of loneliness.

Emeric continues. "When his partner retired, he pushed the academy to let me take the first initiation early, so I could start working cases with him as an apprentice. He was . . ." His voice catches, halts. I pass his kerchief back. "He never let me forget how fallible easy answers can be. Like today. But he always listened. He never made me feel like a nuisance because I was right." Emeric presses his lips together. "He slept in all the time, and then he would be cranky because he missed breakfast. Pastries . . . he didn't like them, but he would eat candied almonds by the handful. Then he would brush the sugar on his coat, just to annoy me. And I'm pretty sure he would have tried to convince you to join the prefects too."

"That would be a terrible idea," I say immediately. "Do you know how fast I would get thrown out? *So* fast."

"Notice *I'm* not trying to convince you," Emeric returns.

My mouth quirks at that. I raise my mug. "To Hubert Klemens." Emeric raises his silently; I don't think he can speak right now. We sit in the quiet a moment. Then I add, "I meant it, earlier. We're going to bring Adalbrecht down."

It takes another moment for Emeric to answer, and when he does, there's iron in his words. "Whatever it takes."

There's a sudden thud from the far wall. The wall my room shares with Emeric's.

Both of us stare at the plaster, holding our breaths. I don't see anything, but a low, muffled scrape seeps out, like furniture's being dragged over the floor.

Poldi crackles with vexation. *"I'll see what's afoot."* The fire dims as he vanishes.

"Tell me your notes aren't in there," I whisper.

Emeric shakes his head. "I'm keeping them at the outpost."

"Nachtmären," growls from the fireplace when the *kobold* returns. *"Making a proper mess. Want me to run 'em off?"*

"Do the honors," I tell him with grim satisfaction. This time his crackling is downright gleeful as he slips away.

The noises from next door abruptly cease. There are a few muffled bangs, then a hush. Poldi pops up in the hearth again, wheezing a bit. *"Tougher this time. The bodies ought to vanish with the next bell."*

"You're a treasure." I turn back to Emeric. "Right, so, you're *definitely* not going back in there until Ragne returns."

That odd look slips through his face again. "If you insist." Then he sets his mug down as I shuffle the cards once more. "You asked me about Hubert to . . . help, didn't you?"

I lay out the cards. "You know the rules, no free questions. Find the Lady."

He picks the middle card again, because the odds favor a new card. And I left the knight there, because that's exactly what I thought he'd do. He gives me a narrow look. "This is a very one-sided interrogation."

"Well, hopefully this will be short." I collect the cards and look him in the eye. "We're cooperating for now, but you still took the *Pfennigeist* case."

He holds up a hand. "Don't waste your question. I don't want you to feel the way you did this morning, *ever* again. As long as we're in this, we're in it together. You have my word."

Together. Once again, he's caught me in the throat.

"Oh" is about all I can muster. Then I shake my head. "I—uh—that wasn't my question, exactly. Even if this all ends with Adalbrecht and Irmgard in a dungeon and me surviving the curse to laugh at them . . . what happens after?"

He gives me a long look. Something's flickering in it like a signal lantern, like there's so much more to say.

"You want to get out of the empire, right?" Emeric asks.

"That's the plan."

Another crooked smile ghosts across his face. There's a challenge in his voice, bone-weary but warm as the wine. "Then I give you a decent head start."

This is when I realize: I want that. I want him to chase me.

But it's not just the chase. I want it to be *him*.

There's a shimmering, intoxicating kind of thrill to it, this game between us. I am his puzzle and he is my lock, and it's an arms race to solve the other first. But somewhere in all the knots and twists and trapdoors, he turned to an arsonist, leaving his embers in my veins, smoke on my tongue, a fire burning softly in my heart.

And it will not die easy.

I want him to chase me. I want to know what it feels like to be caught. I want to burn with him.

Oh, saints and martyrs. I'll be damned.

I think I want him to kiss me.

I'm staring. I'm *panicking*.

I duck my head. "Fair enough. Next question." I splay out the cards, hoping that, between the wine and the fire, my rising blush has an alibi.

He picks the Page of Grails, so we both take a drink. That has to be it, right? It's the wine making me notice the lines of his throat, how he missed the top button on his shirt in his haste. It's *only* the wine gathering the firelight along his narrow jaw, the way his black hair falls over his brow, into something I find handsome.

(It's not the wine. I don't want to talk about it.)

I deal the cards a little too fast. I'm *pretty* sure I know where the queen is.

Then he flips the card over, and I was right. Ugh. "What do you want to know?"

He hesitates, then asks, "What happened with Irmgard von Hirsching?"

"Nothing you haven't already heard."

"I want you to tell your own story."

My stomach clenches, but this was my idea. And part of me, dry and cold as the moraines in Sovabin, aches to be known.

So I tell him a story of a princess, a loyal maid, and a monstrous little countess. I tell him of ruby rings and white pennies. I tell him of Death and Fortune and a deal I had no say in.

And Emeric listens. When I'm done, he runs fingers over his mouth, thinking. Then he asks, "When is your birthday?"

"December thirteenth."

"The day of the wedding?"

"Oh, *scheit*. I think it is." I laugh in disbelief. "Why?"

He pinches his nose, eyes squeezing shut. Then he recites: "'*Upon reaching seventeen years of age, any child of the empire is hereby considered an adult, and granted the full rights of an imperial citizen. They are no longer subject to the custody of their parents or guardians, nor are they subject to their custodian's authority.'"* He blinks. "It's imperial law. You were given to Death and Fortune as a child, right?"

I stare at him. "So when I turn seventeen . . . ?"

"I think, legally, you'll belong to yourself." Emeric rubs the back of his neck. "Or. You should. I mean you should already on principle, but . . ."

I *cannot* believe I'm attracted to a human civics primer. A violent, electric hope sings through me. "I wouldn't have to leave. I—I could go *anywhere.*"

"They're gods, so I don't want to promise anything," he warns.

I barely hear. "I could look for my—"

Then the ruby teardrop gives a twinge.

"Your . . . ?" Emeric prompts.

I swallow hard, looking away as the cold reality catches back up. "It doesn't matter. I may not even make it to seventeen."

"You will."

I say nothing, just shuffle the cards again as Emeric watches.

He can watch all he wants, it won't do him any good. Sure enough, he draws the knight again, and mutters, "Unfortunate."

I decide to lighten the mood. "So," I say slyly. "You have a tattoo."

His ears turn red. "Er. That is, I—not quite. It's a mark from the first initiation. It's not unlike the marks you have from Death and Fortune."

I forgot he could see those. "What does it do?"

"Prefects are contracted like warlocks, but with the Low Gods at large. This part"—he taps two fingers to his heart—"binds me to the gods' rules for us. General 'don't be an evil bastard'–type policies, since no one should have the other mark without them. That mark comes after the second initiation, once I'm fully ordained. It will allow me to utilize the Low Gods' powers myself, within limits."

"Then how the hell did Adalbrecht—" I catch myself, but Emeric is, as ever, too quick to miss it.

"I knew that horse skull in the study was anchoring something powerful, just not *that* powerful," he says quietly. "A full-fledged prefect can't raise mountains or the like, but I've seen Hubert call down fire, speak to the dead . . . He even stopped time once for an emergency. Made himself sick for a week after, though. The human body isn't built to channel that much power, even with the second mark."

"Please tell me you get to pick what the mark looks like," I say. "I really want you to channel the might of the gods through a sexy *loreley*."

Emeric chokes on his wine. "I do not," he coughs, grinning. "More's the pity. I think I'd go for a cat."

It's my turn to snort into my mug. Whatever Ulli Wagner gave him for the witch-ash kickback, I owe them a life debt. I'm already feeling miles better.

Emeric draws the Page of Grails next, and we drain our mugs. Poldi refills them. I splay out the cards, and the queen shows her face again. "Your first theft," Emeric says, resting his fingers on the card. "Tell me about it."

"The von Holtzburgs? It was a mess."

He shakes his head. "You still could have managed your heists as Gisele's maid. So why did you take the pearls?"

I bite my lip. This is a harder tale to tell, even than that of the ruby ring.

And he can tell, because of course he can. "I'm sorry, you don't have to, I can ask something else."

I slide the Queen of Roses free from under his hand, shuffle her back into mine, shaking my head. Even though it hurts, this is what I want: to bleed the poison out.

I tell him of the wolf that came to Sovabin, of the maid who was caught in his teeth. I tell him of how I was expected to walk back into the wolf's jaws to save Gisele.

I tell him the whole ugly tale, thumbing through the cards. When I am done, I look up, steeling myself for questions, skepticism, the little rot of uncertainty.

Emeric's eyes glitter with coldest fury, fists white-knuckled knots on the carpet. "I promise you," he says, low and unsteady, "I will do everything in my power to keep him from *ever* hurting you again. Von Reigenbach will face justice if I have to drag him to it myself."

You would think the most formidable thing in Castle Reigenbach wouldn't be a reedy law library incarnate, but in that moment—he is, because I *believe* him.

He looks away, hands tangling again. "Thank you for telling me."

And—that's all.

"Y-you're taking my word for it?" I stumble.

That's when his eyes return to me, and they do not waver at all. "Why wouldn't I?"

It's not a challenge; it's a quiet, immovable fact. For all my schemes and façades and artifice, I am not prepared in the slightest for the simple, devastating intimacy of being believed.

I take a shaky breath. "Then, if possible, I would like to kick Adalbrecht's teeth in."

"I think that can be arranged."

We don't wait for the Page of Grails to take a long drink.

The next round is easier. He draws the queen again and hands her back to me with a sheepish grin. "How did you pull off the Eisendorf heist?"

"You don't know?" I almost yell, delighted.

"I'm just missing some, some *variables*," he huffs. "You obviously stole the jewelry while you were supposed to be in the guest parlor.

And you fooled the manservant into smuggling the goods out in the toilette bag. But there were guards posted outside the *komte* and *komtessin*'s chambers—"

"Didn't check the windows?"

He scowls. "They were locked from the inside. Besides, it would be impossible to climb to their balcony without ruining your gown, and a toilette bag has no room for a uniform."

I can't help wiggling with glee as I lean forward, ticking off my fingers. "One: There *was* room in the ugly cushions *I* sent Ezbeta a week earlier. They were stuffed with the servant uniform—"

"No," Emeric sputters, "they were still in the parlor—"

"*And* identical slipcovers," I continue with a smirk. "Two: *Cushion batting* can condense enough to fit in a toilette bag. And three: Ezbeta got night sweats from the spiced mead I *also* sent. She left a window open, and I bet she was embarrassed and locked it before you could see. It's all about the details, Junior." I hoist my mug. "To the *komtessin*'s good health."

Emeric stares at me, cogs turning. Then he clinks his mug against mine. "That's . . . brilliant. And terrifying."

I can't help a wicked smile as I shuffle the cards around on the floor. Emeric goes quiet.

Then he picks the Queen of Roses again.

"No," I say indignantly. "Three in a row? You're cheating."

He raises his hands. "I'm not. You have a tell."

"I do *not*!" I gape at him. There's no guile in his face. "What is it?"

He's trying not to laugh. "You know the rules. No free questions."

I'm going to strangle him. Or kiss him like the empire depends on it. Jury's still out. "Fine," I grumble. "Ask."

"Schmidt isn't really your last name, is it?"

That one I didn't see coming. "How did you know?"

"Call it a hunch."

I futz with a lock of hair. "I don't *think* it is. I don't know. When Death and Fortune left me at Castle Falbirg, the housekeeper asked for a family name, and my father was a smith, so. It worked."

"Do you want me to keep using Schmidt?"

I swallow. "Vanja is fine."

He lifts his mug to me. "Then to your health, Vanja."

I didn't expect to like hearing him say my name so much. I *really* didn't expect to giggle, but that at least I can drown in wine.

Then I reach for the cards again. Now the wine *is* going to my head, but I'll be damned if I let Emeric get away with keeping my tell to himself. I know he's going to expect me to leave the queen in the same place again. I slip the Knight of Shields there instead.

Sure enough, he turns over the knight.

"What is my tell?" I demand.

Emeric studies the cards, eyebrows quirking. "The secret isn't to try to watch the cards. That's what *you* want me to do. But right before you stop moving them, you look at the mark."

He leans forward and flips the card on the right. The Queen of Roses stares up at me.

He . . . he knew where she was all along.

"The secret," Emeric says, "is to watch you."

I can feel his gaze on me, and when I look up, I find the firelight snared in his eyes again.

And just like that: I am the firelight, caught in his stare, dancing and burning for it.

The room is suddenly very quiet, but it feels loud as thunder. Everything simmers with a new kind of fever, not just wine-warm but a strange sweet heat in my heartbeat, racing through every inch of me.

An entirely new question coils in the space between us.

We're dangerously close to an answer, if one of us moves—

A sharp knock at the door shatters the silence. We both jerk back. As I scramble to my feet, I discover a *lot* more of the wine has gone to my head than I thought. Emeric isn't in much better shape, stumbling into me. He starts to apologize and I clap my hand over his mouth, silently shush him, then drag him over to stand beside the door. Once it's open, it'll block him from view.

Then I shake out my hands, brush down my skirts, put on my best mild-mannered-servant face, and turn the knob.

Barthl is standing in the hall. He looks faintly surprised but only shifts in place.

"Marthe," he says. "Please pass this message to your mistress. We have received word that the Prince and Dame von Falbirg will be arriving first thing in the morning."

Every bit of that sweet fever drains from me.

"The margrave requests Princess Gisele join them for breakfast, for her parents wish to speak with her." Barthl shifts his weight again. "*Urgently.*"

CHAPTER TWENTY-EIGHT

MIRROR TO MIRROR

IT ISN'T UNTIL I WAKE UP TUESDAY MORNING THAT I REALIZE MY MIS-takes. Plural.

Was it splitting a bottle of wine by the fire with a boy who smells of juniper and keeps popping up one step ahead of me? Well, maybe. Probably. Almost certainly.

But the first undeniable mistake, you see, was depleting the wine too fast for Emeric to attempt taking the trellis back to his room. Adalbrecht couldn't make an attempt on Gisele's life with the von Falbirgs practically on his doorstep, so Poldi would be free to guard Emeric . . . but between the guests and the Wolfhünden, Emeric couldn't exactly sally out of the *prinzessin*'s bedroom unnoticed either.

This paved the way for the second mistake: trying to wait up for sobriety. We made a half-hearted stab at planning the next move. That lasted about a minute, as we found that between the lingering grief, the exhaustion, and the wine, the best we could come up with was "hit Adalbrecht in the head with a shovel and move to Bourgienne."

So instead, we stayed up just—talking. About cases he'd cracked, about close scrapes I'd had, about why he even needed five different knives (it turns out *grimlingen* hate copper, gold is good against curses, and . . . I forgot the others), and when I'd started picking locks (thirteen). About what he wished he could say to Klemens (goodbye, mostly), and what I wished I could say to the von Falbirgs over breakfast (eat glass, mostly).

But the third mistake, the *greatest* mistake, was talking until we both were drowning in yawns, then closing my eyes for only a second. And I know this because as I slowly drift awake now, I realize my pillow is . . . moving. And warm. And it has a heartbeat.

The fire's burned down to embers, but the room glows the mellow blue of the hour before snowy dawn. Enough light to see I am sprawled on my side, my head and half an arm flopped over Emeric's stomach. He looks as if he fell asleep propped against the hearth ledge and gradually slid south, one arm tucked behind his head, the other resting on his chest. I feel the weight of a blanket from the waist down, and I suspect the culprit is also responsible for removing Emeric's spectacles and placing them neatly on the hearthstones. My prime suspect is Ragne, curled up beside them as a black puff of a cat.

She is going to give me *so much* grief for this.

It's quiet in Castle Reigenbach, and so still, and I am the kind of half awake that cuts straight through the lies I tell myself.

I . . . *like* this.

It wasn't the wine, it wasn't my emotions running high. The first and last boy I had feelings for was Sebalt in the stables, who made me laugh every morning as he pitched down fresh hay to lay over Gisele's floor. Then he started courting the baker's daughter, and I sniffled into my scrub bucket for a day and a half, feeling like a fool.

But Emeric isn't the same. I want to think of another puzzle he can't solve. I want to empty his pockets and get caught in the act. I want the simple peace of being known by him; I want this strange, terrible hope he's given me, that I could build a life where I choose, instead of living ready to leave everything behind.

I don't know what's worse: that he's slipped into my heart like a knife, or that I like the feel of him there.

Emeric shifts in his sleep. His hand lifts from his chest and comes to a rest where my pulse beats at the corner of my jaw, fingers loosely tangling in my hair.

I catch my breath. There are too many wolves at my door: the wedding, the curse, the margrave trying to kill us both. The way he's recoiled from any suggestion we might be—more. My own ghost in the mirror, the unlovely face of a thief he has a sacred duty to catch.

Only a fool would hope for anything good to come of this.

In an hour or so, I'll have to get up to face the von Falbirgs and whatever Gisele's monstrous fiancé has to throw at me today. Still, that's an hour off.

I let my eyes slide shut again, leaning into the warmth of his palm. I have this, him, now. I can let myself be a fool a little longer.

༄

It turns out I was smart to defer getting up, because when I finally do, I find Eiswald's curse is done messing around.

Thick rubies run up my ankles to my knees like fat, bloody buttons. All of my breakouts have been relatively discreet until now, but these . . . They're obtrusive enough to poke through my stockings.

Emeric wakes up to me attempting to chip one off with his gold-plated knife. He takes in the room, the hour, and the sight of me chiseling away at a ruby on my shin, and says groggily, "I cannot tell you how many principles of knife safety you are violating right now."

"Where's your sense of adventure?"

"When it comes to stab wounds? On indefinite sabbatical." He sits up with a groan, rubbing his neck, and puts on his spectacles as Ragne unfurls herself on the hearth. "Good morning, Miss Ragne. When did you return?"

"Good morning." Ragne arches her back in a stretch, tail curling. "I came back late. I was very surprised to find you sleeping together."

The knife slips and almost gouges a hole in my calf. "That's not—"

"We didn't—" Emeric sputters at the same time, flushing. "Er."

"I'll explain later, Ragne," I say quickly, and hand Emeric his knife. The rubies are staying, like it or not. "All right. So. We have less than a week now. We need a real plan. Where do we start?"

Emeric gets up to pace, pinching the bridge of his nose. "We know a couple of things. The margrave is responsible for Hubert's murder, and he tried to pin it on the *Pfennigeist*. He's made serious attempts on both our lives, albeit yours typically in the guise of Gisele, even though he wants the wedding to go through."

"Seems like it's to humor the von Hirschings."

"True. Hmm. I also don't know why he would go to the effort of petitioning for prefects, only to murder Hubert. What does that get him? Why is it worth bringing scrutiny from the Order?" He pauses to offer me a hand up, still frowning out the window.

I take it and let him pull me to my feet. "And we still don't know what he's supposed to get out of marrying Gisele."

He shoots me a smile. "I *knew* you read through my notes." I think we both realize he's still holding on to my hand at the same time. He drops it, then rubs the back of his neck. "You'll be stuck with the von Falbirgs at least through the morning, right?"

"Can't wiggle out of that one," I grouse. "But I'll try to make the most of it. Maybe Adalbrecht will let something slip with them here."

Emeric's eyes light up. "That's it. I'll be right back."

"Give me a couple of minutes," I tell him as he heads for the veranda door. "I need to change."

While he's gone, I climb into the longest dress in my wardrobe, a currant-red samite gown embroidered with plump gold roses. It should hide my shins well enough. Adalbrecht will certainly take umbrage to the fact that I'm not in Reigenbach blue, but I can call it close to Falbirg red for filial piety's sake. The thick leather of my boots helps cover the rubies, too, but it still won't hold up to close inspection.

I pull the upper half of my hair back into a serviceable bun, and I'm in the middle of fastening an earring when there's a quiet rap at the veranda door.

"Can I let him in?" Ragne asks, knotting the sash of the dressing gown I left out for her.

I nod, and Emeric steps inside once Ragne turns the doorknob.

"Apparently I've been invited to breakfast as well. Not at the high table with you all, thank the gods, just . . ." Emeric trails off.

"What?" I grab the other earring and walk over. "At the great table in the banquet hall?"

He gives a tiny shake of his head, like a horse vexed by a fly. "Ah. Yes. That . . . that one. We should make sure to arrive separately. Anyway, this is what I wanted to show you." He pulls two silver cases from his waistcoat, round and palm-sized like pocket mirrors, flicks them both open, and hands one to me. Sure enough, there's a mirror set in one half and a generic engraving of a sleeping face in the other, facing the left. "Breathe on the mirror."

When I do, the engraving's eye opens.

"If you close it like this, it will record everything spoken in a ten-foot radius until you breathe on it again," Emeric says. "And we can listen to it later, from my mirror or yours. If you close it *this* way"—he twists it at the hinge, so when it shuts, the mirror faces out—"it will stop recording, but anything you trace onto the mirror will show up on mine."

"Anything?" Ragne peers over my shoulder as I rotate the mirror.

"Yes, like this." He draws a quick spiral on the glass. There's a quick flare of heat from my mirror's case, and then the glass fogs. The spiral appears, fades, reappears. "So you can pass messages undetected. Or . . ." He makes an exasperated noise. "Vanja."

I look up innocently. "Yes?"

Ragne cackles, pointing at my mirror. "That's a *butt*."

"I'm just testing it," I say, straight-faced.

By contrast, Emeric's mouth twists at the corners, like he's trying not to condone my artistic choices. "I'm already regretting this. The point is, if the conversation gets interesting, you can record it." He pauses, then adds, "And if things get bad and you need help, you can let me know. I'll figure something out."

The concern in his voice flips my stomach like the Queen of Roses. I discover this was perhaps not the best moment to have added a small but distinct fart cloud to the butt.

Emeric lets out a long-suffering sigh. "Are you just going to use it to draw crude—"

I stow mine in my pocket before he can take it back. "Only time will tell, Junior."

He's making a valiant attempt at gravitas. Then real somberness steals over his face. "Oh. And . . . one more thing. Here." He hands me a pewter coin stamped with the symbol of the prefects.

"I would like to remind you *how fast* I would get kicked out of the Order," I say.

"It's not a prefect coin, it's an amnesty token." He waves a hand over the coin. Glowing runes and letters rise into the air; I think I see *Vanja Schmidt* among them. "I had Wagner specifically link it to you and this case. We give them to people who are, er, consulting with us. It means none of the prefects can detain you, not even a sanctimonious coatrack of a junior prefect." His voice softens. "I can't ask you to trust me while I have the power to arrest you. So now I don't."

I stare at the pool of pewter in my palm. "How long does it last?"

"It can't be revoked by anyone until after the case it's linked to is closed." He cocks his head. "As you can imagine, we don't hand these out like candy, so I'm going to be very embarrassed and in a lot of trouble if you go on a crime spree in the meantime."

I'm at a loss for words. Probably because I'm having an extraordinary and overwhelming number of feelings right now, and chief among them is outrage that I am *this* attracted to a personified pocket ledger.

There's a knock at the door. I grab the pearls, clasp them around my neck, and flap my hands at Emeric to shoo him out. He's almost gawking at me with a peculiar expression; if I didn't know better, I'd call it dazed.

Cold reality flattens out any fledgling hope in my veins. Right, of course. No one's immune to the pearls. It's just a gut punch to be reminded what they do to him.

What I don't.

I consider tossing the contents of my washbasin at him, but Ragne pushes him out onto the veranda instead. She shrinks herself to a mouse as I answer the door.

Barthl is back. His eyes linger on the ruby teardrop, but he doesn't say anything about it, only escorts me to the entrance hall.

The sun is almost too bright, shattering off the pale marble and alabaster and relenting only on the red-fringed swaths of blue bunting. Adalbrecht's added more golden wolf statues, because of course he has, and now a small fortune in hothouse flowers crowds urns around the hall: cornflower for prosperity, dahlia for promises kept, peony for high hopes . . . white lilies, a loaded choice. They can signify purity, but Death liked to keep some in the house when I lived with her and Fortune. It wasn't until later I learned she took them from funerals.

The margrave himself tromps down from his wing just as the doors of the entrance hall swing open. And then they're here: the Prince and Dame von Falbirg.

The last year looks to have been kind to them; either that or they've gone to considerable expense to make it appear so. I see velvet and miniver instead of fustian and rabbit fur, rosy cheeks instead of sallow, comfort instead of hunger.

Still, a year is not enough to forget who they are. Gisele—the real Gisele—takes after her father, with his broad hunter's build and light brown hair, but the hard gray eyes are all her mother.

And when I see them, a stale frost seizes my heart, my spine, my lungs. I'm bracing for a rebuke. I'm looking over the silver, because there will be no dinner if I missed a spot. I'm stiffening against a tirade because they traveled so far just to see me, and there's a wrinkle on my sleeve, and can't I do *anything* right?

But Dame von Falbirg surges forward in an assault of velvet, throws her arms around my neck, and practically sings, "*My darling!*"

Right. I have the pearls; I am the *Prinzessin* now. I am safe, I tell myself. They *want* to like me.

Still, something in my bones is buzzing on high alert.

I go into a kind of fog, making inoffensive small talk as we head to the banquet hall. It's almost as massive as the ballroom, set just above the kitchens in the north end of the castle, with windows all along the eastern wall to let in the morning light. I'm pretty sure the decorations of evergreen boughs and gilded ivy have been repurposed from the ball.

It's also close to bursting. Its infamous oaken banquet table is a relic from the days of Kunigunde, who made a point of seating her noble guests alongside her soldiers, and ordered a table to accommodate. One of her descendants found that demeaning and added a dais for the high table at some point, but nothing spares us the noise of the guests. Kunigunde's ambitions, too, have been mitigated, for the end nearest the dais is choking with nobles, and the far end left for the common element.

I move through it all in a detached haze. I'm not me, I'm not even my invention of the *Prinzessin*. I'm a bland, unobjectionable, beautiful girl, someone not even the von Falbirgs can find fault in.

When we reach the high table, near sagging with an outlandish floral centerpiece, it gets worse. Not just because I have to sit at the foot, across from Adalbrecht, but because the von Falbirgs are on my left . . . and the von Hirschings to my right.

"They're practically family," Adalbrecht says. "You're acquainted, I believe?"

"We had a lovely little visit, what was it, three years ago?" Irmgard blinks my way through plumes of baby's breath, chin propped on her laced fingers. You would hardly think just two nights ago, she'd been castigating *Markgraf* von Reigenbach for failing to murder me on her schedule.

"Four," I say distantly. "Four years, in less than a week."

Dame von Falbirg reaches over and clasps my left hand, squeezing it in her powder-soft one. "You've both become such *precious* young ladies. I'm sure your father is just as proud of you, *Frohlein* Irmgard, as we are of our little pearl."

I think I'm going to be sick.

What is wrong with me? I've endured Irmgard before, the von

Falbirgs think I'm their key to salvation, and there are too many witnesses for Adalbrecht to do anything. Yet I still feel like at any point, my
throat's about to be slashed from behind.

I slip my right hand into my pocket and find the mirror. The weight,
the cool metal, it steadies me a little. Or it gives me something to grip
until my fingers break. Either way, it helps.

Adalbrecht straightens abruptly, eyes sharpening. "Franziska," he
barks. The steward hurries over. "Go get the Conrad boy, he just walked
in. I need a word."

A different kind of alarm needles through the fog, familiar and almost
welcome. We were careful to stay out of the hallway last night, and none
of the other guests in the riverfront wing should have been out on their
balconies thanks to the cold—but if we *were* seen somehow—no, they
would have spotted him with Marthe the Maid, not the *prinzessin*—

But when Emeric arrives, we discover Adalbrecht means to twist
two knives at once.

Emeric stops before the dais and drops a quick bow, going through
his fidget-shuffle routine and distinctly not looking at me. "Sir?"

Markgraf Adalbrecht stands, circles the table, comes to a halt by
my chair. His hand drops onto my right shoulder, a little too close to
my neck. "I wished to offer my sincerest condolences, Conrad." He
squeezes, a little harder than Dame von Falbirg still clinging to my left
hand. "I heard the news about Prefect Klemens. Truly devastating."

Emeric bows his head and clasps his hands behind his back—but
not before I see them snarl into fists. "Much appreciated. Sir."

"Do you have any idea who would do something so heinous?"
Adalbrecht grips my other shoulder as well, his thumb brushing up
against the string of pearls. I freeze, my face stiffening into a mask of
empty sympathy.

Emeric's eyes flick briefly to me, then away. I'm fairly certain he's reconsidering his stance on stab wounds. To his credit, the only sign is a muscle jumping in his jaw. "I'm not at liberty to say," he says tightly. "Thank you again for your concern, sir. Please excuse me."

Adalbrecht lets me go once Emeric turns his back, and I can breathe again. *Damn* him. Damn it all.

There's one thing I can salvage from this: my fury. It reminds me who I am.

My head clears at least a little. I squeeze the dame's hand and then pull free. The conversation picks back up again with Count von Hirsching pressing Adalbrecht for details on the murder as he returns to his seat. I don a look of genteel horror and find the mirror surface in my pocket, then trace out:

Want
me to
poison
him?

After a moment, I feel the pulse of heat from the case. I sneak the mirror into my lap to read the answer in the fogged glass.

Yes

Then:

<u>*DON'T*</u>

Emeric might know me a little too well.

Irmgard lets out a scandalized squeal, no doubt over some grisly detail—and I realize Adalbrecht may give something away here, with what he knows about Klemens's death. I twist the case lid into the recording mode and slip it back into my pocket.

Prinz von Falbirg speaks up with a strained rumble. "Forgive me, but perhaps business matters would make for better breakfast conversation. *Markgraf* Adalbrecht, do you have the adrogation paperwork here—"

Adrogation. Where have I heard that term before?

He's cut off by a minor furor as breakfast arrives. The table fills with *rohtwurst*, pumpernickel, steaming *damfnudeln*. Irmgard practically leaps for the tureen of *weysserwurst*. Some part of me finds that a little on the nose.

"It's in my study," Adalbrecht says over his coffee. "As long as the paperwork is dealt with before the ceremony, I'm at your leisure."

I pick at the *damfnudeln*, biting my tongue. Adalbrecht isn't at *anyone's* leisure, ever, and he makes sure they know it.

"Very well. Gisele, dear, we've also brought your Imperial Citizenship papers. You should be able to submit them at the end of the month."

Adalbrecht tenses. "Bring those to my study as well. We wouldn't want them getting misplaced in all the"—he slices into a *weysserwurst*, grim-faced—"revelry."

"Certainly not." *Prinz* von Falbirg leans forward to peer down the table at me. "You've barely touched your breakfast. Are you feeling all right?"

"O-of course, Papa," I say. "I'm just so excited."

Irmgard tilts her head, lips pursing. "You must certainly be. We know how much you love your *damfnudeln*."

"Well, eat up," the prince says sternly. "Can't have you fainting on the big day."

But the dame has other priorities. Her eyes are gleaming with pride at my neglected plate. "Leave her be, dear. It's a fine thing for a young lady to mind her figure."

Saints and martyrs. I remember Dame von Falbirg pushing Gisele to eat like a bird when we were younger, but this is my first time being on the receiving end. Why go to the trouble of procuring the pearls only to keep trying to cut her down?

I make myself take an enormous bite, if only to watch the dame's smile falter.

"My poor little moonbeam has such a delicate constitution," Adalbrecht says.

Prinz von Falbirg's brows raise. "Really? She had such a hearty stomach in Sovabin."

"Perhaps Minkjan fare does not agree with her," Irmgard coos with a sympathetic pout.

My throat closes.

"What a lovely ruby." Dame von Falbirg reaches for my face. I flinch back on instinct, then scramble to turn it into a cough. She tilts my cheek when I'm done. "Wherever did you get it?"

"She won't say," Irmgard declares, smirking.

The dame gasps with delight, a gossip hound scenting blood. She always treated these things like a game, a rosebush someone else grows for her, shoving her face in the petals but ignoring the thorns. "Is it a secret? A nameless admirer, perhaps?"

Adalbrecht looks like he's going to flip the table.

"No, no," I stammer. "Just a—a jeweler. Wanted me to show off his latest."

I should have a clever jibe, a riposte, *anything*. I kept my head when Emeric clapped me in irons, when a *nachtmahr* nearly bit my face off, even with a roomful of orphans heckling me. But I can't do it now. Not for the prince and dame.

Some part of me is still scared of them. And it's going to get me caught.

The dame takes a delicate sip of her coffee. "We'll have plenty of time to discuss that later."

"Later?" I croak.

"Your papa and I thought it would be lovely to take tea together after lunch, just the three of us." She smiles. It doesn't reach her eyes. "As a *family*."

There's that razor glimmer again, as her gaze lingers on the ruby. It's drawing out her greed.

I don't want to be alone with her, I don't, I don't—

I gulp. "That would be lovely."

"So, Gisele," the *prinz* says, leaning forward again. "What have you been up to for the last year?"

I switch the mirror back and trace a single, frantic word on the cool glass:

HELP

CHAPTER TWENTY-NINE

❡LD ❡ABITS

I MUMBLE SOME NONSENSE ABOUT CHARITY AND EXPLORING BÓERN, then try to keep breathing while the rest of the table moves on to something else. I don't dare check for a reply until they're distracted.

All the mirror says is: *ON IT.*

A knot in my chest loosens at that. Then, barely ten minutes later, the mirror pulses again. This time the handwriting has changed.

It's Gisele.
What do you need?

She steers me through the remaining hour of breakfast, then hands me an excuse to retreat (I need to lie down after *such* a sumptuous meal). It takes everything in me not to bolt for the riverfront wing as the hour-bells ring in eleven o'clock. A minute after my bedroom door thuds shut, I hear the dead roses rattle on the trellis, then a rap at the veranda door. I set the pearls on the vanity and let Emeric in.

"Are you all right?" is the first thing out of his mouth as he steps inside.

I start to say some watered-down nonsense about how I'm fine, just rattled, until I realize I don't want to lie to him. I'm too tired to keep lying. I can still feel Adalbrecht's fingers digging too close to my throat.

Instead I let my head my head fall forward until it rests on his chest. Emeric goes still. Then one of his hands settles gently over the back of my head, and the steady warmth of it is as calming as the soft beat of his heart.

"I hate him," I whisper. "I hate them all so much I can't think."

It turns out he handed his mirror off to Ragne, who flew it to Gisele for help. Perhaps it was her parents, or her guilt, or she felt she owed me for finding a place for the Gänslinghaus residents. Whatever her cause, Gisele has agreed to take over, at least for the day.

And when Gisele walks into the room in a hastily pilfered servant uniform a little after noon, I'm . . . actually happy to see her. Ragne pokes out of her pocket as a squirrel once the door is shut.

"Here." Gisele hands Emeric his mirror back. "They aren't expecting you until teatime?"

"I said breakfast was too heavy, so I'd skip lunch. Do you need help getting ready?"

Gisele frowns, looking around the room. "No, I can do it myself now, mostly. I may need help figuring out where things are."

"I'll leave you to it." Emeric's been sitting beside me on the trunk at the end of the bed, but he stands, dusting his breeches off. "Vanja, did you record anything?"

I nod. "It's not much, but Adalbrecht said something about paperwork that seemed . . . off."

"Paperwork?" Gisele frowns. "What paperwork?"

Emeric fiddles with his pocket mirror. It plays out the conversation from breakfast like a bard plays a song.

His brow furrows at *adrogation.* I *knew* I'd seen it somewhere.

"*It's a fine thing for a young lady to mind her figure,*" the dame simpers, and Gisele winces.

"Enough, please," she says.

Emeric snaps the mirror shut. "Where have I heard that before? Adrogation?"

"I remember it too!" I jump to my feet. "Which means we saw it together—"

"The night of the ball—"

"In the study—"

"*The law book!*" we say at the same time.

Gisele is looking from me to Emeric, eyes narrowed. Then she clasps her hands together. "That sounds like a solid lead, *Meister* Conrad, why don't you follow up on that now? Vanja and I will have Ragne in case of an emergency, and we'll use the mirror to let you know if we learn anything. We can all reconvene later at the cathedral." She barely lets him nod in agreement before hustling him toward the bedroom door.

"No—out the veranda—" I yank them about-face.

"Oh, right, right." Gisele laughs a bit too sunnily, and pulls the veranda door open just long enough to shove Emeric out. She waits until the trellis sounds its rattle to whirl back to me. Her voice drops to a delighted hiss. "When Ragne said you slept together I didn't think she meant *slept together.*"

"Stop that." I toss Gisele a fine embroidered cambric shift as the castle hour-bells chime. "Here, we don't have much time. Pearls after that, then the dress. And nothing happened last night."

"Really? Because *that* just now was like watching two sweethearts prance around a Maypole."

"I'm allergic to prancing," I say dourly. "We talked things out and fell asleep by the fire, and that was it."

"You were lying very close together," Ragne mews, curled up on the hearth as a cat once more. "What's the word?"

"*Snuggling*, I think," Gisele says with a smirk.

I go foraging in the wardrobe, partially for a gown and mostly to hide my burning face. "It doesn't matter."

She pulls the shift over her head. "You know when we were younger, how I'd ask you to get straw for my floor rushes every day? So you had to keep going to the stables when Sebalt was working?"

I peer around the wardrobe door, over an armful of emerald silk. "You *didn't*."

"I'm just saying, if *I* were you, impersonating, well, me, Gisele would be *very* invested in the *Pfennigeist* case and making sure all her correspondence with the junior prefect were delivered by her maid's hand."

"The Vanja did that," Ragne says brightly. "Well, she asked me to go check on you at the cathedral last night."

Gisele snorts. "I see. Thank you for improving *my* night, then." Then her cheer falters a little. "Ragne told you about . . . us, already, right?"

"She did." I lay the dress out on the bed. "Pearls are on the vanity. We'll put the ruby on last."

I try not to look at Gisele as the pearls go on. Instead I focus on changing into a servant uniform. There's a moment of just rustling fabric. Then Gisele asks, "You aren't mad I didn't tell you?"

"What?" I frown as I paste plaster and gauze over my own ruby. "Of course not. Your parents were . . ." I catch myself before I say something crude. ". . . *clear*. About you carrying on the bloodline. I mean, I'm assuming you only like girls."

"I—I'm pretty sure."

"Then it makes all the sense in the world why you would hide it. It narrows down your prospects."

She nods, face tight. "There are . . . options. I've heard of warlocks who could help me have a child. And a few noble families have daughters they thought were boys at birth, so they might . . . But I've never met them, and Mama never would have paid for me to travel across the empire just for that."

Neither of us says the rotten truth aloud: Dame von Falbirg emptied coffers for the pearls readily enough.

"Knowing your mother, she'd say you did it on purpose just to make her life harder," I say instead. "Like *that's* how it works." I still avoid looking at her, focusing instead on bundling heavy woolen leggings over my stockings. It's hardly an elegant way to hide the rubies, but nobody expects elegance from a chambermaid anyway. Especially not in this cold. "When did you know?"

Gisele's shoulders hunch, so much so I see it from the corner of my eye. "When Irmgard visited. I just remember seeing her for the first time, and thinking that that was how the prince felt in fairy tales, right? When he sees the princess for the first time. She was so pretty, and funny, and Mama liked her so much . . . And then she turned out to be a nightmare."

No wonder Gisele fell for Ragne. It's the same reason Ragne was the first new person I'd call a friend: Ragne loves who she loves without question, without games. "You chose better this time," I say stiffly. "Granted, if you hurt Ragne, you know I will make this last year seem like a romp in the countryside."

Gisele lets out a startled laugh. It's not angry disbelief, more surprise. Then she smiles and says, with more steel in her voice than I've ever heard, "Likewise."

A knock rattles the door. I tap my cheek and whisper, "*Ruby!*" Then I go to answer.

Trudl is there, flanked by another maid. "The Prince and Dame von Falbirg wish to tell Her Ladyship that they have concluded their luncheon and will be proceeding to her parlor shortly. A tea service is on its way."

"Please be sure to include *pfeffernüszen* for my mother," Gisele calls over my shoulder, one hand pressing the ruby to her face as the glue sets. "Thank you!"

Trudl looks a little baffled at the thanks, but bobs a curtsy and hurries off. I close the door. "By the way, they all think my name is Marthe. It's a long story. Come on, I'll take you to the parlor."

This proves to be another mistake. The moment I open the door ahead of Gisele, the prince and dame light up.

"Oh, my little *Rohtpfenni*! How good it is to see you well!" Dame von Falbirg presses a hand to her heart. "Why don't you stay and serve the tea? It will be just like old times."

"She has work to do, Mama," Gisele says quickly.

"Nonsense, what could be more important than family? I'll hear no argument." The dame flicks her hand to dismiss the attendant posted by the door.

The attendant hesitates, looking to Gisele.

Gisele doesn't know how to parse it at first, and I realize she has never once been the mistress of a castle. Not here, not Castle Falbirg.

"It's no trouble, Princess Gisele," I grit between my teeth.

The dame gives another thin smile. "Of course it isn't."

Gisele swallows. Then she nods to the attendant, who bows and leaves, shutting the parlor door behind them.

"The *tea*, Vanja," barks the dame, and miserable instinct takes over. It's so much easier to be quiet, to just do as they ask, no matter how it chafes.

The tea is poured: cream and honey for the prince, a splash of cream for the dame—

Dame von Falbirg wrinkles her nose. "Too much, Vanja. Do it again."

"I'll take it." Gisele plucks the teacup away before her mother can refuse. "That's how I like it these days."

I get it right the second time. Then I retreat to the corner of the room to wait.

Unbidden, I hear Emeric's words from last night: *It wouldn't excuse how I treated you. Or how the von Falbirgs did.*

I wish I could stop thinking about him. I wish I didn't *like* thinking about him.

I can't understand it. By the cold numbers, I should be almost as afraid of Emeric as I am of Adalbrecht. They've both threatened me, hurt me; what does it matter if one did it in the name of duty, and one did it out of hunger?

But the difference, I suppose, is the amnesty nestled in my own pocket. Emeric's had chances to hurt me again, especially with every scar I bared last night. Instead he showed me his own, armed me with ways to hurt him, too, so we would be even. He gave up power over me so I would feel safer.

If Adalbrecht knew even one of the wounds I hide, he would use it to hunt me down. Emeric knows so many of mine, and he chooses to help.

Whatever this game is between us, it doesn't play by the rules of the trinity of want. It isn't about servitude, it isn't a hunt. It's a dance. We're on even ground; I'm not afraid to lose. And that makes all the difference.

"*Vanja!*" The dame's voice breaks through my thoughts. I hate that I jump to attention on reflex. From the look on the dame's face, it's not the first time she's called for me. She holds up her empty teacup, mouth pinched.

"Right away, m'lady." When I get to the table I notice the serving plates have been shuffled around. I remember this move: Dame von Falbirg would always rotate all the sweets gradually out of Gisele's reach, even if she'd had just one. I guess old habits die hard.

She says loftily as I refill her teacup, "I hope you haven't been easy on her, Gisele. She's just going to get lazy."

I meet Gisele's gaze and see her jaw clench. There's a sting to her anger, the same in mine: A year softened our memories of this to an ache.

But it was always this poisonous. And it burns coming back up.

Then Gisele does something new. She sets her own teacup down with an indelicate clatter of porcelain and says, "Don't talk about Vanja that way."

The prince and dame stare at her, mystified. *Prinz* von Falbirg is the one to find words first. "She's your servant," he says, like he's explaining which way is north.

Like Ragne, when she told me she helped because that's what people do. Like Emeric, when I asked what it would cost to save me, and he said I owed him nothing.

Too late, I realize the dame's teacup is overflowing. She leaps to her feet as tea spills onto the table. A few drops land on her velvet skirt.

"You clumsy little *oaf*—" the dame snarls, drawing her hand back.

Gisele's chair falls over with a thud. A tide of emerald silk crashes between me and Dame von Falbirg as Gisele catches her arm. *"NO."*

The pearls lie on the floor. Without them, Gisele's even taller than her mother now.

"Put the pearls back on." The came wrenches her arm free. Her breath is coming faster, but her voice and poise stay icily calm. "You don't want anyone seeing you like this—"

Gisele returns frost with frost. "I'm not afraid to be seen as I am. Like I see *you* for what you are. You used Vanja every day she was under our roof. You bought the von Hirschings with her blood. You have no right to raise a hand to her. The *least* you owe her is respect."

The prince rises from his chair, face darkening. "We took her in when she had nowhere to go. We gave her everything she needed. Didn't we, Vanja?"

I have spent so many hours thinking of exactly what I would say to just this question. What witty, devastating insults I could unleash, what cutting observations I could carve into them. But in the end, only the unvarnished truth spills from my lips.

"You paid me because I worked for you," I say, matching Gisele's chill. "And you worked me to the bone for pennies, so I couldn't afford to leave."

The dame's face twists, that ice growing perilously thin. "You ungrateful little *wretches*. Do you know how lucky you are? The margrave is a true nobleman, and *I* made you his bride. Look at this—" She slashes her hand at the parlor. "Do you think you would have any of this without us? Without those pearls?"

"You sold us to a monster," Gisele returns. "You didn't ask if he was kind, or if he was honorable, because you knew he was neither and you didn't care. You just cared about his money." She snatches up the pearls and heads for the door.

"We're not done," *Prinz* von Falbirg blusters. "Get back here this instant."

Gisele clasps the pearls back on as I catch up to her. "No, we *are* done, because I say so. It's my castle." She opens the door, then shuts it most of the way again and turns, eyes glittering with a ferocious kind of joy. "Oh, and by the way: I'm not even interested in men. Not that you ever asked."

Then she breezes through the door. I follow with a broad, feverish grin, and can't help an *entirely* inappropriate mock-salute as I slip into the hall.

We rush to the bedroom in the stiff, frantic walk of people who need to hurry and are pretending they don't. Once the door shuts behind us, I say numbly, "*Scheit*. You just did that."

"I just did that," she echoes, eyes wide. Then she grabs my arms. "*I did that!*"

"*You did that!*"

And suddenly we're both laughing and crying and jumping in place. It feels like a curse has broken, one older and bitterer than Eiswald's.

It's not just that Gisele defended me. It's that some part of me needed to see it, to understand that the prince and dame *could* be cracked, and we could both walk away.

"What did you do?" Ragne asks, sitting up on the hearth. She's dressed herself again, this time in a shirt tucked into riding breeches.

I grin through my tears. "She told her parents to get stuffed."

"I just," Gisele gasps, "after everything, I couldn't keep lying to myself about how awful they were to you—"

"I can't believe your mother, still pulling that nonsense with the food—"

Gisele scrubs at her face with the heel of her palm. "Saints and martyrs, neither can I. And it's not just that they were cruel to us. You were right, earlier. Umayya and I ran the Gänslinghaus not just to give the children a home, but to make sure it was one where they could still *be* children. You never got that, did you? You always had to look after me."

I duck my head, tears winning for the moment. "Well," I say thickly. "It's over now."

"Here." Ragne holds out two kerchiefs. Once we take them, she winds her arms around Gisele's shoulders. "You both sound happier."

Gisele leans her head against Ragne's and tangles their fingers together. "I know I am. I didn't plan on blowing up at them, but knowing my mother, she'll stay out of our hair from now on, rather than risk me causing a scene."

"Well, damn. I thought we could switch and I'd take a turn yelling at them."

Gisele laughs again. "I just wish I'd done it earlier. I . . . learned a lot in the last year. By the time I made it to Minkja, my money was gone, and Umayya was the only one who would take me in and let me work for my keep. I was so angry at you, because what you did left me powerless. And I kept telling myself I stayed angry because you had all—all of *this*, and you weren't doing anything with it, you weren't helping people. I mean, all it took was one afternoon of forgiving debts and you made me the most popular girl in Minkja."

"Maybe Eiswald should have cursed me sooner," I deadpan.

Gisele sits on the bed, looking around the room. Her eyes linger on Ragne, then me. "But I'm a hypocrite, aren't I? I've been angry because I was left as powerless as you were in my home. And for all my preaching about helping people, you offered this life back and I turned it down." She blows her nose. "The night of the ball, you started to say I should have protected you from Adalbrecht, didn't you?"

I sit on the other end of the bed. Then I nod. "I'm sorry I took this from you, but . . ."

"You were trying to protect yourself," Gisele finishes. "I understand."

We stay quiet for a long moment. There's still a distance between us, one that will take time to close. But the thorns are behind us now.

Finally I say, "Well, that's you and Emeric down, so if my mother shows up for a heartfelt apology by sundown, I'll have a trifecta."

Gisele lets out a very unladylike snort. Then she clenches her fists and takes a deep breath. "If—if your offer's still open . . . I'll do it."

A weight lifts. "You'll come back?"

"*If* we stop Adalbrecht," she says swiftly. "We can help Emeric bring him down before it's too late for either of us. Then I'll take back my life, and your curse should be broken."

I stare at her. The princess and the loyal maid died in the woods together a year ago; we are just two girls trying to survive now. And this is it. This is how we take down the wolf: together.

I sit back and stare at the canopy, shaking my head as I laugh. "Depose the second-most powerful politician in the Blessed Empire of Almandy, who seems to have never-ending nightmare monsters at his disposal. Sure. Why not? How hard can it be?"

CHAPTER THIRTY

Adrogation

THE FIGHT WITH THE VON FALBIRGS BUYS US THE REST OF THE EVE-
ning. I'm not sure who decides Gisele is not well enough to join the
evening festivities, Adalbrecht or her parents, but either way dinner is
sent up for us instead. It's plainer fare, and uninvited, and the message
is clear. Adalbrecht will not tolerate any chance of her making a scene.

It seems he wants to make sure to drive that message home, though,
because he sends a brief missive with the meal: a reminder that Gisele is
expected to join the rest of the guests tomorrow for a hunt.

"That's a death threat, right?" Gisele says, scanning the paper as we
split liver dumpling soup and a plate of Minkja-style kraut. "He's going
to try to kill me."

"Probably," I say around a mouthful of dumpling. "But he also has
to be the best hunter there. He'll be humiliated if anyone else gets the

biggest kill on his wedding hunt. If you hang back with most of the guests, you'll be surrounded by witnesses. Really, Irmgard could be a bigger threat if she gets proactive."

"Will you go with me?"

"I could barely keep up with you when we were younger."

"I could be the Vanja's horse," Ragne offers, picking at a slice of rye. "Then you will keep up for certain."

I think it over. "That could work." I can't help fidgeting with a spoon. "We, uh, told Emeric we'd meet up at the cathedral, right?"

Gisele smirks at me. "We *did*, in fact. And I'm sure Umayya needs a break, she's been managing the children herself for most of the day, so we can give you and Emeric some time alone—"

I throw a scarf at her.

When we arrive at Fortune's cathedral, though, we find that Umayya isn't exactly on her own. The residents of the Gänslinghaus have been given a small wing in the clergy dormitory, though truth be told, it might be larger than their old house. The common room certainly is, with sturdy couches and armchairs whose cushions have been forcibly donated to an impressive fortress, mostly empty baskets of toys, a few heavy tables with the edges sanded down, and a slate wall at the far end. I suspect the room's typically used for children of the clergy, but the orphans have settled right in, most of them gathered around Umayya as she reads aloud by a roaring fireplace.

Emeric's at the slate wall, though, with a handful of stragglers. His hands are on his hips, sleeves rolled up, back to us, one foot tapping irately as he studies a complicated chalk diagram. A few of the children are scribbling on the lower half of the wall to either side of him, adding a rather jarring border of flowers, horses, and soldiers to his work. A little hand tugs at his, and he passes off his own chalk but otherwise stays still, likely for the benefit of a small Gharese girl standing on a chair beside him so she can attempt to put a braid in his hair. She doesn't seem to be having much success.

"Khidren, let the boy think," Joniza calls distractedly from a nearby table, frowning at a sheaf of parchment.

The little girl pouts. "His hair's too short anyway. Can I braid yours?"

Joniza presses her lips together, trying not to laugh. "My hair's already in braids," she says. "And it took a long time, and I paid a nice woman a lot of money to do it, so I think I'll have to pass, thank you."

"You can braid my hair," Gisele informs Khidren as we walk over to the table nearest the slate wall. I see both sets of Emeric's notes wedged between a few volumes of Imperial Law.

Khidren ties a pink ribbon in a bow around Emeric's head, to match the outlandishly fluffy ones clustered on her own glossy dark braid. "There. Now you're pretty."

"Thank you," he says solemnly, spectacles askew. "I've been very concerned."

"You're *welcome*." She overenunciates in the way of a child still nailing down their please-and-thank-yous, then hops down and zooms over to Gisele.

I set my cloak and scarf on the table with the law books and go to squint at the diagram, doing my best to muffle my sheer delight at Emeric's new accessory. "So the lead with the law book didn't pan out?"

"It's definitely part of the picture, I just can't see how it fits," he grumbles, straightening his spectacles. "The mar—excuse me, the *baker* had—"

"Who is the baker?" Ragne asks, dropping her cloak by mine. She only deigned to wear one for the sake of disguise; a thick layer of black fur is still running down her arms.

"*Mäestrin* Umayya allowed me to use the slate wall so long as I remembered I had a, er, younger audience," Emeric explains, "who also might repeat what they read or hear."

I take a closer look at the wall. "'Possible motives for baker to . . . hug *G*'? *Hug*? Really?"

"*G* is for the Gisele, yes?" Ragne crouches on the chair like a wayward gargoyle. "Why is this baker hugging the Gisele?"

"No, it's code for, er—" Emeric draws a finger across his throat. The ribbon flopping in his hair *really* brings the gravity of the situation home.

Ragne brightens. "I know that! The Vanja told me. It means dead." Then she bristles. "Who is hugging the Gisele to death?"

One of the little boys ceases his drawing and whirls around, eyes sparkling. "Who's dead?"

"*Aaaand* it's bedtime," Umayya announces from across the room.

"Let me take care of it, Umayya. You rest. Come on, everyone, pack it up." Gisele starts ushering children toward a hallway.

Joniza sets down her parchment. "That's my cue too. Those little monsters better be happy with one lullaby. I have a gig tonight."

As the room quiets down, strains of a festive Winterfast carol rise from the street, punctuated by jingling bells. Normally the carol-band would be playing in the Göttermarkt so couples could dance in the plaza, but it seems they're making do outside. I can't say I mind. Low Gods don't typically tolerate any *grimlingen* in their temples, but it's good to be doubly sure the *nachtmären* will keep clear of the bells.

Emeric waits until Khidren is out of sight to remove the ribbon, though he absentmindedly winds it around his knuckles as he thinks. I did not expect that to make it *incredibly* difficult to concentrate, but it turns out I'm learning a lot of things about myself these days.

Once the children are out of earshot, he speaks. "I'm afraid I have some dismal news. First, apparently the nearest fully ordained prefects can't make it to Minkja for another week."

My stomach drops. "Does that mean we can't summon the Godly Court, then?"

"Not exactly," Emeric says slowly. "I'm not supposed to, but I can, in an emergency. It . . . It'll be fine. We just have to make a strong case." The ribbon digs into his hand a little too deep. "But that's the other bit of news. I borrowed a couple of law books from the outpost's library so I could look into the section *Markgraf* von Reigenbach bookmarked. It doesn't give us any clear answers."

There's a shuffle behind me. I turn and find Umayya walking up.

"I want to see what this boy's been working on," she explains, bundling her indigo shawl tighter. "I like puzzles, when I'm not picking them up off the floor."

"Princess Gisele brought you up to speed on her situation?" Emeric asks, and she nods. He sets the ribbon on the table. "Then yes, please. The three of you could see what I'm missing."

I pick up a volume that's been left open, and see SECTION 13.2: FILIATION AND GUARDIANSHIP; SUBSECTION 42: ADROGATION AND INTESTACY. That's the one. I pass it to Emeric. "Start by walking us through it. Maybe something will click."

"It's all inheritance law for nobility." He paces back to the slate wall, book in one hand, and picks up a discarded bit of chalk with the other. "Specifically, the inheritance rights of an adopted heir, and the rights of the adopter."

Ragne wrinkles her brow. "Inheritance rights? Why do you need rights to inherit?"

"Because otherwise the aristocracy tend to kill each other while they're carving up an inheritance," Emeric drawls. "So the inheritance laws are all built on the concept of noble houses." He draws two rect-angles, labeling one *Falbirg* and the other *Reigenbach*. "House Falbirg pro-duces *prinzeps-wahlen*, which means Princess Gisele's father is eligible to elect another *prinzeps-wahl* to the Blessed Imperial Throne, or to be elected himself. Under certain conditions, Princess Gisele would inherit the role of *prinzessin-wahl* from her father once she comes of age. Does that make sense so far?"

Ragne nods.

Emeric draws two crowns in the *Falbirg* house, then a plain circle in *Reigenbach*. "Here's the catch. A noble can typically only belong to *one* house: either their ancestral house *or* the house they marry into."

"Do they have to leave their family house if they marry?" Umayya asks, tapping her chin.

Emeric shakes his head. "No, but their spouse marries into their house instead and cannot rise in rank. For example, Dame von Falbirg was Lady von Konstanz before she married *Prinz-Wahl* von Falbirg. Her rank is still the same, but she joined House Falbirg."

Umayya frowns. "Isn't marrying into House Reigenbach a step down in rank for Hil—Gisele?"

"Correct. Though they're more powerful than House Falbirg in practical terms, House Reigenbach gave up their royal designation and became a margrave dynasty following the First Imperial Conclave in Blessed Era four—" Emeric catches himself mid-lecture and sheepishly rolls his wrist. "That's all backstory. In short, yes." Then he draws an arrow from one crown into *Reigenbach*, then puts another plain circle at its terminus. "Marrying into House Reigenbach means Princess Gisele will no longer be eligible for the *Kronwähler* either."

"And *Markgraf* von Reigenbach can't marry *up* into the *Kronwähler* by joining House Falbirg, because he will still be a margrave," Umayya says, to Emeric's nod.

Ragne squints at the charts. "Sovabin is very small, and the margrave is a greedy man. What does he want with the Gisele, then?"

I sling my arm around Ragne's shoulders, grinning proudly at Emeric. "Look at us. Look at how far we've come."

"I'm not sure I want to rejoice in our bad influence," he says dryly. "But yes, that's the big question. Klemens had a theory that most crimes derive from five motives: greed, love, hate, revenge, or fear. I think we can rule out love and fear, at least."

I snort. "He commissioned a portrait of himself standing on his father's corpse. Something tells me hate and revenge are involved."

Emeric nods. "And, as Miss Ragne noted, greed. For the margrave of the largest march in the empire, his behavior suggests he's wildly insecure, so he needs to eliminate any threats. The obvious answer is that Gisele can give him a child who is eligible for the imperial throne. Since House Falbirg will lose their only heir, there's a provision that their title can pass to Gisele's firstborn. But I don't think that's it, because he's trying to kill her even before the wedding."

Umayya leans against Ragne's chair, mouth pursing. "What is this adrogation business? Where does that come in?"

"That's where I'm hitting a wall." Emeric gestures to a list titled *WHY (smudge) BAKER WANTS (smudge) FLOUR.* "Adrogation is the process of adopting an heir when a noble house doesn't have one. It could be a threat for von Reigenbach, if the von Falbirgs use it to name an adrogated ward as an heir rather than wait for Gisele's firstborn."

I blink. Something about that rings a bell, but I can't think of what. "Right," I say slowly. "What if he wants the von Falbirgs to make *him* their heir?"

Emeric shakes his head. "He'd have to give control of Bóern to House Falbirg in the interim. An adrogated heir technically becomes a secondary owner of the house's properties, titles, and debts, but an idiosyncrasy of adrogation is that it goes both ways, since most adrogated heirs are adults with their own assets. House Falbirg would become a secondary owner of Bóern as well, giving them authority by seniority."

Greed, hate, revenge. No, Adalbrecht would never endanger his sovereignty.

"What if the margrave makes the Gisele adopt an heir?" Ragne asks. She's gone from crouching on the chair to sitting cross-legged and backward, arms folded over the chairback.

"That seems like a strong possibility," Umayya says, studying a branch of the diagram that charts it out as she plays with the end of her dark braid. "But would that not be terribly messy? The rest of the empire would notice if he killed her and put their ward on the imperial throne."

"Wait. Stop. Wait." I tug on my own twin braids. I know what stuck out, but why? *Ward.* I've seen that before. *Where* have I seen that before?"

"It's the legal shorthand for an adrogated heir, when the heir is a minor." Emeric stares at me, one hand frozen halfway to adjusting his spectacles. "What is it?"

I can feel it, the tumblers sliding into place, the tension rake twisting in my grasp, the lock *almost* turning. "The von Falbirgs asked about the adrogation forms at breakfast, because *they* need to sign them for Adalbrecht . . . because—because—"

It clicks. The vault swings open.

I know why the margrave wants Gisele dead.

CHAPTER THIRTY-ONE

The Two-Step

I GRAB EMERIC'S ARM. "DO YOU HAVE THE VOLUME ON MARITAL LAW?"

"Here." He fishes out a leather-bound tome from the heap on the table.

"There should be a standard marriage decree for nobles, right?" I crowd beside him as he flips the pages until we spot it, then skim the clauses until I find what I'm looking for. My finger jabs onto the page. "*There*. This is why Adalbrecht wanted everyone to see us sign the marriage decree. Gisele won't be seventeen until late April, so she's still a minor in the eyes of the law. And—"

"'Until the minor reaches the age of seventeen and is enrolled as a full citizen of the Blessed Empire of Almandy and representative of their ancestral house, they will be considered an *adrogated ward* of their spouse, and entitled to full and reciprocal right of intestacy,'" Emeric reads, then drops the book back onto the table like he's been struck by lightning. "Which means that Gisele is his legal heir, but also—"

"He's *hers*," I finish, almost vibrating with excitement. I seize Emeric's wrists. "Because *only* adrogation goes both ways! So now the contract's signed, if she dies before she turns seventeen—"

Emeric's hands close around mine, his face blazing. "Then *he* inherits the von Falbirg title of *prinz-wahl* without giving up Bóern—"

"And becomes eligible to be elected Blessed Emperor—"

"With the backing from the families allied with the von Hirschings!" Emeric spins me around. "That's it, Vanja, that's *exactly* it!"

The carol-band outside picks up, and before I know it we're whirling across the floor in time with the music, giddy with triumph. We fall too easily into a Bóernische two-step, his hand suddenly warm and solid across the middle of my back. Ragne grabs Umayya's hands and swings her into a dance, too, as the older woman laughs.

"*Solved it, we solved it,*" I sing (badly), "*the margrave can eat my—*"

"Those definitely aren't the right lyrics," Gisele observes from the doorway. Umayya trades Ragne to her, catching her breath. Gisele spins by in Ragne's arms. "Why are we celebrating?"

"We finally cracked it!" Emeric twirls me around, grinning ear to ear. "We know why von Reigenbach's trying to kill you!"

"I'm not sure I should be dancing to that!"

"Is *that* what you call it?" Joniza weaves around us to pick up her parchment and collect her *koli* from a shelf beyond the children's reach. "Don't mind me, just enjoying the sound of job security. You have three minutes to explain this murder plot to me. I'm onstage at the Küpperplat in an hour and it's a long way to Südbígn."

"Yes, I would also like to know what my betrothed gets from my demise," Gisele says dryly over Ragne's shoulder as she reels past.

Ragne has a much looser grasp of the steps, but Gisele certainly seems to be enjoying herself.

The carol is winding down anyway, though, and we have work to do. We slow to halt. For a brief second it almost seems like Emeric and I might stay this way, hands clasped, half holding each other— then I realize perhaps I shouldn't be quite so obvious around a boy who started solving murders at age eight. I pull away.

Once we're done explaining, Gisele taps a finger to her lips, thinking.

"My parents also mentioned the Imperial Citizenship papers," she says. "For nobles, those papers have to go all the way to the Chief Imperial Registrar's office in the capital. You're allowed to send them up to four months before your seventeenth birthday, so they'll be processed by the actual birthday. Mine can be sent off December twenty-third. Even if I died before my birthday, the paperwork could still have been filed, and he'd have an ugly legal fight over whether the title reverted to House Falbirg or not. So *that's* why he's rushing all this now, that's why he wants to hold on to the papers."

"So that's it, right?" Joniza asks as she ties on her cloak. "You know that he poisoned Vanja when he thought she was Gisele, you overheard him and the little von Hirsching toad talking about killing her, you know what he gets out of it, and you've all been attacked by *nachtmären* that he probably controls. Is that enough for the Godly Court?"

Emeric runs a hand through his hair. "I'm not sure. He can claim ignorance on the poison, and the incriminating statements came mostly from von Hirsching. The skull in his study could be enough to tie him to the *mahr* attacks, but he'll likely know if we remove it, so we should wait until right before the trial. We'll only have one shot, so the case has to be airtight."

"Then make it airtight." Joniza gives a two-fingered wave. "I'm off. You know where I'll be."

"Knock 'em dead," I call as she slips out the door.

Gisele adds, "Especially if the *baker* is there!"

"You know, Adalbrecht specifically ordered Gisele to attend the wedding hunt tomorrow," I point out. "In writing. If there's an attempt on her life . . ."

Emeric's face darkens. "There *absolutely* will be. Tell me Miss Ragne's going with you, Princess Gisele."

"Both of us are," I say.

He glances from me to Gisele, brows raised. Then he looks away. "I doubt von Reigenbach will be extending me an invitation, so . . . please be careful."

"I will keep them safe." Ragne's hand tightens in Gisele's. "I can come get you tomorrow morning, before sunrise, and sneak you into the castle."

"Then we should let you get some rest," Emeric says, and goes to erase his diagram. "We're still missing a few pieces, but I don't think we'll find them tonight."

I pull on my cloak and scarf, only to realize Ragne isn't doing the same. "If you're going to fly back to the castle, I can take your clothes with me."

I think this is the first time I've seen Ragne blush. "I will be coming back later," she says, inching a little closer to Gisele.

It takes a second for me to get it, and then I knot my scarf very fast. "Oh. Uh. Right. Just remember to get *some* sleep."

Now Gisele is definitely blushing. "*Thank you*, very helpful, now good night—"

"This is my mother's house, kind of!" I say as I head out the door. "She probably knows what you're doing!"

Emeric follows me outside, then hesitates. "Should we be seen walking back together?"

I shrug awkwardly. "Thanks to the, uh, linen closet incident, apparently the castle staff all think we're . . . you know. So we can just say Gisele gave me the night off to go . . ." I swallow, my mouth suddenly dry. "You know," I mumble again.

"I see." Emeric offers me an elbow. "In retrospect, it's likely the mar—*baker* is having at least one of us followed, so it's not safe to go alone either. Shall we?"

I slip my arm through his, glad the frosty night can explain my red cheeks. *Scheit*, I'm a disaster. "What pieces do you think we're still missing?" I ask, more to distract myself than anything else as we head for the Hoenstratz viaduct.

"Ah, hmm." He narrows his eyes, thinking. His voice lowers. "I have some questions about the baker's . . . helpers. The night shift."

It's an absurd way to think of the *nachtmären*, and I can't help huffing a laugh that steams in the air as we crunch over freezing slush. "How he, er, hired them?"

"How many there are. We haven't seen more than one at a time on the job. That's not enough to present a serious threat to the northern——er. Bakeries."

The northern imperial territories, then. "Maybe he plans on *hugging* the competition."

"That's just it. His existing . . . day shift forces are significant, but not enough to manage that. So that's one question."

"What's the other?" My foot slips a little on a patch of ice below the snow.

Emeric pulls me closer to steady me, waiting until I've caught my balance to keep walking. "I still don't know about Hubert," he says quietly as we reach the viaduct stairs and begin to climb. "He was a fully ordained veteran prefect, far from an easy target. It should have been me."

"If Adaaauhhhh the *baker* went for the harder of two targets, then he wanted something only Klemens had. So he was always going to try to kill him, not you." The words dangle in the air like a broken sign, for all the good they do. I gulp, then add, "There was nothing you could have done to stop it. So . . . stop blaming yourself."

When I glance up at Emeric, he's watching me with that peculiar expression, the one from the night of the ball, right before he came back for me. He quickly looks away.

"What?" I ask as we reach the top of the viaduct. It's starting to snow again, but the roadway should stay clear long enough for us to reach Castle Reigenbach.

He adjusts his spectacles, eyes on the cobblestones. "Don't let this scare you, but sometimes, *sometimes*, Vanja, I think you're a much better person than you give yourself credit for."

This is how I discover that despite fielding ludicrous amounts of flattery on Gisele's behalf for the past year, I am completely unprepared for someone I like to say something sincerely nice about *me*.

This is also how I discover my panic response is to laugh so loud a passing donkey brays back.

Oh, *gods*.

I scramble for more familiar territory. "So does this mean you're going to let me off the hook for the teeny tiny bit of theft I may or may not have committed?"

"You mean the jewelry worth roughly five years of income for a skilled laborer? That teeny tiny bit of theft?" His teeth flash in a smile. "Doubtful." Then he sobers a bit. "Though . . . once I'm fully ordained, I'll be able to request access to things like census records. If you wanted to try to track down your birth family someday, we could . . . call a truce."

I know I'm staring, but I can't stop.

I didn't even let myself finish the thought last night, that if I could go anywhere when I turn seventeen . . . I could look for them, my birth family, my hometown, my name.

But I didn't have to say it. He still understood.

I know, I *know* that there's no point in hope. That this amnesty lasts only until the margrave is gone; that unless we time it right, I will die from the curse anyway.

But *damn* if he doesn't make it easy, and heartbreaking, to hope.

"It was just an idea," he says quickly. "You don't have to—"

"I want to," I blurt out. "I—I'd really like that."

The tips of his ears are going pink. "Oh. Then—good."

We reach the bottom of the hill leading up to the castle and begin the climb. A fancy carriage rolls past on its way into Minkja; the evening is still young by aristocrat standards. Guests will likely be coming and going until dawn.

"If we get asked about tonight, we should have our story straight," I say.

"Right." Emeric thinks a moment. "How's this? I spent most of the day in pursuit of the *Pfennigeist*, but you and I met up after dinner." He pauses as we pass the guardhouse, then continues once we're out of their earshot. "We went to the Küpperplat to see *Mäestrin* Joniza perform, *you* had a little too much *glohwein*—"

"Why me?" I demand indignantly.

"—and we walked it off around the Göttermarkt, listening to the carol-bands." His voice shifts in the slightest way, like this is more than just an alibi. "I asked you to dance, and you said yes. When we were ready to go, we left, and now here we are. How does that sound?"

"It sounds like a nice night," I admit. I leave out the rest: It sounds too nice for a girl like me to hope for.

We're almost to the grand front doors. The castle guard won't drag them open for us, but there's a smaller door nearby for commoners and servants. I untangle my arm from Emeric's and pull the bell, shivering a little.

"How does it end?" Emeric asks suddenly.

I turn to blink up at him. "What?"

"It's your story too." That shift in his voice has lingered, honed itself; a soft, hungry sort of curiosity crackles like lightning in the falling snow, sweeping prickles down my arms. His eyes are locked on me, as if we are the only people in Minkja tonight. "How do you want it to end?"

I don't know if he's asking what I think he's asking. I know what I *want* him to be asking. The story. The night. The game between us. I tell myself I don't know how I want them to end, but I do, I do.

It might be the same for all three: with him.

The oak door gives a surly rattle, creaking open with absolutely no regard for the heart attack I'm having.

"You're coming in, *ja?*" croaks the withered turnip of a doorman before muttering something about frisky teenagers.

We scuttle into a torchlit hall, stamping snow off our boots. I can't think of anything to say to Emeric that isn't a variation on the theme of *kiss me like the world is ending.*

"Marthe!" Barthl's voice sails down the hall. He's striding toward us, looking harried as a mother hen. "I've been looking for you. I have fabric samples your lady mistress *must* review as soon as possible."

Ugh. I drop a quick curtsy to Emeric. "Good night to you, *Meister* Conrad."

He flicks his gaze at Barthl in a silent question, and I give a tiny nod. Barthl may have had me deliver a letter to the Wolfhünden, but he's also supposed to be on duty as the understeward in the entrance hall, with guests constantly passing through. Whether or not he has motive to do me harm, he doesn't have *time*.

Emeric bows. "Good night to you, *Frohlein* Marthe."

Barthl clears his throat. I barely resist rolling my eyes and trot over. "Yes, sir?"

"Follow me," he snaps, and turns on a heel. We march down the corridor.

After the third turn, I realize we're headed the way of the wine cellar, nowhere near where any fabric samples could be scrounged up. Something's wrong.

Barthl may not have time for murder, but maybe he's making time.

"My mistress will be expecting me, sir," I say, warning in my tone.

Barthl stops in the empty hall. He looks around, holds his breath a moment as he strains to catch any noise, then whips around to face me again. This time I mark deep shadows under his sunken eyes, darker than I've ever seen on him.

"I think you'll be the judge of that," he hisses. "Won't you, *Princess Gisele?*"

CHAPTER THIRTY-TWO

The Copper Knife

THIS IS WHERE I MUST MAKE A CONFESSION.

I have dedicated a lot of time in the last year to thinking up excuses for if I got caught. If someone spotted me in one of Gisele's fine gowns before I could don the pearls, I would tearfully claim to have just wanted to try it on once like a *real* lady and that I did no harm. If someone witnessed the transformation as I put the pearls on, I would tearfully claim to be cursed with red hair as a child because *Prinz* von Falbirg was rude to the Low God of Rust or the like. (You may notice a pattern here: a lot of tearful claims.)

I have not, however, spent a single moment preparing for someone thinking *Gisele* is real and her maid is the disguise.

I gape at Barthl.

And then I blurt out: "Who's Gisele?"

Then: "Wait. Uh."

"You forgot to cover the ruby last night, you dullard." Barthl jabs a long pale finger in my face. "When you answered the door. You remembered the rest of this ludicrous little getup but forgot that. And don't think I missed all the drunken giggling either. I don't care if you're romping around with the prefect boy, but my family has served House Reigenbach since *Kunigunde,* and I will not have your indiscretion disgracing the name more than Adalbrecht already has—"

He cuts himself off, but it's too late.

"You don't like the margrave?" I whisper.

Barthl eyes me like I have a knife to his throat. He attempts to brandish one of his own. "And you're having an affair."

"I'm really, really not," I say, "or I'd be in a much better mood right now. I saw you lurking outside Adalbrecht's study on the night of the ball. Have you been eavesdropping on him?"

"What were *you* doing sneaking around his wing?" Barthl returns.

We stare at each other a long, tense moment, both hovering on the edge of a dangerous admission, neither of us willing to turn over our cards.

Then gold glimmers at the edge of my sight. Fortune can't help but meddle; my luck is about to turn for the better.

Sure enough, Barthl's eyes narrow. "You're spending a lot of time with the prefect boy."

"I wonder," I say, stretching out each syllable with significance, "why that would be."

Barthl seems to catch on. He hesitates, then matches that meaningfully strung-out tone. "My father . . . was the former margrave's steward. He was the one—"

"Who found the old margrave's body, with the ruined feet," I finish, a fistful of disjointed wisps twisting into the binding thread. "*You tipped off the Order! Were you spying on him this whole time?*"

Barthl's face pales. "Please, Princess Gisele, you must know you're in danger. The margrave has to be stopped. Just leave the prefect boy alone and let him do his job."

It clicks. He still thinks I'm another selfish noble, one who will treat this nightmare like a parlor game, something to giggle about from an armchair.

Well, there's a quick and easy way to dispel him of that notion. I reach for the pearls in my pocket. "Barthl, I think we have a lot to unpack here. Have you heard of the *Pfennigeist?*"

✌

If anyone were to walk into the castle chapel Wednesday morning, the most unusual thing they'd see would be that there are four fools in Minkja devout enough to be praying at this predawn hour. However, we all have excuses (Gisele and I are praying for the hunt to go well, Barthl is getting in his daily dose of piety at the end of his night shift, and Emeric's not exactly from the Order of Agnostic Prefects). Moreover, this is the one place on the castle grounds we can be certain no *nacht-mären* will enter.

We're still keeping our voices low in case of passing clergy, and Gisele's left the pearls dangling around her throat, ready to be clasped in a hurry, but we can speak freely here. Just like Barthl and I did, at length, about ten hours ago.

"Junior, Gisele," I say under my breath, "I'd like you to meet my new best friend. Barthl, you can tell them everything."

Barthl stares up at the vaulted ceiling with its painted saints, as if beseeching the Low Gods for strength. Not to bolster his convictions—

we found quite a lot of common ground in our mutual detestation of Adalbrecht—but more likely to endure the indignity of being referred to as my best friend.

"I've been suspicious of the margrave since he came back from the battlefield with blue eyes," Barthl begins. "If anyone asked, he just insisted his eyes had always been that way and they were imagining things."

Of course he did. That's the true cost of someone who makes you pick your battles: You can cling to a fistful of victories, but they rarely outweigh the thousand little fights lost before they even began.

Barthl's still speaking. "A few years ago, he began sending frequent messages to Count von Hirsching, which I found unusual given their difference in station. I believe he burned his letters until summer, when it was too warm to do it himself."

"So he fobbed it off on Barthl," I say smugly. "Lazy bastard."

Emeric straightens in his pew. "Please tell me you still have them."

"Only the letters sent *to* the margrave, but they paint a clear picture." Barthl glances over his shoulder, and I can't blame him for the paranoia. His father quit and moved all the way to Rósenbor just because he saw the old margrave's body; Barthl knows the deadly dice he's rolling to betray Adalbrecht like this. "Once he holds the title of *prinz-wahl*, the Blessed Empress will be . . . removed. An alliance of southern territories will back his candidacy for emperor to guarantee his election, and in exchange, once crowned, he will dissolve the Free Imperial States and award the lands to the southern nobility."

Gisele's hands knot together. "That should be impossible. The Low Gods would never allow the free states to fall."

"I would hope not, but . . ." Barthl shakes his head. "He's guaranteed it somehow. Multiple letters reference his promise to that effect.

Most of them are from Count von Hirsching, who seems to be coordinating this as the margrave's proxy."

"That aligns with what we overheard the night of the ball," Emeric says. "The letters aren't enough evidence that *he* executed the plans and committed a crime, but they should prove intent and motive beyond a doubt. You won't be participating in the hunt, *Meister* Barthl?"

"No."

"Then once the hunting party's left, I can collect the letters. They should be safe in the outpost. We may be able to search the study again as well."

The hour-bells peal through the chapel, and we all jump. Gisele laughs, a little strained. "We should get going before anyone else arrives. Thank you so much, *Meister* Barthl. You've taken a terrible risk and done the empire a great service."

It's Barthl's turn to look sheepish. He doesn't seem quite prepared to be appreciated, especially not by the noblewoman I've been rudely impersonating for the last year. "M-my husband and I are thinking of starting a family here," he stumbles. "I just want what's best for us all."

"You're *married*?" I ask, amazed. "We're best friends and you didn't even tell me?"

Barthl stands from his pew. "I'm leaving."

"I can meet you outside the banquet hall after the hunting party departs," Emeric tells him as Gisele and I scoot into the chapel aisle as well. Then he catches my arm. "Vanja, wait. Take this with you today." He holds out a knife. I recognize the hilt; it's the one plated in copper. That one I remember: best against *grimlingen*. "Just in case."

❧❦❧

By midafternoon, I'm beginning to wonder whether Adalbrecht's lost his nerve. The biggest problem we've encountered thus far is that Gisele does not like her horse.

There's nothing wrong with it, of course; it's a dappled silver mare, almost as fine a steed as Adalbrecht's stallion. But it's not *her* horse, the one she brought from Sovabin. "It's not the same," she groused this morning as we rode out of Minkja. "Falada's gait is glass compared to this."

I've had no use for her old horse—the rare times I've needed a mount, it's been a sturdy little pony suitable for Marthe the Maid—so it's safe to say Gisele's own gelding is just growing tubby on oats and rolling around in a pasture.

Not that it would have made much of a difference. The wedding hunt is an old tradition but something of a moot point with this many chattering nobles traipsing through the forest outside Minkja. Any wildlife fled long before we arrived, and Gisele and I have stayed at the heart of the crowd, surrounded by too many others for even a beast like Adalbrecht to risk a shot. Instead we're strolling sedately through the sun-streaked snow, the white birch trunks starting to gild with the honey glow of a clear winter afternoon waning.

The real hunters have gone far ahead, including the margrave. It's supposed to be good luck to bring in large game for the wedding feast, and knowing Adalbrecht, he'll want to make sure his kill is the first, and the biggest.

Gisele's mare tosses her head, no doubt picking up on Gisele's frustration. If this were Sovabin, she'd be at the front of the pack. Instead she's stuck here, picking at her pearls.

"How much longer, do you think?" Gisele asks me quietly, so the others don't hear. I'm far from the only lady's maid here, but it's still unusual for her to keep my company over, say, Sieglinde von Folkenstein's.

"Not long. The roads will start freezing over again after sundown." My hands tighten on the reins. The bridle is purely ornamental; I couldn't stop Ragne from bolting if I wanted to, but at this point I'd trust she had good cause. She snorts as if in agreement.

I don't say that I *hope* it ends soon, because the cold is making me ache everywhere a gem has erupted. Including the two new rings of bulbous pearls around my wrists, hidden under lambswool-lined leather gloves. I'm bundled up in a riding costume like Gisele's, with thick leggings, woolen breeches, a long tunic, and a heavy coat under a heavier cloak, but it's still not quite enough to keep the chill at bay.

A horn sounds through the woods. The hunters are on the chase again. Every time, they've come up empty. The rest of the party moves into a reluctant trot, in no rush to catch up.

Then the horn sounds again. A strange sort of shiver pulses through the leaves.

The golden sunlight softens and bleeds to silver, like it's passing through a cloud—but the sky is crystal clear. Shadows on the snow blur into a sea of blue.

The horn sounds a third time.

The hunting party surges into a canter, snow spraying like water. Ragne lets out a startled whinny and leaps forward to keep pace.

"What's happening?" I shout.

Gisele doesn't answer.

When I look to where she rides to my left, I see a blue-silver glow has fogged over her eyes, and her mare's. Everyone else seems caught in the same trance, eyes milky and unseeing. Only Ragne and I have escaped. Whispers of frosty sunlight flicker among the riders, manes and tails and ghostly teeth, phantom horses in the tide.

"It is like the *Wildejogt*," Ragne calls to me, "but it is wrong!"

The Wild Hunt. I saw them pass Castle Falbirg once on a cold, clear night, with the Spindle-dam at the head; I could have sworn she looked straight at me. Sometimes she leads the hunt, pulling riders from roads and dreamers from their beds; sometimes it's Waul of the Winds, sometimes the shadowy blur of the Knight Unseen.

None of them leads us now. And it is getting colder.

The horn sounds a fourth time, closer. An answering howl snakes through the bone-pale trees, closer even than the horn.

"Why didn't it take us?" I call to Ragne.

Ragne shakes her head, distressed. "It is the horses, the call is to the horses, and the riders are prisoners with them!"

Then we have to get Gisele off her mare. But I can't just shove her from the saddle, there are a thousand ways that could go wrong—her foot could get caught in the stirrup, she could fall and be trampled—

I grip the copper knife. *Don't panic.*

"We need to push her away from the rest of the riders." I huddle close to Ragne's neck, moving my left leg up and away from her side. This is about to get rough.

Ragne shoulders into the silver mare, not hard enough to knock Gisele from the saddle, but enough to send her dancing wide of the pack. We weave around trees, driving the mare into open snow. Then I cut through my reins and loop the loose end around Gisele's stomach, grabbing her arms and freeing the foot I can reach from its stirrup. She's still entranced and doesn't even fight. "Ragne, stop on the count of three—one—two—*three*—"

The mare keeps cantering, sides lathering with sweat. Ragne digs in her hooves. Between her and me, we drag Gisele from the saddle.

She crashes into the snow, then sits up, eyes clear and alarmed. "What was *that*?"

Before I can answer, hoofbeats pound through the woods. Adalbrecht appears as if from nowhere, spear in hand, bow strung and strapped to his back. I go even colder than the frost. He very well may try to kill us both here, while the guests are still caught in the hunt.

But confused shouts pierce through the woods. It seems breaking Gisele out shattered the *Wildejogt*'s hold.

Anger darts through Adalbrecht's face before it's masked with dismay. "My blossom, what's wrong?"

This time, a growl answers.

A massive, starving gray wolf leaps out of the trees, bound for Gisele.

She shrieks and throws herself out of its way. Adalbrecht's face is impassive, evaluating. This close, I can see the flicker of blue in the wolf's eyes, smell the rot in its fur. It's a *mahr*, like the one in Lähl.

A dark spike thrusts into my sight against the snow: Death watching from the edge of the clearing, her face shifting, shifting, shifting. Gisele's features keep surfacing.

Voices rise. Figures rush through the trees.

Ragne flings a hoof at the *nachtmahr*'s side, but it whips away. She screams her fury.

That seems to bother Adalbrecht's stallion, its pink nostrils flaring. "Rear and try to scare his horse," I whisper to Ragne.

She obliges, throwing her forelegs into the air and bellowing as I tumble from her back. The copper knife is still unsheathed in my hand. I slash it at the wolf-*mahr*. It snarls, but the copper scares it back, buying Gisele and me space.

From the corner of my eye I see a handful of hunters and nobles have nearly reached us. No doubt Adalbrecht staged it just so: They'll witness a mindless beast tearing his bride to pieces.

But now his stallion is rearing too. He drops his spear to grab the reins.

And Gisele swoops for it. The spear shudders as she levers it to push herself back up, snow raining from her cloak. Even with the illusion of the pearls, I recognize the way her eyes sharpen, the angle of her shoulders, the comfort of the weapon in her hands.

The wolf-*mahr* charges for her again. This time she leans back, readies herself—and drives the spear into its belly.

It lets out a hissing howl, thrashing in the snow. I pass her the copper knife. She slashes it across the *mahr*'s throat.

It goes still. A stinking stain spreads into the snow.

Adalbrecht looks like he wants to obliterate Gisele here and now. The many, many nobles gathered around us look like they've witnessed the birth of a saint.

And when I look for Death, she's gone.

Gisele hands the knife back to me as a hush falls in the woods. The sunlight warms to gold again.

"Too bad we can't serve wolf," she says smoothly. "Will someone find my horse?"

CHAPTER THIRTY-THREE

Unwanted

DARK IS FALLING WHEN WE MAKE IT BACK TO CASTLE REIGENBACH. Gisele and I endure a rowdy, quick dinner banquet with the rest of the hunting party, where the tale of her victory is sung again and again. I can't help but notice Count von Hirsching looking increasingly uneasy with the number of nobles clapping Gisele on the shoulder. That I file away for later. If Gisele's star is on the rise, it means further murder attempts are going to draw more scrutiny than Adalbrecht can afford.

Ragne is waiting for us in the bedroom. Almost immediately after the hallway door shuts, there's a knock at the veranda. I let Emeric in.

He's surprisingly pale, almost rattled; his sleeves have a myriad of wrinkles from being rolled and unrolled over and over. "I heard a wolf attacked you," he says the moment he steps in. His hands close over my shoulders, as if to verify I'm still in one piece. "Are you hurt? Was it the margrave?"

"It was the margrave," Ragne answers. Emeric blinks over at her. I'd almost swear he forgot she was there.

Gisele hangs her cloak on the rack. "We're all fine. But that copper knife came in handy."

"The wolf was a *mahr*. I've seen bigger," I say. "But I'm also on your side now, horses are absolutely cursed."

He lets me go, looking a bit flustered, and mumbles, "They just *bite* things for no reason."

I pull the copper dagger from my belt and hand it back to him, a grin unfurling across my face. "You were worried about us, weren't you?"

Emeric starts futzing with a sleeve. "Of course I was."

"Did you find anything in the study?" Gisele asks, sitting on the trunk to undo her boots.

Emeric shakes his head. "Von Reigenbach left two soldiers posted outside the door this time. I can handle it, but they'll know what hit them, so . . ."

"We should save that for right before the Godly Court is called." I set my gloves on the vanity.

Emeric catches my wrist with just his fingertips, eyes on the new outbreak of pearls. Each one is as wide across as a white penny. "It's getting worse, isn't it?"

I duck my head. "Full moon is Sunday night, after the wedding. If we haven't brought Adalbrecht down by then, I have bigger problems."

No one seems to know what to say.

I know what Gisele is thinking: She could take her place back now, but that would only be to help me. That might even make the curse worse. I know what Ragne is thinking: Her mother's curse is killing her first friend.

I'm never quite sure what Emeric is thinking; I just know his fingers tighten the briefest moment before he drops my wrist.

Gisele tries and fails to stifle a yawn. Emeric starts at that. "I should go," he mumbles. "You all need to rest. Good night."

Before I can tell him he's welcome to stick around, he's slipped out the door.

Gisele sighs. "Sorry, Vanja."

"For what?"

Ragne and Gisele trade looks. "I think," Ragne says delicately, "that the Emeric wanted to be alone with you."

I laugh too loud. "No, he didn't, he wanted to make sure we were fine after the hunt."

Gisele raises her eyebrows. "Sure." Then she yawns again.

I lunge for the opening to change the subject. "You can sleep here, if you want. The cathedral's a long walk, and if you aren't wearing the pearls, Adalbrecht may mistake you for a servant and try something desperate."

"I don't want to inconvenience you," Gisele says, but I can tell she's exhausted.

I also suspect it's been too long since she slept on anything but a straw pallet. "You and Ragne can take the bed, and I'll sleep by the hearth."

That does the trick. We divvy up blankets and blow out candles, and soon the dark fills with the soft snores I remember from Castle Falbirg. I watch the red embers in the fireplace, waiting for sleep to claim me, too, but for some reason it doesn't come.

I don't know if it's the chill still lingering in the jewels or the other angle of familiarity to this, with Gisele in the feather bed and me by the hearth. Perhaps it's the ache I can't quite articulate, the one that knots in my belly every time Gisele or Ragne teases me about Emeric.

I don't know how to explain it to them, that it just reminds me of what I'm not, what I will never have. That just because he and I are playing outside the rules of the trinity of want . . . doesn't mean he wants a girl like me.

That girls like me, neither lovely of face nor sweet of temper, are not courted. They are simply used to pass the time.

I want him to chase me, because it means I'm more than that. It means for once in my life, I am seen.

I realize, suddenly, what is keeping me awake. It is what links all those things: fear.

It's been over a year since I stole the pearls, since I threw myself into this grand lie, since I decided to set off on my own. It's been almost four years since I paid the price for loyalty. Thirteen years since I watched my mother's lantern vanish into the night.

And if you saw me now, sleeping by a fireplace, giving up everything for Gisele, letting new people into my heart, daring even an ember of hope . . . Well.

Only a fool would look at me now and think I had learned anything, *anything* at all.

⚭

Most of Thursday goes by in a blur. Gisele and I trade duties: She does the stiff, awkward meals with her parents and Adalbrecht, I handle tea parties with the locals who've been buttering me up all year. She handles the final meetings with the decorators, I handle the final dress fitting.

We probably should have swapped those; I have to take care to keep the outbreaks on my hands and shins hidden. Worse is the sight of myself in brilliant Reigenbach blue, the swaths of brocade and ermine worthy of a queen. Worst of all is the weight of the Reigenbach family bridal crown, a massive work of gold, diamonds, and sapphires, which makes my head hurt after wearing it for just five minutes. All I can hope is that neither Gisele nor I have to put it back on.

At least her popularity is still climbing. The local nobility was already fawning over her as a proxy for the margrave; now aristocracy from across the empire are begging her to tell them, again, how she slew the wolf. The only who's more annoyed than Adalbrecht is Irmgard von Hirsching.

A mirror-message calls us back to Fortune's cathedral that evening, earlier than we'd planned. Joniza, Barthl, and Emeric are waiting for us in the clergy dormitory library, a close little room that's mostly worn armchairs and overflowing bookshelves arranged around a fireplace. A square table has been dragged from the corner it clearly belongs in, charcoal sticks and papers spilling over its surface from a leather satchel. Emeric's standing over it, scribbling furiously on a large sheet, a razor edge to his focus. The stiff lines of his shoulders say something grim has dropped into our laps.

"What's wrong?" I sidestep into the room and drop my own satchel and cloak into an armchair that lets out a wheeze of dust and beeswax.

Emeric looks up at me, face taut. "You were right about Hubert. The margrave wanted something only he had. When the outpost was preparing his body for final rites, the priests found . . ." His voice hitches. "The tattoo was cut off his back."

My stomach turns. "The one from the second initiation?"

Emeric nods. "The mark that bound Hubert to the Low Gods' power. But not the one that bound him to their rules."

"What can Adalbrecht do with that?" Gisele sounds ill.

"A lot, I suspect," Emeric says tightly. "None of it good."

"That must be how he's delivering the free states," Joniza says, tucked under a blanket in an armchair by the fireplace. "I bet he'll do something to keep the Low Gods out of the picture. Maybe, since the mark binds him to their power, he can bind *them* right back."

Ragne climbs onto an armchair herself, this time perching on the sturdy back. I'm pretty sure she knows how chairs work by now and is just choosing to ignore it. "If he has bound himself to anything, then he must wear a mark of some kind on his body. Especially if he wants to use the powers of the Low Gods."

I edge around the table to look at what Emeric's writing. It's different angles of the case, a series of lists, and the evidence we have. "You're going to summon the court, then?"

He gives a thin-lipped nod. "With Hubert's binding mark in the mix, it's safe to say what he's planning to do with it won't be subtle. That means he has to do it after the wedding, so at least his right to the Blessed Imperial Throne can't be challenged. If we call the court before Sunday, we beat him."

This is it. This is how we take down the wolf.

But I can see Emeric's hands are shaking.

I place one of mine on the paper. "Walk me through it."

Emeric takes a deep breath and stands up straight, scanning his chart. "We can prove he's bound himself to *nachtmären* with the skull from his study and, as Ragne said, whatever mark he's bearing. We *may* be able to audit the skull's history of spellwork, but if we can't, Ragne, myself, Gisele, and Vanja can still testify to the *mahr* attacks. Even if we can't prove he ordered them, there's a clear pattern of targeting us when it benefits him. And his possession of Klemens's tattoo will implicate him in that murder. We'll establish motive with the letters from von Hirsching and the marital adrogation loophole. The letters, in context of everything else, also give us an implicit admission of guilt."

"Will that be enough?" Gisele reaches for Ragne's hand.

Emeric goes quiet a moment. Something is weighing on him, something that sits ill with me. "It should be. But we need to time it right. Bystanders will be able to observe the trial, and if I fail to convince the Low Gods, you will need people with the political power to bring the margrave to justice."

I don't miss the change in pronouns. "What do you mean, you?" He doesn't answer. I go cold. "*Emeric.* What happens if you fail?"

He stares at the tabletop, stone-faced. "No matter what . . . summoning the Godly Court will kill me."

"No," I say immediately, "*no—*"

"If I win the case, the Low Gods will bring me back to life," he pushes on. "If I lose . . . they don't have patience for junior prefects wasting their time."

"We'll find another way."

"There isn't one."

"I said we'll find one!"

"And *I* said I'd bring him to justice, whatever it took." Emeric's voice rises. "I'm not letting y—I'm not letting him get away. He has to answer for what he's done."

The protest withers on my tongue. Of course. He wants revenge for Klemens. He wants it enough to die for it.

He wants it more than—

Me.

What a vain, stupid thing hope is.

What a vain, stupid thing I am, to have hoped for more.

Of course Klemens is more important; I'm a girl he barely knows, even if—even if I let myself think there might be an *after* for us. Years have passed, and I'm just the same little fool sniveling into a washrag because the boy she liked chose something else. Something that mattered more.

"Why the hell does it work like that?" Joniza asks. "It doesn't make sense to spend all that time training you and then kill you the first time you put it to the test."

"If I were fully ordained, it wouldn't be an issue," Emeric explains. "It's like with the witch-ash. Junior prefects may have the tools, but the risk keeps us from abusing them. The second tattoo is what allows a prefect to survive channeling the gods' powers."

I'm not giving up. "How does the summoning work? Can we, I don't know, diffuse it somehow?"

"No, it requires an incantation that's specific to the prefect coin and—" He catches himself, then swallows. "That's all I'm going to say."

I don't know what hurts more, that he thinks I'd sabotage the summoning, or that he's caught me fishing for a way to do just that.

He knows what I am, after all: selfish. I wear that mark plain on my face. I would let Minkja burn if I could drag at least us from the ashes.

"All our lives have been on the line at one point or another," Emeric adds, trying to soften the edge. "And if the margrave wins, none of us are making it out of here alive—"

"Oh, I definitely am," Joniza says flatly. "Are you kidding? I'm not dying in this mud pit."

"No one is." I lean on the table, trying to think. My hand lands on Emeric's satchel and accidentally shoves it off in a tumble of charcoal sticks. I wave him back and crouch to clean it up. "No, I've got it."

"What about the gala on Saturday evening?" Barthl speaks up for the first time. He's been lurking in the corner, antsy as ever, though I can't say I blame him. "Adalbrecht will be away from his study, so we can take the skull. Representatives from the Imperial Court will be there, with their security details, and plenty of other nobility who aren't part of the von Hirsching alliance. Even in the worst-case scenario, you'll have an audience who can hold Adalbrecht to account if the Low Gods won't."

I drop the last of the charcoal sticks back in the satchel—then freeze at a familiar canvas-bound book.

Yannec's ledger is still in there.

No, I tell myself. This isn't the time. I return the satchel to the table.

"I'm booked to play the gala too," Joniza says. "You can coordinate around my song cues again."

"Perfect. Barthl and I will handle the study guards and get the skull, then bring it to the gala. I will summon the court." Emeric stares at the ceiling, thinking. "If we win the case . . . Gisele, the adrogation works in your favor. You may have some challenges for the title, but whatever punishment von Reigenbach faces, you'll likely inherit everything. That means you should take the pearls for the gala, with Ragne for protection."

"I can work with that." Gisele smiles at Ragne.

"Wait," I say. "Let me handle getting the skull. It's not like having guards at the door ever kept me out before, and if you have to knock them out, they could be discovered. Besides, you need someone to pick the lock on—"

Barthl clears his throat. "I have keys."

"As long as we get out and get to the gala, it doesn't matter if the guards are discovered," Emeric says. "It's a safer bet."

"Then what do you want me to do?" I ask.

There's a stiff, uneasy silence, and then I understand. Gisele has the pearls, Barthl has the keys, Joniza has the stage, Ragne has her claws, and Emeric has his coin. They have no need for a thief and a liar.

I am not needed.

Somehow, that scares me more than maybe even Adalbrecht von Reigenbach.

"Irmgard," Gisele says quickly. "Someone needs to keep an eye on Irmgard. You could come to the gala as my attendant, and Ragne can hide with you, and if Irmgard tries anything you can stop her."

Gisele, always handing out her charity pennies. We can all hear what a weak excuse it is. I nod, pressing my tongue against the roof of my mouth until it aches.

"Sure" is all I say.

"I think that works best for everyone," she adds.

Gisele has no reason to know why those words strike an agonizing chord in me. She doesn't see the lantern at the crossroads; she doesn't hear my mother leaving me to Death and Fortune with the same excuse.

I only listen with half an ear as they talk through signals, timing, locations. It's fine, because none of it depends on me. None of *them* depend on me.

This shouldn't be personal but it is.

It's the fear that gnawed at my belly last night, breaking its teeth on something harder to swallow. Not only have I learned *nothing* in the last thirteen years, I've made a new and terrible mistake.

At the end of the day, Gisele will likely have Castle Reigenbach, she will have Ragne, she will have wealth and power and a fairy-tale ending. I will be lucky to keep my pocket full of gold. I may not even have the boy I stupidly care for.

But that s not my new mistake.

Somehow, I've let all these people, even Barthl, matter to me. I've found them shelter and smuggled them around the castle and fought monsters and somehow, *somehow*, I have let myself be—loyal.

And now they don't need me. No more than they trust me.

What a terrible, foolish mistake, to think loyalty would ever serve me in kind.

Greed, hate, love, revenge, fear. One way or another, they are all my motives.

I'll help stop Adalbrecht. I'll save Gisele to break the curse. Then I will take my money and run, and I will remember this lesson when I've left the Blessed Empire behind: There is one person in this world who I can trust to need me, and that is myself alone.

They may not need a thief and a liar, but I do. I do, if I want to survive.

When I leave Fortune's cathedral late that night, it's with Yannec's ledger buried deep in my satchel.

CHAPTER THIRTY-FOUR

Nothing Stolen

Friday morning breaks cold and brittle, the silver sky bright and flat as a white penny, and it finds me in the tidy cobblestone streets of the Obarmarkt. Anyone who sees me with my satchel and House Reigenbach servant badge will think I'm on an errand for the wedding; the gatehouse guards certainly bought the lie easily enough.

No one has to know I'm carrying around a small fortune in Eisendorf jewelry in this bag.

It was all too simple to figure out who Yannec was selling to. Just as I'd hoped, he kept his ledger in charcoal, and it survived its trip in the Yssar. All I had to do was skim through the deliveries he made after each of my thefts. One customer came up every time: a goldsmith by the name of Frisch, with an address near the Salzplatt.

I don't even have to worry about coming up with an excuse for the *Prinzessin* to spend the morning in her bedroom, because the real Gisele spent the night again, and I slept on the hearth again, and she's having breakfast in the banquet hall right now, and if I think about it too much I'm going to forget to breathe. Even Ragne is with her now, for safety.

Joniza said nothing stolen was ever really mine. It's just . . . gutting, to see how much of my life was stolen, even my time with her. How fast it's all slipping away.

An icy wind sweeps down the lane, and all of my jewel outbreaks ache in answer. More rubies erupted overnight, this time as seeds starting from my ankles and the undersides of my wrists. Unlike the older breakouts, these keep growing. Every hour I feel another one emerge along the lines of my arteries, creeping closer to my heart like blood poisoning from infected wounds.

Worse, I can feel the buds of jewels swelling in my belly now, hard little lumps that roll under my fingertips. I don't know how large they can grow before it becomes a problem, but one thing is clear:

Today, tomorrow, Sunday. That's all I have left.

A sign flashes gold ahead, swinging on its hooks in the breeze. Three rings and the name *Frisch*, all in gilt. I pick up the pace, if only to get out of the cold, and hide the Reigenbach badge in my pocket.

A bell rings over the door as I step inside. There's a bland little man at the counter, meticulously polishing a stunning collar of silver and sapphire sparkling on a bed of black velvet. I'm fairly certain I stole the thumbnail-sized stone at its center from Irmgard von Hirsching's vanity. "*Meister* Frisch?"

The man nods, still absorbed in the collar. "What can I help you with, *frohlein*?"

"I believe you did business with an associate of mine," I say, shutting the door behind me. "Yannec Kraus."

Frisch sets down his brush and sits upright, sizing me up. There's an edge in his voice when he says, "Perhaps I did."

"That business is mostly over." I set my satchel on the counter. "But I was hoping you'd make one last deal."

For something that took so long, the exchange is quick and to the point. Frisch seems as eager to stash away the Eisendorf jewelry as I am to part with it. I leave with two hundred *gilden*, more than I expected and much more than Yannec estimated. I knew he took a cut, but we agreed to a tenth of the money, not a fifth. But it's not like I ever caught him in the act, so who knows how long he was breaking our deal.

I think through the plan as I start back to the castle. I will pack today, while Gisele is out. I won't pack much, just one outfit worthy of a princess, and one worthy of a maid. And, of course, my *gilden*.

Once it's clear that she's taken her place and my curse is broken, I will steal away, hopefully no later than Sunday. I will pretend to be a servant one last time and hire a coach, claiming my lady, a wedding guest, got drunk and gave her coach away as a gift to the bride. Then the next morning I will use the stolen gown, stolen powders, stolen manners, and become a *prinzessin* for the final time. And I will take that coach . . . anywhere.

Well, not anywhere. Adalbrecht's border wars have carved up the south and the east, even gnashing into Eiswald Forest. But I can go west or north, as far as I care to.

I know Emeric said he would follow, but that was before he made it clear Klemens's revenge matters more. That's on me, though, for believing him. I won't make that mistake again.

A thunderous *crack* nearly makes me leap out of my boots as I set foot in the Salzplatt. The bronze statue of Kunigunde has brought her spear crashing down on the marble pedestal. I hold my breath, convinced she's going to point me out for a cheat—but instead she freezes again, scowling.

A bright flash of blue catches my eye from across the plaza. Adalbrecht's coach is parked in front of the city hall, a small crowd gathered around it. He emerges from the double doors, smiling and waving with a toothy kind of triumph. The von Falbirgs must have found the leisure to sign the marital adrogation forms.

That makes his paperwork robbery complete.

I don't want to wait for him to spot me, or for Kunigunde to single me out. I hurry from the Salzplatt and hope I don't see either of them again on my way back to the castle.

The clothing is easy enough to pack up and hide in the wardrobe. It takes longer to count out the *gilden*, then double-count to make sure I have a thousand. Both times I come in just a little over.

I start counting a third time, not because I think I'm wrong, but because when I see the stacks of coins lined up before me—it feels real. I've done it. It feels like freedom.

I've just reached three hundred when there's a pulse of heat at my thigh. At first I think it's another jewel erupting, then I remember I'm still carrying the message-mirror. I pull it out. Emeric's writing scrawls across the fogged surface:

> We need
> to talk.

There must be a change in plans. I write back: *Where?*

When I walk into Fortune's cathedral a quarter hour later, I expect to see everyone knotted together and anxious as some new miserable development narrows our chances. I didn't even bother with braids; I just hid the gold, grabbed a cloak and a scarf, and left with my hair flying loose like a madwoman's in a pageant.

But Gisele, Ragne, Barthl, and Joniza are nowhere in sight. Instead, Emeric is waiting for me in the vestibule, alone. The sanctuary itself is mostly empty, save for the acolyte Fortune possessed the first time I came here, side-eyeing me as she sweeps the aisle between pews. There's no way to know for certain when one of Fortune's services will be, for her priestesses roll bones to see if they'll hold ceremonies every six hours. (Fortune once told me she did that just to keep them on their toes.)

Emeric tips his head at a smaller chapel off to the side. I follow him in, tucking my cloak under my arm. The room is a little smaller than the clergy library, with only a few small windows high above, but it's lined with rows of flickering vow candles on dark walnut shelves. The smell of burnt wick and melting beeswax weighs on the air. A shallow altar sits at the far end, empty but framed in an arch of gold leaves twining around animal bones.

This is the Gambler's Altar, where people light a candle and swear to perform a deed in Fortune's name. She's supposed to favor them if they succeed, and neglect them if they fail.

Maybe Emeric wants to light a candle for the trial.

I drop my cloak on the plain stone bench. The chapel doors latch behind me, and I spin on a heel, suddenly nervous. "What's going on?"

Emeric's back stays to me, his hands still on the doors. "I could ask you the same." He sighs, then turns around. Even in the dim flickering light, I can see shadows under his eyes. "What are you doing, Vanja?"

I narrow my stare. "What are you talking about?"

He takes off his spectacles and runs a hand over his brow. "The day after you dropped me in the Yssar, I paid a visit to a *Meister* Frisch. I told him the prefects had reason to believe he was buying the *Pfennigeist*'s stolen jewelry, based on Yannec Kraus's ledger, and that I would ask for clemency if he agreed to send a messenger to the outpost *immediately* after anyone tried to sell him the Eisendorf jewels." He pinches his nose. "And then I completely forgot about it. At least, until this morning, when the messenger arrived and I discovered you'd stolen the ledger."

Scheit.

"It's none of your concern," I say. At least—it shouldn't be. Not if he's keeping his promise to let the *Pfennigeist* case go until after Adalbrecht's handled.

"Is this because of the plan for tomorrow?" he asks exhaustedly, returning his spectacles to his face. "Because I know it's not perfect, but it's the best for—"

The best for everyone. That's a little too close to home. So, of course, I lie. "*No.* It's not about the plan, it's just a loose end." Then I realize exactly why he cares. "You're the only one who knows I sold stolen jewelry. You won't get in trouble for me doing it while I have an amnesty token unless you snitch on yourse—"

"What? No, I don't . . ." Emeric waves a stiff hand. "I don't care about that. What do you mean, loose end?"

I look away. "It's clear everything will go fine without me, so . . . I have business to take care of."

The *before I go* is implied.

There's a strange, splintering crackle in the air between us, static lightning flickering over a powder keg. I want to fight, to scream, to run. I want to have something to hope for again. More than anything, I want him to ask me to stay.

Instead he just shakes his head, incredulous. "Business. I can't believe you."

"I said it was none of your concern."

"But it's *killing* you!" he explodes. "You being selfish just feeds the curse! I can't believe that after—after everything, you still only care about yourself!"

"BECAUSE I'M THE ONLY ONE WHO DOES!"

My voice rings in the chapel like an hour-bell. Emeric stares at me, utterly floored.

"You have *no right*," I snarl, "to tell me a *damned* thing about what I care for. I have nothing after this but what I take myself. I am a commoner and an orphan and a servant, and I have *only* survived by being selfish, because *who else* will care about a girl like me?"

"Vanja—" he starts, but I am not done.

He's nicked an artery, and I am bleeding words.

"When all this is over, what do I go back to? The mother who left me for dead? The godmothers who only wanted a servant? Gisele gets to go back to Ragne and the castle her parents bought her when they *sold me*. And *if* you survive, you get to go back to your family, your prefects." I scrub a fist over my eyes, ashamed at the rattle in my voice. "Which is *only* an 'if' because you'd rather kill yourself getting revenge for Klemens than—than—"

"It's you," Emeric says, abrupt.

That stops me cold.

He's gone very pale, a tense current strung in every line of him, like he faces a different kind of execution. "It's . . . it's for you. I could wait for the other prefects to get here, if I just wanted justice for Hubert. But it would be too late. You can't break the curse while von Reigenbach is a threat."

I shake my head, wholly confounded, *refusing* to comprehend. He's not saying what I think he's saying. No, I'm not hearing right, I know what I am, it's impossible—

Emeric crosses the stone floor to me, leaving charged inches between us. "I'm scared too," he admits softly. "And I don't want to go." Unsteady fingertips rise, hesitate, trace the line of my jaw, careful, featherlight like before, like it could be the last. They stray to the corner of my mouth, and a helpless note spills into his voice. "But please, Vanja. Don't ask me to watch you die."

Fury and fear are written in his eyes, familiar like my heart is a mirror, like I traced them onto the glass myself. Fury and fear—and the same desperate, searching heat.

Emeric's head tilts, bows, halfway to me. He's waiting. Asking. I can still run. I should, I should, everything in me wants to run—

To him.

It was always going to end with him.

I wrap my fingers in his collar and pull him the rest of the way.

We crash together like magnets at first, moved by forces we don't understand. It's not so much a kiss as a stunned breath caught, soft and bewildered, between us; we're almost frozen, afraid to ruin what we've won. Neither of us knows what we're doing. We just know what we want.

But I am selfish, I want more. My hand slides into his hair and he kisses me again, an arm slipping around my waist to draw me closer.

The feel of it, everywhere we press together, sets a match to lantern oil in my blood. Any caution goes up in smoke. What we lack in expertise we make up for in a catastrophic ferocity, claws out, all instinct, all greed. I feel—I feel like I am cracking apart, a glacier tumbling into a heady thaw, the taste of him burning sweet on my tongue. When we finally break apart for air, we're both staring wild-eyed and entirely astonished.

"So," I manage to stammer, "about the—the—improper interest."

Emeric leans his brow to mine, cradling my face in his shaking hands. "*Nothing*," he says feverishly, "about how I feel for you . . . is proper." He lets out a ragged laugh. "It hasn't been for days."

"What?" I demand. "No. What?"

"You didn't notice when the pearls started working differently on me? I almost walked into the door, I couldn't stop thinking——" He cuts himself off, flushing even darker.

My stomach knots a little. "Oh, right, well," I babble, "that's what the enchantment makes me into, it's supposed to be prettier——" It's my turn to cut myself off as his lips brush my temple.

"Vanja," he says, his voice roughening, "what I was thinking of . . . did not involve the pearls."

That does something *entirely* different to my stomach.

"Oh," I say, very faintly.

Part of me is furious with the indignity, with what a fool this is turning me into. The rest of me has other priorities.

"Say it again." My own voice is shaking. He makes a questioning noise and I feel it in his throat, in every inch of me. "My name." My face is burning, I'm a mess and a fool and I don't care even a little. "Please."

His mouth grazes my ear as he shifts closer. Then he breathes, "Vanja."

A shiver curves my spine, arches me into him, and I feel the answering curve of Emeric's smile against my jaw. I'd be embarrassed and annoyed, but I can barely think, even less so when he moves to my cheekbone.

"Vanja," he says again, like it tastes as sweet to him as to me.

I fist my hands in his hair as a shudder sweeps through me. I can't believe I told him how to unravel me like this. Damn him, *damn* him——

"*Vanja*," he whispers against my mouth, and I am undone. We melt into another kiss, stumbling back until I collide with the plain altar. I find myself swiftly hefted onto it, my back flush to the wall, eye to eye with Emeric as I pull him against me again. I could get lost on his mouth, in the way his touch makes me feel like a knot untied. I don't know if this is love like in the ballads, but I'm starting to understand why they write them.

His fingers tangle in mine. Then he presses closer, easing our twined hands to the wall—

And suddenly, horribly, I can't breathe.

It's like when I fell below the waterfall, the memory dragging me under, Adalbrecht pinning my hands, ramming me against a wall too much like this, digging at my bodice like a pig, the humiliation, the terror—

I am pinned—helpless—frozen—

This is a trap—it isn't real—

My feet hit the bottom, the closest thing to a rationalization.

I should have known when he brought up the pearls. It's all a lie, all a trick, and I fell for it. I should have known better. I should have *known*.

I never escaped the trinity of want.

I am not a thing to be loved.

I am a thing to be used.

I need to get out, I need—I need—

I tear a hand free, seize the first of his knives I find. It sings free of its sheath. Candlelight zips along the gold-plated blade as I snap it to his throat.

Emeric goes very still.

For a moment, the only sound is both of us struggling for breath.

"You almost got me," I rasp, bitter as cyanide. I yank my other hand away, then shove myself off the altar as Emeric reels back. This is just one more narrow escape in the end, I reason, the cruelest trap I've evaded. And I speak that language perfectly. "You almost . . . No wonder I'm not part of the plan. The amnesty's a—a fake. You were going to arrest me here. Today."

Emeric takes another step away from me, hands half raised between us, like he can't decide whether to keep me at a distance or show he's unarmed. His lips part, still flushed. Something awful flickers in his eyes, almost like grief. His voice is so quiet I barely hear it. "I gave you my word."

No—no, my fear is never wrong. It can't be wrong.

Distantly I remember sitting together in the alcove the night of the ball, the strain in his voice when he said he can't fake anything like this. He had no reason to lie then.

He has no reason to lie now.

I can't be wrong about him. I can't be.

Because if I am, I found someone I cared for, someone who knew my scars, someone who cared for a girl like me.

And when he bared his throat to me, I answered with a knife.

I made sure he will never trust me, never touch me again.

I can't be wrong. My fear can't be wrong.

Nothing stolen is ever mine. But there's another truth on the other side of that coin: What is mine can always be stolen.

I will not be anyone's servant, not even my own; I will always be a thief. I am never going to let myself be happy.

I'm always, always going to steal it from myself.

I press my fists over my eyes. Panic roars through me, and I cannot keep the tide at bay, I am falling through shame and horror, I'm a fool, I can't do anything right, I will always be haunted by myself—

The golden knife clatters to the floor.

"This was a mistake," I say brokenly. Then I shove past Emeric, seize my cloak, and do what I should have done in the first place: run.

CHAPTER THIRTY-FIVE

Sweet Dreams

THE BEDROOM IS EMPTY AND STILL WHEN I STUMBLE IN, ALMOST JAR-ringly so. I'm trembling, cold and hot and furious and ruined, and the worst part is I know I have done this to myself. I am falling, falling, and the longer I plummet, the harder I know I will crash.

The tears are coming, I know they are. If I stop for even a moment it will all overthrow me. Instead I tell myself to go back to packing, to count the gold, to be ready to run—

A slip of paper crackles under my boot. I must have knocked it off the credenza. I pick it up and find a short message from Gisele:

> The "baker" decided he doesn't need to socialize this
> afternoon, so I'm doing the same. Ragne and I will
> be keeping an eye on the children tonight to give

*Umayya a break. Ragne may be back later, and I'll
see you tomorrow. 6
P.S. If security's a concern, I know someone who
might be willing to spend the night again!*

I didn't realize until this moment that I wanted to talk to her. Or
Ragne. Or Joniza. Even my mothers, just once. Someone.

Damn *everything*, I—I want to talk to Emeric.

But apparently I can't without holding a knife to his throat.

That's when it catches me.

I choke back a sob, but another wells up in its place, then another.
The paper crumples in my hand. I let it fall to the floor and stagger
to the bed. Some remote part of me remembers to kick off my boots
before I crawl beneath the blankets, though I only remember to untie
my cloak after.

Something's off about the bed. It takes me a moment to realize: It
smells like lavender.

I am already good as gone.

I curl up and bury my face in a pillow as another sob rattles me like
a loose door in a storm. I thought I could beat it, my fear, my past, the
wolf still at my heels. I thought I could win this game.

But it's a draw at best. I will leave Minkja with my life and my
gold and a promise of freedom. Two weeks ago, that would have been
enough.

Two weeks ago, I didn't know how much more there was to lose.

I cry into the pillow until my sobs dry to gasping heaves, and when
those are spent, I lie in the dull, sore haze of defeat. My head pounds
from weeping, my jewels ache, and every time I think of the look on
Emeric's face my heart shatters all over again.

The day cools to afternoon, then to early evening. The room is mostly shadows when I hear his footsteps in the hall. I hate that I know they're his. They slow by my door a moment . . . then carry on.

Of course. Emeric has bigger problems.

Evidently Adalbrecht is too busy for dinner, too, for I hear Trudl bringing trays to the riverfront wing. Emeric's muffled thanks is a punch in the stomach. I don't answer when she knocks on the door, because Gisele took the pearls with her, and I have no time to cover the lines of rubies marching toward my heart. I hear the bump of a tray left in the hall before she moves on.

Not long after, the message-mirror pulses warm in my pocket.

Iron shoots through my veins. I don't want to look, I don't want to face the damage I've done—but I'd be lying if I said I wasn't starving for even a scrap of hope.

I pull the case out, heart in my throat, and unfold the mirror. Words trace across the fogged glass:

> *Vanja—*
> *I can't*

I wait. There has to be more. There has to be more, it's Emeric and he wouldn't do less than a three-part proposal, with footnotes and a bibliography.

The fog fades, reappears. And it spells out again:

> *Vanja—*
> *I can't*

Something in me breaks. I stare at the mirror, watching the words scrawl out again and again. Pain ripples through me, the jewels glittering as they swell larger. Maybe it's just the curse, reminding me I only have two more days. Maybe it's just my own greed.

I am too much for him. I am not enough.

In the end, I find I still have tears left after all.

At some point I fade into fitful sleep.

I don't know what wakes me up. It's dark still—but not quite. A chilly blue light fills the room, but it's too deep a blue to be frigid dawn.

"Get up."

I wrench around.

Adalbrecht is standing at my bedside, a granite mountain glowering down at me.

His eyes burn the same blue, his blond hair hanging stringy and loose around his stone-hard face. He's wearing only breeches and boots, his naked chest pale, twitching, glistening with sweat.

An iron horseshoe is nailed, points-down, over his heart. Icy light gasps from it with every beat.

I scream. My hands skid on the sheets as I try to push away. He just snatches my upper arm and drags me off the bed.

"Stop that noise," he barks, dumping me on the ground still tangled in blankets. "No one in this castle will help you."

The dinner. "You poisoned them." But then—Emeric—

"Don't be stupid. I'm not cleaning up such a mess." He turns around and heads for the door. "They'll sleep as long as I want them to."

Angry black-threaded welts stitch a bleeding ring between his shoulder blades, around a patch of gray skin inked with complicated wheels of runes.

Bile surges in my throat. It's Klemens's tattoo. Adalbrecht has sewn it into his own back.

And suddenly I piece it together. The horseshoe, the skull, the vision of the horse head. He hasn't used the mark to bind himself to all the Low Gods. He's used it to bind himself to all the *nachtmären*. And there are as many as there are dreamers.

That's how he'll overrun the free states and any territory that resists. That's why he wants the Göttermarkt for the wedding: to make sure that, for whatever he's planning, the temple bells will be silent.

My eyes sweep around the bedroom as I struggle to my feet, looking for any way out. The pearls are with Gisele—I don't know what he wants with me, I don't have time to chase those threads—and Ragne's not here either. The veranda—no, I can't get down the trellis and to the Lovers' Road fast enough. The windows are the same. He's blocking the hallway door. The fireplace—

Is burning frosty blue.

I feel even sicker. "What did you do to Poldi?"

"I reminded the *kobold* who's master of this castle," Adalbrecht says. "Stop dragging your feet and come with me."

I don't have a way out. Yet. I follow him to the hallway.

Bodies are scattered up and down it, like they simply fell asleep where they stood. Lurching, giggling *nachtmären* squat on each one, stroking their ears, tying knots in their hair. Of course—one for every dreamer. And Adalbrecht can command sleep itself now.

This is beyond anything I could have planned for.

I glance toward the stairs. The hallway's open, maybe I can make a break for it.

Then I realize Adalbrecht is leading me to Emeric.

I have no choice but to go along.

The same blue flames cast an uncanny pallor over Emeric's room as Adalbrecht throws the door open. Emeric's collapsed over his desk, head cushioned on his wrists; he didn't even take his spectacles off, one wire arm digging into a temple.

A pale, grinning *mahr* hunches on his shoulders, hugging its knees and rocking back and forth.

Adalbrecht reaches over to the *nachtmahr* and grips its shoulder, closing his eyes as if listening to a distant song. A moment later, he sighs. "I see. I was right." He thinks a moment. "I believe you've been informed how my father died. If you'd like to avoid Conrad bleeding out through his feet, you will listen very closely to me now. Am I understood?"

I nod.

"Am I *understood*?" he repeats.

"Yes," I say aloud. His eyes flare blue, and I realize what he's waiting for. The word sticks like coal in my teeth. "M'lord."

"I've known you were a fake for nearly two weeks," he says shortly. "The *nachtmahr* told me everything it dug up in your head: the pearls, the curse, even *his*"—he gestures disdainfully at Emeric—"ridiculous façade. That was the real Gisele in your room the night of the ball, wasn't it? I couldn't recall where I'd seen her, until I remembered that filthy orphanage from your dreams."

"You're bluffing," I say. "If you knew where she was, you could have exposed me days ago."

"And let the empire know an embarrassing little parasite had burrowed into my castle? I think not. I meant to kill you as a gift to Gisele, and then come to her as a savior. She would have been delivered from her misery, a *prinzessin* reborn."

"And then you would murder her," I bite out.

Adalbrecht shrugs. "Of course. But she would have died happy, and you took that from her too. I do owe you, you know. It's impossible to find a binding mark like this anywhere else; the prefects don't let that secret out of their sight. The *Pfennigeist* gave me an excuse to call them in without getting my hands dirty. After that, all I had to do was make sure you and the boy kept each other occupied."

My belly feels like it's turned to lead. I did this. I made this possible. The dance, the guest room, the charade of *improper interest*—in the end, I was always something to be used.

Adalbrecht touches the *nachtmahr* again. It convulses, then begins to shrink. Emeric doesn't so much as stir a finger.

"Do you know what we do to thieves in Bóern?" Adalbrecht asks calmly.

The answer to this kind of question is, as ever, no. Or: "No, m'lord."

"It depends on what's stolen. What do you think the punishment would be for a treacherous maid who stole her mistress's name? Who stole her life?" Adalbrecht watches the *mahr* shrivel to the size of a beetle. It slithers over Emeric's throat.

"I—I don't know, m'lord," I stammer.

The *mahr* crawls into Emeric's ear.

Adalbrecht's blazing eyes flick over to me as he rests a hand on the back of Emeric's skull. "Think harder."

The answer should be no, but— "Hanging," I say, desperate. *Little thieves go to the gallows.*

A jolt runs through Emeric, his brow furrowing with pain. Adalbrecht looks at me, waiting.

He wants worse.

"Hanging," I say swiftly, "but—but the maid drops into a barrel, one that's been lined with nails. So she tears herself to pieces thrashing on the noose."

Emeric quiets.

"Good girl," Adalbrecht says. "That will do."

What have I done?

Adalbrecht enlightens me, shaking out his hands. "As thanks for bringing me the prefect, I will give you a choice. Tomorrow night, I will arrest Gisele von Falbirg's maid for the crimes of the *Pfennigeist*. The day after, Gisele will marry me in the afternoon. Her maid will be hanged, just as you've described, at the end of the wedding ceremony. Gisele herself will die after the wedding night. You can play either role, and so can she. So here is my gift to you: a day to decide which of you goes to the gallows, and which of you goes to the altar."

My fists clench in my skirts. "There's nothing to keep her from running."

"You are a thief and a liar. I am certain you can be convincing." Adalbrecht brushes a bit of grime from Emeric's shoulder. "And if you aren't . . . we will find out how large a *mahr* needs to grow before it pulps a boy's skull from the inside."

I'm going to vomit.

He's smiling in the gentle, savage way that says he knows it's over.

He knows he's got me. He knows I'll do it, because I wear my own greed on my face.

I hate him so much. I want to seize the copper knife and see if all his blood burns blue. But he'll kill Emeric before I can put even a scratch on him.

"Why are you doing this?" I spit instead. "You were born into *everything*. A family, power, wealth——"

"Don't be so dramatic," he says flatly. "So long as Bóern is strong, it is a threat to the imperial throne, unless that throne is *mine*. I watched my father send my brothers to their deaths, one after the other to thank House Reigenbach for keeping the empire safe. He bowed to an empress when we deserved to be kings. Then he sent me, and all I had on the battlefield were my nightmares. You should understand better than any-one. This isn't about petty squabbles or silly games; it's about taking con-trol of my own life. I'm doing this to survive."

And for just a moment, the mountain shudders, candor cleaving down to the raw bedrock. He believes it. He believes that he is a vic-tim, because the life he has is not the one he thinks he is owed. That in that way, the world betrayed him, just as it betrayed me. That in this, he knows me; in this, we are the same.

But he will never understand that girls like me become liars, thieves, ghosts, all to survive men like him.

"I stole from spoiled nobles who barely missed the money," I hiss. "If you didn't like your life, you could have vanished into the empire. You could have lived like the rest of us, but you didn't want to lose your castle. This isn't about survival, it's about comfort. You're nothing but a murderer and a monster."

Adalbrecht closes the distance between us in a stride. He catches my chin in those iron-hard fingers and drags me in close, smiling that awful smile. "And you still dream of me."

He tosses me aside like a rag. I crash into the footboard hard enough to knock the wind from my lungs. When I pick myself up, he's gone.

Emeric is motionless, still crumpled over the desk. The fire still burns unforgiving blue, the only noise in the frigid silence. Poldi can't save me now.

I am on my own.

CHAPTER THIRTY-SIX

The Thief and the Lie

I DON'T KNOW HOW MUCH TIME PASSES WHILE I HUDDLE BY THE BED, fighting panic and failing.

I fail and I fail and I fail. No matter how many times I tell myself not to panic, it never puts down roots.

The hour-bells begin to chime.

I close my eyes. I tell myself I can panic for as long as the bell tolls. I can feel that fear, I can let myself fall until the silence tells me I've hit the bottom.

So I do. For eleven more droning rings, I let myself be terrified. Angry. Selfish. I let it course through me like a poison, breathe in everything ugly and little and quivering. I am dying. I am not enough. I am a broken girl in a world that wants me in smaller pieces still.

I let this malignant terror find my edges, spill over.

Then the bells go quiet.

The fear is still there, but I've let it have its time.

I make myself stand. I take a deep, clean breath, waiting for the fear to settle. And then I dust myself off, and start thinking about how exactly I'm going to pick this lock.

Greed, love, hate, revenge, fear. Ragne, Gisele, Joniza, Barthl. These are my picks; I am the rake. If I shift everything in just the right order, I can get us all out.

But Emeric is the lock, and if I get this wrong, he will break.

I need to test that first. As long as Adalbrecht keeps Emeric off the board, my hands are tied. He keeps the real threat at bay: the justice of the Godly Courts.

There has to be a way to get the *nachtmahr* away from Emeric. I gently turn his face to look in his ear. All I see are two pinpricks of blue light staring back.

Maybe Ragne can shrink down to tear it out—no, it just has to start growing and I'll lose Emeric and Ragne both. I could pour tallow into Emeric's ear to try to drown it, but Adalbrecht knows when one of his creatures dies.

Maybe we can lure it out somehow . . . but Adalbrecht seemed to be giving it unspoken orders. I don't know what those were, only the threatened consequences.

I let my fingers linger on Emeric, telling myself I'm just checking his pulse, trying to ignore the glimmer of pearls spelling my end across my skin. His heartbeat is soft and steady as ever, and neither of us has time for sentiment; I make myself move on. Maybe he's left some prefect gadget lying around. I look around the desk.

He's holding the message-mirror in one hand. It's still flashing *Vanja—I can't*, over and over. But below his elbow is an open notebook, charcoal smudging his sleeve. The page looks nearly full. I lift his elbow and slip it out.

It's a draft of a letter. One for me.

> Vanja—
> ~~I want~~
> ~~You mean more~~
> I can't watch you die. You said you didn't think me a coward, but ~~that's what I am~~ I am terrified of losing you, whether it's to the curse or because I failed you. I thought I didn't believe in bravery. I just didn't know what it was until I met you. You've lived with monsters for thirteen years, and you keep choosing to face them, to fight them, to walk back into their homes. I know bravery is real because I see you choose it every day.
>
> I'm afraid I will be one more person who fails you. ~~I know~~ I think you're afraid of that too. ~~Please don't run~~ I can't ask you to choose ~~me this us~~ to stay, but I want to be with you more than I fear losing you. If you want me to chase you, I will chase you. If you want me to find you, I will find you. If you'll have me, I will choose you every time.
> ~~Maybe I've finally learned to be brave.~~

The absolute *bastard*. I'm—I'm going to—I'm going to save him, just so I can strangle him for making me cry again. I might kiss him first. But *then* I'm going to strangle him.

He must have been in the middle of tracing this onto the mirror when he fell asleep. He wasn't giving up on me. And now . . .

How can he ask me to stay, when I'm so close to losing him?

The veranda door rattles. A black cat is pawing at the glass. I let Ragne in.

"What has happened?" she yowls, tail bushed out as she leaps up onto the desk. "The *kobold* is sick, and I smell *nachtmären*, and——what is wrong with the Emeric? Why is everything wrong?"

"Adalbrecht got him." I scrub my face on a sleeve, wincing as the linen catches on jewels bristling over my forearm. "He knows everything. There's a *mahr* in Emeric's ear, and if we don't do as the margrave says, he'll die."

Ragne's ears flatten to her skull. Then she bumps my elbow with her head. "What can we do?"

I take another breath, tilting on a knife's edge.

If I don't use each of us *exactly* right, this lock will break.

I've failed as a thief. I need to do this as a liar.

I shove the message-mirror at Ragne. "We can't do anything alone. Can you get Gisele and Joniza? Bring them up through the servant corridors. You can take them behind the waterfall as a bear."

Ragne turns to an enormous black owl, the silver mirror-case flashing in her talons as she flies back out the open door. As soon as she's gone, I shut it and begin pacing, mumbling to myself, working through the snags of the lie I am about to spin.

I talk through the loops and threads and knots as the fire burns down to eerie blue coals; I take a spill-stick from the copper urn on the hearth and light enough candles to see by, but even those flames are blue. I don't know what Adalbrecht did to Poldi. I don't know if a bowl of honey and grits will save him.

Every so often Emeric's hand twitches, or his lips part, or he shifts in the chair, and I hold my breath. Once, he mumbles something that sounds like my name. But he doesn't wake up.

I don't know what I'll do if he won't wake up.

By the time Gisele and Joniza arrive, dawn is only a few hours away. Ragne arrives after them, bundled into her dressing gown. The temperature in the castle is plummeting; it's a shallow heat rolling off the blue flames, and it does not last.

Gisele runs over to Emeric and shakes his shoulder, pale. "Is it true?" she asks. "Ragne said there's a *mahr* in—in—"

"If we don't do what Adalbrecht wants, it'll grow until it kills Emeric." My voice is shaking. "He used the *nachtmahr* to see into Emeric's mind. He knows the entire plan, so we need a new one."

Joniza is still standing in the doorway, strung tight as a bow. "Without him, there is no plan."

"No, we can—we can pull this off still." I give her and Gisele both a strained look. "We don't need the Godly Court. Barthl said representatives from the Imperial Court will be at the gala, so we can fool Adalbrecht into revealing himself there. He has Klemens's tattoo on his back and a horseshoe on his heart, we can prove everything if we make him show those. Gisele, you can pose as my maid, and I'll be you, and Barthl will get the skull. We can—"

"It won't work," Gisele says slowly. "It's not enough."

I shake my head, frantic. "No, no, we can pull it off! The Imperial Court guards can bring Adalbrecht in."

"If he knows everything, then he'll recognize Gisele pretending to be your maid," Joniza points out. "And once he realizes something's up, he'll just kill Conrad too."

"Then—then we'll have Ragne do it. Or . . ." I trail off.

Gisele's voice is low, mournful. "Vanja, I'm sorry, but . . . I don't think there's a way to save him. I think we just have to save ourselves."

"I won't," I say immediately. "I won't leave him."

"That's your choice to make. But I have too much to live for." Gisele takes Ragne's hand. "I . . . I'll go through with the wedding ceremony. Then I'll leave Minkja."

"I'll go with you," Joniza says heavily. "I'm sorry, Vanja. You can come with us."

"No—please—you have to help me—I have to save him—" I turn to Ragne, who's stayed quiet this whole time. "Ragne. Ragne, *please.*"

She looks from me to Gisele, red eyes wide and uncertain. Gisele lays a hand on her shoulder. Ragne swallows. "I promised . . . I would protect the Gisele."

A hollow, nauseating hush falls over the bedroom.

Then I pick up the spill-stick urn and throw it at Gisele's feet. Copper clangs against the stone as the wooden splinters scatter. "*GET OUT!*" I scream. "*DAMN YOU, GET OUT!*"

She opens her mouth, then closes it, and sweeps from the room without another word. Joniza follows. Ragne wavers a moment—then she, too, slips through the door.

I hear my bedroom door open, then close. I almost laugh. Of *course* that's where they went.

Emeric still isn't moving.

I let all my fury and sorrow loose in a feral sob and sink to the floor beside him.

Then I take his hand in mine, tears rolling down my face, and trace into his palm like the mirror, writing out my last, most desperate plea:

Stay.

Stay.

Stay.

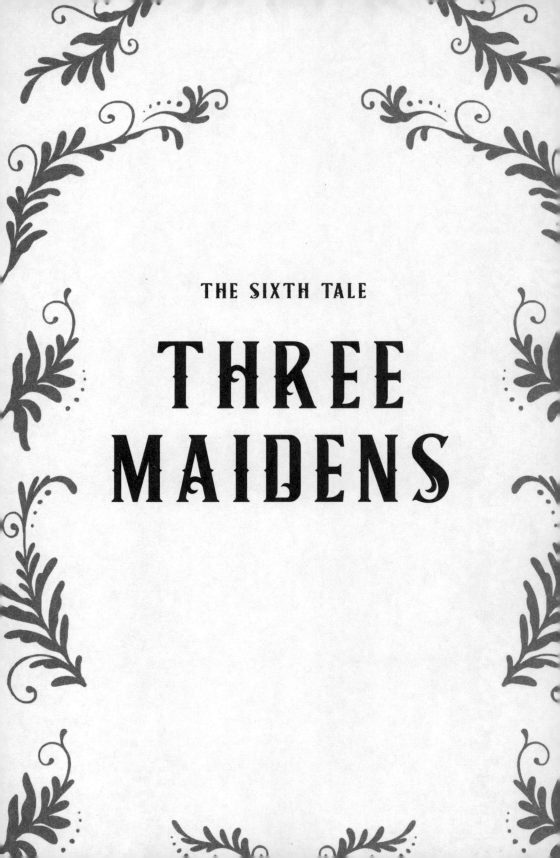

THE SIXTH TALE

THREE MAIDENS

ONCE UPON A TIME, THREE MAIDENS WENT TO A WOLF'S WEDDING.

The night before the wedding, the first maiden sat in a cold, dark bedroom, grieving a life that could have been hers. She was alone with her choices, good and ill; she was in a prison of her own making, behind bars she'd forged herself. And when the wolf's guards came to take her, she went with them, for there was no saving her from herself.

The night before the wedding, the second maiden dressed herself in finest silk and went to dance with the wolf. She twirled and smiled and played the role of *prinzessin* to a fault; she let the wolf's groomsmen "steal" her to the far side of the hall and make the wolf ransom her back in beer and praise and promises. She made sure when she laughed, they could see her teeth, for she would marry the wolf the next day, and he was not the only one with fangs.

The night before the wedding, the third maiden slipped on a face that was not her own, but one she knew well. It was a face that had served her and hurt her, the face of a friend, the face of a liar, the face of a loyal maid. And she waited on her princess as she danced with the wolf. She knew creatures like the wolf well. She knew if no one was there to see it, he would eat the princess whole.

(Now remember—don't follow the cards. Keep your eyes on the real mark.)

The day of the wedding, the second maiden dressed herself in the wolf's own blue and donned the wolf's heavy crown. It was all too heavy, but she bore it anyway, holding her head high as the loyal maid set the crown upon her and made certain it would stay there.

The day of the wedding, the third maiden walked into the ceremonial house the wolf had built in the Göttermarkt, wearing the wolf's own blue. She was not there for the same reason as most of the guests; she was there to be married.

The day of the wedding, the first maiden was marched into the

Göttermarkt, up to the gallows the wolf had built alongside his houses. She stood, iron-faced and alone, as the hangman placed a noose around her neck. Below her waited a barrel full of nails, ready to eat her whole.

You have watched the cards move, shields and grails, roses and bells, knights and pages and queens and kings. I think it's only fair for you to take a guess now at where the Lady lies. There are maidens three: a loyal maid, a bride in her crown, a thief at the gallows.

Which of the maidens was I?

CHAPTER THIRTY-SEVEN

Find the Lady

It's a beautiful day in Minkja, and I am about to die.

"Good people of Bóern," Adalbrecht booms, "we have two causes to celebrate today." His voice echoes over the Göttermarkt, which looks like someone sucker punched the treasury and it spewed all over the plaza. (Adalbrecht. Adalbrecht was the one doing the punching.)

The ceremonial houses are tiny cathedrals unto themselves, one draped in Falbirg red, one draped in Reigenbach blue, and the open-faced altar house between them draped in cloth of gold. Gisele's house is the only spot of Falbirg red; the rest of the decorations are an onslaught of blue and gold silk, great arches of hothouse flowers, fans of gilded holly and fir, Bóernische flags flapping in the gentle breeze. Thick carpets have been laid over the paving stones, and chairs arranged for the gentry, all facing the golden altar house at one end of the plaza. Braziers have been placed around the rows to keep the guests warm, and a glittering dome spreads overhead, the work of a streetwitch guild. It will keep any snow at bay, though even the weather seems to have bowed to Adalbrecht, offering nothing but unbroken blue afternoon sky.

At the other end of the plaza stands a gallows, the strange platform I saw them building last week. It's a little humbling to know the margrave was planning this for a while.

And he's savoring his triumph as he stands in the middle of the central aisle, which he will walk down with his bride once the vows are spoken. He's borrowed the officiant's ceremonial staff, which has another streetwitch guild specialty: a charm to amplify his voice. It carries over the seated nobility and into the standing crowds ringed around the plaza to watch.

"I am pleased," Adalbrecht announces, "to tell you that, thanks to hard work and perseverance of the city guard, the *Pfennigeist* has been caught. She was masquerading as a servant of the princess . . ." He gestures to Gisele beside him. She gives him a smile as pale and hard as the pearls around her neck but does not look my way even once, not even as he tips his hand to me. ". . . and is about to learn what we do to thieves in Minkja."

Oh, *please*.

"We have given her the honor of being the first guest to dance at our wedding!" Adalbrecht continues, grinning up to me on the gallows. "Albeit at the end of a rope."

An uncomfortable laugh ripples through the crowds.

"Shitty wedding tradition," I mutter. Everything aches in the chill; some of the jewels have grown so large they scrape against each other under my sleeves. The rubies are almost to my heart now. It doesn't help that my hands have been manacled behind my back. "Whatever happened to 'something borrowed'?"

One of the two guards on the platform gives me a look. I glare at him until he turns away.

Adalbrecht keeps talking, but I'm barely listening. I'm a little distracted by the hangman shoving my head through a noose. Perhaps I'm just being fussy, but the rope is *awfully* scratchy. Trust Adalbrecht to be a cheapskate to the end.

Though I did get a perfect view of the barrel waiting below the gallows' trapdoor on my way up. Apparently hundreds of nails are in the budget.

There's a ruffle of applause. Adalbrecht tosses the officiant's staff back to her. He and Gisele walk to the end of the aisle, then pace, solemn and stiff, to their respective houses as the band strikes up a garishly chipper wedding march. There are doors on either side of the house, one facing me, one facing the altar—another bit of (absurd) symbolism. Whatever ills cling to the spouses-to-be are meant to be shut in the houses with them, then left behind.

They stay in the houses, supposedly to give themselves a moment to pray to the gods for a happy marriage. I suspect Gisele and Adalbrecht are both praying for something else.

The wedding march comes to an end. The second doors swing open. Adalbrecht and Gisele emerge and proceed to the gold awning of the altar house.

All eyes are on them. I slip a hairpin out of my sleeve and go to work on the lock.

"*Hey.*" The same guard is looking again. He strides over and plucks the hairpin from my hand, holding it up for the hangman. "The little terror's trying some foolishness."

The hangman laughs. "Put it in her hair, so she's pretty when she meets Death," he suggests.

"I've already met Death," I sneer. "She doesn't care if I'm pretty."

The hangman scowls. "Check her pockets. There should be nothing but the Ferryman's due."

The guard does a quick search and pulls out only the single red penny everyone gets before they're hanged. "Nothing," the guard says, returning the penny to my pocket.

"Keep an eye on her. If she doesn't hang, the margrave will string us up too."

"Yes, sir." The guard stations himself at my back, the better to keep an eye on my manacles.

The officiant plants her staff on a stand, then reaches out and takes both Gisele's and Adalbrecht's hands.

"Gisele-Berthilde Ludwila von Falbirg," the officiant begins. "Do you come to this altar of your own free will, to marry this man?"

I can't see Gisele clearly from this far off, but I can hear the edge in her voice when she says, "I do."

The officiant turns to Adalbrecht. "And do you, sir, come to this altar of your own free will, to marry—"

"I do," he answers quickly.

No one speaks, but I see flutters in the crowd as people trade glances. The margrave is not known for being retiring, but to be so hasty on his wedding day? I can see the calculations: There will be an heir before year's end.

I want to scream at them that there will be no heir at all.

"Do you swear, my lady, swear to keep your marriage with honor and trust, to be faithful and true, until death do you part?"

"I do." Gisele's steadied her voice.

That's the first signal.

A hairpin falls into my palm.

"And do you swear, my lord, to keep your marriage with honor and trust, to be faithful and true, until death—"

"I do," Adalbrecht interrupts again. This time there are titters in the throngs clustered around the plaza.

Joniza's doing a remarkable job as officiant for someone who was ordained as a temporary delegate of Fortune overnight, but I'd be shocked if she's not rolling her eyes this very moment.

She waits until the laughter dies down and then continues, glancing briefly up to me. It seems like Adalbrecht's composed himself now, but he still seems impatient, even from this distance. Joniza's doing her best to strike a balance. We timed this yesterday, working through how long she'd have to drag out the rest of the vows while my pin worked away at these manacles, how much wiggle room I had. (Not much.)

Sure enough, I feel the latching mechanism slide open just as Joniza declares, "In the name of the High Gods and the Low, by the laws mortal and divine, I proclaim you wed. You may kiss—"

Gisele is the one to move a little too fast this time. She all but leaps into Adalbrecht's arms.

Well, not quite.

We'll come back to that. Because right then, the hangman pulls the lever for the trapdoor. It drops open into the gaping, bristling mouth of the barrel, the jaws of a monstrous wolf.

But the only thing that falls into it are the manacles.

I've wrapped my hands above the noose knot, keeping my weight from pulling it tight even as my feet dangle over the gap.

If this were a normal hanging, this would be a short fall and I would already be dead. But because *somebody* wasn't happy with a garden-variety execution, the rope had to be long enough for me to pass into the barrel below the platform. And that, friend, *that* bought me enough time to seize it and hold on for dear life.

Maybe after today Adalbrecht will realize that every time he gives me room for error, I'm going to use it.

You may be wondering what the long game is here, though. And that's a valid question! I'm still dangling over a barrel full of nails, and my upper-arm strength really isn't where I'd like it to be, which is "enough to hold this rope indefinitely."

The answer is the arm around my waist, pulling me back onto the platform. A blur of steel slices through the rope.

"So that's what the steel one's for," I wheeze, pulling off the noose as I turn to face Emeric.

"They're knives, Vanja, they're all good against ropes." He wraps both arms around me, and I think we've reached an unspoken agreement to pretend neither of us is shaking with relief. Even in a stolen guard's uniform, he smells like juniper. I wish I could chalk it up to a mysterious boy power, but I know precisely why.

⚜

And I *know* you're wondering how we pulled this one off.

Fine, since you've been so patient, I'll tell you just this once.

Let's wind back the clock to a little over a day ago, still in Emeric's room. Joniza, Gisele, and Ragne had just given the performance of their lives. They were waiting in my bedroom to see if the gambit paid off, and meanwhile I was busy weeping like a girl whose kitten just got carried off by a hawk before her eyes. (Oddly specific imagery, I know. I saw a *lot* of grim things in Sovabin.)

And the tears certainly weren't all fake. I was terrified this wouldn't work, terrified I was wrong, terrified I'd lose Emeric. I'd written as much to Gisele in the message-mirror Ragne brought her: *Everything I tell you about Emeric will be true. Everything I tell you about how to fix it will be a lie. Trust me. Refuse to help.*

Everything I'd traced into his palm was true. I needed him to stay.

Then I made myself go quiet and still, deepen my breath, nearly nod off. And a few minutes later, I heard a rustle as the *mahr* crept from Emeric's ear.

Adalbrecht had kept touching it to give it orders. Knowing that rat bastard, he'd want to hear exactly what we were planning, so I'd fed the *mahr* a juicy tale to report.

And when it scurried onto the floor, no doubt to slip to Adalbrecht and back before I woke, I seized the copper spill-stick urn—*conveniently empty* after I threw it at Gisele—and slammed it down over the squalling *mahr*.

"Grow into *that*, you little shit," I snapped. Then I stood, looking for something heavy to set on it, just in case this particular *nachtmahr* was a masochist and enjoyed throwing itself against copper.

I had just dropped a stack of books onto the urn when a single sound froze me in my tracks:

"*Vanja?*" Emeric was pushing himself up from the desk, blinking and befuddled. I may have knocked him out of his chair throwing my arms around his neck. (I did. I did do that.)

He still seemed thoroughly bewildered, but he buried his face in my hair nonetheless, holding me so tight to him I nearly forgot to breathe.

I half laughed, half sobbed into his shoulder, gasping, "I can't believe you were going to write all that out on the mirror."

Then I explained to him about the *mahr*, and why he shouldn't touch the urn on the floor, and why we were going to get to Fortune's cathedral as fast as we could. And, more painfully, I told him why I ran.

And then he told me why he would always follow.

And then—well. It took a few extra minutes for us to leave his bedroom and cross the trellis to mine. You can probably figure out why.

(I'm still impressed that he managed to find a place that wasn't covered in jewels to leave a kiss mark. Not thrilled it was on my neck, but in the moment I absolutely did not mind. I did later, when Joniza saw it and died laughing, but since he was as mortified as I was, I let him off the hook this once. At least it's scarf weather.)

Now let's come back to the wedding, where a lot of confused people are trying to figure out what's going on, chief among them the hangman.

He's probably going to have more questions after Emeric returns his spectacles to his face, says, "I do apologize for this," and then kicks him down the gallows' stairs.

"Don't apologize, he almost killed me," I say indignantly.

The wedding guests are turning in their seats, watching the commotion on the scaffold. The remaining guard eyes us, no doubt weighing his options against his pay grade, and finding the latter wanting.

Then everyone finds an entirely new distraction.

"STOP! STOP THE WEDDING AT ONCE!"

Adalbrecht von Reigenbach, Margrave of Bóern, bursts from the Reigenbach ceremonial house, disheveled, sweating, and a little charred.

You see, when he walked into that house for his moment of prayer and reflection, he found two things.

One: the same banishing spell that Emeric used to slow the *nachtmahr* in Lähl. (With a slight modification to muffle any shouting. It was Adalbrecht. There was sure to be a lot of shouting.)

And two: Ragne, wearing his face and waiting in the traditional Reigenbach family wedding regalia. Virtually identical, just a bit older, and much easier for Barthl to sneak out.

It's always, always about the details.

So when the real Adalbrecht storms up to the altar, where Gisele's still clinging to Ragne in his likeness, everyone's attention is solely on them.

Exactly where I want it.

CHAPTER THIRTY-EIGHT

Thieves at the Altar

"That is a fake!" Adalbrecht roars, pointing at Ragne. His jacket is smoking a little, and I cannot adequately express how much joy I take in that. "I was attacked! That—that's a fraud! A *grimling* or a—something!"

Emeric and I hurry off the gallows while Gisele gasps, clutching Ragne even tighter. "How dare you speak about my darling Adalbrecht this way! How do we know *you're* not an imposter?"

Emeric's hand tightens around mine. Everything in this plan has to go perfectly, but this moment more than anything.

"Please, my lady, step back." Joniza steps between Gisele and Ragne. Ragne has maintained Adalbrecht's look of constipated outrage this entire time, and it's almost a little too convincing. Joniza reaches her hands out to both Adalbrechts. Her voice rolls, crystal clear, through the Göttermarkt. "This is very simple. Clearly there are wicked forces at work here, but if one of you is a *grimling*, there will be a mark on your body."

Ragne nods solemnly and begins to undo her collar, never one to mind a little public nudity. "I am not afraid," she says in Adalbrecht's aloof tones. We coached her on this moment for *hours*. "I have nothing to hide."

The real Adalbrecht sputters in fury, reaching for his own buttons—then stops.

Emeric and I have skirted the edge of the plaza, ducking around the flower arches and behind flags, and we're close enough now to see the moment it dawns on the margrave.

If he takes off his shirt, everyone will see the horseshoe nailed to his heart, the dead man's tattoo on his back.

And if the assembled nobility of the Blessed Empire of Almandy have questions *now*, they are nothing compared to the ones that will follow.

Adalbrecht looks from Ragne, merrily unbuttoning her waist-coat, to Gisele, staring at him in wide-eyed dismay. Then he looks to the gallows—and finds it empty.

The real nail in the coffin, though, is when Barthl steps out of the Falbirg ceremonial house, holding the horse skull from the study.

You know, the one covered in the runes of a binding spell that scream, *I am up to some illegal and blasphemous shenanigans? That* skull.

Adalbrecht sees that. And Barthl. And then he does the *last* thing I, personally and professionally, would recommend: he panics.

Adalbrecht slashes a hand through the air. Blue light sweeps across the Göttermarkt, and the wedding guests slump in their seats, out cold. I hear a shuddering thud as the crowds all around the plaza fall where they stand.

But Emeric, Gisele, Joniza, Barthl, Ragne, and I all stay on our feet.

We weren't quite sure what we were up against with Adalbrecht, so we came prepared. Ulli Wagner worked all through the night after sabbath, forging the coins I gave them into warding charms at the Order of Prefects' outpost. The copper for *grimlingen* was easy enough to salvage from pennies, and for curses . . . I just happened to have a few spare bits of gold.

With everyone fallen, Adalbrecht finally sees me and Emeric. His eyes widen with comprehension—then rage.

His lips start moving in a silent chant. There's a whispery, songlike rush, a vicious lullaby, and then *mahr* after *mahr* appears from thin air, crouching on the shoulders of every sleeper. Adalbrecht's jacket smokes and blackens over the iron horseshoe, his eyes smoldering blue with power and hate.

Here's the thing about men like Adalbrecht von Reigenbach: They assume that once something's in their control, it will *stay* in their control. They tell their subordinates that they want an entire temple district to go silent? It goes silent. They see little things like lost signet rings as inconveniences, not liabilities. They can never imagine a world in which someone else commands the same kind of power.

Which is why Gisele spent a decent part of her day yesterday shepherding a group of older orphans around to the temples closest to the plaza, explaining that she had persuaded her fiancé to do a bit of *charity*. Couldn't these bright young orphans be the ones to sound the wedding bells from the (conveniently *grimlingen*-proof) temples?

And no one would refuse written orders, all sealed with the margrave's own signet ring.

Adalbrecht von Reigenbach thinks he's in control, because I want him to think he's in control. So he doesn't see it coming when Joniza leans over to the officiant's staff, which will carry her voice all across the Göttermarkt, and calmly says: "All right, little monsters. Let 'em ring."

Bells peal from their towers, throaty and raucous and undeniable. It's not the measured blow of hour-bells chiming, but all-out war on every side. The *nachtmären* scream, glass bursting around the plaza. Below their howls I hear Adalbrecht screaming too. The *nachtmären* are splitting like the horse-*mahr* did in Lähl, fraying in every direction, peeling into a fractured host.

The bells keep ringing. Adalbrecht crashes to his knees, hands over his ears. Emeric and I grip each other's hands tighter. This is it. We have the horse skull, we have the letters, we have a margrave on his knees. We can call the Godly Court and bring this to an end.

Then I hear a horrid, splintering whine.

I look over to Barthl. The horse skull is shaking—*thrashing*—in his hands. Every rune blisters and smokes. Fissures spiderweb across the bone.

And then the skull—you know, the binding skull? The key piece of evidence?

The one that keeps all these monsters leashed together, bound to Adalbrecht's will?—*that* skull . . .

. . . shatters.

That was not in the plan.

The *nachtmären* spiral into a shrieking, giggling, sobbing wheel, a thousand blazing blue eyes darting through putrescent white flesh.

Then they converge on Adalbrecht. He doesn't even have time to scream.

Gisele pulls Joniza and Ragne back from the altar as boiling gray-white swells around the margrave in a mass of shifting limbs. Then, horribly, it begins to warp into—what, exactly, I cannot tell you.

It's like the *mahr* from the night of the ball, reeling between horse and man. I see Adalbrecht's eyes in a human face stretched sickeningly over a horse's skull; I see a long, muscled neck lined with hundreds of gnashing mouths; I see blond hair in a stringy, dirty mane; I see arms like a man's but stretched and gnarled into a horse's forelegs, the fingers ending in hard iron hooves.

Oh, and perhaps I should mention—it's almost as tall as the nearest temple. And it's still growing.

Emeric, with a martyr's air of vindication, says faintly, "*Horses.*"

Adalbrecht lets out a roar from scores of mouths. A moment later a clanging *bang* answers from all over the Göttermarkt. The bells go silent.

A new wave of screams erupts as the sleepers start waking. Nobles and commoners alike stampede from the plaza, and Emeric, Barthl, and I duck behind the Falbirg ceremonial house to get out of their path.

"*THIEVES!*" Adalbrecht's tortured voice tears across the Göttermarkt. "*MINE! THE GIRL IS MINE! THE EMPIRE IS MINE! HOW DARE YOU STEAL FROM ME?*"

I peer around the corner as the wave of fleeing people subsides. Gisele, Ragne, and Joniza are huddled behind the wreck of the altar house. The monstrous Adalbrecht is lurching around the plaza, crushing chairs and knocking over braziers. He swings one massive fist into the Reigenbach ceremonial house. It collapses in a heap of blue silk and gilt.

Emeric pushes away from the Falbirg house. "I have to call the court before this gets any worse."

There's another crash from the plaza, but I'd swear it's my heart. "We just lost our biggest piece of evidence."

Emeric pulls the letters from his jacket. "I'd say Adalbrecht himself is convincing evidence at this point. And we can prove everything else with these."

"Can we?" I ask.

His jaw clenches, his eyes on the paving stones. All he says is "I promised you."

"Ragne, wait!"

Gisele's cry reaches us. We all turn and see Ragne run into the plaza, falling to all fours. She shifts to a black lioness, red eyes burning—and then she swells even larger, until she's almost as big as Adalbrecht.

She did say she would be greater on the full moon. I just hadn't expected that to translate to size as well.

Ragne hurls herself at him, claws out.

They topple over onto the plaza, Adalbrecht screaming as she drags him over spilled coals from the braziers. The ground shakes, the paving stones splitting beneath them. Smoke rises from the carpets, tongues of flame springing up from broken chairs. Adalbrecht smashes the side of Ragne's head with an iron-shod fist, but she sinks her teeth into his foreleg and jerks. There's a crunch like a felled tree—then an earsplitting howl from Adalbrecht.

I hear a muffled *thwip*. Emeric staggers forward with a startled cry.

A crossbow bolt sprouts from the back of his left shoulder, so close to his heart, I think for a terrible moment he's—gone. His arm jerks, spilling the letters onto the ground.

In a flurry of golden skirts, *fucking* Irmgard von Hirsching sweeps them up.

She moves out of range, stuffing the letters under an arm, and levels a crossbow at me. She must have picked one up off a fleeing guard. I brace Emeric as he fights to keep on his feet; he's still here, still with me, but I can't imagine the pain he's in. It gives me only the feeblest satisfaction to see Irmgard's dress has been ruined beyond repair, her gleaming tresses tangled.

Doesn't change that she's still pointing a crossbow my way.

"Oh, *Rohtpfenni*," she simpers. "You thought you could stop this? Adalbrecht's going to rule Almandy with me. You're just a little bitch who squeaks when she's whipped."

I stay very still. One wrong move and I won't have to worry about the curse anymore—or anything else at all. And if we can't get the letters back . . .

We have to get the letters back. I have to be smart about this.

Irmgard, as ever, sees my hesitation. "Get on your knees," she sings. "Beg. Beg me to let you live." Then she tilts her head, smirking. The crossbow shifts to point to Emeric. "Beg me to let *him*—"

I tackle her before she finishes the sentence.

Irmgard's head smacks against the paving stones. The crossbow fires. The shot goes wide. Then I hear Ragne scream, and look up.

She's rearing back, one paw fumbling at her eye. Vivid red streaks down her cheek. Then she vanishes—no, she's a crow, tumbling and flapping as she plummets, slows—then a cat again, shaking her head.

She had to shift to heal. But that takes the most out of her.

Ragne streaks toward Gisele. Her fur bristles with terror as Adalbrecht lumbers after her, sides heaving with hungry laughter.

What else could possibly hold him off?

I hear a distant *boom*. Then another, closer. Another. Another. Even Adalbrecht stops to see what's coming.

Then *she* appears.

She leaps over the Yssar, spear aloft. Thunder rattles the Göttermarkt when she lands. More follows as she sprints toward the plaza, face cold and furious, each footfall leaving an ox-sized dent in the street.

I don't know whether it's a Low God or the ghost of Kunigunde von Reigenbach in that statue, but I am certain of one thing: She is here to reckon with Adalbrecht.

Irmgard blinks dizzily at the bronze statue charging into the plaza.

I yank the crossbow from her grasp and throw it onto the coals of a nearby overturned brazier.

She grins up at me.

Then she lifts her other fist, now full of her father's letters, and throws them, too, into the fire.

CHAPTER THIRTY-NINE

Moonrise

"**N**o!" I scramble after the letters, but they're gone in a flash.

That was—that was all the evidence we had left.

Emeric can't call the court now. He doesn't have a case.

Kunigunde may be the only way left to stop Adalbrecht. And even if she isn't, it really, really helps to watch her swing her bronze spear into his head.

He lets out a guttural scream-roar as I look to Gisele and Ragne. I see two glowing red eyes in the bundle of fur huddled in Gisele's arms. At least Ragne saved her eye, but between healing and keeping up the shape of a temple-sized lion, I'm sure she's out of the fight for good. Not even the full moon can give her infinite energy.

The full moon.

Oh, *scheit*.

I look up. The sun is sinking behind Castle Reigenbach, golden light searing over the Göttermarkt, flashing over broken glass and silent belfries and the wreckage of the wedding houses.

I have a matter of minutes before the full moon rises.

The ground leaps and shudders as Kunigunde takes a tumble. Adalbrecht snaps his teeth at her, only to bite down on unyielding bronze. There's a horrible *crack*. He shakes his head, voice hoarse with a fresh howl, bits of fang scattering across the plaza. Then he bowls into Kunigunde, shoving her into spilled coals. He's clutching one bleeding foreleg to his chest, but he brings the other down on her shin. The metal bends and twists.

Then I discover I shouldn't have counted Irmgard down for the count either, as she drives a knee into my gut. I falter, crying out.

Surprisingly, Irmgard also screams, jerking her leg back. Blood stains her golden skirt.

I look down. Thorns of rubies are breaking through my prison dress. She kicked right into those

Irmgard rolls away, then gets to her feet, making a limping break for the nearest temple. She's watching Kunigunde and Adalbrecht over one shoulder as she runs.

She misses Gisele setting Ragne down, getting to her feet, and picking up the enormous, heavy Reigenbach bridal crown.

Gisele swings. And she does not miss Irmgard.

This time, Irmgard stays down.

That's for the best, because when I try to stand, I find my whole foot has gone numb. Rubies and pearls are bursting through my ruined stockings.

My time is almost up.

Like Eiswald warned me, I am become my greed.

Emeric kneels in front of me, face taut with pain, left arm still dangling. "Vanja. I have to do it. I'm the only one who can stop this."

He has the prefect coin, and only he knows what to say to call the court.

I hang my head. "I know."

I know this, and still. And still. And still.

Kunigunde is barely holding Adalbrecht off now. There's a cacophonous clang as he strikes the spear from her hands. It flies across the plaza, landing in the gallows.

Emeric cradles my face with his good hand. I make myself look him in the eye. It's the least I can do for him now.

All I can think is that he is a good person, one ready to die because it will save countless strangers, and I—I am dying of my own selfishness.

The story is ending with him. And I am not ready for it.

The full moon begins to crest over his shoulder.

His lips move, like he's struggling to find the words. I still them with my fingertips, while they're still mine. Judging by the numbness spreading up from my knees, the curse won't let me keep my hands much longer.

"Tell me after," I say softly. Then I kiss him one last time. We linger only for the briefest moment, stolen as the monster rages behind us, as the curse devours me from within.

Emeric reaches into his pocket for the prefect coin. His eyes shut as he pulls it out, white-knuckled and shaking. "In the name of Emeric Conrad," he whispers, "initiate of Hubert Klemens of the Helligbrücke First Office of the Order of Prefects of the Godly Courts, I convene the Court of the Low Gods."

There's a long, brutal silence as he waits for the axe to fall.

It doesn't.

In this moment, I am grateful for three things.

Emeric opens his eyes, uncomprehending.

As he unfurls his hand, I am grateful that mine have only just now crusted over into solid ruby.

I am grateful that he has not seen my lips move to say his name, not caught the words I am barely breathing aloud as my lungs calcify into pearl.

And I am grateful that this beautiful damned boy left his prefect coin in the same pocket he always does.

In his palm sits a single red penny.

"—of the Godly Courts," I gasp, "I convene—"

"Vanja, *NO*—" He seizes my arm, cutting himself on the rubies.

It's too late. With the last of my breath, I squeeze out the final words of the incantation: ". . . the Court of the Low Gods."

CHAPTER FORTY

Vanja, Yes

TIME IS THE FIRST LOW GOD TO ARRIVE. OR AT LEAST, THE FIRST I notice. But Time is hard to miss.

The world goes silent in a way you don't hear outside the realm of the Low Gods. It reminds me of living with Death and Fortune in their cottage; it's a kind of quiet that nothing can break, not even you. I could cry and laugh and yell as loud as I wanted, and no one would tell me to hold my tongue.

Time sweeps into the plaza in a flowing, glittering gown, surveying the scene. "Huh," he says. "Isn't *this* a mess?"

Death arrives second. "Vanja, what have you done?" she demands. Her face is frozen in my features.

That's when I realize with a jolt that I am standing—well, in myself. I seem to have both feet planted in a mass of rubies and pearls. It's my body, or what's left of it.

I can't help but laugh. It killed me, just as Emeric said it would. Now I really *am* the Penny Phantom. At least my ghost isn't carrying the jewel curse.

It stops being funny when I see Emeric's frozen face, bleak with horror.

Fortune makes her entrance in about the same emotional state as Death. "Have you lost your mind? You could have just called one of us for help!"

"Oh, *could* I?" I ask sharply.

We don't have time to get into it before the rest of the court arrives. I've heard that the Court of the Low Gods is supposed to be Time, Justice, and Truth at minimum, usually with the addition of a few local deities who want entertainment.

Yssar and Eiswald are here, but many, many more are packing the plaza, from the Spindle-dam and Waul of the Winds to the Silversmith, Hunger, the Eadalisk, even littler gods of distant mountains and farther shores.

It as if they've been waiting for a call.

There's a *crack* like jaws snapping shut. Justice has come.

She stands nearly as tall as Adalbrecht's warped form, draped in robes of unfurling scrolls. The text upon them shifts constantly, immeasurable laws written and unwritten to suit the world. Twin lanterns burn where her eyes should be—or where they would be, if her face was more than a blank skull. Above her floats Truth, who has taken the form of a wheel of eyes today. (As one does.)

"The Court of the Low Gods is convened," Justice declares, rapping her staff against the ground. "Truth. How do we speak of you for this trial?"

Truth spins a moment, then says, "I am 'they' for now."

"Understood. We will begin with the opening remarks. If Truth hears anything egregiously false, they may interrupt. Is that understood, Prefect . . ." Justice looks down, and while a skull can't frown, she is absolutely *nailing* the same feeling. "What is this? Who are you?"

"Vanja, Your Honor," I say. "I have convened the court."

"You are no prefect. You do not have the right."

Oh, this is already going badly. I gesture to the frozen mayhem and destruction of the Göttermarkt. "It's kind of an emergency?"

"This court was convened in the name of Emeric Conrad," Justice crackles. "How did you come by his coin? How did you know the words?"

I lick my lips. "Let me preface this by pointing out that the margrave of Bóern is currently half man, half *mahr*, and all murderous bastard—"

"She stole the coin," Truth whispers, and somehow it rolls through every inch of the plaza. "She tricked him into saying the words."

"I never liked you anyway," I mutter under my breath.

"That is mostly true," Truth whispers again.

"You still should not have been able to convene the court without a connection to the gods," Justice booms.

"She's our goddaughter," Death says from my side. "Mine and Fortune's."

Justice regards them both a long moment, lantern flames flickering, then deadpans, "Well, *that* explains it." I don't think she means just the connection. She bends closer to me. "You have paid with your life to summon the court, but if you fail, do you understand that you will not be restored?"

"I do." I shrug. "I was about to die anyway."

"You summoned us in the name of Emeric Conrad. Do you wish to allow him to assist you in making the case?"

"Oh, like you wouldn't believe," I burst out.

Justice taps her staff again. "Very well. Time, let the junior prefect go."

Emeric crashes forward. I try to catch him—and my hand passes through his shoulder. He looks up at me, then at the assembly of Low Gods. Then he returns to me, shaking his head, and asks, "*Why?*"

"I had seconds left," I say quietly. "You have years." He still looks devastated, so I add, "Besides, do you know how much money that coin's worth? I'm guessing at *least* five horses."

"That is incorrect," Truth sighs.

I glare up at them. "Must you?"

Their eyes blink at me, slow and unsynchronized. "Yes."

"Someone fix the boy's arm," Fortune interrupts. "He's bleeding all over the place. You can't expect him to be much help like that."

Emeric's shoulder jerks, and there's a clatter as the crossbow bolt falls out. He lets out a breath, and I can't help but share the relief as he gets to his feet.

"Let us begin." Justice cracks her staff down once more. "Prefect, you may assist this girl in making your case. First, both of you, state who you are for the assembled court."

Emeric straightens his spectacles. "Junior Prefect Emeric Conrad, born September 9, 742 Blessed Era, in Rabenheim, dispatched on behalf of the Helligbrücke First Office."

The Low Gods look at me.

I shuffle my feet. "Vanja," I say. "My name is Vanja. I don't know where I was born, or what my family name is, and I think I'm sixteen."

Death coughs. "Seventeen. As of today."

She always knows.

Something about that steadies me. "I am the daughter of Death and Fortune, of Sovabin and Minkja. I have been an orphan, a servant, a thief, and a princess."

"And which are you now?" Justice asks.

"Vanja," I answer. "That is the best I have."

Truth blinks again. "That is true."

Justice draws a ring on the plaza stones with her staff. "Vanja, who do you accuse?"

"*Markgraf* Adalbrecht von Reigenbach of Bóern."

Justice taps the stone. The monster that was grappling with Kunigunde vanishes. Adalbrecht appears in the ring, stripped down to a human again, bloody, bedraggled, and clutching a broken forearm. The iron horseshoe is gone, but it's left a searing brand over his heart, one that still oozes blue light.

His head whips around as he takes in the Low Gods, then Emeric and me. He lunges for me—and slams into a flare of light as he tries to step over the ring.

A murmur runs through the assembled gods.

"Hmm," Justice grunts. "Vanja, of what is this man accused?"

I hadn't really thought that out beyond "half man, half *mahr*, all bastard" because I felt like that summed it up pretty well. I look at Emeric.

"Just what we can prove," he says, voice low. "With testimony and physical evidence alone, I think we can show he bound himself to the *nachtmären* with intent to cause harm." He presses his lips together. "It should get him a curse, and probably banishment from the march."

I look at Adalbrecht. He's holding his head high, defiant, the curling wick of a smirk on his face.

He knows it's my word against his. That what we can prove is not enough.

The horseshoe burn simmers on his chest. Something about that tugs at a loose thread in my own skull.

We all know how Adalbrecht loves his image as the Golden Wolf. And *nachtmären* take any form, so . . . why use a horse skull? Why did I see a horse head with the Augur's Tears? Why is he going all in on the horses?

I take a deep breath. "I accuse him of binding himself to *nachtmären* with intent to cause harm."

Adalbrecht's smile slices deeper.

Then I add, "And of attempted murder, solicitation of murder, conspiracy to commit—what's the word? *Impericide?*"

Emeric is staring at me. "Vanja, *no.*"

"Vanja, yes. *Regicide,* that's it!" I snap my fingers. "Conspiracy to commit regicide. He did that. And conspiracy to, uh, invade? He was planning to dissolve the Free Imperial States, so whatever you want to call that. I'm pretty sure that's illegal too."

"Correct," Truth whispers.

"I might like you after all, Truth."

I would say Truth winks at me, but they have an untold myriad of eyes, so honestly it's anyone's guess.

Adalbrecht isn't smiling anymore.

Emeric tries to grab my shoulder and wafts right through it. "What are you doing?" he hisses frantically. "You have to prove *all* of those things or they won't bring you back to life!"

"I have to try, or else he's just going to do worse in a few more years." I flap a hand. "Sometimes you just have to throw *spätzle* at the wall and see what sticks, Junior."

"You *absolutely* do not, that is how you get *ruined spätzle*—"

Justice clears her throat. "It's time for your opening statement, Vanja."

"Right." I turn to Emeric. "What is that?"

Emeric gathers himself a moment, pinching the bridge of his nose, and I'm fairly certain he's interrogating a lot of the life choices that brought him to this point. "Just . . . explain why we think von Reigenbach did all those things, and how. Tell the story. And remember you can call witnesses after to back everything up. But that's *all* you have."

"I know. I can be convincing."

He looks like he wants to kiss me. And a little like he wants to strangle me. We *are* meant for each other.

Then he swallows and says, "I trust you. So you've already convinced at least me."

Damn it, now *I* want to kiss him. All the more motivation to win the case.

Tell the story. I know how to do that. And when I look at Adalbrecht's rigid, furious face, I remember why I want to.

So I step forward, and I tell the Low Gods a tale.

CHAPTER FORTY-ONE

The Price

I TELL THE LOW GODS OF WOLVES IN SOVABIN.

I tell them of dead margraves and hungry ones, I tell them of prefects and *grimlingen*, letters and loopholes, poisons and skulls. I tell them of thieves. I tell them of fires. I tell them of bells.

And when I am done, I call my witnesses.

I call Ragne. Joniza. Barthl. They all arrive startled and unsure, but they tell what they've seen and heard, Truth softly confirming their stories.

Adalbrecht is given the opportunity to respond after each account. He dissembles and excuses, weaving words cleverly so Truth hums and grumbles, "He believes that is . . . *true*." He claims he desired a young bride like so many men do. He claims he wished to protect Bóern with the *nachtmären*. He claims he did not give the order to kill Klemens the night of the ball, that the Wolfhünden were afraid to face the prefect's scrutiny.

Each time, the Low Gods whisper among themselves.

I let them. I know how this story ends.

I call Irmgard and watch her squirm as Truth patiently says, "That is a lie," again and again until Justice sends Irmgard from the court. Adalbrecht doesn't even bother responding.

I call Emeric, and he holds my gaze with his own as I ask for his tale.

Finally, I call Gisele. I ask her to stand by me, to say my story is true.

And this time, she does.

There is winter in her words, the same Sovabin cold in me, the scars of old ice tearing at the stone for years as it drags itself down to the valley. We know the wounds we've left on each other, and we have answered for them. We have crossed the thorns. We know the way off the mountain.

When she is done, Justice asks Adalbrecht, "How do you respond?"

He plants his feet in the ring, barely hiding his confidence. "Everything I did, I did because I believed it the best for everyone."

Truth wheels and spins, twisting and twisting and twisting. Finally they say, "He believes it to be . . . mostly true."

Justice taps her fingers against her staff. I can tell she's unhappy, and I know why.

We've laid out the damage done. We've explained why Adalbrecht had motive to do it. We have shown how he benefited from it. But without the letters or the skull, we have nothing that irrefutably shows he's responsible. Even though there was power to seize, loopholes to exploit, and murder to solicit, we cannot prove that Adalbrecht deliberately did so.

But I know what can.

So when Justice turns to me and asks, "Do you have anyone else to call?" I smile.

"Yes." Then I turn to Gisele and ask, "What was your horse's name?"

She gives a tiny shake of her head, almost in disbelief. "What?"

"From Sovabin. I can never remember."

Emeric goes still. I see that fire light in his eyes. He's *definitely* going to kiss me when all this is over.

"Falada," Gisele says. "But—"

"I call Falada," I tell Justice.

"The *horse?*" Justice asks, as bewildered as Gisele. I nod. She raises her hands as if to say, *Sure, why not, let's bring in the horse.* Then she raps her staff against the ground.

Chips of bone rattle toward us from all across the plaza.

Adalbrecht's face is almost enough to bring me back to life on the spot.

See, here's the other thing about Adalbrecht von Reigenbach. He'll spend money on *his* wedding, *his* armies, *his* plans, even if he's digging it out of other people's pockets. And he'll be cheap about everything else.

Before he bound himself to all the *nachtmären* with Klemens's tattoo, he bound himself to enough of them to keep terrorizing us. And he did it with the skull on his wall, one whose ghost seeped into every *mahr* it made.

I know a thief when I see one, little or great. And I know if he was going to sacrifice a horse for a binding spell, he wouldn't use his own.

The shattered skull pulls itself together before us as Gisele covers her mouth, tears welling in her eyes. Wisps of silvery light weave into a long muzzle and graceful withers, and then the ghost of the gelding stands before us, shaking his head.

"Falada," I say conversationally, "you were used to bind *nachtmären* to Adalbrecht von Reigenbach, correct?"

"Let me get a translator." Justice twists to wave at the assembly behind her. Something lets out a cry that sounds like every language in the world at once. Justice tilts her head. "That'll work."

A forlorn, eldritch wail shudders from Falada. When he speaks, it sounds like mourning. "*By margrave's hand was I slain, to bind himself to sleeper's bane.*"

Of *course* the dead talking horse is rhyming. I'll put up with it, though, because there's a much more important question for him to answer: "Through your bond, did you know his intentions? His choices?"

"*I saw every choice, twisted and cruel. I saw his desire to devour and rule.*"

(This is where I have to admit I'm impressed he's coming up with the rhymes on the fly. Not bad for, you know, a horse.)

"Falada, did he use you to try to kill us?"

"*Bone by bone, he fed me to the beasts. Mahr after mahr on his foes was unleashed.*"

"Beasts? Unleashed? Not your best work." I wave off a glare from the gelding. "Why did he want to marry Gisele?"

"*To steal the empire for his own, to crush us all beneath his throne.*"

"Truth?" I prompt.

Truth does not hesitate. "I detect no lies."

"All right, then. That's all."

Falada lays his head on Gisele's shoulder a moment. Then a soft wind blows, and he is gone.

I plant my hands on my hips and look to Justice. "I feel like the ghost horse summed it up pretty well."

Justice's lanterns flicker. She brings her staff down on the plaza one last time, and a sound like a bell peals from the stones. "Low Gods, have you heard enough?"

The gods roar in answer.

"Does anyone speak for Adalbrecht von Reigenbach?"

That same opaque silence fills the air.

"Who among us says he is innocent of these charges?"

You could hear a hairpin drop.

I think this is where Adalbrecht realizes he is alone. I think this because I know that dread on his face, that rush of helplessness.

I saw it in the mirror with the Augur's Tears. I saw it in the ghost of the girl I'd been. I saw it every time I wanted to call for help and knew it came at a price I couldn't pay.

But I chose a different way.

"Who among us says he is guilty?"

Another deafening roar.

Justice nods. "Then it is decided. Eiswald, this is your territory. Render the sentence as you see fit." One by one the gods begin to vanish. Justice points her staff at me, but she's looking—at least I *think* she is—at Emeric. "Vanja, you will be restored per our agreement. You, Junior Prefect. I'm telling Helligbrücke you're due for a promotion. And you might want to think about recruiting her."

"He tried," I say. "I'm more of a freelancer."

Did you know a skull with lanterns for eyes can still roll them? I didn't.

All the Low Gods vanish save three: Death, Fortune, and Eiswald. Fortune, I think, wants to speak with me. I suspect I know why, but I'll ignore it a little longer. Eiswald is here for the margrave. And Death . . .

Even though time is still frozen, Death wears Adalbrecht's face now.

I think she's enjoying herself smiling at him. He's certainly not enjoying himself, trapped in Justice's glowing ring.

Eiswald turns my way. Then in a blink she's standing before me, peering down. The once-dark orb balanced between her branch-antlers is now a disc of gleaming silver: the full moon. Of course. "You broke my gift, little Vanja."

"I did?" I turn to where the gnarled lump of my body had been. It's dissolved into a pile of rubies and pearls.

"You cared for something above yourself, with your whole heart," she says. "You made up for your greed."

A hand brushes mine, warm and heartbreakingly familiar. *Alive.*

Emeric looks like he can't quite believe it either, lifting my face like a holy relic. "You did it," he says wonderingly, "you—you beautiful terror, you *did* it—" Then he pulls me into that kiss I predicted, and I find that it's all the sweeter for coming *after* the kiss I thought was our last.

Eiswald makes a supremely annoyed noise. "Out of respect for what you've done, I will give you another gift."

"*PASS,*" I mumble emphatically against Emeric's mouth, with a rude gesture for a flourish. "I'm busy."

He pulls back anyway, consternation in his face. We both know gifts from gods are rarely good news.

But Eiswald doesn't have riddles up her bearskin sleeves this time. "I think you will enjoy this one. I give you a choice: What shall become of *Markgraf* Adalbrecht von Reigenbach?"

There are very few things in this world as delicious as the look of a man who has spent his life adored, believed, stepping on everyone, answering to no one . . . realizing who, exactly, has come to settle the account.

I look at Eiswald, then at the rubies and pearls I have shed. And then I smile.

"I think," I tell her, resting my cheek on Emeric's chest, "he should learn the price of being wanted."

Ragne lets out a ferocious cackle, back to her human form and looking better in Adalbrecht's second-finest suit than he currently does in the remains of his best. For someone who seems allergic to sitting in a chair properly, she's still figured out the right way to sit on Irmgard's back to keep her from going anywhere.

Eiswald's red eyes flare with glee. She turns to Adalbrecht.

"No," he protests, "you don't understand, my father——"

"You killed your father, and you were not satisfied." Eiswald reaches through the glowing ring and seizes his head in one red-knuckled hand. "So you will become your greed."

She tosses him into the middle of the plaza. He lands on all fours, convulsing, as the statue of Kunigunde rises, then kneels before Eiswald. Time is bleeding back into motion.

A tinge of gold begins to blush through Adalbrecht's hands.

Kunigunde rises, the dents in her bronze gone—but she isn't just Kunigunde anymore. She has Gisele's face, my twin braids, her own eyes. A torn wedding dress, an ancient crown, a pair of broken manacles. She strides across the plaza to pick up her spear.

When she returns to Adalbrecht, he's fallen on his side, writhing as his limbs swell and bend. Molten gold sprouts in tufts from his shifting flesh.

And then they go still: the statue of a great golden wolf cowering on his back, and the bronze girl holding her spear to his throat, greater still.

"Poetic," Emeric drawls.

I cling to his jacket, wide-eyed. "Do you know how much that statue is worth?"

"Five horses?"

"*So many* horses!"

"It cannot be melted down or destroyed," Eiswald says dryly. "It is meant to be a warning, not an inspiration."

"Fine, but do Irmgard now," I say.

Eiswald shakes her head. "I think she is best left to your justice. I am going back to my trees, to fix the damage he did to them. May we meet next on a friendlier road."

I narrow my eyes, doing a bit of unpleasant math as she begins to fade away. Adalbrecht's battlefields were just beginning to chew into Eiswald's domain. "Wait. Stop. Wait. You didn't . . . Eiswald. Did you curse me so I would stop Adalbrecht?"

The bear skull seeps into the night sky, but I'd swear she's laughing. "I told you, it would be what you made of it."

Emeric is shaking. It takes a moment to realize he's laughing too.

"It's not funny," I growl.

"She tricked *you*," he says with unabashed delight, "into deposing a tyrant. That's *very* funny."

Fortune's voice breaks between us. "Vanja, dear. We need to talk."

She and Death are still here. And something about the way she's knotting her hands sends a chill down my spine. "You called the court. And that means you called us for help."

I go still as the statues in the plaza. I was hoping, *hoping* they wouldn't make that connection.

Emeric's hands press tighter into my back. "That—that can't—"

Death's face is back to its endless shifting beneath her hood. Her words are loaded with an odd sort of strain. "As her parents, we gave her a choice, and we have waited"—she draws out the syllables—"for *four years* for her to make it. We are Low Gods, and we cannot go back on our word."

"Wait. Vanja—wait. It's the thirteenth." Emeric looks from me to Death and Fortune, then back. "It's your birthday. You're seventeen. You belong to yourself."

I stare up at him.

I'm seventeen today.

"I'm seventeen," I say blankly. Then, fervently, "*I'm seventeen.*"

"Enough," Death interrupts. I can almost hear relief in her voice. "She's seventeen. We can no longer claim authority over her as our child."

That's when it hits me.

Death always knows.

Fortune looks almost sheepish, her halo of coins and coal rattling. "Now, obviously, gods can't be wrong, Vanja. Death told you, we just . . . wanted to protect you."

"Gods can't be wrong," Death says, "but mothers can."

Fortune lays a hand on my cheek. "As gods, we can no longer shake the world to keep you safe. But if you need us, we will come to you, as your mothers. And you will always see our hands at work." Then she winks. "We may nudge things for you here and there. You are, after all, our daughter."

I don't have to run anymore.

I don't have to leave Almandy.

I can go anywhere. And for once in my life—I can stay.

"And you, boy," Death rumbles as she and Fortune begin to fade. "You're courting the daughter of Death and Fortune, and we want her to be happy. We are only a prayer away. You'd be well served to . . . *bear* that in mind."

They vanish into the swelling night. Once the last trace is gone, Emeric says under his breath, "So that's where you get it from."

I start laughing, and then he starts laughing, and then we can't stop, holding each other for dear life and kissing through the laughter and spinning through the pile of rubies like dancing drunks under the full moon.

I am delirious, happier than I knew I could be, trembling with joy and relief and exhilaration.

I am seventeen, I am a daughter, I am no one's servant but my own.

I am wanted.

I am *free*.

CHAPTER FORTY-TWO

The Queen of Roses

I LAY SEVEN CARDS OUT ON THE LOW TABLE AND WAIT.

The other six faces at the table know the drill. They hold their breath as Ragne waves her hand over the array, then pounces on a card. She doesn't lift it yet, thinking. Then she says, "Have you ever tasted your own earwax?"

She flips over the card: the Page of Grails. Barthl slumps in his chair. "This is beneath me."

"It's Winterfast," *Markgräfin* Gisele sings, "you have to play the game!"

Ragne's sitting on the floor of the cozy library, but she scoots closer to lay her head on Gisele's knee, a wide grin on her face. She's the official ambassador for Eiswald now, which gives her all the time in the world to spend with the new margravine of Bóern.

(She may also be Gisele's wife? We're not sure, and no one's asking. They both seem too happy to care.)

Barthl covers his face with his hands. To my surprise and delight, he has turned out to be a complete lightweight; it took just two glasses of *glohwein* for him to start slurring. "I have not tasted," he says slowly, "my *own* earwax."

"Awfully specific," Emeric says into his own goblet beside me. My mouth twists, and he shoots me a sideways smile, eyes creasing at the corners.

I shuffle the cards and lay them out again. "Barthl, your turn."

Barthl's hand slaps onto a card. "Favorite habit . . . of your sweetheart."

He turns over the Queen of Shields. There's an awkward pause as Umayya fixes her shawl. She's moved into the castle, along with the rest of the Gänslinghaus residents; she, Trudl, and Gisele are working on converting the lower levels into a school for many, many more children than just the ones from the Gänslinghaus. I never asked, but I always assumed that left Umayya with little time for sweethearts.

I've assumed wrong. "He pets every cat and dog we see," she admits.

The room erupts with shouts of astonishment. Apparently I'm not the only one who made assumptions; Joniza's jaw is on the floor.

It's just us seven in the riverfront wing's library. Eight, if you count Poldi, who we found burning resentfully in Adalbrecht's study after the wedding. He's lounging on the hearth with a jug of mead, though. He can't pick up cards without setting them ablaze.

Technically, with this being the first night of Winterfast, one would expect a grander party from the new margravine. The new margravine, however, is doing things her own way.

The official explanation is that the trial changed her, like it changed

Kunigunde and Adalbrecht. She's embraced the idea, because it gives her further excuses to chase the wolves from this castle, to help the Order of Prefects flush the Wolfhünden from the streets.

And tonight, Gisele's way means enough tasteful garlands to make the room smell of fresh fir, a hot kettle of *glohwein*, and a card game.

Umayya picks the next card. "Who in this room would you sell for ten thousand *gilden*?"

It's the Queen of Grails.

"Everyone," Joniza answers with zero hesitation. She's also moved into the castle now. It's a much better stage than the bard-in-residence of Castle Falbirg. "Ten thousand? Done. And then I'd hire Vanja to steal you back."

"I should raise my rates," I say.

Ragne yawns. It's been over a week since the Göttermarkt acquired a new set of statues, and we're getting closer to the new moon. She likes being a human around Gisele as much as possible, but I'm sure the day is wearing on her.

"Last question for the night." I spread out the cards.

Joniza's watched me carefully. And she's one of the two people at this table who know what to look for when I'm dealing. Sure enough, she flips the Queen of Roses. "Where are you going after this?"

I sweep the cards back into the deck. "The inn."

"You know what I mean."

"Still not sure," I admit. "I'll tell you when I am."

Emeric's studying me again, but he keeps his thoughts to himself.

We leave Castle Reigenbach together. The guards at the gatehouse are still very confused about how things have shaken out; one calls me Vanja and one calls me Marthe, and I hear them debating as Emeric and I head down the hill, arm in arm.

Once I moved out of the riverfront wing last week, he went back to the prefect outpost. I'd be lying if I said I wasn't at least a little bit touched. I'd also be lying if I said I didn't make sure the inn I chose was close to the outpost.

I couldn't stay in Castle Reigenbach. They cleaned out the margrave's wing, uncovering hidden caches with plenty of evidence to confirm he richly deserved to be turned into an embarrassing statue. Letters, plans, collections of animal skulls . . . and that was just the study.

I couldn't stay there. Not even after Gisele gave her mother the pearls back and asked her parents to leave.

Too many shadows, too many memories, too many ghosts. It's my own ceremonial house now; I will shut my ills there and leave them behind.

That's both literal and figurative. Irmgard's in one of the dungeons. I thought about going to see her, going to taunt her, and then I realized she had to live with the fact that I was running around, free as a bird, while she was locked up in a cold, grim cell.

(I went and taunted her anyway. No regrets. Eiswald tricked me into bringing down Adalbrecht; she didn't trick me into sainthood.)

And then I took the thousand *gilden* and carried it to city hall. When I left, not a single citizen of Minkja owed the march a single red penny.

I mean, it was just common sense. I walked out of the Göttermarkt with my weight—my actual, mathematical weight—in rubies and pearls. I might be set for life. I'm *certainly* set for as long as it takes me to decide what to do next. (I see a future filled with horses.) Another thousand *gilden* on top was just gilding the lily.

Besides, everyone knows the *Pfennigeist* was hanged the day of the disastrous wedding. Vanja, however, has a chance to start things off on the right foot.

Emeric and I reach the bottom of the hill and cross the High

Bridge. As we get closer to the Göttermarkt, the strains of a carol-band bounce through the air.

The night is still young, the waning half-moon still low in the sky. Emeric looks at me. There's a trick to it, one I haven't figured out yet. All I know is that every time he does, I feel warm and giddy, as if I've downed enough *glohwein* to floor even Ezbeta von Eisendorf.

"Would you care to dance, *Frohlein* Vanja?" he asks.

"I think I would, *Meister* Conrad."

The Göttermarkt plaza has been cleared of the wreckage from the wedding, and *sakretwaren* stalls wasted no time moving back in, even with the temple clergy themselves still sweeping up broken glass and patching empty windows against the winter. Tonight the plaza's alive with bright-colored lanterns and bonfires and music, couples whirling through the falling snow.

We join them, dancing until we're both breathless, sipping mugs of *glohwein* for a break, leaping back into the fray. We dance to fast songs and slow, merry and sweet, until the band finally lays down their instruments and, one by one, the lanterns begin to go dark.

Emeric and I sit on a bench together. I rest my head on his shoulder, and he settles his chin on the crown of my head, and I think this may be the best night of my life, and I think that is why I am bracing for it to end.

He pulls something from his coat and passes it to me, suddenly fidgety. "I, er. Made this for you. For your birthday. I apologize that it's so late."

"I think we had other things to worry about," I say, pulling the paper off. "What do you mean, you *made* . . ."

I trail off. It's a little journal, leather-bound like his. The cover has been stamped with an intricate pattern of roses and stained a rich red.

"It was a guess," he says quickly, "I thought that might be your favorite flower. And color. If it's wrong I can—"

I pull his face to mine and proceed to convey that he, as always, got it right.

When we break apart I spread my fingers over the wool of his coat's breast pocket, letting myself commit every fiber, every breath of this moment to memory. Then I ask, "What's the bad news?"

He sighs. "Zimmer and Benz."

Those are the fully ordained prefects who arrived last week to help Emeric. I don't know what aggrieved them more: that this case is so sprawling and complicated it requires an unprecedented amount of paperwork, or that they got stuck with it because an upstart junior prefect solved the case before they arrived.

"They're halfway done with the reports," he continues. "It should be wrapped up by the end of Winterfast next week. After that, we have orders to return to Helligbrücke."

"You need to complete the second initiation anyway."

"I do. I just . . ." He huffs a laugh. "I could have waited. I wanted more than a week."

"I could steal the reports, so they'd have to redo them," I propose. "I'm almost certainly going back to a life of crime the second those rubies run out anyway."

"I really wish you wouldn't say that when it is going to be my professional obligation to stop you." Emeric's got a tilt to his mouth that says he'll let this one slide. Then he skims his knuckles against my cheek. "You could come with me. If I'm going to be fully ordained soon . . . we could start looking for your birth family together."

He remembered. And it's not just a *someday*, not an *after*; it's *soon*. It's *together*. It makes me want to cry.

This was, perhaps, not the best time to have shackled him to the bench.

Emeric looks down to find an iron cuff around one of his wrists. "*Vanja.*"

"You shouldn't carry manacles around if you don't want me to use them," I inform him before I kiss him again. And this much I know: I want this. I want him to chase me. I want him to be part of my story.

From the heat of his mouth on mine, I believe he wants me to be part of his story too.

I push myself away from the bench, walking backward so I can grin at him. I tap my chest, right where his coat's breast pocket would be.

"Is that where you left the key?" Emeric grumbles, fishing with his free hand. But instead of a key, he pulls a single card from his pocket: the Queen of Roses.

He looks up at me, a question in his eyes.

"I want you to catch me," I answer, and it is alien and thrilling to say it aloud.

And I slip into the night, knowing he will keep his word, and follow.

THE SEVENTH TALE

THE LITTLE THIEF

ONCE UPON A TIME, THERE WAS A GIRL COLD AS WINTER, GREEDY AS a king, lonely as an orphan. She was a liar, a thief, and a wicked maid, who stole from the family that took her in and threw her lady mistress to the wolves. She did what it took to survive, and would not martyr herself for anyone.

She was a little thief, and everyone said she died at the gallows.

One day, she told her own story, and everything changed.

I will keep telling it, this seventh tale, as long as I wish.

(Seven is lucky, don't you know?)

I am the daughter of Death and Fortune; I have come down from the mountain with my sisters. We have passed through the thorns. We have thrown out the wolf. We have told our own stories, named our destinies ourselves. If I fall, I fall without fear.

So I will tell you: My name is Vanja.

And this is the story of how I am caught.

GLOSSARY

Noble Titles and Governing Bodies

Blessed Emperor: ruler of the Blessed Empire of Almandy. Elected from one of the seven royal bloodlines by the Kronwähler.

komte / komtessin: count / countess. Nobles who manage smaller territories within margraviates and principalities, and serve as vassals to the higher-ranked ruling families.

Kronwähler: the somewhat-inconsistent body of electors who can elect an emperor. Comprised of the seven *prinzeps-wahl*, and up to twenty-seven other cardinals and delegates representing various imperial interests and factions.

markgraf / markgräfin: margrave / margravine. A noble rank for rulers of the border marches of the empire, which command the most powerful of the empire's armies. In exchange for military strength, these noble families have given up their eligibility for any member to be elected as Blessed Emperor.

prinz-wahl / prinzessin-wahl / prinzeps-wahl: prince / princess / princeps-elector. A noble descended from one of the seven royal bloodlines, who rule over principalities in the empire. The royal houses vary in power and influence, but beyond a small security force, they cannot maintain their own military. One designated member of the family is eligible to be elected Blessed Emperor . . . if there's a job opening.

All Things Wicked and Godly

grimling / grimlingen: Lesser malevolent supernatural creatures.

kobold: Hearth spirits who protect the home . . . so long as they're shown the proper respect.

loreley / loreleyn: Beautiful water-women with fish-like tails who lure fishers to their deaths.

Low Gods: Manifestations of human beliefs, imbued with various powers. Unlike the unnameable and unknowable High Gods, Low Gods have specific names and roles, but these change regionally in response to local lore.

nachtmahr/nachtmären: *Grimlings* that control and feed on bad dreams, occasionally stealing the dreamer and riding them through the night.

sakretwaren: Holy wares sold outside temples, such as prayer incense, luck charms, makeshift relics, pre-made offerings, ritual supplies, etc.

Wildejogt: The Wild Hunt, led by various Low Gods in the dead of night. Riders may be other spirits, local gods, human volunteers, or those who have displeased the leader.

Currency

gelt/gilden: Gold coin, worth ten white pennies, fifty sjilling, or five hundred red pennies.

rohtpfenni: Red penny, made of copper. Lowest form of imperial currency.

sjilling: Shilling, made of bronze. Worth ten red pennies.

weysserpfenni: White penny, made of silver. Worth five sjilling.

Miscellaneous Terms and Expressions

damfnudeln: Steamed sweet dumplings.

glohwein: Sweetened spiced red wine, served warm in the winter.

mietling/mietlingen: Hireling, the polite-neutral term for a sex worker.

Pfennigeist: The Penny Phantom, and none of your business.

scheit: Crap, crud. Strongly favored by discerning narrators.

sjoppen: Mug, pint.

ACKNOWLEDGMENTS

This book is, above all, for the ones who told their stories. Whether it was easy or agonizing, on a national stage or to a blank page, whether it left scar tissue or a smoking crater. Thank you for saying the words, and know that it changed something, even if that change seems immeasurable.

We are now three books into this toad's wild ride, and the fact that I'm not wandering a salt marsh in sackcloth is an achievement that lies solely on the shoulders of my incredible team. Tiff, thank you for seeing the statue in the block of marble with this one, for putting up with my endless fussing, and *especially* for letting me get away with sausage-based bullying. What would this be without your magic?

V, thank you for coming out swinging even back when we were still calling the book *Untitled Goose Girl,* and keeping the pugilism dialed to eleven even with a toddler on your hip and a pandemic in the background. I don't think there's a catastrophe out there that won't run screaming from you (though . . . this is 2021, let's not put it to the test.)

Thank you to the fabulous marketing and publicity Voltron of Morgan, Jollegra, Teresa, Molly, Allison, Caitlin, and Melissa at Mac Kids, who *also* have to put up with my endless fussing and, with the grace and patience of the saints, have refrained from starting a GoFundMe to launch me into the sun. Soft skills, people. Hopefully by the time this is out, it will be safe for me to buy you all the drinks I absolutely owe you. Also owed libations and perhaps a burnt offering: Mike Corley and Angela Jun, for making the world's prettiest book. Just look at it! She's a stunner!

The writing community continues to be one of the greatest resources out there for people looking to talk about the highs and lows of their publication journeys (or, let's be real, looking to procrastinate on deadlines.) Early readers and reviewers, Petty DM Buddies, the PW Class of '15, and Lake Denizens in Protagonist Jackets, you've all been the highs of my journey. If I call you out by name we're going to be here for an hour, and no one brought refreshments. Just know that you are the unlikely shapeshifting friend to this gremlin.

To my friends and family: In my hubris, I joked about you surviving wildfires in my last set of acknowledgments, and then the entire West Coast burst into flame for a month, so. Thank you, as always, for putting up with my publishing rants, which are probably like if Leslie Knope prepared a presentation on Pepe Silvia. Fingers crossed for a significantly less Old Testament year for us all! (Unless we're drinking tyrants under the table and then beheading them, in which case, you better call.)

My cats were marginally useful for this book, at least for research purposes, so that earns them a single acknowledgment. I will not elaborate further.

And lastly, to all the terrible girls: It's a lie. You deserve the world.

DISCARD